LOVER UNBOUND

BY J. R. WARD

THE BLACK DAGGER BROTHERHOOD SERIES

Dark Lover

Lover Eternal

Lover Awakened

Lover Revealed

Lover Unbound

Lover Enshrined

*The Black Dagger Brotherhood:
An Insider's Guide*

Lover Avenged

Lover Mine

Lover Unleashed

Lover Reborn

Lover at Last

NOVELS OF THE FALLEN ANGELS

Covet

Crave

Envy

Rapture

Possession

J.R.WARD

LOVER
UNBOUND

A NOVEL OF THE BLACK DAGGER BROTHERHOOD

 NEW AMERICAN LIBRARY

New American Library
Published by the Penguin Group
Penguin Group (USA) LLC, 375 Hudson Street,
New York, New York 10014

USA | Canada | UK | Ireland | Australia | New Zealand | India | South Africa | China
penguin.com
A Penguin Random House Company

Published by New American Library, a division of Penguin Group (USA) LLC. Previously published
in Signet Eclipse and Signet editions.

First New American Library Printing, December 2013

 REGISTERED TRADEMARK—MARCA REGISTRADA

NEW AMERICAN LIBRARY HARDCOVER ISBN: 978-0-451-23995-2

Printed in the United States of America
1   3   5   7   9   10   8   6   4   2

Set in Garamond
Designed by Patrice Sheridan

Dedicated to: *You.*
I got you wrong in the beginning
and you have my apologies.
It's just so like you that you stepped in anyway,
and saved not only him,
but also me in this endeavor.

• • •

With immense gratitude to the readers
of the Black Dagger Brotherhood,
and a shout-out to the Cellies!
I'm not even going to bring up the couch.
I can't count that high.

Thank you so very much:
Karen Solem, Kara Cesare, Claire Zion, Kara Welsh.

Thank you, Dorine and Angie,
for taking such very good care of me—
and thanks also to S-Byte and Ventrue for everything
you do out of the goodness of your hearts!

As always with gratitude to my executive committee:
Sue Grafton, Dr. Jessica Andersen, Betsey Vaughan, and my Partner.
And with much respect to the incomparable
Suzanne Brockmann.

To DLB—guess what? ya mummy still loves ya xxx
To NTM—as always, with love and gratitude.
As you well know.

And I have to say,
none of this would be possible without:
my loving husband, who sticks by me always;
my wonderful mother, who's been with me since . . .
well, hey, the very beginning;
my family (both those of blood and those by choice);
and my dearest friends.

GLOSSARY OF TERMS
AND PROPER NOUNS

ahvenge (v.) Act of mortal retribution, carried out typically by a male loved one.

attendhente (n.) Chosen who serves the Scribe Virgin in particularly close manner.

Black Dagger Brotherhood (pr. n). Highly trained vampire warriors who protect their species against the Lessening Society. As a result of selective breeding within the race, Brothers possess immense physical and mental strength as well as rapid healing capabilities. They are not siblings for the most part, and are inducted into the Brotherhood upon nomination by the Brothers. Aggressive, self-reliant, and secretive by nature, they exist apart from civilians, having little contact with members of the other classes except when they need to feed. They are the subjects of legend and the objects of reverence within the vampire world. They may be killed by only the most serious of wounds, e.g., a gunshot or stab to the heart, etc.

blood slave (n.) Male or female vampire who has been subjugated to serve the blood needs of another. The practice of keeping blood slaves has largely been discontinued, though it has not been outlawed.

the Chosen (pr. n.) Female vampires who have been bred to serve the Scribe Virgin. They are considered members of the aristocracy, though they are spiritually rather than temporally focused.

They have little or no interaction with males, save for the Primale, but can be mated to Brothers at the Scribe Virgin's direction. They have the ability to prognosticate. In the past, they were used to meet the blood needs of unmated members of the Brotherhood, and that practice has been adopted once again.

cohntehst (n.) Conflict between two males competing for the right to be a female's mate.

Dhunhd (pr. n.) Hell.

doggen (n.) Member of the servant class within the vampire world. *Doggen* have old, conservative traditions about service to their superiors, following a formal code of dress and behavior. They are able to go out during the day, but they age relatively quickly. Life expectancy is approximately five hundred years.

ehros (n.) A Chosen trained in the matter of sexual arts.

the Fade (pr. n.) Nontemporal realm where the dead reunite with their loved ones and pass eternity.

First Family (pr. n.) The king and queen of the vampires, and any children they may have.

ghardian (n.) Custodian of an individual. There are varying degrees of *ghardians*, with the most powerful being that of a *sehcluded* female.

glymera (n.) The social core of the aristocracy, roughly equivalent to Regency England's ton.

hellren (n.) Male vampire who has been mated to a female. Males may take more than one female as mate.

leahdyre (n.) A person of power and influence.

leelan (n.) A term of endearment loosely translated as "dearest one."

Lessening Society (pr. n.) Order of slayers convened by the Omega for the purpose of eradicating the vampire species.

lesser (n.) De-souled human who targets vampires for extermination as a member of the Lessening Society. *Lessers* must be stabbed through the chest in order to be killed; otherwise they are ageless. They do not eat or drink and are impotent. Over time, their hair, skin, and irises lose pigmentation until they are blond, blushless, and pale-eyed. They smell like baby powder. Inducted into the society by the Omega, they retain a ceramic jar thereafter into which their heart was placed after it was removed.

lewlhen (n.) Gift.

lheage (n.) A term of respect used by a sexual submissive to refer to his or her dominant.

mahmen (n.) Mother. Used both as an identifier and a term of affection.

mhis (n.) The masking of a given physical environment; the creation of a field of illusion.

nalla (n.f.) or **nallum** (n.m.) Beloved.

needing period (n.) Female vampire's time of fertility, generally lasting for two days and accompanied by intense sexual cravings. Occurs approximately five years after a female's transition and then once a decade thereafter. All males respond to some degree if they are around a female in her needing. It can be a dangerous time, with conflicts and fights breaking out between competing males, particularly if the female is not mated.

newling (n.) A virgin.

the Omega (pr. n.) Malevolent, mystical figure who has targeted the vampires for extinction out of resentment directed toward the Scribe Virgin. Exists in a nontemporal realm and has extensive powers, though not the power of creation.

pherarsom (adj.) Term referring to the potency of a male's sexual organs. Literal translation something close to "worthy of entering a female."

princeps (n.) Highest level of the vampire aristocracy, second only to members of the First Family or the Scribe Virgin's Chosen. Must be born to the title; it may not be conferred.

pyrocant (n.) Refers to a critical weakness in an individual. The

weakness can be internal, such as an addiction, or external, such as a lover.

rahlman (n.) Savior.

rythe (n.) Ritual manner of assuaging honor granted by one who has offended another. If accepted, the offended chooses a weapon and strikes the offender, who presents him- or herself without defenses.

the Scribe Virgin (pr. n.) Mystical force who is counselor to the king as well as the keeper of vampire archives and the dispenser of privileges. Exists in a nontemporal realm and has extensive powers. Capable of a single act of creation, which she expended to bring the vampires into existence.

sehclusion (n.) Status conferred by the king upon a female of the aristocracy as a result of a petition by the female's family. Places the female under the sole direction of her *ghardian*, typically the eldest male in her household. Her *ghardian* then has the legal right to determine all manner of her life, restricting at will any and all interactions she has with the world.

shellan (n.) Female vampire who has been mated to a male. Females generally do not take more than one mate due to the highly territorial nature of bonded males.

symphath (n.) Species within the vampire race characterized by the ability and desire to manipulate emotions in others (for the purposes of an energy exchange), among other traits. Historically, they have been discriminated against and during certain eras hunted by vampires. They are near extinction.

tahlly (n.) A term of endearment loosely translated as "darling."

the Tomb (pr. n.) Sacred vault of the Black Dagger Brotherhood. Used as a ceremonial site as well as a storage facility for the jars of *lessers*. Ceremonies performed there include inductions, funerals, and disciplinary actions against Brothers. No one may enter except for members of the Brotherhood, the Scribe Virgin, or candidates for induction.

trahyner (n.) Word of mutual respect and affection used between males. Translated loosely as "beloved friend."

transition (n.) Critical moment in a vampire's life when he or she transforms into an adult. Thereafter, they must drink the blood of the opposite sex to survive and are unable to withstand sunlight. Occurs generally in the mid-twenties. Some vampires do not survive their transitions, males in particular. Prior to their transitions, vampires are physically weak, sexually unaware and unresponsive, and unable to dematerialize.

vampire (n.) Member of a species separate from that of Homo sapiens. Vampires must drink the blood of the opposite sex to survive. Human blood will keep them alive, though the strength does not last long. Following their transitions, which occur in their mid-twenties, they are unable to go out into sunlight and must feed from the vein regularly. Vampires cannot "convert" humans through a bite or transfer of blood, though they are in rare cases able to breed with the other species. Vampires can dematerialize at will, though they must be able to calm themselves and concentrate to do so and may not carry anything heavy with them. They are able to strip the memories of humans, provided such memories are short-term. Some vampires are able to read minds. Life expectancy is upward of a thousand years, or in some cases even longer.

wahlker (n.) An individual who has died and returned to the living from the Fade. (S)he is accorded great respect and is revered for his/her travails.

whard (n.) Equivalent of a godfather or godmother to an individual.

LOVER UNBOUND

PROLOGUE

Greenwich Country Day School
Greenwich, Connecticut
Twenty years ago

"Just take it, Jane."

Jane Whitcomb grabbed the backpack. "You're still coming, right?"

"I *told* you this morning. *Yes.*"

"Okay." Jane watched her friend head down the sidewalk until a horn beeped. Straightening her jacket, she squared her shoulders and turned toward a Mercedes-Benz. Her mother was staring out of the driver's-side window, her eyebrows clenched.

Jane hustled across the street, the rogue backpack with the contraband making too much noise, as far as she was concerned. She hopped in the backseat and stashed the thing at her feet. The car started rolling before she got the door shut.

"Your father is coming home this evening."

"What?" Jane pushed her glasses up on her nose. "When?"

"Tonight. So I'm afraid the—"

"No! You promised!"

Her mother looked over her shoulder. "I beg your pardon, young lady."

Jane teared up. "You promised me for my thirteenth birthday. Katie and Lucy are supposed to—"

"I've already called their mothers."

Jane fell back against the seat.

Her mother's eyes lifted to the rearview mirror. "Take that expression off your face, thank you. Do you think you're more important than your father? Do you?"

"Of course not. He's *god.*"

The Mercedes swerved to the shoulder with a lurch and the brakes squealed. Her mother twisted around, lifted her hand, and held the pose, her arm trembling.

Jane shrank back in horror.

After a moment of suspended violence, her mother turned away, smoothing her perfectly smooth hair with a palm that was steady as boiling water. "Yo . . . you will not be joining us for dinner this evening. And your cake will be disposed of."

The car started moving again.

Jane wiped her cheeks and looked down at the backpack. She had never had a sleepover before. Had begged for months.

Ruined. It was all ruined now.

They were silent the whole ride home, and when the Mercedes was in the garage Jane's mother got out of the car and walked into the house without looking back.

"You know where to go," was all she said.

Jane stayed in the car, trying to collect herself. Then she picked up the backpack and her books and dragged herself in through the kitchen. Richard, the cook, was bent over the trash bin pushing a cake with white icing and red and yellow flowers off a plate.

She didn't say anything to Richard because her throat was tight as a fist. Richard didn't say anything to her because he didn't like her. He didn't like anyone but Hannah.

As Jane went out the butler's door into the dining room, she didn't want to run into her younger sister and prayed Hannah was in bed. She'd been sick this morning. Probably because she'd had a book report due.

On the way to the staircase, Jane saw her mother in the living room.

The couch cushions. Again.

Her mother was still in her pale blue wool coat with her silk scarf in her hand, and no doubt she was going to stay dressed like that until she was satisfied with the way the cushions looked. Which might be a while. The standard against which the things were measured was the same as the hair standard: total smoothness.

Jane headed up to her room. Her only hope at this point was that her father would arrive after dinner. That way, although he would still find out she was grounded, at least he wouldn't have to look at her empty seat. Like her mother, he hated anything out of order, and Jane not at the table was big-time out of order.

The length of the lecture she'd get from him would be longer that way, because it would have to include both how she'd let the family down with her absence at the meal as well as the fact that she'd been rude to her mother.

Upstairs, Jane's buttercup yellow bedroom was like everything else in the house: smooth as hair and couch cushions and the way people talked. Nothing out of place. Everything in the kind of frozen perfection you saw in house magazines.

The only thing that didn't fit was Hannah.

The rogue backpack went into the closet, on top of the rows of penny loafers and Mary Janes; then Jane changed out of her school uniform into a Lanz flannel nightgown. There was no reason to put real clothes on. She was going nowhere.

She took her stack of books to her white desk. She had English homework to do. Algebra. French.

She glanced over at her bedside table. *Arabian Nights* waited for her.

She couldn't think of a better way to spend her punishment, but homework came first. Had to. Otherwise she would feel too guilty.

Two hours later she was on her bed with *Nights* in her lap when the door opened and Hannah's head poked in. Her curly red hair was another deviation. The rest of them were blonds. "I brought food."

Jane sat up, worried for her younger sister. "You'll get in trouble."

"No, I won't." Hannah slipped in, a little basket with a gingham napkin, a sandwich, an apple, and a cookie in her hand. "Richard gave this to me so I'd have a snack tonight."

"What about you?"

"I'm not hungry. Here."

"Thanks, Han." Jane took the basket as Hannah sat on the foot of the bed.

"So what didja do?"

Jane shook her head and bit into the roast beef sandwich. "I got upset with Mom."

"'Cuz you couldn't have your party?"

"Uh-huh."

"Well . . . I gots something to cheer you up." Hannah slid a folded piece of construction paper onto the duvet. "Happy birthday!"

Jane looked at the card and blinked fast a couple of times. "Thanks . . . Han."

"Don't be sad, I'm here. Look at your card! I made it for you."

On the front, drawn in her sister's messy hand, were two stick figures. One had straight blond hair and the word *Jane* written under it. The other had curly red hair and the name *Hannah* at its feet. They were holding hands and had big smiles on their circle faces.

Just as Jane went to open the card, a pair of headlights swept the front of the house and started coming up the driveway.

"Papa's home," Jane hissed. "You better get out of here."

Hannah didn't seem as concerned as she'd usually be, probably because she didn't feel good. Or maybe she was distracted by . . . well,

whatever Hannah got distracted by. She was mostly in her day-dreams, which was probably why she was happy all the time.

"Go, Han, seriously."

"Okay. But I'm really sorry thats your party got quitted." Hannah shuffled over to the door.

"Hey, Han? I like my card."

"You didn't look inside."

"Don't have to. I like it because you made it for me."

Hannah's face split into one of her daisy smiles, the kind that reminded Jane of sunny days. "It's about you and me."

As the door shut, Jane heard her parents' voices drift up from the foyer. In a rush she ate Hannah's snack, shoved the basket into the folds of the drapes next to the bed, and went to the stack of her schoolbooks. She took Dickens's *The Pickwick Papers* back with her to the bed. She figured if she was working on school stuff when her father came in, it would buy her some brownie points.

Her parents came upstairs an hour later and she tensed, expecting her father to knock. He didn't.

Which was weird. He was, in his controlling way, as reliable as a clock, and there was a strange comfort in his predictability, even though she didn't like dealing with him.

She put *Pickwick* aside, turned the light out, and tucked her legs under her frilly duvet. Beneath the canopy of her bed she couldn't sleep, and eventually she heard the grandfather clock at the head of the stairs chime twelve times.

Midnight.

Slipping from bed, she went to the closet, got out the rogue knap-sack, and unzipped it. The Ouija board fell out, flipping open and landing faceup on the floor. She grabbed it with a wince, as if it might have broken or something, then got the pointer thingy.

She and her friends had been looking forward to playing the game because they all wanted to know who they were going to marry.

Jane liked a boy named Victor Browne, who was in her math class. The two of them had been talking a little lately, and she really thought they could be a couple. Trouble was, she wasn't sure what he felt for her. Maybe he just liked her because she gave him answers.

Jane laid out the board on her bed, rested her hands on the pointer, and took a deep breath. "What is the name of the boy I'm going to marry?"

She didn't expect the thing to move. And it didn't.

A couple more tries and she leaned back in frustration. After a minute she rapped on the wall behind her headboard. Her sister knocked back, and a little later Hannah sneaked in through the door. When she saw the game, she got excited and jumped on the bed, bouncing the pointer into the air.

"How do you play!"

"Shh!" God, if they got caught like this, they were totally grounded. Forever.

"Sorry." Hannah tucked her legs up and held on to them to keep from spazzing. "How do—"

"You ask it questions and it tells you the answers."

"What can we ask?"

"Who we're going to marry." Okay, now Jane was nervous. What if the answer wasn't Victor? "Let's start with you. Put your fingertips on the pointer, but don't push down or anything. Just—like that, yup. Okay . . . Who is Hannah going to marry?"

The pointer didn't move. Even after Jane repeated the question.

"It's broken," Hannah said, pulling away.

"Let me try another question. Put your hands back up." Jane took a deep breath. "Who am I going to marry?"

A squeaky little noise rose up from the board as the pointer began to move. When it came to rest on the letter *V*, Jane trembled. Heart in her throat, she watched it move to the letter *I*.

"It's Victor!" Hannah said. "It's Victor! You're going to marry Victor!"

Jane didn't bother shushing her sister. This was too good to be—

The pointer landed on the letter *S. S?*

"This is wrong," Jane said. "This has to be wrong—"

"Don't stop. Let's find out who it is."

But if it wasn't Victor, she didn't know. And what kind of boy had a name like *Vis*—

Jane fought to redirect the pointer, but it insisted on going to the letter *H*. Then *O, U,* and once more to *S*.

VISHOUS.

Dread coated the inside of Jane's rib cage.

"I told you it was broken," Hannah muttered. "Who's called Vishous?"

Jane looked away from the board, then let herself fall back onto her pillows. This was the worst birthday she'd ever had.

"Maybe we should try again," Hannah said. When Jane hesitated, she frowned. "Come on, I want an answer, too. It's only fair."

They put their fingers back on the pointer.

"What will I get for Christmas?" Hannah asked.

The pointer didn't move.

"Try a *yes* or *no* to get it started," Jane said, still freaked out over the word she'd been given. Maybe the board couldn't spell?

"Will I get anything for Christmas?" Hannah said.

The pointer started to squeak.

"I hope it's a horse," Hannah murmured as the pointer circled. "I should have asked that."

The pointer stopped on *no.*

They both stared at the thing.

Hannah's arms went around herself. "I want some presents, too."

"It's just a game," Jane said, closing the board up. "Besides, the thing really is broken. I dropped it."

"I want presents."

Jane reached out and hugged her sister. "Don't worry about the stupid board, Han. I'll always get you something for Christmas."

When Hannah left a little later, Jane got back between the sheets.

Stupid board. Stupid birthday. Stupid everything.

As she closed her eyes, she realized she'd never looked at her sister's card. She turned the light back on and picked it up off the bedside table. Inside it said, *We will always hold hands! I love you! Hannah*

That answer they'd been given about Christmas was so wrong. Everyone loved Hannah and got her presents. Jeez, she could even sway their father on occasion, and no one else could do that. So of course she would get things.

Stupid board . . .

After a while Jane fell asleep. She must have, because Hannah woke her.

"You okay?" Jane said, sitting up. Her sister was standing by the bed in her flannel nightie, an odd expression on her face.

"I gotta go." Hannah's voice was sad.

"To the bathroom? You gonna be sick?" Jane pushed the covers away. "I'll go with y—"

"You can't." Hannah sighed. "I gotta go."

"Well, when you're finished doing whatever, you can come back here and sleep if you wanna."

Hannah looked to the door. "I'm scared."

"Being sick is scary. But I'll always be here for you."

"I gotta go." When Hannah glanced back, she looked . . . all grown-up somehow. Nothing like the ten-year-old she was. "I'll try and come back. I'll do my best."

"Um . . . okay." Maybe her sister had a fever or something? "You want to go wake up Mother?"

Hannah shook her head. "I only want to see you. Go back to sleep."

As Hannah left, Jane sank back against her pillows. She thought about going and checking on her sister in the bathroom, but sleep claimed her before she could follow through on the impulse.

*   *   *

The following morning Jane woke up to the sound of heavy footfalls running outside in the hall. At first she assumed someone had dropped something that was leaving a stain on a carpet or a chair or a bedspread. But then the ambulance sirens came up the driveway.

Jane got out of bed, checked the front windows, then poked her head into the hall. Her father was speaking to someone downstairs, and the door to Hannah's room was open.

On tiptoe, Jane went down the Oriental runner, thinking that her sister wasn't usually up this early on a Saturday. She must really be sick.

She stopped in the doorway. Hannah was lying still on her bed, her eyes open toward the ceiling, her skin white as the pristine snowy sheets she was on.

She wasn't blinking.

In the opposite corner of the room, as far away from Hannah as possible, their mother was sitting in the window seat, her ivory silk dressing robe pooling on the floor. "Go back to bed. *Now.*"

Jane raced for her room. Just as she shut her door, she saw her father coming up the stairs with two men in navy blue uniforms. He was talking with authority and she heard the words *congenital heart* something.

Jane jumped into her bed and pulled the sheets up over her head. As she trembled in the darkness, she felt very small and very scared.

The board had been right. Hannah got no Christmas presents and married no one.

But Jane's little sister kept her promise. She did come back.

ONE

"*I* am *so* not feeling all this cowhide."

Vishous looked up from his bank of computers. Butch O'Neal was standing in the Pit's living room with a pair of leathers on his thighs and a whole lot of you've-got-to-be-kidding-me on his puss.

"They don't fit you?" V asked his roommate.

"Not the point. No offense, but these are wicked Village People." Butch held his heavy arms out and turned in a circle, his bare chest catching the light. "I mean, come on."

"They're for fighting, not fashion."

"So are kilts, but you don't see me rocking the tartan."

"And thank God for that. You're too bowlegged to pull that shit off."

Butch assumed a bored expression. "You can bite me."

I wish, V thought.

With a wince, he went for his pouch of Turkish tobacco. As he took out some rolling paper, laid down a line, and twisted himself a cig, he did what he spent a lot of time doing: He reminded himself that Butch was happily mated to the love of his life, and that even if he weren't, the guy didn't play like that.

As V lit up and inhaled, he tried not to look at the cop and failed. Fucking peripheral vision. Always did him in.

Man, he was a perverted freak. Especially given how tight the two of them were.

In the last nine months, V had grown closer to Butch than anyone he'd ever met in his over three hundred years of living and breathing. He'd roomed with the male, gotten drunk with him, worked out with him. Been through death and life and prophesies and doom with him. Helped bend the laws of nature to turn the guy from human to vampire, then healed him when he did his special business with the race's enemies. He'd also proposed him for membership in the Brotherhood . . . and stood by him when he'd been mated to his *shellan*.

While Butch paced around like he was trying to get comf with the leathers, V stared at the seven letters that were carved in Old English across his back: MARISSA. V had done both the *A*s, and they'd come out well, in spite of the fact that his hand had been shaking the whole time.

"Yeah," Butch said. "I'm not sure I'm feeling these."

After their mating ceremony, V had vacated the Pit for the day so the happy couple could have their privacy. He'd gone across the compound's courtyard and shut himself up in a guest room at the big house with three bottles of Grey Goose. He'd gotten saturated drunk, real rice-paddy flooded, but hadn't been able to meet the goal of making himself pass out. The truth had kept him mercilessly awake: V was attached to his roommate in ways that complicated things and yet changed nothing at all.

Butch knew what was doing. Hell, they were best friends, and the guy could read V better than anyone could. And Marissa knew it

because she wasn't stupid. And the Brotherhood knew it because those old-maid fool idiots never let you keep secrets.

They were all cool with it.

He wasn't. He couldn't stand the emotions. Or himself.

"You going to try the rest of your gear on?" he asked on an exhale. "Or you want to whine about your pants a little more?"

"Don't make me flip you off."

"Why would I deprive you of a favorite hobby?"

"Because my finger's getting sore." Butch walked over to one of the couches and picked up a chest harness. As he slid it onto his broad shoulders, the leather contoured to his torso perfectly. "Shit, how'd you get it to fit so well?"

"I measured you, remember?"

Butch buckled the thing in place, then bent down and ran his fingertips across the lid of a black-lacquered box. He lingered over the gold crest of the Black Dagger Brotherhood, then traced the Old Language characters that spelled out *Dhestroyer, descended of Wrath, son of Wrath.*

Butch's new name. Butch's old, noble lineage.

"Oh, for fuck's sake, open the thing." V stabbed out his cig, rolled another, and lit up again. Man, it was a good thing vampires didn't get cancer. Lately he'd been chain-smoking like a felon. "Go *on.*"

"I still can't believe this."

"Just open the damn thing."

"I really can't—"

"Open. It." At this point, V was twitchy enough to levitate out of his frickin' chair.

The cop triggered the solid-gold lock mechanism and lifted the top. Lying on a bed of red satin were four matching black-bladed daggers, each precisely weighted to Butch's specs and honed to a lethal edge.

"Holy Mary, Mother of God . . . They're beautiful."

"Thanks," V said on another exhale. "I make good bread, too."

The cop's hazel eyes shot across the room. "You did these for me?"

"Yeah, but it's no big thing. I do them for all of us." V lifted up his gloved right hand. "I'm good with heat, as you know."

"V . . . thank you."

"Whatever. Like I said, I'm the blade man. Do it all the time."

Yeah . . . just maybe not with quite as much focus. For Butch, he'd spent the past four days straight on them. The sixteen-hour marathons working his cursed glowing hand over the composite steel had made his back burn and his eyes strain, but goddamn it, he'd been determined to get each one worthy of the male who would wield them.

They still weren't good enough.

The cop took one of the daggers out, and as he palmed it his eyes flared. "Jesus . . . feel this thing." He began working the weapon back and forth in front of his chest. "Never held anything so well weighted. And the grip. God . . . perfect."

The praise pleased V more than any he'd ever received.

So it irritated the shit out of him.

"Yeah, well, they're supposed to be like that, true?" He stabbed the hand-rolled out in an ashtray, crushing the fragile glow at its tip. "No sense you going out in the field with a set of Ginsus."

"Thank you."

"Whatever."

"V, seriously—"

"Make that fuck you." When there was no slappy comeback, he looked up.

Shit. Butch was standing right in front of him, the cop's hazel eyes dark with a knowledge V wished the guy didn't have.

V dropped his stare to his lighter. "Whatever, cop, they're just knives."

The black tip of the dagger slid under V's chin and angled his head up. As he was forced to meet Butch's stare, V's body tensed. Then trembled.

With the weapon linking them, Butch said, "They're beautiful."

V closed his eyes, despising himself. Then he deliberately leaned into the blade so that it bit into his throat. Swallowing the flare of pain, he held it in his gut, using it as a reminder that he was a fucked-up freak, and freaks deserved to get hurt.

"Vishous, look at me."

"Leave me alone."

"Make me."

For a split second V almost launched himself at the guy, prepared to punch the bastard out cold. But then Butch said, "I'm just thanking you for doing something cool. No BFD."

No big fucking deal? V's eyes flipped open and he felt his stare glow. "That's bullshit. For reasons you are *very* fucking aware of."

Butch removed the blade, and as the male's arm dropped, V felt a trickle of blood ease down his neck. It was warm . . . and soft as a kiss.

"Don't say you're sorry," V muttered into the silence. "I'm liable to get violent."

"But I am."

"Nothing to be sorry for." Man, he couldn't take living here with Butch anymore. Make that Butch and Marissa. The constant reminder of what he couldn't have and shouldn't want was killing him. And Christ knew he was already in bad shape. When was the last time he'd slept through the day? Weeks and weeks.

Butch sheathed the blade in the chest holster, handle down. "I don't want you to hurt—"

"We are *so* not discussing this further." Putting his forefinger to his throat, V caught the blood he'd drawn with the blade he'd made. As he licked it off, the hidden door to the underground tunnel opened and the scent of the ocean filled the Pit.

Marissa came around the corner, looking Grace Kelly–fine as usual. With her long blond hair and her precision-molded face, she was known as the great beauty of the species, and even V, who didn't go for her type, had to show love.

"Hello, boys—" Marissa stopped and stared at Butch. "Good . . . Lord . . . look at those pants."

Butch winced. "Yeah, I know. They're—"

"Could you come over here?" She started backing down the hall to their bedroom. "I need you to come back here for a minute. Or ten."

Butch's bonding scent flared to a dull roar, and V knew damn well the guy's body was hardening for sex. "Baby, you can have me for as long as you want me."

Just as the cop left the living room, he shot a look over his shoulder. "I'm *so* feeling these leathers. Tell Fritz I want fifty pairs of them. Stat."

Left by himself, Vishous leaned over to the Alpine and cranked up MIMS's *Music Is My Savior*. As the rap pounded, he thought about how before, he'd used the shit to drown out the thoughts of others. Now that his visions had dried up and that whole mind-reading thing had gone *poof!*? He used the bass beats to keep him from hearing his roommate making love.

V rubbed his face. He *really* had to get out of here.

For a while he'd tried to get them to move out, but Marissa maintained that the Pit was "cozy" and that she liked living in it. Which had to be a lie. Half the living room was eaten up by the foosball table, ESPN was on mute twenty-four/seven, and hard-core rap was always playing. The refrigerator was a demilitarized zone marked with decaying casualties from Taco Hell and Arby's. Grey Goose and Lagavulin were the only drinks in the house. Reading material was limited to *Sports Illustrated* and . . . well, back issues of *Sports Illustrated*.

So, yeah, not a whole lot of duck-and-bunny-adorable going down. The place was part frat house, part locker room. With decor by Derek Jeter.

As for Butch? When V had suggested a little U-Haul action to the guy, the cop had shot a level stare across the couch, shook his head once, and gone into the kitchen for more Lagavulin.

V refused to think they stayed because they were worried about him or some shit. The very idea made him mental.

He got to his feet. If there was going to be a separation, he was going to have to be the one who initiated it. The trouble was, not having Butch around all the time was . . . unthinkable. Better the torture he had now than an exile.

He checked his watch and figured he might as well hit the underground tunnel and head over to the big house. Even though the rest of the Black Dagger Brotherhood lived in that rock-faced monster of a mansion next door, there were plenty of extra rooms. Maybe he should just try one on for size. For a couple of days.

The thought made his stomach churn.

On his way to the door, he caught the bonding scent wafting from Butch and Marissa's bedroom. As he thought about what was happening, his blood heated even as shame made his skin go Popsicle.

With a curse, he walked over to his leather jacket and took out a cell phone. As he dialed, his chest was warm as a meat locker, but at least he felt as if he was doing something about this obsession of his.

When the female voice answered, V sliced through her husky hello. "Sundown. Tonight. You know what to wear, and your hair will be off your neck. What do you say to me?"

The reply was a purr of submission. "Yes, my *lheage*."

V hung up and tossed the cell phone on the desk, watching as it bounced and came to rest against one of his four keyboards. The submissive he'd chosen for tonight liked things especially hard-core. And he was going to deliver.

Fuck, he truly was a pervert. Down to the marrow. A confirmed, unrepentant sexual deviant . . . who was somehow famous within the race for what he was.

Man, it was absurd, but then, the tastes and motivations of females had always been bizarre. And his fancy reputation was no more significant to him than his subs were. All that mattered was that he had volunteers for what he needed sexually. What was said about him, what the females needed to believe about him, was just oral masturbation for mouths that needed to be otherwise occupied.

As he went down into the tunnel and headed for the mansion, he was thoroughly bitched. Thanks to that stupid rotation schedule the Brotherhood was on, he wasn't allowed in the field tonight, and he hated that. He'd much rather be hunting and killing the undead slayers who went after the race than parked on his ass.

But there were ways to burn off a case of the eye-splitting frustrates.

That was what restraints and willing bodies were made for.

Phury walked into the mansion's industrial-sized kitchen and froze the way you did when confronted with an accidental injury of the bloody variety: The soles of his feet got stuck to the floor, his breath stopped, his heart skipped then scrambled.

Before he could back out through the butler's door, he got caught. Bella, his twin's *shellan*, looked up and smiled. "Hi."

"Hello." *Leave. Now.*

God, she smelled good.

She waved the knife in her hand over the roasted turkey she was working on. "Would you like me to make you a sandwich, too?"

"What?" he said like an idiot.

"A sandwich." She pointed the blade at the bread loaf and the almost empty jar of mayonnaise and the lettuce and tomatoes. "You must be hungry. You didn't eat much at Last Meal."

"Oh, yeah . . . no, I'm not . . ." His stomach put the kibosh on the lie by growling like the empty beast it was. *Bastard.*

Bella shook her head and went back at the turkey's breast. "Get yourself a plate and have a seat."

Okay, this was the last thing he needed. Better to be buried alive than sit alone in the kitchen with her as she prepared food for him with her beautiful hands.

"Phury," she said without looking up. "Plate. Seat. Now."

He complied because in spite of the fact that he came from a warrior bloodline and he was a member of the Brotherhood and he outweighed her by a good hundred pounds, he was lame and weak when it came to her. His twin's *shellan* . . . his twin's pregnant *shellan* . . . was not someone Phury could deny.

After sliding a plate over next to hers, he sat down across the granite island and told himself not to look at her hands. He'd be okay as long as he didn't look at her long, elegant fingers and her short, buffed nails and the way—

Shit.

"I swear," she said as she sliced more breast meat off, "Zsadist wants me big as a house. Another thirteen months of him pestering me to eat and I won't fit into the swimming pool. I can barely get my pants on anymore."

"You look good." Hell, she looked perfect, with her long dark hair and her sapphire eyes and her tall, fit body. The young inside of her didn't show beneath her baggy shirt, but the pregnancy was obvious in her glowing skin and the way her hand frequently went to her lower belly.

Her condition was also evident in the anxiety behind Z's eyes whenever he was around her. As vampire pregnancies carried high maternal/fetal death rates, they were a blessing and a curse for the *hellren* who had bonded with his mate.

"Do you feel okay?" Phury asked. After all, Z wasn't the only one worried about her.

"Pretty much. I get tired, but it's not all that bad." She licked her fingertips, then grabbed the mayonnaise jar. As she fished around inside, the knife made a rattling noise, like a coin being shaken up and down. "Z's driving me nuts, though. He's refusing to feed."

Phury remembered what her blood tasted like and looked away as his fangs elongated. There was no nobility in what he felt for her, none at all, and as a male who had always prided himself on his honorable nature, he couldn't reconcile his emotions with his principles.

And what was doing on his end was definitely not reciprocated. She'd fed him that one time because he'd needed it desperately and because she was a female of worth. It had not been because she was driven to sustain him or because she craved him.

No, all of that was for his twin. From the first night she'd met Z, he'd captivated her, and fate had provided that she be the one who truly saved him from the hell he'd been locked in. Phury may have rescued Z's body from that century of being a blood slave, but Bella had resurrected his spirit.

Which was, of course, just one more reason to love her.

Damn, he wished he had some red smoke on him. He'd left his frickin' stash upstairs.

"So how are you doing?" she asked as she dealt out thin slices of turkey, then layered on lettuce leaves. "Is that new prosthesis still giving you problems?"

"It's a little better, thanks." Technology these days was light-years ahead of what he'd had a century ago, but considering all the fighting he did, his lost lower leg was a constant management issue.

Lost leg . . . yeah, he'd lost it, all right. Shot it off to get Z away from that sick bitch Mistress of his. The sacrifice had been worth it. Just like the sacrifice of his happiness was worth Z being with the female they both loved.

Bella topped the sandwiches with bread and slid his plate across the granite. "Here you go."

"This is just what I needed." He savored the moment as he sank his front teeth into the thing, the soft bread giving way like flesh. While swallowing, he was struck with a sad joy that she had prepared this food for his belly, and she had done it with a certain kind of love.

"Good. I'm glad." She bit into her own sandwich. "So . . . I've wanted to ask you something for a day or so."

"Oh? What?"

"I've been working down at Safe Place with Marissa, as you know. It's such a great organization, full of great people. . . ." There was a long pause—the kind that made him brace himself. "Anyway, a new social worker has come in to counsel the females and their young." She cleared her throat. Wiped her mouth with a paper towel. "She's really great. Warm, funny. I was kind of thinking that maybe—"

Oh, God. "Thanks, but no."

"She's really nice."

"No, thanks." With his skin shriveling up tight around his body, he started eating at a dead run.

"Phury . . . I know it's not my business, but why the celibacy?"

Shit. Faster with the sandwich. "May we change the subject?"

"It's because of Z, right? Why you've never been with a female. It's your sacrifice to him and his past."

"Bella . . . please—"

"You're over two hundred years old, and it's time you started to think about yourself. Z's never going to be completely normal, and no one knows that better than you and me. But he's more stable now. And he's going to get even healthier over time."

True, provided Bella survived this pregnancy of hers: Until she came out of the delivery healthy, his twin wasn't out of the woods yet. And by extension, neither was Phury.

"Please let me introduce you—"

"No." Phury stood up and chewed like a cow. Table manners were very important, but this conversation had to end before his head exploded.

"Phury—"

"I don't want a female in my life."

"You would make a wonderful *hellren*, Phury."

He wiped his mouth on a dish towel and said in the Old Language, *"Thank you for this meal made by thine hands. Blessed evening, Bella, beloved mate of mine twin, Zsadist."*

Feeling cheap that he didn't help clean up, but figuring it was better than him having an aneurism, he pushed through the butler's door into the dining room. Halfway down the thirty-foot-long table, he ran out of gas, pulled free a random chair, and dropped into the thing.

Man, his heart was pounding.

When he looked up, Vishous was standing on the other side of the table, staring down at him. *"Christ!"*

"Little tense there, my brother?" At six-feet-six, and descended of the great warrior known only as the Bloodletter, V was a massive male. With his blue-rimmed ice white irises, his jet-black hair, and his angular, cunning face, he might have been considered beautiful. But the goatee and the warning tattoos at his temple made him look evil.

"Not tense. Not at all." Phury splayed his hands out on the glossy table, thinking about the blunt he was going to light up the instant he got to his room. "Actually, I was going to come find you."

"Oh, yeah?"

"Wrath didn't like the vibe at this morning's meeting." Which was an understatement. V and the king had ended up chin-to-chin on a couple of things, and that wasn't the only argument that flew. "He's taken us all off rotation tonight. Said we need some R and R."

V arched his brows, looking smarter than a matched set of Einsteins. The genius air wasn't just an appearance thing. The guy spoke sixteen languages, developed computer games for kicks and giggles, and could recite the twenty volumes of the Chronicles by rote. The brother made Stephen Hawking seem like a candidate for vo-tech.

"All of us?" V said.

"Yeah, I was going to hit ZeroSum. Wanna come?"

"Just scheduled some private biz."

Ah, yes. V's unconventional sex life. Man, he and Vishous were on such opposite ends of the sexual spectrum: Him knowing nothing, Vishous having explored everything, and most of it on the extremes . . . the untrodden path and the Autobahn. And that wasn't

the only difference between them. Come to think of it, the two of them had absolutely nothing in common.

"Phury?"

He shook himself to attention. "Sorry, what?"

"I said, I dreamed of you once. Many years ago."

Oh, God. Why hadn't he just gone straight to his room? He could be lighting up right now. "How so?"

V stroked his goatee. "I saw you standing at a crossroads in a field of white. It was a stormy day . . . yeah, lots of storms. But when you took a cloud from the sky and wrapped it around the well, the rain stopped falling."

"Sounds poetic." And what a relief. Most of V's visions were scary as hell. "But meaningless."

"None of what I see is meaningless, and you know it."

"Allegorical then. How can anyone wrap up a well?" Phury frowned. "And why tell me now?"

V's black brows came down over his mirrorlike eyes. "I . . . God, I have no idea. I just had to say it." With a nasty curse, he headed for the kitchen. "Is Bella still in there?"

"How did you know she was—"

"You always look ruined after you see her."

TWO

alf an hour and a turkey sandwich later, V materialized to the terrace of his private downtown penthouse. The night was a bitch, all March cold and April wet, the bitter wind weaving around like a drunk with a nasty attitude. As he stood before the panorama of Caldwell's bridge, the postcard view of the twinkling city bored him.

And so did his prospects for the evening's fun and games.

He supposed he was similar to a long-standing coke addict. The high had once been intense, but now he serviced the monkey on his back with no particular enthusiasm. He was all need, no ease.

Planting his palms on the terrace ledge, he leaned way over and got sandblasted in the face with a rush of icy air, his hair blowing back all fashion-model and shit. Or maybe . . . more like in superhero comics. Yeah, that was a better metaphor.

Except he would be a villain, wouldn't he?

He realized his hands were stroking the flat stone they rested on,

caressing it. The ledge was four feet high and ran around the building like the lip of a serving tray. The top of it was a three-foot-wide shelf just begging to be leaped off of, with the thirty feet of thin air on the other side the perfect breezy prelude to death's hard fuck.

Now, this was a view that interested him.

He knew firsthand how sweet that free fall was. How the force of the wind pushed at your chest, making it hard to breathe. How your eyes watered and the tears streaked up your temples, not down your cheeks. How the ground rushed up to greet you, a host ready to welcome you to the party.

He wasn't sure he'd made the right decision to save himself that time he'd jumped. At the last moment, though, he dematerialized back up to the terrace. Back into . . . Butch's arms.

Fucking Butch. Always came back to that son of a bitch, didn't it.

V turned away from the urge to pull another flier and unlocked one of the sliders with his mind. The penthouse's three walls of glass were bulletproof, but they didn't filter sunlight. Not that he would have stayed here during the day even if they did.

This was not a home.

As he stepped inside, the place and what he used it for pressed into him as if the force of gravity were different here. The walls and the ceiling and the marble floors of the sprawling one-room spread were black. So were the hundreds of candles that he could light at his will. The only thing that could be classified as furniture was a king-size bed that he'd never used. The rest was equipment: The table with the restraints. The chains mounted into the wall. The masks and the ball gags and the whips and the canes and the chains. The cabinet full of nipple weights and steel clips and stainless-steel tools.

All for the females.

He took off his leather jacket and tossed it onto the bed, then ditched his shirt. He always kept his leathers on during the sessions. The subs never saw him completely naked. No one did except for his brothers during ceremonies in the Tomb, and that was only because the rituals demanded it.

What he looked like down below was no one else's fucking biz.

Candles flared at his command, the liquid light rebounding off the glossy floor before being sucked up by the black dome of the ceiling. There was nothing romantic in the air. The place was a cave where the profane was performed on the willing, and the illumination was only to ensure proper placement of leather and metal, hands and fangs.

Plus, candles could be used for a purpose other than illumination.

He went to the wet bar, poured himself a couple of inches of Grey Goose, and leaned back against the short stretch of counter. There were those among the species who thought coming here and withstanding intercourse with him was a rite of passage. Then there were others who could find their satisfaction only with him. And still more who wanted to explore how pain and sex could mix.

The Lewis-and-Clark types were the ones who interested him least. Usually they couldn't handle it and had to use the safe word or safe hand signal he gave them in the middle. He always let them go readily, though any tears were theirs to soothe, not his. Nine out of ten times they wanted to try again, but that was a no-go. If they broke too easily once, they'd probably do it again, and he wasn't interested in coaching lightweights into the lifestyle.

The ones who could take it called him *lheage* and worshiped him, not that he gave a shit about their reverence. The edge in him had to get dulled, and their bodies were the stone he used to grind himself down on. End of story.

He walked over to the wall, picked up one of the lengths of steel chain, and let it slide through his palm, link by link. Although he was a sadist by nature, he didn't get off hurting his subs. His sadistic side was fed by his *lesser* kills.

For him, the control over his subs' minds and bodies was what he

was after. The things he did to them sexually or otherwise, the things he said, what he made them wear . . . it was all carefully calibrated for effect. Sure, there was pain involved, and yeah, maybe they cried from the vulnerability and the fear. But they begged him for more.

Which he gave to them, if he felt like it.

He glanced at the masks. He always put them in masks, and they were never to touch him unless he told them where and how and with what. If he had orgasms during the course of a session, it was unusual and regarded by the subs with great pride. And if he fed, it was only because he had to.

He never degraded those who came here, never made them do some of the nasty things he knew damn well some Doms favored. But he did not comfort them in the beginning, the middle, or the end, and the sessions were on his terms only. He told the people where and when, and if they pulled any jealous entitlement horse-shit, they were out. For good.

He checked his watch and lifted the *mhis* that surrounded the penthouse. The female who was coming tonight could track him because he'd taken her vein a couple months ago. When he was through with her, he would fix it so she would leave with no memory of the location where she'd been.

She would know what happened, though. The marks of the sex would be all over her.

As the female materialized on the terrace, he turned around. Through the sliders she was an anonymous shadow of curves in a black leather bustier and a long, loose black skirt. Her dark hair was coiled up high on her head, as he'd required.

She knew to wait. Knew not to knock.

He opened the door with his mind, but she also knew better than to come in without being summoned.

He looked her over and caught her scent. She was totally aroused.

His fangs elongated, but not because he was particularly inter-ested in the wet sex between her legs. He needed to feed, and she was female and she had all kinds of veins to tap into. It was biology, not bewitchment.

V extended his arm and crooked his finger at her. She came forward, trembling, as well she should. He was in a particularly sharp mood tonight.

"Lose that skirt," he said. "I'm not feeling it."

She immediately unzipped the thing and let it fall to the floor in a rush of satin. Underneath, she wore a black garter and black lace-topped hose. No panties.

Hmm . . . yeah. He was going to cut that lingerie off her hips with a dagger. Eventually.

V walked over to the wall and picked out a mask with only one opening. She was going to have to breathe through her mouth if she wanted air.

Tossing it to her, he said, "On. Now."

She covered her face without a word.

"Get up on my table."

He didn't help her as she fumbled around, just watched, knowing she'd find her way. They always did. Females like her always found the way to his rack.

To pass the time, he took a hand-rolled out of his back pocket, put it between his lips, and picked a black candle from its holder. As he lit his cigarette, he stared at the little pool of liquid wax at the foot of the flame.

He checked on how the female was progressing. Well-done. She'd positioned herself faceup, arms out, legs spread.

After he restrained her, he knew exactly where to start tonight.

He kept the candle in his hand as he stepped forward.

Under the caged lights of the Brotherhood's gym, John Matthew assumed the ready position and focused on his training opponent. The two of them were as well matched as a pair of chopsticks, both thin and insubstantial, easily broken. As all pretrans were.

Zsadist, the Brother who was teaching the hand-to-hand tonight, whistled through his teeth, and John and his classmate bowed to each other. His opponent said the appropriate acknowledgment in the Old Language, and John returned the statement using American Sign Language. Then they engaged. Small hands and bony arms flew around to no great effect; kicks were thrown out like paper airplanes; dodges were made with little finesse. All their moves and positions were shadows of what they should have been, echoes of thunder, not the bass roar itself.

The thunder came from elsewhere in the gym.

In the middle of the round, there was a tremendous *WHOOMP!* as a solid body hit the blue mats like a bag of sand. Both John and his opponent glanced over . . . and abandoned their meager mixed-martial-arts attempts.

Zsadist was working with Blaylock, one of John's two best friends. The redhead was the only trainee who'd been through the change so far, so he was twice the size of everyone else in the class. And Z had just rugged the guy.

Blaylock sprang to his feet and once more faced off like a trooper, but he was just going to get his ass handed to him again. As big as he was, Z was a giant as well as a member of the Black Dagger Brotherhood. So Blay was facing a Sherman tank with a fuckload of fighting experience.

Man, Qhuinn should be here to see this. Where was the guy?

All eleven trainees let out a "Whoa!" as Z calmly clipped Blay off balance, tossed him sunny-side down on the mats, and cranked him into a bone-bending submission hold. The instant Blay tapped out, Z got off him.

As Zsadist stood over the kid, his voice was as warm as it ever got. "Five days out of your transition and you're doing good."

Blay smiled, even though his cheek was mashed into the mat like it had been glued down there. "Thank you . . ." He panted. "Thank you, sire."

Z extended his hand and hooked Blay off the floor just as the sound of a door opening echoed through the gym.

John's eyes bulged at what came in. Well, *shit* . . . that explained where Qhuinn had been all afternoon.

The male coming slowly across the mats was a six-foot-four-inch, two-hundred-and-fifty-pound likeness of someone who'd weighed about as much as a bag of dog food the day before. Qhuinn had been through the transition. God, no wonder the guy hadn't Y-messy'd or texted during the day. He'd been busy growing a new body.

As John lifted his hand, Qhuinn nodded back like his neck was stiff or maybe his head was pounding. The guy looked like shit and moved as if every bone in his body hurt. He also fiddled with the collar of his new XXXL fleece like the feel of it was bugging him, and he kept jacking his jeans up with a wince. His black eye was a surprise, but maybe he'd bumped into something in the middle of the transition? Word had it you flailed around a lot when you were changing.

"Glad you showed," Zsadist said.

Qhuinn's voice was deep as he replied, a totally different cadence from before. "I wanted to come even though I can't work out."

"Good call. You can chill over there."

As Qhuinn went to the sidelines he met Blay's eyes and they both smiled real slow. Then they looked at John.

Using American Sign Language, Qhuinn's hands spelled out, *After class we go to Blay's. Have a shitload to tell both of you.*

As John nodded, Z's voice cracked through the gym. "Kibitzing break's over, ladies. Don't make me lap your asses, because I will."

John faced his little partner and settled into his ready position.

Even though one of the trainees had died from the change, John couldn't wait for his to hit. Sure, he was pants-down terrified, but better to be dead than stuck in the world as a sexless scrap of flesh at the mercy of others.

He was beyond ready to be male.

He had family business to take care of with the *lessers*.

*   *   *

Two hours later, V was as satisfied as he ever got. Not surprisingly, the female was in no shape to dematerialize home, so he put her in a robe, hypnotized her into a stupor, and took her down in the building's freight elevator. Fritz was waiting at the curb with the car, and the elderly *doggen* didn't ask any questions after her address was given.

As always, that butler was a godsend.

Alone again in the penthouse, V poured himself some Goose and sat down on the bed. The rack was covered with hardened wax, blood, her arousal, and the results of his orgasms. It had been a messy session. But the acceptable ones always were.

He took a long pull from his glass. In the dense silence, in the aftermath of his perversions, in the cold slap of his zero reality, a cascade of sensual images came to him. What he'd seen weeks ago and now remembered had been caught by mistake, but he'd macked the scene like a pickpocket anyway, stashing it in his frontal lobe even though it didn't belong to him.

Weeks ago he'd seen Butch and Marissa . . . lying together. It had been when the cop was at Havers's clinic on quarantine. A video camera was set up in the corner of the hospital room, and V had caught the two of them on a computer monitor: she dressed in a vibrant peach gown, he in a hospital john. They'd been kissing long and hot, their bodies straining for sex.

V had watched with his heart in his throat as Butch had rolled over and mounted her, his john breaking open to reveal his shoulders and his back and his hips. While he'd started in with a rhythm, his spine had flexed and released as her hands slid onto his ass and her nails dug in.

It had been beautiful, the two of them together. Nothing like the sex with hard edges V had had all his life. There had been love and intimacy and . . . kindness.

Vishous let his body fall loose and slap back onto the mattress, his glass tipping until it almost spilled as he lay out. God, he wondered what it would be like to have that sort of sex. Would he even like it? Maybe it would get claustrophobic. He wasn't sure he'd be into someone with their hands all over him, and he couldn't imagine being fully naked.

Except then he thought of Butch and decided it probably just depended on who you were with.

V covered his face with his good hand, wishing like hell his feelings would go away. He hated himself for these thoughts, for this attachment, for his useless pining, and the familiar litany of shame brought on a whitewash of fatigue. As bone-deep exhaustion Tom Sawyer'ed him from head to foot, he fought the wave, knowing it was dangerous.

This time he didn't win. Didn't even get a vote. His eyes slammed shut even as fear licked up his spine and left his skin in a quilt of goose bumps.

Oh . . . shit. He was falling asleep. . . .

Panicked, he tried to open his lids, but it was too late. They had become masonry walls. The vortex had him and he was being sucked down no matter how much he tried to pull himself free.

His grip loosened on the glass in his hand and dimly he heard the thing hit the floor and splinter. His last thought was that he was just like that tumbler of vodka, shattering and spilling, unable to hold himself inside anymore.

THREE

A couple of blocks to the west, Phury picked up his martini and eased back into a leather banquette at Zero-Sum. He and Butch had been pretty quiet since landing at the club about a half hour ago, the two of them just doing the people-watching thing from the Brotherhood's table.

God knew there was plenty to see around here.

On the other side of a waterfall wall, the club's dance floor was tweaking with techno music as humans rode waves of Ecstasy and coke and did dirty deeds in designer clothes. The Brotherhood never hung on the general-pop side, though. Their little slice of real estate was in the VIP section, a table all the way in the back next to the fire escape. The club was a good spot to R & R. People left them alone, the booze was top-drawer, and it was smack-dab in downtown, where the Brotherhood did most of their hunting.

Plus it was owned by a relative, now that Bella and Z were mated. Rehvenge, the male who ran it, was her brother.

Also happened to be Phury's drug dealer, too.

He took a good long one from the rim of his shaken-not-stirred. He was so going to have to make another buy tonight. His stash was weighing low again.

A blond woman shimmied past the table, her breasts bobbing like apples under silver sequins, her postage-stamp skirt flashing her ass cheeks and her lamé thong. The getup made her look like something more than just half-naked.

Dirty was maybe the word he was looking for.

She was typical. Most of the human females in the VIP section were within an inch of getting arrested for indecent exposure, but then, the ladies tended to be either professionals or the civilian equivalent of whores. As the prostitute hit the next banquette over, for a split second he wondered what it would be like to buy some time with someone like her.

He'd been celibate for so long, it seemed totally off the page even to think like that, much less follow through on the idea. But maybe it would help him get Bella out of his mind.

"See something you like?" Butch drawled.

"I don't know what you're talking about."

"Oh? You mean you haven't noticed that blonde who just flashed by here? Or the way she was checking you?"

"She's not my type."

"Then look for a long-haired brunette."

"Whatever." As Phury finished his martini, he wanted to throw the glass into a wall. Shit, he couldn't believe he'd even thought about paying for sex.

Desperate. Loser.

God, he wanted a blunt.

"Come on, Phury, you have to know that all the chicks here case you when you come. You should just try one."

Okay, *way* too many people were pushing him tonight. "No, thanks."

"I'm just saying—"

"Fuck you and shut it."

Butch cursed under his breath and didn't comment any further. Which made Phury feel like an asshole. As he should. "I'm sorry."

"Nah, it's cool."

Phury waved down a waitress, who came right over. As his empty was taken away, he muttered, "She tried to set me up with someone tonight."

"Excuse me?"

"Bella." Phury picked up a soggy cocktail napkin and started folding it up into squares. "Said there was some social worker at Safe Place."

"Rhym? Oh, she's very cool—"

"But I'm—"

"Not interested?" Butch shook his head. "Phury, man, I know you're probably going to bite my head off again, but it's time for you to get interested. This shit with you and the females? Gotta end."

Phury had to laugh. "Be blunt, why don't you?"

"Look, you need to live a little."

Phury nodded over at the bionic blonde. "And you think that buying sex constitutes living a little?"

"With the way she's looking at you, you wouldn't have to pay."

Phury forced his brain to try on the scenario. He pictured himself getting up and walking over to the woman. Taking her by the arm and moving her into one of the private bathrooms. Maybe she'd blow him. Maybe he'd prop her up on the sink and spread her legs and pump into her until he came. Total elapsed time? Fifteen minutes, tops. After all, he might be a virgin, but the mechanics of sex were pretty simple. All his body would need was a tight hold and some friction and he'd be good to go.

Well, in theory. He was limp in his trousers right now. So even if he wanted to bust his cherry tonight, it wasn't going to happen. At least, not with her.

"I'm good," he said as his fresh martini arrived. After he swirled the olive around with a finger, he popped it into his mouth. "Really. I'm good."

The two of them went back to the silent routine, with nothing between them but the dim thumping from the music on the other side of the waterfall wall. Phury was about to bring up sports because he couldn't handle the quiet when Butch stiffened.

A female across the VIP area was staring their way. It was that security chief, the one who was jacked like a male and had a male's haircut. Talk about a hard-ass. Phury had seen her cuff drunken human men around like she was whapping dogs with a newspaper.

But wait, she wasn't looking at Phury. She was all about Butch.

"Whoa, you've had her," Phury said. "Haven't you."

Butch shrugged and swallowed the Lag in his glass. "Only once. And it was before Marissa."

Phury glanced back at the female and had to wonder what that sex had been like. She seemed like the kind who could make a male see stars. And not necessarily in a fun way.

"Is anonymous sex any good?" he asked, feeling like he was twelve.

Butch's smile was slow. Secret. "I used to think it was. But when that's all you know, sure, you think cold pizza is fantastic."

Phury took a pull on his martini. Cold pizza, huh. So that's what was out there waiting for him. How inspiring.

"Shit, I don't mean to be a buzz kill. It's just better with the right person." Butch tossed back his Lag. As a waitress headed over to pick up for a refill, he said, "Nah, I stop at two now. Thanks."

"Wait!" Phury said, before the woman took off. "I'll have another one. Thanks."

Vishous knew the dream had come to him, because he was happy in it. The nightmare always started out with him in a state of bliss. He was, in the beginning, wholly happy, utterly complete, a Rubik's Cube solved.

Then the gun went off. And a bright red stain bloomed on his shirt. And a scream sliced through air that seemed dense as a solid.

Pain hit him like he'd been ripped into by bomb shrapnel, like he'd been doused in gasoline and matched up, like his skin had been taken off in strips.

Oh, God, he was dying. No one lived through this kind of agony.

He fell to his knees and—

V shot up from the bed like he'd been boot-licked in the head.

In the penthouse's cage of black walls and night-backed glass, his breath sounded like a hacksaw going through hardwood. Shit, his heart was pounding so fast he felt like he should put his hands up to keep it in place.

He needed a drink . . . *now.*

On sloppy legs he went to the bar, grabbed a fresh glass, and poured himself about four inches of Grey Goose. The long-tall was almost at his lips when he realized he wasn't alone.

He unsheathed a black dagger from his waistband and whirled around.

"It is only I, warrior."

Jesus Christ. The Scribe Virgin stood before him swathed in black robes from head to foot, her face covered, her tiny form dominating the penthouse. From beneath her hem a glow spilled out onto the marble floor, bright as the noonday sun.

Oh, this was an audience he wanted right now. *Yup, yup.*

He bowed and stayed put. Tried to figure out how he could keep drinking in this position. "I am honored."

"How you lie," she said dryly. "Lift thyself, warrior. I would see your face."

V did his best to marshal some hi-how're-ya onto his puss, in hopes of camoing the oh-fuck-me that was there. *Goddamn it.* Wrath had threatened to turn him in to the Scribe Virgin if he couldn't pull it together. Guess that dime been dropped.

As he eased upright, he figured sucking some Goose would be perceived as an insult.

"Yes, it would," she said. "But do what you must."

He swallowed the vodka like it was water and put the glass on the wet bar. He wanted more, but hopefully she wouldn't be staying long.

"The purpose of my visit has naught to do with your king." The Scribe Virgin floated over, stopping when she was just a foot away. V fought the urge to step back, especially as she reached out her glowing hand and brushed his cheek. Her power was like that of a lightning bolt: deadly and precise. You didn't want to be her target. "It is time."

Time for what? But he kept a lid on himself. You didn't ask questions of the Scribe Virgin. Not unless you wanted to add being used as floor wax to your résumé.

"Your birthday draws near."

True, he was going to be three hundred and three years old soon, but he couldn't think why that would warrant a private visit from her. If she wanted to fly him some birthday jollies, quick something in the mail would be just fine. Fuck it, she could rock out an e-card from Hallmark and call it a day.

"And I have a gift for you."

"I am honored." *And confused.*

"Your female is ready."

Vishous jerked all over, like someone had goosed him in the ass with a jackknife. "I'm sorry, what—" *No questions, dumb ass.* "Ah . . . with all due respect, I have no female."

"You do." She dropped her glowing arm. "I have picked her from among all the Chosen to be your first mate. She is the most pure of blood, the finest of beauty." As V opened his mouth, the Scribe Virgin steamrolled right over him. "You will be mated, and the two of you will breed, and you will also breed with the others. Your daughters shall replenish the ranks of the Chosen. Your sons shall become

members of the Brotherhood. This is your destiny: to become the Primale of the Chosen."

The word *Primale* dropped like an H-bomb.

"Forgive me, Scribe Virgin . . . ah . . ." He cleared his throat and reminded himself that if you pissed Her Holiness off, they'd need barbecue tongs to pick up your steaming pieces. "I mean no offense, but I will take no female as my own—"

"You will. And you will lie with her in the proper ritual and she will bear your young. As will the others."

Visions of getting trapped on the Other Side, surrounded by females, unable to fight, unable to see his brothers . . . or . . . God, Butch . . . snapped the hinge on his mouth. "My destiny is as a fighter. With my brothers. I am where I should be."

Besides, with what had been done to him, could he even sire young?

He expected her to hit the fan at his insubordination. Instead she said, "How fearless of you to deny your station. You are so like your father."

Wrong. He and the Bloodletter had *nothing* in common. "Your Holiness—"

"You shall do this. And you shall submit of your own volition."

His reply shot out, hard and cold. "I'd need a good goddamned reason."

"You are my son."

V stopped breathing, his chest going concrete on him. Surely she meant that in the broader sense.

"Three hundred and three years ago you were born of my body." The Scribe Virgin's hood rose off her face of its own volition, revealing a ghostly, ethereal beauty. "Lift thy so-called cursed palm and know our truth."

Heart in his throat, V brought up his gloved hand, then ripped the leather off with messy tugs. In horror he stared at what was behind his tattooed skin: The glow in him was just like hers.

Jesus Christ . . . Why the hell hadn't he made the connection before?

"Your blindness," she said, "afforded your denial. You did not want to see it."

V stumbled away from her. When he hit the mattress, he let his ass go down and told himself now was not the time to lose his mind—

Oh, wait . . . he'd already lost it. Good deal, or he'd be totally freaking out right now.

"How . . . is this possible?" Sure, that was a question, but who the fuck cared at this point?

"Yes, I think I shall pardon your inquiry this one time." The Scribe Virgin floated around the room, moving without walking, her robes unaffected by the trip, as if they were carved from stone. In the silence she made him think of a chess piece: the queen, the one among the others on the board who was free to move in all directions.

When she finally spoke, her voice was deep. Commanding. "I wanted to know conception and birth physically, so I assumed a form sufficient to perform the sexual act and went to the Old Country in a fertile condition." She paused before the glass doors in front of the terrace. "I chose the male based on what I believed were the most desirable masculine attributes for the survival of the species: strength and cunning, power, aggression."

V pictured his father and tried to imagine the Scribe Virgin having sex with the male. Shit, that must have been a brutal experience.

"It was," she said. "I received exactly what I had gone out to find in full measure. There was no going back once the rutting started, and he was characteristic to his nature. At the end, though, he withheld himself from me. Somehow he knew what I was after and who I was."

Yeah, his father had excelled at finding and exploiting the motivations of others.

"It was perhaps foolish of me to think I could pass for something I was not with a male like him. Cunning, indeed." She looked across the room at V. "He told me he would give me his seed only if a male young would be placed with him. He had never successfully begotten the live birth of a son, and his warrior loins wanted that satisfaction.

"I, however, wanted my son for the Chosen. Your father may have understood tactics, but he was not the only one. I knew well his weakness too, and had it within me to guarantee the sex of the young. We agreed that he would have you three years after the birth for three centuries, and that he could train you to fight on this side. Thereafter you would be for my purpose."

Her purpose? His father's purpose? Shit, didn't he get a vote?

The Scribe Virgin's voice got lower. "Having reached our accord, he forced me beneath him for hours, until the form I was in nearly died from it. He was possessed by the need to conceive, and I endured him because I was the same."

Endured was right. V, like the rest of the males in the warrior camp, had been forced to watch his father have sex. The Bloodletter hadn't distinguished between fighting and fucking and had made no allowances for females' size or weakness.

The Scribe Virgin began shifting around the room again. "I delivered you unto the camp on your third birthday."

V became dimly aware of a humming in his head, like a train was gathering speed. Thanks to his parents' little bargain, he'd been living his life in ruins, stuck dealing with the aftermath of his father's cruelty as well as the war camp's vicious lessons.

His voice dropped to a growl. "Do you know what he did to me? What they did to me there?"

"Yes."

Throwing all rules of etiquette into the shitter, he said, "Then why the *fuck* did you let me stay there."

"I had given my word."

V burst to his feet, his hand going to his privates. "Glad to know your honor stayed intact, even if I didn't. Yeah, that's a fair fucking exchange."

"I can understand your anger—"

"Can you, *Mom*? That makes me feel *so* much better. I spent twenty years of my life fighting to stay alive in that cesspool. What did I get? A scrambled head and fucked-up body. And now you want me to breed for you?" He smiled coldly. "What if I can't impregnate them? If you know what happened to me, you ever think of that?"

"You are able."

"How do you know?"

"Think you there is any part of my son I cannot see?"

"You . . . *bitch*," he whispered.

A blast of heat came out of her body, hot enough to singe his eyebrows, and her voice cracked through the penthouse. "Do *not* forget who I am, warrior. I chose your father unwisely, and we both suffered for the mistake. Do you think I remained unharmed as I saw what course your life laid? Think you I watched from afar unaffected? *I died every day for you.*"

"Well, aren't you Mother fucking Teresa," he shouted, aware that his own body had started to heat up. "You're supposed to be all-powerful. If you'd given a shit, you could have stepped—"

"Destinies are not chosen, they are conferred—"

"By who? You? Then are you the one I should hate for all the shit that was done to me?" Now he was glowing all over; he didn't even have to look down at his forearms to know that what was within his hand had spread throughout him. Just. Like. Her. "God . . . *damn* you."

"My son—"

He bared his fangs. "You do not call me that. *Ever.* Mother and son . . . we aren't that. My mother would have done something. When I couldn't help myself, my mother would have been there—"

"I wanted to be—"

"When I was bleeding and torn up and terrified, my mother would have been there. So don't fly me that sonny-boy *bullshit*."

There was a long silence. Then her voice came clear and strong. "You will present yourself to me following my sequester, which starts this night. You will be shown your mate as a formality. You will return when she is suitably prepared for your use, and you will do what you were birthed to do. And you will do it of your own free choice."

"The hell I will. And *fuck you*."

"Vishous, son of the Bloodletter, you will do this because if you do not, the race will not survive. If there is any hope of withstanding the onslaughts of the Lessening Society, more Brothers are needed. You of the Brotherhood are but a handful now. In past epochs there were twenty and thirty among you. Where may yet more come but from selective breeding?"

"You let Butch into the Brotherhood, and he wasn't—"

"Special dispensation for a prophecy realized. Not the same at all, and well you know it. His body will never be as strong as yours. If not for his innate power, he could never function as a Brother."

V looked away from her.

Survival of the species. Survival of the Brotherhood.

Shit.

He walked around and ended up by his rack and his wall of toys. "I'm the wrong guy for this kind of thing. I'm not the hero type. I'm not interested in saving the world."

"The logic is in the biology and cannot be countered."

Vishous lifted his glowing hand, thinking about the number of times he'd used it to incinerate things. Houses. Cars. "What about this? You want a whole generation cursed like me? What if I pass this down to my offspring?"

"It is an excellent weapon."

"So's a dagger, but it doesn't light up your friends."

"You are blessed, not cursed."

"Oh, yeah? Try living with the thing."

"Power requires sacrifice."

He laughed in a hard rush. "Well, then, I'd give this shit up in a heartbeat to be normal."

"Regardless, you have a duty to your species."

"Uh-huh, right. Just like you had one to a son you birthed. You'd better pray I'm more conscientious with my responsibility."

He stared out over the city, thinking of the civilians he'd seen battered, beaten, dead at the hands of the Omega's *lessers*. There had been centuries of innocents slain by those bastards, and life was hard enough without being hunted. He should know.

Man, he hated that she had a point about the logic. There were only five in the Brotherhood now, even with Butch's membership: Wrath couldn't fight by law, because he was the king. Tohrment had disappeared. Darius had died last summer. So there were five against an ever-replenishing enemy. Making it worse, the *lessers* had an endless supply of humans to pull into their undead ranks, whereas Brothers had to be born and raised and had to survive their transitions. Sure, the trainee class being worked on back at the compound would go out as soldiers eventually. But those boys would never possess the kind of strength, endurance, or healing capabilities that males from the Brotherhood bloodlines would.

And as for making more Brothers . . . Small pool of sires to choose from. By law Wrath as king could lie with any female in the species, but he was fully bonded to Beth. So too were Rhage and Z to their females. Tohr, assuming he was still alive and ever came back, wasn't going to be in any frame of mind to get members of the Chosen pregnant. Phury was the only other possibility, but he was a celibate with a broken frickin' heart. Not really man-whore material.

"Shit." While he chewed on the situation, the Scribe Virgin stayed quiet. As if she knew one word from her, and he would drop the whole thing and to hell with the race.

He turned around to face her. "I'll do it on one condition."

"Which is."

"I live here, with my brothers. I fight with my brothers. I'll go to the Other Side and"—*Holy shit. Oh, God*—"lay with whoever. But my home is here."

"The Primale lives—"

"This one won't, so take me or leave me." He glared at her. "And know this. I am enough of a selfish bastard that if you don't agree, I will walk, and then where will you be? After all, you can't make me fuck females for the rest of my life, not unless you want to work my cock yourself." He smiled coldly. "And how's that for some biology, true?"

Now it was her turn to move around the room. As he watched her and waited, he hated that they seemed to think in the same manner—with motion.

She stopped by the rack and reached out a glowing hand, hovering it above the hardwood slab. The remnants of the sex he'd had vanished into thin air, the mess cleaned up, as if she didn't approve. "I thought perhaps you would like a life of ease. A life where you were protected and didn't have to fight."

"And lose all that careful training I had at my father's fist? Now, that would be *such* a waste. As for protection, I could have used it three hundred years ago. Not now."

"I thought perhaps . . . you would like a mate of your own. The one I chose for you, she is the best of all the bloodlines. A pure-blood with grace and beauty."

"And you picked my father, right? So you'll excuse me if I don't get all excited."

Her gaze drifted over to his equipment. "You favor such . . . hard couplings."

"I'm my father's son. You said it yourself."

"You could not participate in this . . . sexual endeavor with your mate. It would be shameful and frightening for her. And you could not be with anyone other than the Chosen. It would be a disgrace."

V tried to imagine giving up his proclivities. "My monster needs to get out. Especially now."

"Now?"

"Come on, *Mom*. You know everything about me, right? So you know my visions have dried up and I'm half-psychotic from lack of sleep. Hell, you gotta know I took a jump off this building last week. Longer this goes on, the worse I'm going to get, especially if I can't get a . . . workout in."

She waved her hand, dismissing him. "You see nothing because you are at a crossroads in your own path. Free will cannot be exercised if you are aware of the ultimate outcome, therefore the prescient part of you naturally suppresses itself. It will return."

For some crazy reason that eased him, even though he'd fought the intrusions of other people's fates since they started appearing to him centuries ago.

Then something dawned on him. "You don't know what's going to happen to me, do you. You don't know what I'm going to do."

"I would have your word that you shall fulfill your duties on the other side. That you shall take care of what must be done there. And I would have it now."

"Say it. Say you don't know what you see. If you want my vow, you give me this."

"Why for?"

"I want to know you're powerless about something," he bit out. "So you know how *I* feel."

The heat of her rose until the penthouse was like a sauna. But then she said, "Your destiny is mine. I know not your path."

V crossed his arms over his chest, feeling like a noose was around his neck and he was standing on a rickety chair. Fuck. Him. "You have my bonded word."

"Take this and accept your nomination as Primale." She held out a heavy gold pendant on a black silk cord. When he took the thing, she nodded once, a sealing of their pact. "I shall go forth and inform the Chosen. My sequester ends several days hence. You will come to me then and be installed as the Primale."

Her black hood lifted without hands. Just before it lowered over her glowing face she said, "Until we meet hence. Be well."

She disappeared without sound or movement, a light extinguished.

V went over to the bed before his knees let go. As his ass hit the mattress, he stared at the long, thin pendant. The gold was ancient and marked with characters in the Old Language.

He didn't want young. Never had. Although he supposed that under this scenario, he was nothing more than a sperm donor. He wasn't going to have to be a father to any of them, which was a relief. He wouldn't be good at that shit.

Shoving the pendant into the back pocket of his leathers, he put his head in his hands. Visions of growing up in the warrior camp came to him, the memories crystal-clear and sharp as glass. With a nasty curse in the Old Language, he reached over to his jacket, took his phone out, and hit speed dial. When Wrath's voice came on the line, there was a whirring noise in the background.

"You got a minute?" V said.

"Yeah, what's doing?" When V didn't hold forth, Wrath's voice got lower. "Vishous? You all right?"

"No."

There was a rustling, then Wrath's voice came from a distance. "Fritz, can you come back and vacuum a little later? Thanks, my man." The whirring noise shut off and a door closed. "Talk to me."

"Do you . . . ah, do you remember the last time you got drunk? Like, really drunk?"

"Shit . . . ah . . ." In the pause, V pictured the king's black eyebrows sinking down behind his wraparounds. "God, I think it was with you. Back in the early nineteen hundreds, wasn't it? Seven bottles of whiskey between the two of us."

"Actually, it was nine."

Wrath laughed. "We started at four in the afternoon and it took us, what, fourteen hours? I was faced for a whole day afterward. Hundred years later and I think I'm still hungover."

V closed his eyes. "Remember just as dawn was coming, I, ah . . . told you I'd never known my mother? Had no clue who she was or what happened to her?"

"Most of it's fog, but yeah, I recall that."

God, they'd both been so polluted that night. Drunk off their asses. And that had been the only reason V had yakked even a little about what rotted in his head twenty-four/seven.

"V? What's doing? This have something to do with your *mahmen*?"

V let himself fall back on the bed. As he landed, the pendant in his back pocket bit into his ass. "Yeah . . . I just met her."

FOUR

On the Other Side, in the sanctuary of the Chosen, Cormia sat on a cot in her white room with a small white candle glowing beside her. She was dressed in the traditional white robe of the Chosen, her feet bare on white marble, her hands folded in her lap.

Waiting.

She was used to waiting. It was the nature of your life as a Chosen. You waited for the calendar of rituals to offer up activity. You waited for the Scribe Virgin to make an appearance. You waited for the Directrix to give you duties to perform. And you waited with grace and patience and understanding, or you disgraced the entirety of the tradition you serviced. Herein no one sister was more important than another. As a Chosen, you were part of a whole, a single molecule among many that formed a functioning spiritual corpus . . . both critical and utterly unimportant.

So woe be the female who failed in her duties lest she contaminate the rest.

Today, though, the waiting carried an inescapable burden. Cormia had sinned, and she was awaiting her punishment with dread.

For a long time she had wanted for her transition to be given upon her, had been secretly impatient for it, although not for the benefit of the Chosen. She'd wanted to be fully realized as herself. She'd wanted to feel a significance in her breath and her heartbeat that pertained to her being an individual in the universe, not a spoke in a wheel. Her change had struck her as the key to that private freedom.

Her change had been conferred unto her just recently, when she'd been invited to drink of the cup in the temple. At first she'd been elated, assuming that her clandestine desire had gone undetected and yet was fulfilled. But then her punishment had arrived.

Glancing down at her body, she blamed her breasts and her hips for what was about to happen to her. Blamed herself for wanting to be someone specific. She should have stayed as she had been—

The thin silk curtain over the doorway swept aside, and the Chosen Amalya, one of the Scribe Virgin's personal *attendhentes*, walked in.

"And so it is done," Cormia said, tightening her fingers until her knuckles stung.

Amalya smiled beneficently. "It is."

"How long?"

"He comes at the conclusion of Her Highness's sequester."

Desperation made Cormia ask the unthinkable. "Cannot it be another of us who is called forth? There are others who want this."

"You have been chosen." As tears were born unto Cormia's eyes, Amalya came forward, her bare feet making no sound. "He will be gentle with thine body. He will—"

"He will do no such thing. He is the son of the warrior the Bloodletter."

Amalya jerked back. *"What?"*

"Did the Scribe Virgin not tell you?"

"Her Holiness said only that it was arranged with one of the Brotherhood, a warrior of worth."

Cormia shook her head. "I was told earlier, when she first came unto me. I thought all knew."

Amalya's concern drew her brows together. Without a word, she sat on the cot and gathered Cormia to her.

"I do not want this," Cormia whispered. "Forgive me, sister. But I do not."

Amalya's voice lacked conviction as she said, "All will be well . . . truly."

"What goes on herein?" The sharp voice yanked them apart sure as a pair of hands.

The Directrix stood in the doorway, her stare suspicious. With a book of some sort in one hand and a strand of black worship pearls in the other, she was the perfect representation of the Chosen's proper purpose and calling.

Amalya stood up quickly, but there was no denying the moment. As a Chosen, you were to rejoice in your station at all times; anything less was considered a specious deviation for which you had to render penitence. And they had been caught.

"I shall talk to the Chosen Cormia now," the Directrix announced. "Alone."

"Yes, of course." Amalya went to the door with her head down. "If you will excuse me, sisters."

"You shall progress to the Temple of Atonement, will you not."

"Yes, Directrix."

"Stay there for the rest of the cycle. If I see you on the grounds, I will be most displeased."

"Yes, Directrix."

Cormia squeezed her eyes shut and prayed for her friend as the female left. A whole cycle in that temple? You could go mad from the sensory deprivation.

The Directrix's words were clipped. "I would send you there, too, were there not things you need to attend."

Cormia brushed off her tears. "Yes, Directrix."

"You shall begin your preparations now by reading this." The leather-bound book landed on the bed. "It details the Primale's rights and your obligations. When you have finished, you will have your sexual tutorial."

Oh, dear Virgin, please, not the Directrix . . . please, not the Directrix . . .

"Layla will instruct you." As Cormia's shoulders sagged, the Directrix snapped, "Shall I take offense at your relief that it shall be not I who teaches you?"

"Not at all, my sister."

"Now you offend with untruth. Look at me. *Look at me.*"

Cormia lifted her eyes and couldn't help but draw back in fear as the Directrix pinned her with a hard stare.

"You shall do your duty and do it well or I shall cast you out. Do you understand me? You shall be cast out."

Cormia was so stunned she couldn't reply. Cast out? Cast out . . . to the far side?

"*Answer me.* Are we clear?"

"Y-yes, Directrix."

"Mistake this not. The survival of the Chosen and the order I have established herein are of the only significance. Any one individual who obstacles either will be eliminated. Remind you that when you feel the urge to pity yourself. This is an honor, and it shall be revoked with attendant consequences by my hand. Are we clear? *Are we clear?*"

Cormia couldn't find her voice, so she nodded.

The Directrix shook her head, a strange light coming into her eye. "Save for your bloodline, you are wholly unacceptable. As of fact, the entirety of this is wholly unacceptable."

The Directrix left in a whisper of robing, her white silk sheath flowing around the doorjamb in her wake.

Cormia put her head in her hands and bit her lower lip as she contemplated her station: Her body had just been promised to a

warrior she'd never met . . . who was begotten of a brutish and cruel sire . . . and upon her shoulders the noble tradition of the Chosen rested.

Honor? Nay, this was a punishment—for the audacity of wanting something for herself.

As another martini arrived, Phury tried to remember whether it was his fifth? Or sixth? He wasn't sure.

"Man, good thing we ain't fighting tonight," Butch said. "You're drinking that shit like water."

"I'm thirsty."

"Guess so." The cop stretched in the booth. "How much longer you plan on rehydrating there, Lawrence of Arabia?"

"You don't have to hang—"

"Move over, cop."

Both Phury and Butch glanced up. V had appeared in front of the table from out of nowhere, and something was up. With his wide eyes and his pale face, he looked like he'd been in an accident, though he wasn't bleeding.

"Hey, my man." Butch scooted to the right to make room. "Didn't think we'd see you tonight."

V sat down, his leather biker's jacket bunching up and making his big shoulders look positively immense. In an uncharacteristic move, he started drumming his fingers on the tabletop.

Butch frowned at his roommate. "You look like roadkill. What's doing?"

Vishous linked his hands together. "This isn't the place."

"So let's go home."

"No fucking way. I'm going to be trapped there all day long." V lifted his hand. When the waitress came over, he put a hundred on her tray. "Keep the Goose coming, true? And that's just for the tip."

She smiled. "My pleasure."

As she took off for the bar like she was on roller skates, V's eyes sifted through the VIP area, his brows down low. Shit, he wasn't checking out the crowd. He was trolling for a fight. And was it possible that the Brother was . . . glowing a little?

Phury looked to the left and tapped his ear twice, sending a request to one of the Moors that guarded a private door. The security guard nodded and spoke into a wristwatch.

Moments later a huge male with a cropped Mohawk came out. Rehvenge was dressed in a perfectly tailored black suit and had a black cane in his right hand. As he came slowly over to the Brotherhood's table, his patrons parted before him, partly out of respect for his size, partly out of fear from his reputation. Everyone knew who he was and what he was capable of: Rehv was the kind of drug lord who took a personal interest in his livelihood. You crossed him and you turned up diced like something off the Food Channel.

Zsadist's half-breed brother-in-law was proving to be a surprising ally for the Brotherhood, although Rehv's true nature complicated everything. It wasn't smart to get in bed with a *symphath*. Literally or figuratively. So he was an uneasy friend and relative.

His tight smile barely showed any fangs. "Evening, gentlemen."

"Mind if we use your office for a little private biz?" Phury asked.

"I'm not talking," V ground out as his drink arrived. With a flip of the wrist he tossed the thing back like he had a fire in his gut and the shit was water. "Not. Talking."

Phury and Butch locked eyes, and a perfect accord was met: Vishous was so going to convo.

"Your office?" Phury said to Rehvenge.

Rehv lifted an elegant eyebrow, his amethyst eyes shrewd. "Not sure you'd want to use it. The place is wired for sound, and every syllable goes on record. Unless . . . of course . . . I'm in there."

Not ideal, but anything that hurt the Brotherhood hurt Rehv's sister, as Z's mate. So even though the guy was part *symphath*, he had the motivation to be tight about whatever went down.

Phury slid out of the booth and stared at V. "Bring your drink."

"No."

Butch got up. "Then you're leaving it. Because if you won't go home, we talk here."

V's eyes gleamed. And they weren't the only thing. "Fuck—"

Butch leaned down onto the table. "Right now you're throwing off an aura like your ass is plugged into the wall. So I strongly encourage you to drop the I-am-an-island bullshit and get your sorry excuse for a personality into Rehv's office before we have a situation. Dig?"

There was a long stretch of nothing but V and Butch looking at each other. Then V got to his feet and headed for Rehv's office. On the way, his anger carried a toxic chemical smell, the kind that stung your nose raw.

Man, the cop was the only one who had a chance with V when the male was like this.

So thank God for the Irishman.

The group of them went through the door guarded by the pair of Moors and took up res in Rehvenge's cave of an office. As the door shut, Rehv went behind his desk, reached under it, and a beeping sound went off.

"We're clear," he said, lowering himself into a black leather chair.

They all stared at V . . . who promptly went zoo animal, all pacing around and looking like he wanted to eat someone. The brother finally stopped across the room from Butch. The recessed light above him wasn't as bright as what was shining under his skin.

"Talk to me," Butch murmured.

Without saying a word, V took something out of his back pocket. As his arm came forward, a heavy gold pendant swung on the end of a silken cord.

"Seems I got a new job."

"Oh . . . shit," Phury whispered.

The setup in Blay's bedroom was SOP for John and his buddies: John was on the foot of the bed. Blay was cross-legged on the floor.

Qhuinn was in full lounge, his new body hanging half on, half off a beanbag chair. Coronas were open, and bags of Doritos and Ruffles were being passed around.

"Okay, so spill," Blay said. "What was your transition like?"

"Screw the change, I got laid." As Blay and John both bug-eyed, Qhuinn chuckled. "Yeah. I did. Got my cherry popped, so to speak."

"Get. The. Fuck. Out," Blay breathed.

"For real." Qhuinn tossed his head back and swallowed half his beer. "I will say, though, that transition . . . man . . ." He looked at John, his mismatched eyes narrowing. "Get ready, J-man. It's hard-core. You wish you would die. You pray for it. And then shit gets critical."

Blay nodded. "It is awful."

Qhuinn finished his beer and tossed the empty into a wastepaper basket. "Mine was witnessed. Yours, too, right?" When Blay nodded, Qhuinn cracked open the minifridge and took out another Corona. "Yeah, I mean . . . that was weird. My father in the room. Her father, too. All while my body was whacking out. I would have been embarrassed, but I was too busy feeling like ass."

"Who did you use?" Blay asked.

"Marna."

"Niiiiiiice."

Qhuinn's eyelids got heavy. "Yeah, she was *very* nice."

Blay's mouth fell open. "Her? She was the one you—"

"Yup." Qhuinn laughed as Blay collapsed back on the floor like he'd been shot in the chest. "Marna. I know. I can barely believe it myself."

Blay lifted his head. "How did it happen? And so help me God, I will whup your ass if you leave anything out."

"Ha! Like you were so forthcoming with your shit."

"Don't dodge the question. Start barking like the dog you are, buddy."

Qhuinn sat forward, and John took the cue, moving to the very edge of the bed.

"Okay, so it was all over, right? I mean . . . the drinking was done, change was finished, I was lying on the bed just . . . yeah, train-wrecked. She was hanging out in case I needed more from her vein, like in a chair in the corner or something. Anyway, her father and mine were talking and I kind of passed out. Next thing I know, I'm alone in the room. Door opens and it's Marna. Says she forgot her sweater or some shit. I took one look at her and . . . well, Blay, you know what she looks like, right? Instant hard-on. Can you blame me?"

"Not in the slightest."

John blinked and leaned in even closer.

"Anyway, there was a sheet over me, but somehow she knew. Man, she was totally looking me over and smiling, and I was like, 'Oh, my God . . .' But then her father calls her name from down the hall. The two of them had to stay over because it was daylight by the time I was through, but he clearly didn't want her bunking in with me. So as she leaves, she tells me she'll sneak back in later. I didn't really believe her, but I had my hopes. Hour goes by, I'm waiting . . . I'm jonesing. Another hour. Then it's like, fine, she ain't showing. I call my dad on the house phone and tell him I'm crashing. Then I get up, drag my ass into the shower, come back out . . . and she's in the room. *Naked. On the bed.* Christ, all I could do was stare. But I got over that fast." Qhuinn's eyes fixated on the floor and he shook his head back and forth. "I took her three times. One right after the other."

"Oh . . . shit," Blay whispered. "Did you like it?"

"What do you think? Duh." As Blay nodded and lifted his Corona to his lips, Qhuinn said, "When I was done, I put her in the shower, cleaned her off, and went down on her for half an hour."

Blay choked on his beer, spraying it all over himself. "Oh, God . . ."

"She tasted like a ripe plum. Sweet and syrupy." As John's eyeballs popped clear out of his head, Qhuinn smiled. "I had her all over my face. It was fantastic."

The guy took a long swallow, like he was so the man, and made no effort to hide his body's reaction to what he was no doubt reliving in his head. As his jeans got tight at the zipper, Blay covered up his hips with a fleece.

Having nothing to conceal, John looked down at his bottle.

"Are you going to mate her?" Blay asked.

"For God's sake, no!" Qhuinn's hand lifted and he gently prodded his black eye. "It was just . . . a thing that happened. I mean, *no*. She and I? Never."

"But wasn't she a—"

"No, she wasn't a virgin. Of course she wasn't. So no mating. She would never have me like that anyway."

Blay looked over at John. "Females of the aristocracy are supposed to be virgins before they're mated."

"Times have changed, though." Qhuinn frowned. "Still, don't say anything to anyone, okay? We had a good time, and it was no big deal. She's good peeps."

"Lips sealed." Blay took a deep breath, then cleared his throat. "Ah . . . it's better with someone else, isn't it?"

"Sex? By miles, buddy. Doing yourself takes the edge off, but it's nothing like the real thing. God, she was so soft . . . especially between her legs. I loved being on top of her, working my shit in deep, hearing her moan. I wish you guys could have been there. You'd have really dug it."

Blay rolled his eyes. "You having sex. Yeah, now, there's something I need to see."

Qhuinn's smile was slow and a little evil. "You like watching me fight, right?"

"Well, sure, you're good at it."

"Why should sex be any different? It's just something you do with your body."

Blay seemed nonplussed. "But . . . what about privacy?"

"Privacy is a matter of context." Qhuinn got out a third beer. "And, Blay?"

"What?"

"I'm really good at sex, too." He cracked the top and took a pull. "So here's what we need to do. I'm going to take a couple days to get strong, and then we're going out to the clubs downtown. I want to do it again, but it can't be with her." Qhuinn looked over at John. "J-man, you're coming with us to ZeroSum. I don't care if you're a pretrans. We go together."

Blay nodded. "The three of us are a good vibe. Besides, John, you're going to be where we are soon."

As the two started making plans, John got quiet. The whole picking-up-chicks thing was unfathomable, and not just because the transition had yet to hit him. He had a bad history with things of a sexual nature. The worst.

For a split second, he had a vivid memory of the dirty stairwell it had happened in. He felt the gun at his temple. Felt his jeans being yanked down. Felt the unthinkable as it was done to him. He remembered his breath scratching up and down his throat and his eyes watering and how, when he'd pissed himself, it had gotten on the tips of the guy's cheap sneakers.

"This weekend," Qhuinn announced, "we are going to get you taken care of, Blay."

John put his beer down and rubbed his face as Blay's cheeks got red.

"Yeah, Qhuinn . . . I don't know—"

"Trust me. I'm going to make it happen for you. Then, John? You're next."

John's first response was to shake his head no, but he stopped himself so he didn't look like an idiot. He was already feeling behind the eight ball, all small and unmanly. Turning down an offer to get laid would put him solidly in Loserland.

"So we got a plan?" Qhuinn demanded.

As Blay fiddled with the bottom of his T-shirt, John got the distinct impression the guy was going to say no. Which made John feel so much better—

"Yeah." Blay cleared his throat. "I . . . ah, yeah. I'm, like, juiced as shit. It's almost all I can think about, you know? And it's, like, painful, for real."

"I know exactly what you mean." Qhuinn's mismatched eyes sparkled. "And we are going to have us some good times. Shit, John . . . will you tell your body to get its groove on?"

John just shrugged, wishing he could leave.

"So, time for some sKillerz?" Blay asked, nodding to the Xbox on the floor. "John's going to beat us again, but we can still fight for number two."

It was a royal relief to get focused on something else, and the three of them got wound up by the game, yelling at the TV, throwing candy wrappers and beer caps at one another. God, John loved this. On the video screen they competed as equals. He was not small and left behind; he was better than they were. In sKillerz, he could be the warrior he wanted to be.

As he tanned their hides, he looked over at Blay and knew the guy had picked this game specifically to make John feel better. But then, Blay tended to know where people were in their heads, and how to be kind without embarrassing someone. He was an excellent friend.

Four six-packs, three trips to the kitchen, two full games of sKillerz, and a Godzilla movie later, John checked his watch and got off the bed. Fritz would be coming for him soon, because he had an appointment at four A.M. every night that he had to make or he was kicked out of the training program.

See you tomorrow in class? he signed.

"Good deal," Blay said.

Qhuinn smiled. "IM later, 'kay?"

Will do. He paused at the door. *Oh, hey, meant to ask.* He tapped his eye and pointed to Qhuinn. *What's up with the shiner?*

Qhuinn's stare stayed absolutely steady, his smile bright as ever. "Oh, it's nothing. Just slipped and fell in the shower. Really stupid, huh."

John frowned and glanced at Blay, whose eyes hit the floor and stayed there. Okay, something was—

"John," Qhuinn said firmly, "accidents happen."

John didn't believe the kid, especially given that Blay's peepers were still down for the count, but as someone who had his own secret he wasn't into the prying thing.

Yeah, sure, he signed. Then he whistled a quick good-bye and took off.

As he closed the door, he heard their deep voices and put his hand on the wood. He wanted to be where they were so badly, but the sex stuff . . . No, his transition was about becoming male so he could avenge his dead. It was not about banging chicks. Matter of fact, maybe he should take a page from Phury's book.

Celibacy had plenty of things to recommend it. Phury had been abstaining for, like, ever, and look at him. He was totally tight in the head, a real together kind of guy.

Not bad footsteps to follow in.

FIVE

"You're going to be the what?" Butch blurted.

As he looked at his roommate, Vishous could barely choke out the fucking word. "The Primale. Of the Chosen."

"What the fuck is that?"

"Basically, a sperm donor."

"Wait, wait . . . so you're going to do, like, IVF?"

V dragged a hand through his hair and thought how good it would feel to put his fist through the wall. "It's a little more hands-on than that."

Speaking of hands-on, it had been a long time since he'd had straight sex with a female. Could he even get off during the formal, ritualistic mating of the Chosen?

"Why you?"

"Has to be a member of the Brotherhood." V paced around the dark room, figuring he'd keep his mother's identity under wraps a

little longer. "It's a small pool to choose from. One that's getting smaller."

"Will you live over there?" Phury asked.

"Live over where?" Butch cut in. "You mean you won't be able to fight with us? Or, like . . . hang?"

"No, I made that a condition of the deal."

As Butch exhaled in relief, V tried not to get sapped out that his roommate cared about seeing him as much as he cared about being seen.

"When does it happen?"

"Few days."

Phury spoke up. "Does Wrath know?"

"Yup."

As V thought about what he'd signed on for, his heart started kicking in his chest, a bird flapping its wings to get out of his rib cage. The fact that he had two of his brothers and Rehvenge giving him the hairy eyeball made the panic worse. "Listen, you mind excusing me for a while? I need to . . . shit, I need to get out."

"I'll go with you," Butch said.

"No." V was in a desperate frame of mind. If there was ever a night he might be tempted to do something grossly inappropriate, it was now. Bad enough what he felt for his roommate was an unspoken undercurrent; making it a reality by acting on it would be a catastrophe neither he, Butch, nor Marissa could handle. "I need to be by myself."

V shoved the godforsaken pendant back in his ass pocket and left the crushing silence of the office. As he fast-tracked it out the side door into an alley, he wanted to find a *lesser*. Needed to find one. Prayed to the Scribe Vir—

V stopped dead. *Well, shit.* He sure as hell wasn't praying to that mother of his anymore. Or using that phrase.

God . . . damn.

V settled back against the cold brick of ZeroSum's building, and, much as it pained him, he couldn't help but think back to his life in the warrior camp.

The camp had been situated in middle Europe, deep in a cave. Some thirty soldiers had used it as a home base, but there had been other residents. A dozen pretrans had been sent there for training, and another dozen or so whores fed and serviced the males.

The Bloodletter had run it for years and had churned out some of the best fighters the species had. Four members of the Brotherhood had gotten their start there under V's father. Many others, of all levels, hadn't survived, however.

V's first memories were of being hungry and cold, of watching others eat while his stomach moaned. Through his early years, hunger had driven him, and like the other pretrans, his sole motivation had been to feed himself, no matter how he had to do it.

Vishous waited in the shadows of the cave, staying out of the flickering light thrown by the camp's fire pit. Seven fresh deer were being consumed in a bawdy frenzy, the soldiers slicing meat off bones and chewing like animals, blood marking their faces and hands. On the fringes of the meal, all the pretrans trembled with greed.

Like the others, V was sharpened to an edge from starvation. But he didn't stand with his fellow young. He waited in the faraway darkness, eyes locked on his prey.

The soldier he tracked was fat as a hog, with folds of flesh falling over his leathers and facial features indistinct for the puffy padding. The glutton went without a tunic most of the time, his bulbous chest and distended belly jiggling while he paraded around kicking the stray dogs that lived in camp or going after the whores. For all his sloth, however, he was a vicious killer, what he lacked in speed being made up for in brute strength. With hands as big as a grown male's head, he was rumored to snap the limbs off lessers and eat them.

At every meal he was among the first to get to the meat, and he ate with speed, though he was hampered by a lack of accuracy. He didn't pay

a lot of attention to what actually made it into his mouth: Pieces of deer flesh and streams of blood and segments of bone would coat his stomach and chest, a gory tunic knit of his sloppy ministrations.

This night the male finished early and eased back onto his haunches, a deer flank in his fist. Though he was through, he lingered next to the carcass he'd been working on, pushing other soldiers away for amusement.

When it was time for the sparring punishments to be dealt out, the fighters moved from the fire pit to the Bloodletter's platform. In the light of torches, soldiers who had lost during practice were bent over at the foot of the Bloodletter and violated by those who'd bested them, to the sneers and slaps of the others. Meanwhile, the pretrans fell on what was left of the deer while the females of the camp watched with hard eyes, waiting their turn.

V's prey wasn't much interested in the humiliations. The fat soldier watched for a little while, then lumbered off, the deer leg hanging from his hand. His filthy pallet was all the way at the far edges of where the soldiers slept, because even to their noses, his stench offended.

Stretched out, he looked like an undulating field, his body a series of hills and valleys. The deer leg lying across his belly was the prize at the top of the mountain.

V stayed back until the soldier's beady eyes were covered by fleshy lids and his hefty chest went up and down with a slowing rhythm. Soon fish lips fell open, and one snore escaped, followed by another. It was then that V closed in on his bare feet, making no sound over the dirt floor.

The foul smell of the male didn't deter V, and he cared not about the grime on the deer's fresh muscle. He reached forward, small hand splayed, inching toward the bone joint.

Just as he ripped it free, a black dagger streaked down next to the soldier's ear and its penetration into the packed cave floor snapped open the male's eyes.

V's father loomed like a chain-mail fist about to fall, legs planted, dark eyes leveled. He was the biggest of all in the camp, rumored to be the largest male born into the species, and his presence inspired fear for two reasons: his size and his unpredictability. His mood was ever-changing, his whims violent and capricious, but V knew the truth behind the variable temper: There was nothing that was not calibrated for effect. His father's malicious cunning ran as deep as his muscle was thick.

"Awake," the Bloodletter snapped. "You laze whilst you are feloned by a weakling."

V cringed away from his father, but started to eat, sinking his teeth into the meat and chewing as fast as he could. He would be beaten for this, likely by the both of them, so he had to consume as much as possible before the blows landed upon him.

The fat one made excuses until the Bloodletter kicked him in the sole of the foot with a spiked boot. The male went gray in the face but knew better than to cry out.

"The whys of this happenstance bore me." The Bloodletter stared at the soldier. "What shall you do about it, is my inquiry."

Without taking a breath the soldier curled up a fist, leaned over, and slammed it into V's side. V lost the mouthful he had as the impact drove the breath from his lungs and the meat from his mouth. As he gasped, he picked the piece up from the dirt and pushed it back between his lips. It tasted salty from the cave's floor.

As the beating commenced, V ate through the blows until he felt his calf bone bend until it nearly snapped. He let out a scream and lost the deer leg. Someone else picked it up and ran away with it.

All along, the Bloodletter laughed without smiling, the barking sound coming from lips that were straight and thin as knives. And then he ended it. With no effort at all he grabbed the fat soldier by the back of the neck and threw him against the rock wall.

The Bloodletter's spiked boots planted in front of V's face. "Get me my dagger."

V blinked dry eyes and tried to move.

There was a creak of leather, and then the Bloodletter's face was before V. "Get me my dagger, boy. Or I will have you take the whores' place tonight in the pit."

The soldiers who had gathered behind his father cackled, and some-one threw a stone that hit V where his leg had been injured.

"My dagger, boy."

Vishous speared his little fingers into the dirt and dragged himself over to the weapon. Though a mere two feet from him, the blade seemed miles away. When he finally closed his palm upon it, he needed both hands to free it from the dirt, he was so weak. His stomach was rolling from pain, and as he pulled at the blade, he threw up the meat he had stolen.

After the retching passed, he held up the dagger to his father, who had risen back to his full height.

"Stand," the Bloodletter said. "Or think you I should bow to the worthless?"

V struggled into a sitting position and couldn't fathom how he was going to get his full body up, as he could barely lift his shoulders. He switched the dagger to his left hand, planted his right one on the dirt, and pushed. The pain was so great his eyesight went black . . . and then a miraculous thing occurred. Some kind of radiant light overtook him from the inside out, as if sunshine had swept into his veins and cleaned the pain until he was free of it. His eyesight returned . . . and he saw that his hand was glowing.

Now was not the time to wonder. He peeled himself from the ground, rising up while trying to put no weight on his leg. With a hand that shook, he presented the dagger to his father.

The Bloodletter stared back for a heartbeat, as if he'd never expected V to get to his feet. Then he took the weapon and turned away.

"Someone knock him back down. His boldness offends me."

V landed in a heap when the order was followed, and at once, the radiance left him and agony returned. He waited for other blows to land, but when he heard a crowd's roar, he knew that the losers' punishments would be the amusement for the day, not him.

As he lay in the swamp of his misery, as he tried to breathe through the pounding of his battered body, he pictured a little female in a black robe coming unto him and wrapping him up in her arms. With soft words she cradled him and stroked his hair, easing him.

He welcomed the vision. She was his imaginary mother. The one who loved him and wanted him to be safe and warm and fed. Verily, the image of her was what kept him alive, giving him the only peace he knew.

The fat soldier leaned down, his fetid, humid breath invading Vishous's nose. "You steal from me again and you shall not heal from what I bring unto you."

The soldier spat in V's face then picked him up and slung him like useless debris away from the dirty pallet.

Before V passed out, his last sight was of another pretrans finishing the deer leg with relish.

SIX

With a curse, V disengaged from his memories, his eyes flying around the alley he was standing in, like old newspapers caught in the wind. Man, he was a wreck. The seal on his Tupperware had cracked open and his leftovers had leaked out all over the place.

Messy. Very messy.

Good thing he hadn't known then what a crock of shit the whole my-mommy-who-loves-me thing was. That would have hurt him more than any of the abuse coming his way.

He took the Primale's medallion out of his back pocket and stared at it. He was still looking at it minutes later when the thing dropped to the ground and bounced like a coin. He frowned . . . until he realized that his "normal" hand was glowing and had burned through the silk cord.

Goddamn, his mother was an egomaniac. She'd brought the species into being, but that wasn't enough for her. Hell, no. She wanted herself in the mix.

Fuck it. He wasn't going to give her the satisfaction of hundreds of grandchildren. She'd sucked as a parent, so why should he give her another generation to screw over.

And besides, there was another reason why he shouldn't be the Primale. He was, after all, his father's son, so cruelty was in his DNA. How could he trust himself not to take it out on the Chosen? Those females were not to blame, and didn't deserve what would come between their legs if he were their mate.

He wasn't going to do this.

V lit a hand-rolled, picked up the medallion, and left the alley, hanging a right on Trade. He badly needed a fight before the dawn came.

And he banked on finding some *lessers* in downtown's concrete maze.

It was a safe bet. The war between the Lessening Society and the vampires had one and only one rule of engagement: No fighting around humans. The last thing either side needed was human casualties or witnesses, so hidden battles were the name of the game, and urban Caldwell presented a fine theater for small-scale combat: Thanks to the 1970s retail exodus to the burbs, there were plenty of dark alleys and vacated buildings. Also, what few humans were on the streets were primarily worried about servicing their various vices. Which meant they were otherwise occupied, giving the police plenty to do.

As he went along, he stayed out of the pools of light cast by street lamps and splashed by cars. Thanks to the bitter night there were few pedestrians around, so he was alone as he passed McGrider's Bar and Screamer's and a new strip club that had just opened. Farther up, he walked by the Tex-Mex buffet and the Chinese restaurant that were sandwiched between competing tattoo parlors. Blocks later he went by the apartment building on Redd Avenue where Beth had lived before she met Wrath.

He was about to turn around and go back toward the heart of

downtown when V stopped. Lifted his nose. Inhaled. The scent of baby powder was on the breeze, and since old biddies and babies were out of commission this late, he knew his enemy was close by.

But there was something else in the air, something that made his blood run cold.

V loosened his jacket so he could get at his daggers and started to run, tracking the scents to Twentieth Street. Twentieth was a one-way off Trade, bracketed by office buildings that were asleep this hour of night, and as he pounded down its uneven, slushy pavement, the smells got stronger.

He had a feeling he was too late.

Five blocks in he saw that he was right.

The other scent was the spilled blood of a civilian vampire, and as the clouds parted, moonlight fell on a gruesome spectacle: A post-transition male dressed in torn club clothes was beyond dead, his torso twisted, his face battered past any hope of recognition. The *lesser* who had done the killing was going through the vampire's pockets, no doubt hoping to find a home address as a lead for more carnage.

The slayer sensed V and looked over its shoulder. The thing was white as limestone, its pale hair, skin, and eyes matte like chalk. Big, built rugby-player solid, this one was well past his initiation, and V knew it not just because the bastard's natural pigmentations had faded out. The *lesser* was all business as he leaped to his feet, hands going up to his chest, body surging forward.

The two ran at each other and met as cars crashing at intersections did: grille-to-grille, weight-to-weight, force against force. In the initial meet-and-greet, V took a ham-handed smash to his jaw, the kind of punch that made your brains slosh around in your skull. He was momentarily dazed, but managed to return the favor hard enough to spin the *lesser* like a top. Then he went after his opponent, grabbing onto the back of the bastard's leather jacket and flipping him off his combat boots.

V liked to grapple. And he was good at the ground game.

The slayer was fast, though, popping up off the icy pavement and throwing out a kick that shuffled V's internal organs like a deck of cards. As V stumbled backward, he tripped on a Coke bottle, blew his ankle out, and took a seat on the express train down to the asphalt. Letting his body go loose, he kept his eyes on the slayer, who moved in fast. The bastard went for V's off ankle, grabbing the shit-kicker attached to it and twisting with all the power in his massive chest and arms.

V popped a holler as he flipped face-first onto the ground, but he shut out the pain. Using his bad ankle and his arms as leverage, he pushed himself off the asphalt, brought his free leg up to his chest and hammered it back, catching the motherfucker in the knee and shattering his joint. The *lesser* flamingoed, his leg bending in the absolute wrong way as he fell on V's back.

The two of them clinched up hard-core, their forearms and biceps straining as they rolled around and ended up next to the slaughtered civilian. When V was bitten in the ear, his shit really got cranked out. Tearing himself free of the *lesser's* teeth, he fisted the bastard's frontal lobe, laying a bone-on-bone crack that stunned the fucker long enough for him to get free.

Kind of.

The knife went into his side just as he was pulling his legs out from under the slayer. The sharp, shooting pain was a bee sting on 'roids, and he knew the blade had broken skin and penetrated muscle just below his rib cage, on the left.

Man, if an intestine had been nicked, things were going to go bad, fast. So it was time to put the fight to bed.

Energized by the injury, V grabbed the *lesser* by the chin and the back of the head and twisted the son of a bitch like he was a beer bottle. The snap of the skull popping free of the spinal cord was like a branch cracking in half and the body went instantaneously loose, its arms flopping to the ground, its legs going still.

V grabbed his side as his crest of power faded. Shit, he was covered in cold sweat and his hands were shaking, but he had to finish the job. He quickly patted down the *lesser*, looking for ID before he poofed the bastard.

The slayer's eyes met his, its mouth working slowly. "My name . . . was once Michael. Eighty . . . three . . . years ago. Michael Klosnick."

Flipping open the wallet, V found a current driver's license. "Well, Michael, have a nice trip to hell."

"Glad . . . it's over."

"It's not. Haven't you heard?" Shit, his side was killing him. "Your new town house is the Omega's body, buddy. You're going to live there rent-free for fucking ever."

Pale eyes cracked wide. "You lie."

"Please. Like I'd bother?" V shook his head. "Doesn't your boss mention that? Guess not."

V unsheathed one of his daggers, heaved his arm up over his shoulder, and drove the blade square into that wide chest. There was a burst of light bright enough to show off the whole alley, then a pop and . . . *shit*, the burst caught the civilian, lighting him up as well thanks to a heavy gust of wind. As the two bodies were consumed, all that was left on the cold breeze was the thick smell of baby powder.

Fuck. How could they notify the civilian's family now?

Vishous searched the area, and when he didn't find another wallet, he propped himself against a Dumpster and just sat there, breathing in shallow sucks. Each inhale made him feel like he was being stabbed again, but going without oxygen was not an option, so he kept at it.

Before he got out his phone to call for help, he looked at his dagger. The black blade was covered with the inky blood of the *lesser*. He ran through the fight with the slayer and imagined another vampire in his place, one not as strong as he was. One who didn't have the breeding he had.

He brought up his gloved hand. If his curse had defined him, the Brotherhood and its noble purpose had shaped his life. And if he had been killed tonight? If that blade had gone into his heart? They'd be down to four fighters.

Fuck.

On the chessboard of his godforsaken existence, the pieces were lined up, the play preordained. Man, so many times in life you didn't get to pick your path because the way you went was decided for you.

Free will was *such* bullshit.

Forget his mother and her drama—he needed to become the Primale for the Brotherhood. He owed the legacy he served.

After wiping the blade on his leathers, he resheathed the weapon handle down, struggled to his feet, and patted down his jacket. Shit . . . his phone. Where was his phone? Back at the penthouse. He must have left it there after he talked to Wrath—

A shot rang out.

A bullet hit him right between his pecs.

The impact popped him off his heels and sent him on a slow-mo fall through thin air. As he went back flat on the ground, he just lay there as a crushing pressure made his heart jump and his brain fog out. All he could do was gasp, little quick breaths skipping up and down the corridor of his throat.

With his last bit of strength, he lifted his head and looked down his body. A gunshot. Blood on his shirt. The screaming pain in his chest. The nightmare realized.

Before he could panic, blackness came and swallowed him whole . . . a meal to be digested in an acid bath of agony.

"What the *hell* do you think you're doing, Whitcomb?"

Dr. Jane Whitcomb looked up from the patient chart she was signing and winced. Manuel Manello, M.D., chief of surgery at St. Francis Medical Center, was coming down the hall at her like a bull. And she knew why.

This was going to get ugly.

Jane scribbled her sig at the bottom of the drug order, handed the chart back to the nurse, and watched as the woman took off at a dead run. Good defensive maneuver, and not uncommon around here. When the chief got like this, folks took cover . . . which was the logical thing to do when a bomb was about to go off and you had half a brain.

Jane faced him. "So you've heard."

"In here. *Now.*" He punched open the door to the surgeons' lounge.

As she went in with him, Priest and Dubois, two of St. Francis's best GI knives, took one look at the chief, scrapped their vending-machine cuisine, and beat feet out of the room. In their wake, the door eased shut without even a whisper of air. Like it didn't want to catch Manello's attention, either.

"When were you going to tell me, Whitcomb? Or did you think Columbia was on a different planet and I wasn't going to find out?"

Jane crossed her arms over her chest. She was a tall woman, but Manello topped her by a couple of inches, and he was built like the professional athletes he operated on: big shoulders, big chest, big hands. At forty-five, he was in prime physical condition and one of the best orthopedic surgeons in the country.

As well as a scary SOB when he got mad.

Good thing she was comfortable in tense situations. "I know you have contacts there, but I thought they'd be discreet enough to wait until I decided whether I wanted the job—"

"Of course you want it or you wouldn't waste time going down there. Is it money?"

"Okay, first, you don't interrupt me. And second, you're going to lower your voice." As Manello dragged a hand through his thick dark hair and took a deep breath, she felt bad. "Look, I should have told you. It must have been embarrassing to get blindsided like that."

He shook his head. "Not my favorite thing, getting a call from Manhattan that one of my best surgeons is interviewing at another hospital with my mentor."

"Was it Falcheck who told you?"

"No, one of his underlings."

"I'm sorry, Manny. I just don't know how it's going to go, and I didn't want to jump the gun."

"Why are you thinking about leaving the department?"

"You know I want more than what I can have here. You're going to be chief until you're sixty-five, unless you decide to leave. Down at Columbia, Falcheck is fifty-eight. I've got a better chance of becoming head of the department there."

"I already made you chief of the Trauma Division."

"And I deserve it."

His lips cracked a smile. "Be humble, why don't you."

"Why bother? We both know it's the truth. And as for Columbia? Would you want to be under someone for the next two decades of your life?"

His lids lowered over his mahogany-colored eyes. For the briefest second, she thought she saw something flare in that stare of his, but then he put his hands on his hips, his white coat straining as his shoulders widened. "I don't want to lose you, Whitcomb. You're the best trauma knife I've got."

"And I have to look to the future." She went over to her locker. "I want to run my own shop, Manello. It's the way I am."

"When's the damn interview?"

"First thing tomorrow afternoon. Then I'm off through the weekend and not on call, so I'm going to stay in the city."

"Shit."

There was a knock on the door.

"Come in," they both called out.

A nurse ducked her head inside. "Trauma case, ETA two minutes.

Male in his thirties. Gunshot with probable perforated ventricle. Crashed twice so far on transport. Will you accept the patient, Dr. Whitcomb, or do you want me to call Goldberg?"

"Nope, I'll take him. Set up bay four in the chute and tell Ellen and Jim I'm coming right down."

"Will do, Dr. Whitcomb."

"Thanks, Nan."

The door eased shut, and she looked at Manello. "Back to Columbia. You'd do the exact same thing if you were in my shoes. So you can't tell me you're surprised."

There was a stretch of silence, then he leaned forward a little. "And I won't let you go without a fight. Which shouldn't surprise you, either."

He left the room, taking most of the oxygen in the place with him.

Jane leaned back against her locker and looked across to the kitchen area to the mirror hanging on the wall. Her reflection was crystal-clear in the glass, from her white doctor's coat to her green scrubs to her blunt-cut blond hair.

"He took that okay," she said to herself. "All things considered."

The door to the lounge opened, and Dubois poked his head in. "Coast clear?"

"Yup. And I'm heading down to the chute."

Dubois pushed the door wide and strode in, his crocs making no sound on the linoleum. "I don't know how you do it. You're the only one who doesn't need smelling salts after dealing with him."

"He's no problem, really."

Dubois made a chuffing noise. "Don't get me wrong. I respect the shit out of him, I truly do. But I don't want him pissed."

She put her hand on her colleague's shoulder. "Pressure wears on people. You lost it last week, remember?"

"Yeah, you're right." Dubois smiled. "And at least he doesn't throw things anymore."

SEVEN

The T. Wibble Jones Emergency Department of the St. Francis Medical Center was state-of-the-art, thanks to a generous donation from its namesake. Open for just a year and a half now, the fifty-thousand-square-foot complex was built in two halves, each with sixteen treatment bays. Emergency patients were admitted alternately to the A or the B track, and they stayed with whatever team they were assigned until they were released, admitted, or sent to the morgue.

Running down the center of the facility was what the medical staff called "the chute." The chute was strictly for trauma admits, and there were two kinds of them: "rollers," who came by ambulance, or "roofers," who were flown into the landing pad eleven stories up. The roofers tended to be more hard-core and were helicoptered in from about a hundred-and-fifty-mile radius around Caldwell. For those patients, there was a dedicated elevator that dumped out right into

the chute, one big enough to fit two gurneys and ten medical personnel at one time.

The trauma facility had six open patient bays, each with X-ray and ultrasound equipment, oxygen feeds, medical supplies, and plenty of space to move around. The operational hub, or control tower, was smack in the middle, a conclave of computers and personnel that was, tragically, always hopping. At any given hour there were at least one admitting physician, four residents, and six nurses staffing the area, with typically two to three patients in-house.

Caldwell was not as big as Manhattan, not by a long shot, but it had a lot of gang violence, drug-related shootings, and car accidents. Plus, with nearly three million residents, you saw an endless variation of human miscalculation: nail gun goes off into someone's stomach because a guy tried to fix the fly of his jeans with it; arrow gets shot through a cranium because somebody wanted to prove he had great aim, and was wrong; husband figures it would be a great idea to repair his stove and gets two-fortied because he didn't unplug the thing first.

Jane lived in the chute and owned it. As chief of the Trauma Division, she was administratively responsible for everything that went down in those six bays, but she was also trained as both an ED attending and a trauma surgeon, so she was hands-on. On a day-to-day basis, she made calls about who needed to go up one floor to the ORs, and a lot of times she scrubbed in to do the needle-and-thread stuff.

While she waited for her incoming gunshot, she reviewed the charts of the two patients currently being treated and looked over the shoulders of the residents and nurses as they worked. Every member of the trauma team was handpicked by Jane, and when recruiting, she didn't necessarily go for the Ivy Leaguer types, although she was Harvard-trained herself. What she looked for were the qualities of a good soldier, or, as she liked to call it, the No Shit, Sherlock mental set: smarts, stamina, and separation. Especially the separation. You

had to be able to stay tight in a crisis if you were going to W-II the chute.

But that didn't mean that compassion wasn't mission-critical in everything they did.

Generally, most trauma patients didn't need handholding or reassurance. They tended to be drugged up or shocked out because they were leaking blood like a sieve or had a body part in a freezer pack or had seventy-five percent of their dermis burned off. What the patients needed were crash carts with well-trained, levelheaded people on the business ends of the paddles.

Their families and loved ones, however, needed kindness and sympathy always, and reassurance when that was possible. Lives were destroyed or resurrected every day in the chute, and it wasn't just the folks on the gurneys who stopped breathing or started again. The waiting rooms were full of the others who were affected: husbands, wives, parents, children.

Jane knew what it was like to lose someone who was a part of you, and as she went about her clinical work she was very aware of the human side of all the medicine and the technology. She made sure her people were on the same page she was: To work in the chute, you had to be able to do both sides of the job, you needed the battlefield mentality *and* the bedside manner. As she told her staff, there was always time to hold someone's hand or listen to their worries or offer a shoulder to cry on, because in the blink of an eye you could be on the other side of that conversation. After all, tragedy didn't discriminate, so everyone was subject to the same whims of fate. No matter what your skin color was or how much money you had, whether you were gay or straight, or an atheist or a true believer, from where she stood, everyone was equal. And loved by someone, somewhere.

A nurse came up to her. "Dr. Goldberg just called in sick."

"That flu?"

"Yes, but he got Dr. Harris to cover."

Bless Goldberg's heart. "Our man need anything?"

The nurse smiled. "He said his wife was thrilled to see him when she was actually awake. Sarah is cooking him chicken soup and in full fuss mode."

"Good. He needs some time off. Shame he won't enjoy it."

"Yeah. He mentioned she was going to make him watch all the date movies they've missed in the last six months on DVD."

Jane laughed. "That'll make him sicker. Oh, listen, I want to do grand rounds on the Robinson case. There was nothing else we could have done for him, but I think we need to go over the death anyway."

"I had a feeling you'd want to do that. I set it up for the day after you get home from your trip."

Jane gave the nurse's hand a little squeeze. "You are a star."

"Nah, I just know our boss, is all." The nurse smiled. "You never let them go without checking and rechecking in case something could have been done differently."

That was certainly right. Jane remembered every single patient who had died in the chute, whether she had been their admitting physician or not, and she had the deceased cataloged in her mind. At night, when she couldn't sleep, the names and faces would run through her head like an old-fashioned microfiche until she thought she would go mad from the roll call.

It was the ultimate motivator, her list of the dead, and she was damned if this incoming gunshot was going on it.

Jane went over to a computer and called up the lowdown on the patient. This was going to be a battle. They were looking at a stab wound as well as a bullet in his chest cavity, and given where he'd been found, she was willing to bet he was either a drug dealer doing business in the wrong territory or a big buyer who'd gotten the shaft. Either way, it was unlikely he had health insurance, not that it mattered. St. Francis accepted all patients, regardless of their ability to pay.

Three minutes later, the double doors swung open and the crisis came in at slingshot speed: Mr. Michael Klosnick was strapped to a gurney, a giant Caucasian with a lot of tattoos, a set of leathers, and a goatee. The paramedic at his head was bagging him, while another one held the equipment down and pulled.

"Bay four," Jane told the EMTs. "Where are we?"

The guy bagging said, "Two large-bore IVs in with lactated ringers. BP is sixty over forty and falling. Heart rate is in the one-forties. Respiration is forty. Orally intubated. V-fibbed on the way over. Shocked him at two hundred joules. Sinus tachycardia in the one-forties."

In bay four, the medics stopped the gurney and braked it while the chute's staff coalesced. One nurse took a seat at a small table to record everything. Two others were on standby to bust out supplies at Jane's direction, and a fourth got ready to cut off the patient's leather pants. A pair of residents hovered to watch or help as needed.

"I got the wallet," the paramedic said, handing it over to the nurse with the scissors.

"Michael Klosnick, age thirty-seven," she read. "The picture on the ID is blurry, but . . . it could be him, assuming he dyed his hair black and grew the goatee after it was taken."

She handed the billfold over to the colleague who was taking notes and then started removing the leathers.

"I'll see if he's in the system," the other woman reported as she logged onto a computer. "Found him—wait, is this . . . Must be an error. No, address is right, year's wrong, though."

Jane cursed under her breath. "May be problems with the new electronic records system, so I don't want to rely on the information in there. Let's get a blood type and a chest X-ray right away."

While blood was drawn, Jane did a quick preliminary examination. The gunshot wound was a tidy little hole right next to some kind of scarification on his pectoral. A rivulet of blood was all that showed externally, giving little hint of whatever mess was inside. The knife wound was much the same. Not much surface drama. She hoped his intestines hadn't been nicked.

She glanced down the rest of his body, seeing a number of tattoos— *Whoa.* That was one hell of an old groin injury. "Let me see the X-ray, and I want an ultrasound of his heart—"

A scream ripped through the OR.

Jane's head snapped to the left. The nurse who'd been stripping the patient was down on the floor in full seizure with her arms and legs flapping against the tile. In her hand she had a black glove the patient had been wearing.

For a split second everyone froze.

"She just touched his hand and went down," someone said.

"Back in the game!" Jane clipped. "Estevez, you see to her. I want to know how she is immediately. Rest of you get tight. Now!"

Her commands snapped the staff into action. Everyone refocused as the nurse was carried over to the bay next door and Estevez, one of the residents, started to treat her.

The chest X-ray came out relatively fine, but for some reason the ultrasound of the heart was of poor quality. Both, however, revealed exactly what Jane expected: pericardial tamponade from a right ventricular gunshot wound: Blood had leaked into the pericardial sac and was compressing the heart, compromising its function and causing it to pump poorly.

"We need an ultrasound of his abdomen while I buy us some time with his heart." With the more pressing injury ascertained, Jane wanted more information on that knife wound. "And as soon as that's done, I want both machines checked. Some of these chest images have an echo."

As a resident went to work on the patient's belly with the ultrasound wand, Jane took a twenty-one-gauge spinal needle and plugged it into a fifty-cc syringe. After a nurse Betadined the man's chest, Jane pierced his skin and navigated the bone anatomy, breaching the pericardial sac and drawing out forty ccs of blood to ease the pericardial tamponade. Meanwhile, she gave out orders to prepare OR two upstairs and get the cardiac bypass team on the ready.

She gave the syringe to a nurse for disposal. "Let's see the abdominal."

The machine was definitely misbehaving, as the images were not as clear as she'd like. They did, however, show some good news, which was confirmed as she palpated the region. No major internal organs appeared to be affected.

"Okay, abdomen appears sound. Let's move him upstairs, stat."

On her way out of the chute, she put her head into the bay where Estevez was working on the nurse. "How's she doing?"

"Coming around." Estevez shook his head. "Her heart stabilized after we hit her with the paddles."

"She was fibrillating? Christ."

"Just like the telephone guy we had in yesterday. Like she'd been hit with a load of electricity."

"Did you call Mike?"

"Yeah, her husband's coming in."

"Good. Take care of our girl."

Estevez nodded and looked down at his colleague. "Always."

Jane caught up with the patient as the staff wheeled him down the chute and into the elevator that went to the surgical suite. One floor up she scrubbed in while the nurses got him onto her table. At her request, a cardiothoracic surgical kit and the heart/lung bypass machine had been set up, and the ultrasounds and X-rays taken downstairs were glowing on a computer screen.

With both hands latexed and held away from herself, she reviewed the chest scans again. Truth be told, both of them were subpar, very grainy and with that echo, but there was enough to orient herself. The bullet was lodged in the muscles of his back, and she was going to leave it there: The risks inherent in removing it were greater than letting it rest in peace, and in fact, most gunshot victims left the chute with their lead trophy wherever it ended up.

She frowned and leaned in closer to the screen. Interesting bullet. Round, not the typical oblong shape she was used to seeing inside her patients. Still, appeared to be made of garden-variety lead.

Jane approached the table where the patient had been hooked up to the anesthesia machines. His chest had been prepped, the regions around it draped in surgical cloth. The orange wash of Betadine made him look like he had a bad fake tan. "No bypass. I don't want to use up the time. Tell me we have blood for him on hand?"

One of the nurses spoke up from the left. "We do, although his blood didn't type."

Jane glanced across the patient. "It didn't?"

"The sample reading came back unidentifiable. But we have eight liters of O."

Jane frowned. "Okay, let's do this."

Using a laser scalpel, she made an incision down the patient's chest, then sawed through the sternum and used a rib spreader to pull open the heart's iron bars, exposing—

Jane lost her breath. "Holy . . ."

"Shit," someone finished.

"Suction." When there was a pause, she looked up at her assisting nurse. "Suction, Jacques. I don't care what it looks like, I can fix it—provided I get a clear shot at the damn thing."

There was a hissing sound as the blood was removed, and then she got a good gander at a physical anomaly she'd never seen before: a six-chambered heart in a human chest. That "echo" she'd seen on the ultrasounds was, in fact, an extra pair of chambers.

"Pictures!" she called out. "But make it quick, please."

As photographs were taken, she thought, *Boy, the Cardiology Department is going to go nuts over this.* She'd never seen anything like it before—although the hole torn in the right ventricle was totally familiar. She'd known a lot of them.

"Suture," she said.

Jacques slapped a pair of grips into her palm, the stainless-steel instrument carrying a curved needle with a black thread clipped onto the end. With her left hand, Jane reached in behind the heart, plugged the back end of the hole with her finger, and stitched the front impact site closed. Next move was to lift the heart out of its pericardial sac and do the same underneath.

Total elapsed time was under six minutes. Then she released the spreader, put the rib cage back where it was supposed to be and used stainless-steel wire to close the two halves of the sternum together. Just as she was about to staple him from his diaphragm to his collarbone, the anesthesiologist spoke up and machines started to beep.

"BP is sixty over forty and falling."

Jane called out the heart-failure protocol and leaned down to the patient. "Don't even think about it," she snapped. "You die on me and I'm going to be really ticked off."

From out of nowhere, and against all medical rationale, the man's eyes blinked open and focused on her.

Jane jerked back. Good God . . . his irises held the colorless splendor of diamonds, shining so bright they reminded her of the winter moon on a cloudless night. And for the first time in her life, she was stunned into immobility. With their locked stares, it was as if they were linked body-to-body, twisted and intertwined, indivisible—

"He's V-fibbing again," the anesthesiologist barked.

Jane snapped back to attention.

"You stay with me," she ordered the patient. "You hear me? *You stay with me.*"

She could have sworn the guy nodded at her before his lids shut. And she got back to work saving his life.

"You so need to lighten up about that potato-launcher incident," Butch said.

Phury rolled his eyes and eased back in the banquette. "You broke my window."

"Of course we did. V and I were aiming for it."

"Twice."

"Thus proving that he and I are outstanding marksmen."

"Next time can you please pick someone else's . . ." Phury frowned

and lowered the martini from his lips. For no apparent reason, his instincts were suddenly alive, all lit up and ringing like a slot machine. He glanced around the VIP section, looking for some flavor of trouble. "Hey, cop, do you—"

"Something's not right," Butch said as he rubbed the center of his chest, then took his thick gold cross out from under his shirt. "What the hell is doing?"

"I don't know." Phury ran his stare through the crowd again. Man, it was as if a foul odor had sneaked into the room, coloring the air with something that made your nose want a new job description. And yet there was nothing wrong.

Phury took out his phone and dialed his twin. When Zsadist got on the line, the first thing the Brother asked was whether Phury was okay.

"I'm fine, Z, but you're feeling it, too, huh?"

Across the table, Butch put his cell up to his ear. "Baby? You all right? You okay? Yeah, I don't know. . . . Wrath wants to talk to me? Yeah, sure, put him on. . . . Hey, big man. Yeah. Phury and me. Yeah. No. Rhage is with you? Good. Yeah, I'm calling Vishous next."

After the cop hung up, he punched a couple of keys and the phone went back to his ear. Butch's brows came down. "V? Call me. As soon as you get this."

He ended the call just as Phury got off with Z.

The two of them sat back. Phury fiddled with his drink. Butch played with his cross.

"Maybe he went to his penthouse to work on a female," Butch said.

"He told me he was going to do that first thing tonight."

"Okay. So maybe he's in the middle of a fight."

"Yeah. He'll call us right back."

Although all of the Brotherhood's phones had GPS chips in them, V's didn't work if the phone was on him, so calling back to the compound and putting a trace on his RAZR wasn't going to help much. V blamed that hand of his for throwing off the functionality, maintaining that whatever made his palm glow caused an electrical or magnetic disturbance. Sure as hell affected call quality. Whenever you talked to V on a phone there was fuzz on the line, even if he was on a landline.

Phury and Butch lasted about a minute and a half before they looked at each other and spoke at the same time.

"You mind if we just swing by—"

"Let's just go—"

They both stood up and headed for the club's emergency side door.

Outside in the alley, Phury looked up to the night sky. "You want me to dematerialize over to his place real quick?"

"Yeah. Do that."

"I need the address. Never been there before."

"Commodore. Top floor, southwest corner. I'll wait here."

For Phury it was the work of a moment to put himself on the windy terrace of a flashy penthouse some ten blocks closer to the river. He didn't even bother approaching the wall of glass. He could sense that his brother wasn't there, and was back at Butch's side in a heartbeat.

"Nope."

"So he's hunting—" The cop froze, an odd, fixated expression hitting his face. His head whipped around to the right. *"Lessers."*

"How many?" Phury asked, opening his jacket. Ever since Butch had had his run-in with the Omega, he'd been able to sense slayers like you read about, the bastards coins to his metal detector.

"A pair. Let's make this quick."

"Damn right."

The *lessers* came around the corner, took one look at Phury and Butch, and fell into the ready position. The alley right outside Zero-

Sum was not the best place for a fight, but luckily because the night was so cold, there weren't any humans around.

"I'm on cleanup," Butch said.

"Roger that."

The two of them lunged at their enemy.

EIGHT

Two hours later Jane pushed the door to the Surgical Intensive Care Unit wide. She was packed up and ready to go home, her leather bag on her shoulder, car keys in her hand, her windbreaker on. But she wasn't leaving without seeing her gunshot patient first.

As she walked over to the nursing station, the woman on the other side of the counter looked up. "Hey, Dr. Whitcomb. Come to check on your admit?"

"Yeah, Shalonda. You know me—can't leave 'em alone. What room did you give him?"

"Number six. Faye's in with him now, making sure he's comfortable."

"See why I love you guys? Best SICU staff in town. By the way, has anyone come to see him? We find a next of kin?"

"I called the number on his medical record. Guy who answered said he'd lived in the apartment for the last ten years and had never

heard of a Michael Klosnick. So the addy was a false one. Oh, and did you see the weapons they found on him? Talk about packing with nothing lacking."

As Shalonda rolled her eyes, the two of them said at the same time, "Drug-related."

Jane shook her head. "I'm not surprised."

"Neither am I. Those tats on his face don't exactly play him as an insurance adjuster."

"Not unless he's pushing paper for a bunch of pro wrestlers."

Shalonda was laughing as Jane waved and headed down the corridor. Number six was all the way back, on the right, and as she went she looked in on two other patients she'd operated on, one who'd had a perforated bowel from liposuction gone wrong and another who'd been impaled on a fence rail in a motorcycle accident.

SICU rooms were twenty by twenty square feet of all business. Each one was glass-fronted, with a curtain that could be pulled for privacy, and they were not the kind of digs that had a window or a Monet poster or a TV with Regis and Kelly on it. If you were well enough to worry about what you were watching on the tube, you didn't belong here. The only screens and pictures were from the monitoring equipment orbiting the bed.

When Jane got to six, Faye Montgomery, a real veteran, looked up from checking the patient's IV. "Evenin', Dr. Whitcomb."

"Faye, how are you?" Jane put her bag down and reached for the medical record that was in a pocket holder by the door.

"I'm good, and before you ask, he's stable. Which is amazing."

Jane flipped through the most recent stats. "No kidding."

She was about to close up the medical record when she frowned at the number on the left-hand corner. The ten-digit patient ID was thousands and thousands of numbers away from the ones given to new admits, and she checked the date the file had first been opened: 1971. Flipping through, she found two admits to the ED: one for a knife wound, the other for a drug overdose; '71 and '73 were the dates.

Ah, hell, she'd seen this before. Zeros and sevens could look alike when you wrote them fast. The hospital hadn't made the move to computerized records until late in 2003, and before that everything had been handwritten. This record had clearly been transcribed by data processors who misread what was there: instead of '01 and '03, the person had transcribed the date back into the seventies.

Except . . . the DOB didn't make sense. With the one listed, the patient would have been thirty-seven three decades ago.

She closed the folder and rested her palm on it. "We have to get better precision from that transcription service."

"I know. I noticed the same thing. Listen, you want some time alone with him?"

"Yeah, that'd be great."

Faye paused by the door. "Heard you were pretty awesome in the OR tonight."

Jane smiled a little. "The team was awesome. I just did my part. Hey, I forgot to tell Shalonda I'm taking UK in Spring Madness. Would you—"

"Yup. And before you ask, yes, she's Duke again this year."

"Good, we can abuse each other for another six weeks."

"That's why she picked 'em. Public service so the rest of us can watch you guys go at it. You two are such givers."

After Faye left, Jane pulled the privacy curtain into place and went over to the bedside. The patient's respiration was machine-driven through his intubation, and his oxygen levels were acceptable. Blood pressure was steady, although low. Heart rate was sluggish, and it read funny on the monitor, but then again, he had six chambers beating.

Christ, that heart of his.

She leaned over him and studied his facial features. Caucasian in derivation, most likely middle European. A looker, not that that was relevant, although the handsome thing was thrown off a little by those tattoos on his temple. She moved in closer to study the ink in

his skin. She had to admit it was beautifully done, the intricate designs like Chinese characters and hieroglyphics combined. She figured the symbols must be gang-related, although he didn't seem like a boy to play at warfare; he was more fierce, like a soldier. Maybe the tats were a martial-arts thing?

When she glanced at the tube inserted in his mouth, she noticed something odd. With her thumb she pushed his upper lip back. His canines were very pronounced. Shockingly sharp.

Cosmetic, no doubt. People were doing all kinds of freaky stuff to their appearances these days, and he'd already marked up his face.

She lifted up the thin blanket that covered him. The wound dressing on the chest was fine, so she worked her way down his body, pushing the covers out of her way while she went. She inspected the stab wound's dressing, then palpated his abdominal area. As she gently pushed to feel his internal organs, she looked at the tattoos above his pubic area, then focused on the scars around his groin.

He'd been partially castrated.

Given the messy scarring, it hadn't been a surgical removal, more likely the result of an accident. Or at least, she hoped it had been accidental, because the only other explanation would be torture.

She stared at his face as she covered him up. On impulse, she put her hand on his forearm and squeezed. "You've led a hard-core life, haven't you."

"Yeah, but it's done me good."

Jane wheeled around. "Jesus, Manello. You scared me."

"Sorry. Just wanted to check in." The chief went around to the other side of the bed, his eyes going over the patient. "You know, I don't think he would have lived under someone else's knife."

"Have you seen the pictures?"

"Of his heart? Yeah. I want to send them to the boys at Columbia for a little look-see. You can ask them what they think when you're there."

She gave that one a pass. "His blood wouldn't type."

"Really?"

"If we can get his consent, I think we should do a total workup on him down to the chromosomes."

"Ah, yes, your second love. Genes."

Funny that he remembered. She'd probably mentioned only once how she'd almost ended up in genetics research.

With a junkie's rush, Jane pictured the inside of the patient, saw his heart in her hand, felt the organ in her grip as she saved his life. "He could present a fascinating clinical opportunity. God, I would love to study him. Or at least participate in studying him."

The soft beeping of the monitoring equipment seemed to swell in the silence between them until moments later some kind of awareness tickled the back of her neck. She glanced up. Manello was staring at her, his face grave, his heavy jaw set, his brows down low.

"Manello?" She frowned. "Are you okay?"

"Don't go."

To avoid his eyes she looked down at the bedsheet that she'd folded once and tucked under her patient's arm. Idly she smoothed the white expanse—until it reminded her of something her mother had always done.

She stilled her hand. "You can get another surg—"

"Fuck the department. I don't want you to go because . . ." Manello pushed a hand through his thick dark hair. "Christ, Jane. I don't want you to go because I'd miss you like hell, and because I . . . shit, I need you, okay? I need you here. With me."

Jane blinked like an idiot. In the last four years there'd never been any suggestion that the man was attracted to her. Sure, they were tight and all. And she was the only one who could calm him down when he lost his temper. And okay, yeah, they talked about the inner workings of the hospital all the time, even after hours. And they ate together every night when they were on duty and . . . he'd told her about his family and she'd told him about hers. . . .

Crap.

Yeah, but the man was the hottest property on hospital grounds. And she was about as feminine as . . . well, an operating table.

Certainly had as many curves as one.

"Come on, Jane, how clueless can you be? If you gave me a thin inch, I'd be inside your scrubs in the next heartbeat."

"Are you insane?" she breathed.

"No." His eyes grew heavy-lidded. "I'm very, very lucid."

In the face of that summer-night sultry expression, Jane's brain took a vacation. Just flew right out of her skull. "It wouldn't look right," she blurted.

"We'd be discreet."

"We fight." What the hell was coming out of her mouth?

"I know." He smiled, his full lips curving. "I like that. No one stands up to me but you."

She stared across the patient at him, still so dumbfounded she didn't know what to say. God, it had been so long since she'd had a man in her life. In her bed. In her head. So damned long. It had been years of coming home to her condo and showering alone and falling into bed alone and waking up alone and going to work alone. With both her parents gone she had no family, and with the hours she pulled at the hospital, she had no outside circle of friends. The only person she really talked to was . . . well, Manello.

As she looked at him now, it occurred to her that he truly was the reason she was leaving, though not just because he was standing in her way in the department. On some level she'd known this heart-to-heart was coming, and she'd wanted to run before it hit.

"Silence," Manello murmured, "is not a good thing right now. Unless you're trying to frame something like, 'Manny, I've loved you for years, let's go back to your place and spend the next four days horizontal.'"

"You're on tomorrow," she said automatically.

"I'd call in sick. Say I've got that flu. And as your chairman, I would order you to do the same." He leaned forward over the pa-

tient. "Don't go to Columbia tomorrow. Don't leave. Let's see how
far we can take this."

Jane looked down and realized she was staring at Manny's
hands . . . his strong, broad hands that had fixed so many hips and
shoulders and knees, saving the careers and the happiness of so many
athletes, professional and amateur alike. And he didn't just operate
on the young and in shape. He had preserved the mobility of the
elderly and the injured and the cancer-stricken as well, helping so
many continue to function with arms and legs.

She tried to imagine those hands on her skin.

"Manny . . ." she whispered. "This is crazy."

Across town, in the alley outside of ZeroSum, Phury rose from the
motionless body of a ghost-white *lesser*. With his black dagger he'd
opened up a yawning slice in the thing's neck, and glossy black blood
was pumping out onto the slush-covered asphalt. His instinct was to
stab the thing in the heart and poof it back to the Omega, but that
was the old way. The new way was better.

Although it cost Butch. Dearly.

"This one's ready for you," Phury said, and stepped back.

Butch came forward, his boots crunching through icy puddles.
His face was grim, his fangs elongated, his scent now carrying the
baby-powder sweetness of their enemies. He had finished with the
slayer he had fought with, done his special business, and now he would
do it again.

The cop looked both motivated and in pain as he sank to his
knees, planted his hands on either side of the *lesser*'s pasty face, and
leaned down. Opening his mouth, he positioned himself above the
slayer's lips and began a long, slow inhale.

The *lesser*'s eyes flared as a black mist rose out of its body and was
sucked into Butch's lungs. There was no break in the inhale, no pause
in the draw, just a steady stream of evil passing out of one vessel and
into another. In the end, their enemy became nothing but gray ash,

its body collapsing, then fragmenting into a fine dust that was carried away by the cold wind.

Butch sagged, then gave out altogether, falling to his side onto the alley's slushy road. Phury went over and reached his hand—

"Don't touch me." Butch's voice was a mere wheeze. "I'll make you sick."

"Let me—"

"No!" Butch shoved at the ground, pushing himself up. "Just gimme a minute."

Phury stood over the cop, guarding him and keeping an eye on the alley in case more came. "You want to go home? I'll go look for V."

"Fuck, no." The cop's hazel eyes lifted. "He's mine. I'm going to find him."

"Are you sure?"

Butch got up onto his feet, and though his body waved like a flag, he was nothing but green light. "Let's go."

As Phury fell into step with the guy and the two of them went down Trade Street, he didn't like the look on Butch's face. The cop had the loose-goose expression of someone whose blender was on frappé, but it didn't seem like he was going to quit unless he fell over.

As the two of them scoured the urban armpit of Caldwell and came up with jack shit, the no-V situation clearly made Butch even sicker.

They were on the very fringes of downtown, all the way out by Redd Avenue, when Phury stopped. "We should turn back. I doubt he'd come this far."

Butch stopped. Looked around. In a dull voice he said, "Hey, check it. This is Beth's old apartment building."

"We need to double back."

The cop shook his head and rubbed his chest. "We've got to keep going."

"Not saying we stop looking. But why would he be this far out?

We're on the edge of residential land. Too many eyes for a fight, so he wouldn't come here looking for one."

"Phury, man, what if he got jacked? We haven't seen another *lesser* out tonight. What if something big went down, like they bagged him?"

"If he was conscious, that would be highly unlikely, given that hand of his. Helluva weapon, even if he got stripped of his daggers."

"What if he was knocked out?"

Before Phury could respond, the Channel Six NewsLeader van tore by at a dead run. Two streets down its brakelights flared and the thing hung a louie.

All Phury could think was, *Shit.* News vans didn't show up in a rush like that because some old lady's cat was in a tree. Still, maybe it was just human shit, like a gang-related lead shower.

Trouble was, some horrible, crushing prescience told Phury that wasn't the case, so when Butch started walking in that direction, he went along. No words were spoken, which meant the cop was probably thinking exactly what he was: *Please, God, let it be someone else's tragedy, not ours.*

When they came up to where the TV van was parked, there was your typical crime convention, with two Caldwell Police Department cruisers parked at the entrance to Twentieth Street's dead-end alley. As a reporter stood spotlit and addressing a camera, men in uniform walked around within a circle of yellow tape, and kibitzers huddled together, drama-feeding and yakking.

The gust of wind barreling down the alley carried the smell of V's blood as well as the sweet baby-powder stench of *lessers.*

"Oh, God . . ." Butch's anguish rolled out into the cold night air, adding a sharp, shellaclike tang to the mix.

The cop lurched forward toward the tape, but Phury grabbed the guy's arm to stop him—only to blanch. The evil in Butch was so palpable, it shot up Phury's arm and landed in his gut, making his stomach roll.

He held on to his friend anyway.

"You stay the fuck back. You probably worked with some of those badges." When the cop opened his mouth, Phury talked right over him. "Pop your collar, pull your brim, and hold tight."

Butch tugged on his Red Sox hat and tucked his jaw in. "If he's dead—"

"Shut up and worry about keeping yourself on your feet." Which was going to be a challenge, because Butch was a ragged mess. Jesus . . . if V was dead, not only would that kill each and every one of the Brothers, but the cop had special problems. After he pulled that Dyson routine with the slayers, V was the only thing that could get the evil out of him.

"Go on, Butch. It's too much exposure for you. Go on now."

The cop walked off a couple yards and propped himself up against a parked car in the shadows. When it looked like the guy was going to stay there, Phury went over and joined the hangers-on at the edge of the yellow tape. Surveying the scene, the first thing he noticed were the residuals from where a *lesser* had been offed. Fortunately, the police weren't paying attention to them. They probably thought the glossy puddle was just oil spilled from a car and the scorched place leftover from a homeless person's makeshift fire. No, the badges were concentrating on the center of the scene, where Vishous had clearly lain in a pool of red blood.

Oh . . . God.

Phury glanced at the random human next to him. "What happened?"

The guy shrugged. "Gunshot. Some kind of fight."

A young kid dressed in rave clothes spoke up, all hyped out, like this was the coolest thing ever. "It was in the chest. I saw it happen, and I was the one who called nine-one-one." He waved his cell phone like it was a prize. "The police want me to stick around so they can interview me."

Phury looked over at him. "What went down?"

"God, you wouldn't have believed it. It was right outta *The World's Most Shocking Moments Caught on Tape* show. You know that show?"

"Yeah." Phury checked out the buildings on either side of the alley. No windows. This was probably the only witness. "So what happened?"

"Well, all's I was doing was walking down Trade. My friends ditched me at Screamer's and I got no ride, you know? Anyway, I'm walking and I see this bright flash of light up ahead. It was like a massive strobe thingy coming out of this alley. I walked a little faster, 'cause I wanted to see what was going down, and that's when I heard the gunshot. It was like a pop sound. Actually, I didn't even know it was a gunshot until I got here. You'd think it'd be louder—"

"When did you call nine-one-one?"

"Well, I waited a little bit, 'cause I figured someone would come running out of the alley and I didn't want to be shot. But, like, no one came, so I figured they'd disappeared out some back way or something. Then when I walked down here, I saw that there's no other way out. So maybe he shot himself, you know?"

"What the guy look like?"

"The vic?" The kid leaned in. "Vic is what the police call the victim. I heard 'em."

"Thanks for the clarification," Phury muttered. "So what did he look like?"

"Dark hair. With a goatee. Lot of leather. I stood over him while I called nine-one-one. He was bleeding, but alive."

"You didn't see anyone else?"

"Nope. Just the one. So, like, I'm going to get interviewed by the police. Like, for real. Did I tell you that?"

"Yeah, congratulations. You must be thrilled." Man, Phury totally had to resist popping the kid a fat lip.

"Hey, don't hate. This is cool stuff."

"Not for the guy who got shot, it isn't." Phury looked over the scene again. At least V wasn't in *lesser* hands, and he hadn't been dead

at the scene. Chances were the slayer had shot V first, but the Brother had still had enough strength to poof the bastard before passing out.

But wait . . . the shot came after the flash. So a second *lesser* must have come on the scene.

From the left, Phury heard a well-modulated voice: "This is Bethany Choi of the Channel Six NewsLeader team reporting live from the scene of another downtown shooting. According to police, the victim, Michael Klosnick—"

Michael Klosnick? Whatever, likely V had copped the *lesser*'s ID and it had been found on him.

"—was taken to St. Francis Medical Center in critical condition with a gunshot wound to the chest . . ."

Okay, this was going to be a long night: Vishous injured. In human hands. And they had only four hours until daylight.

Rapid-evac time.

Phury dialed the compound while he walked back over to Butch. As the cell rang, he talked at the cop. "He's alive at St. Francis with a gunshot."

Butch sagged and said something that sounded like, *Praise God.* "So we're going to get him out?"

"You got it." Why wasn't Wrath picking up? *Come on, Wrath . . . pick up.* "Shit . . . those goddamned surgeons must have gotten the surprise of their human lives when they opened him up— Wrath? We've got a situation."

Vishous came awake in an out-of-it body, becoming fully conscious, though he was trapped in a cage of comatose flesh and bones. Unable to move his arms or legs, and with his eyelids shut so tight it was like he'd been crying rubber cement, it appeared that his hearing was the only thing working: There was a conversation going on above him. Two voices. A female's and a male's, neither of which he recognized.

No, wait. He knew one of them. One of them had ordered him around. The female. But why?

And why the hell had he let her?

He listened to her talk without really following the words. Her cadence of speech was like a male's. Direct. Authoritative. Commanding.

Who was she? Who—

Her identity hit him like a slap, stunning some sense into him. The surgeon. The *human* surgeon. Jesus Christ, he was in a human hospital. He'd fallen into human hands after . . . Shit, what had happened?

Panic energized him . . . and got him exactly nowhere. His body was a slab of meat, and he had a feeling the tube down his throat meant a machine was working his lungs. Clearly they'd sedated the shit out of him.

Oh, God. How close to dawn was it? He needed to get the hell away from here. How was he going to—

His escape planning came to a crashing halt as his instincts fired up, took the wheel, grabbed control.

It wasn't the fighter in him coming out, though. It was all those possessive male impulses that had always been dormant, the ones he'd read about or heard about or seen in others, but had assumed he'd been born without. The trigger was a scent in the room, the scent of a male who wanted sex . . . with the female, with V's surgeon.

Mine.

The word came from out of nowhere and arrived with a matched set of urge-to-kill luggage. He was so outraged his eyes flipped open.

Turning his head, he saw a tall human woman with a short cap of blond hair. She wore rimless glasses, no makeup, no earrings. Her white coat read, JANE WHITCOMB, MD, CHIEF OF TRAUMA DIVISION, in black cursive letters.

"Manny," she said, "this is crazy."

V shifted his stare to a dark-haired human male. The guy was also in a white coat, with his reading, MANUEL MANELLO, MD, CHAIRMAN, DEPARTMENT OF SURGERY, at the right of the lapel.

"There's nothing crazy about it." The guy's voice was deep and demanding, his eyes way too fricking fixated on V's surgeon. "I know what I want. And I want you."

Mine, V thought. *Not yours. MINE.*

"I can't not go down to Columbia tomorrow," she said. "Even if there were something between us, I'd still have to leave if I want to lead a department."

"Something between us." The bastard smiled. "Does that mean you'll think about it?"

"It?"

"Us."

V's upper lip pulled off his fangs. As he started to growl, that one word rolled around his brain, a grenade with the pin out: *Mine.*

"I don't know," V's surgeon said.

"That's not a no, is it. Jane? That is not a no."

"No . . . it isn't."

"Good." The human male glanced down at V and seemed surprised. "Someone's awake."

You'd better fucking believe it, V thought. *And if you touch her, I'm going to bite your godforsaken arm off at the socket.*

NINE

Faye Montgomery was a practical woman, which was why she made a great nurse. She'd been born levelheaded, just like she'd come out with dark hair and dark eyes, and she was outstanding in a crisis. With a husband in the Marines and two kids at home and twelve years of working in intensive care units, it took a lot to rattle her.

Sitting behind the SICU's nursing station, she was rattled now.

Three men the size of SUVs were standing on the other side of the partition. One had long, multicolored hair and a pair of yellow eyes that didn't seem real, they were so bright. The second was mind-bendingly beautiful and so sexually magnetic, she had to remind herself she was happily married to a man she still had the hots for. The third was hanging back, nothing but a Red Sox cap, a pair of sunglasses, and an air of pure evil that didn't match his handsome face.

Had one of them asked a question? She thought so.

As none of the other nurses seemed capable of speech, Faye stammered, "I'm sorry? Er . . . what did you say?"

The one with the fantastic hair—God, was that stuff for real?—smiled a little. "We're looking for Michael Klosnick, who came up from the ED. Admitting told us he was brought here after he was operated on?"

God . . . those irises were the color of buttercups in the sunshine, a true, resonating gold. "Are you family?"

"We're his brothers."

"Okay, but I'm sorry, he's just out of the OR and we don't—" For no good reason, Faye's brain changed directions, kind of like a toy train that had been picked up off one track and put down on another. She found herself saying, "He's down the hall, room six. But only one of you can go in and just for a short time. Oh, and you have to wait until his doctor—"

At that moment Dr. Manello came striding up to the desk. He looked over the men and asked, "Everything okay here?"

Faye nodded as her mouth said, "Yes, just fine."

Dr. Manello frowned as he met the men stare for stare. Then he winced and rubbed his temples like he had a headache. "I'll be in my office if you need me, Faye."

"Okay, Dr. Manello." She glanced back at the men. What had she been saying? *Oh, right.* "You'll have to wait until his surgeon leaves, though, okay?"

"He's in there now?"

"*She's* in there now, yes."

"All right, thank you."

Those yellow eyes bored into Faye's . . . and suddenly she couldn't remember if there was a patient in six after all. Was there? Wait . . .

"Tell me," the man said, "what is your user name and password?"

"Excuse . . . me?"

"For the computer."

Why would he— Of course, he needed the information. Absolutely. And she needed to give it to him. "FMONT2 in caps is the login, and the password is 11Eddie11. *E* in uppercase."

"Thank you."

She was about to say, *You're welcome,* when the thought popped into her head that it was time for a staff meeting. Except why would that be? They'd already had one at the beginning of the—

No, it was definitely time for a staff meeting. They urgently needed to have a staff meeting. Right now—

Faye blinked and realized she was staring into space over the nursing station's counter. Weird, she could have sworn she'd just been talking to someone. Someone male and—

Staff meeting. Now.

Faye massaged her temples, feeling like she had a vise clamped onto her forehead. She didn't usually get headaches, but it had been a hectic day, and she'd had a lot of caffeine and not much food.

She glanced over her shoulder at the other three nurses, all of whom were looking a little confused. "Let's head into the conference room, guys. We have to do a patient review."

One of Faye's colleagues frowned. "Didn't we already do that tonight?"

"We need to do it again."

Everyone got up and went into the conference room. Faye kept the double doors open and sat at the head of the table so she could watch over the hall outside as well as the monitor that showed the status of every patient on the floor—

Faye stiffened in her chair. *What the hell?* There was a man with multicolored hair behind the nurses' station, leaning over a keyboard.

Faye started to get up, ready to call security, but then the guy looked over his shoulder. As his yellow eyes met hers, she suddenly forgot why it would be wrong for him to be at one of their computers. She also realized that she needed to talk about the patient in five right away.

"Let's review the status of Mr. Hauser," she said in a voice that got everyone's attention.

After Manello left, Jane stared down at her patient in disbelief. In spite of all the sedatives in his veins, his eyes were open and he was staring up out of his hard, tattooed face with full cognition.

God . . . those eyes. They were unlike any she'd seen before, the irises unnaturally white with navy blue rims.

This was not right, she thought. The way he looked at her wasn't right. That six-chambered heart beating in his chest wasn't right. Those long teeth in the front of his mouth weren't right.

He was not human.

Except that was ridiculous. First rule of medicine? When you hear hoofbeats, don't think zebras. What were the chances that there was an undetected humanoid species out there? A yellow Lab to Homo sapiens' golden retriever?

She thought about the patient's teeth. Yeah, maybe make that Doberman pinscher to the retriever.

The patient stared back at her, somehow managing to loom even though he was on his back, intubated, and only two hours out of trauma surgery.

How the *hell* was this guy conscious?

"Can you hear me?" she asked. "Nod your head if you can."

His hand, the one with the tattoos, clawed at his throat, then grabbed onto the tube going into his mouth.

"No, that has to stay in." As she leaned over to take his hand off of it, he whipped the thing back from her, moving it as far away as his arm would allow. "That's right. Please don't make me restrain you."

His eyes went utterly wide in terror, just peeled right open as his big body started to shake on the bed. His lips worked against the tube down his throat as if he were crying out, and his fear touched her: There was such an animalistic edge to his desperation, like the way a wolf might look at you if his leg was caught in a trap: *Help me and maybe I won't kill you when you set me free.*

She put her hand on his shoulder. "It's all right. We don't have to go that route. But we need that tube—"

The door to the room opened, and Jane froze.

The two men who came in were dressed in black leather and looked like the type who'd carry concealed weapons. One was probably the biggest, most gorgeous blond she'd ever eyeballed. The other scared her. He had a Red Sox hat pulled down low and a horrible air of malevolence about him. She couldn't see a lot of his face, but going by his gray pallor, he seemed ill.

Looking at the pair, Jane's first thought was that they had come for her patient, and not just to bring him flowers and yak it up.

Her second thought was that she was going to need security, stat.

"Get out," she said. "Right now."

The guy with the Sox cap completely ignored her and went over to the bedside. As he and the patient made eye contact, Red Sox reached out and the two linked hands.

In a hoarse voice, Red Sox said, "Thought I'd lost you, you son of a bitch."

The patient's eyes strained as if he were trying to communicate. Then he just shook his head from side to side on the pillow.

"We're going to get you home, okay?"

As the patient nodded, Jane didn't bother with any more Chatty-Cathy, you-need-to-leave shit. She lunged for the nursing station call button, the one that signaled a cardiac emergency and would bring half the floor to her.

She didn't make it.

Red Sox's buddy, the beautiful blond, moved so fast she couldn't track him. One moment he was just inside the door; the next he'd grabbed her from behind and popped her feet off the floor. As she started to holler, he clamped his hand over her mouth and subdued her as easily as if she were a child throwing a tantrum.

Meanwhile, Red Sox systematically stripped the patient of everything: the intubation, the IV, the catheter, the cardiac wires, the oxygen monitor.

Jane went ballistic. As the machines' alarms started going off, she hauled back and kicked her captor in the shin with her heel. The blond behemoth grunted, then squeezed her rib cage until she got so busy trying to breathe she couldn't soccer-ball him anymore.

At least the alarms would—

The shrill beeping fell silent even though no one touched the machines. And she had the horrible sense that nobody was coming from down the hall.

Jane fought harder, until she strained so hard her eyes watered.

"Easy," the blond said in her ear. "We'll be out of your hair in a minute. Just relax."

Yeah, the hell she would. They were going to kill her patient—

The patient took a deep breath on his own. And another. And another. Then those eerie diamond eyes shifted over to her, and she stilled as if he'd willed her to do so.

There was a moment of silence. And then in a rough voice, the man whose life she had saved spoke four words that changed everything . . . changed her life, changed her destiny:

"She. Comes. With. Me."

Standing inside the nursing station, Phury did a quick hack job on the hospital's IT system. He wasn't as smooth or flashy with the keyboard as V was, but he was good enough. He located the records under the name Michael Klosnick and contaminated the findings and notes pertaining to Vishous's treatment with random scripting: All the test results, the scans, the X-rays, the digital photographs, the scheduling, the postop notes, it all became unreadable. Then he entered a brief notation that Klosnick was indigent and had checked out AMA.

God, he loved consolidated, computerized medical records. What a snap.

He'd also cleaned up the memories of most if not all of the OR staff. On the way up here he'd swung by the operating suite and had a little tête-à-tête with the nurses on duty. He'd lucked out. The shift hadn't changed, so the folks who had been in with V were all present and he'd scrubbed them. None of those nurses would have distinct recollections of what they'd seen when the Brother had been operated on.

It wasn't a perfect erase job, of course. There were people he hadn't gotten to and maybe some ancillary records that had been printed out. But that wasn't his problem. Whatever confusion occurred in the wake of V's disappearance would be absorbed into the frantic workings of a tremendously busy urban hospital. Sure, there might be a review or two of patient care, but they wouldn't be able to find V by then, and that was all that mattered.

When Phury was finished with the computer, he jogged down the SICU floor. As he went, he fritzed out the security cameras that were embedded at regular intervals in the ceiling so all they'd show was fuzz.

Just as he came up to room six, the door opened. Vishous was death warmed over in Butch's arms, the Brother pale and shaky and in pain, his head tucked into the cop's neck. But he was breathing and his eyes were open.

"Let me take him," Phury said, thinking Butch looked almost as bad.

"I've got him. You deal with our management issue and ride herd on the security cameras."

"What management issue?"

"Wait for it," Butch muttered as he headed for a fire door at the far end of the hall.

A split second later, Phury got a load of the problem: Rhage walked out into the hall with a rip-shit human female in a choke hold. She was fighting him tooth and nail, the muffled yelling suggesting she had a vocabulary like a trucker.

"You gotta knock her cold, my brother," Rhage said, then grunted. "I don't want to hurt her, and V said she had to come with us."

"This was not supposed to be a kidnap operation."

"Too fucking late. Now knock her out, would ya?" Rhage grunted again and switched his grip, his hand leaving her mouth to catch one of her flailing arms.

Her voice came through loud and clear. "So help me, God, I'm going to—"

Phury took her chin in his hand and forced her head up. "Relax," he said softly. "Just ease up."

He locked his stare on hers and began to will her into calmness . . . will her into calmness . . . will her into—

"Fuck you!" she spat. "I'm not letting you kill my patient!"

Okay, this wasn't working. Behind those rimless glasses and dark green eyes, she had a formidable mind, so with a curse he brought out the big guns, mentally shutting her down completely. She sagged like a mop.

Removing her glasses, he folded them up and put them in the breast pocket of his coat. "Let's bust out of here before she comes around again."

Rhage flipped the woman over, draping her like a shawl off his heavy shoulder. "Get her bag from the room."

Phury ducked in, picked up a leather tote and the folder marked with the name KLOSNICK, then beat feet from the room. When he came back into the hall, Butch was having a run-in with a nurse who'd come out of a patient room.

"What are you doing!" the woman said.

Phury got on her like a tent, jumping in front of her, staring her into a stupor, planting the urgent need in her frontal lobe to get to a staff meeting. By the time he caught up with the evac again, the woman in Rhage's arms was already throwing off the mind control, shaking her head back and forth as it bobbed to the beat of Holly-wood's get-up-'n-go.

As they came up to the stairwell's fire door, Phury barked, "Hold up, Rhage."

The Brother stopped on a dime and Phury clamped his hand on the side of the woman's neck, putting her out cold with a pressure lock.

"She's gone. S'all good."

They hit the back stairs and hauled ass. Vishous's rasping breath was testimony to how much the express-train action was killing him, but he was hard-core as always, hanging in, in spite of the fact that he'd turned the color of pea soup.

Each time they came to a landing, Phury pulled a little scramble with a security camera, running an electrical surge through the things so they blinked out. His big hope was that they'd make it to the Escalade without tangling with a bunch of security guards. Humans were never targets for the Brotherhood. That being said, if there was a risk of the vampire race being exposed, there was nothing that wouldn't be done. And as hypnotizing large groups of agitated and aggressive humans had a low success rate, that left fighting. And death for them.

Some eight flights down the stairwell bottomed out, and Butch stopped in front of a metal door. Sweat poured down his face and he was weaving, but his eyes were soldier-strong: He was going to get his buddy out, and nothing was going to stand in his way, even his own physical weakness.

"I'll do the door," Phury said, jumping to the head of the pack. After taking care of the alarm, he held the slab of steel open for the others. On the far side, a maze of utility halls branched out.

"Oh, shit," he muttered. "Where the hell are we?"

"Basement." The cop marched ahead. "Know it well. Morgue's on this level. Spent a lot of time here in my old job."

Some hundred yards farther, Butch hooked them up with a shallow corridor that was more a shaft full of HVAC piping than any kind of hallway.

And then there it was: salvation in the form of an emergency access door.

"Escalade's out here," the cop said to V. "Sitting pretty."

"Thank . . . God." V's lips pressed flat again, like he was trying not to throw up.

Phury did another jump ahead, then cursed. This alarm setup was different from the others, operating on a more complex circuitry. Which he should have expected. Exterior doors were frequently wired more heavily than interior ones. Trouble was, his little mental tricks weren't going to work here, and it wasn't like he could call a time-out to disarm the thing. V was looking roadkill bad.

"Brace yourself for a screamer," Phury said before punching the bar handle.

The alarm went off like a banshee.

As they rushed out into the night, Phury wheeled around and looked up at the ass end of the hospital. He located the security camera over the door, got it to misread, and stayed locked with its blinking red eye as V and the human female were dumped inside the Escalade and Rhage got behind the wheel.

Butch took shotgun and Phury hopped into the back with the cargo. He checked his watch. Total elapsed time from when they'd first parked back here to Hollywood's foot slamming down on the gas pedal was twenty-nine minutes. The op had been relatively clean. All that was left to do now was get everyone to the compound in one piece and scrap the plates on the SUV.

There was just one complication.

Phury shifted his eyes to the human woman.

One big, huge complication.

TEN

ohn was antsy as he waited in the mansion's brilliantly colored foyer. He and Zsadist always went out for an hour before dawn, and there had been no change of plans as far as he was aware. But the Brother was nearly half an hour late.

To kill some more time, John took another trip across the mosaic floor. As always he felt as if he didn't belong in all the grandeur, but he loved and appreciated it. The foyer was so outrageously fancy it was like standing in a jewelry box: Columns in red marble and some kind of green-and-black stone supported walls festooned with gold-leafed curlicue thingies and light fixtures with crystals. The staircase up was a majestic expanse of red carpet, the kind of thing a movie star would pause dramatically at the top of, then swoop down to a black-tie party. And the pattern beneath your feet was of an apple tree in bloom, the bright palate of spring resplendent and glimmering thanks to millions of sparkling pieces of colored glass.

His favorite thing, though, was the ceiling. Three stories up there

was an astonishing stretch of painted scenes, with warriors and stallions leaping to life as they went into battle with black daggers. They were so real it was as if you could reach up and touch them.

So real it was as if you could be them.

He thought back to when he'd first seen it all. Tohr had been taking him to meet Wrath.

John swallowed. He'd had Tohrment for such a short time. Mere months. After a lifetime of feeling ungrounded, after having floated along for two decades without any family-gravity to anchor him, he'd been given a glimpse of what he'd always wanted. And then with one bullet both his adoptive father and mother were gone.

He'd like to be big enough to say he was grateful he'd known Tohr and Wellsie for the time he had, but that was a lie. He wished he'd never met them. The loss of them was so much harder to bear than the amorphous ache he'd had when he'd been by himself.

Not really a male of worth, was he?

Without warning, Z strode out of the hidden door under the grand staircase, and John stiffened. He couldn't help it. No matter how many times he saw the Brother, Zsadist's appearance always made him think twice. It wasn't just the facial scar or the skull trim. It was the deadly air that hadn't been lost, even though he was now mated and going to be a father.

Plus tonight, Z's face was cast-iron tight, his body even tighter. "You good to go?"

John narrowed his eyes and signed, *What's going on?*

"Nothing you need to worry about. Are you ready." Not a question, a command.

When John nodded and zipped up his parka, the two of them went out through the front vestibule.

The night was the color of a dove, the stars faded by a thin saturation of clouds that was backlit by a full moon. According to the calendar spring was coming, but it was just in theory, if you went by the landscape: The fountain in front of the mansion remained out of commission for the winter, empty and waiting to be refilled. The trees were like black skeletons reaching to the sky, pleading with their bony arms for the sun to get stronger. Snow lingered on the lawns, stubbornly hanging in over ground that was still frozen solid.

The wind held a cheek-slapping chill as he and Zsadist walked over to the right, the pebbles of the courtyard shifting under their boots. The compound's security wall was off in the distance, a twenty-foot-tall, three-foot-thick bulwark that encircled the Brotherhood's property. The thing was strung with security cameras and motion detectors, a good soldier packing a shitload of ammo. But all that was just small potatoes, really. The true keep-out was the 120 volts of electrical charge that ran across the top in curls of barbed wire.

Safety first. Always.

John followed Z down the snow-patched lawn, passing battened-down flower beds and the drained swimming pool in the back. After a gentle decline they reached the forest edge. At this point the monster wall hung a sharp louie and shot down the mountainside. They didn't follow it, but penetrated the tree line.

Beneath thick pines and densely branched maples there was a pad of old needles and leaves and not much undergrowth. Here, the air smelled like earth and cold air, a combination that made the inside of his nose tingle.

As usual, Zsadist led. The paths they took each night were different and felt random, but they always ended at the same place, a short-stack waterfall: The brook that came down the mountainside threw itself off a little cliff, then formed a shallow pool some nine feet across.

John went over and put his hand into the gurgling rush. As his palm pierced the tumble, his fingers numbed out from the cold.

In silence Zsadist crossed the stream, leaping from rock to rock to rock. The Brother's grace was that of the water, flowing and strong, his footing so sure it was clear he knew precisely how his body would react to each shift of muscle.

On the far side he walked up to the waterfall so he was across from John.

Their eyes met. *Oh, man, Z had something to say tonight, didn't he.*

The walks had started up after John had attacked another class-mate and laid the kid out cold in the locker room shower. Wrath had made them a condition upon John staying in the training program, and he'd dreaded them at first, figuring Z was going to try to crawl all around his head. Up until now, however, they had always been about silence.

That wasn't going to be the case tonight.

John retracted his arm, walked downstream a little, and crossed over without Zsadist's confidence or dexterity.

As he came up to the Brother, Z said, "Lash is coming back."

John crossed his arms over his chest. Oh, great, the asshole John had put on a gurney. Granted, Lash had been beyond asking for it, coming after John, heckling and pushing him, turning on Blay. But still.

"And he's gone through the change."

Terrific. Even frickin' better. Now the bastard would be gunning for him with muscle.

When? John signed.

"Tomorrow. I've made it clear if he pulls any shit, he's out for good. You have problems with him, you come to me, we clear?"

Shit. John wanted to take care of himself. He didn't want to be watched over like a kid.

"John? You come to me. Nod your damn head."

John did so slowly.

"You will not aggress on the fucker. I don't care what he says or what he does. Just because he gets up in your face doesn't mean you have to react."

John nodded, because he had a feeling Z was going to ask him to again if he didn't.

"I catch you going all Dirty Harry, you're not going to like what happens."

John stared into the rushing water. *God . . .* Blay, Qhuinn, now Lash. All changed.

Paranoia took root and he looked at Z. *What if the transition doesn't happen for me?*

"It will."

How do we know for sure?

"Biology." Z nodded at a huge oak tree. "That thing is going to leaf up when the sun hits it. Can't help it, and the shit's the same with you. Your hormones are going to kick in hard-core, and then it happens. You can feel them already, can't you?"

John shrugged.

"Yeah, you can. Your patterns of eating and sleeping are different. So is your behavior. You think a year ago you would have taken Lash down onto the tile and pounded on him until he was breathing blood?"

Definitely not.

"You're hungry, but you don't like to eat, right? Restless and exhausted. Short-tempered."

Jesus, how did the Brother know all that?

"Been through it myself, remember."

How much longer? John asked.

"Until it hits? As a male, you tend to take after your father. Darius went through his a little on the early side. But you never really know. Some people can be where you are for years."

Years? *Shit. What was it like afterward for you? When you woke up?*

In the quiet that followed, the eeriest change came over the Brother. It was like a fog crept in and he disappeared—despite the fact that John could still see every detail of his scarred face and big body clear as ever.

"You talk to Blay and Qhuinn about that."

Sorry. John flushed. *Didn't mean to pry.*

"Whatever. Look, I don't want you to worry about it. We've got Layla lined up for you to feed from, and you're going to be in a safe environment. I'm not going to let anything bad go down."

John stared up at that ruined warrior face and thought about the classmate they'd lost. *Hhurt died, though.*

"Yeah, that happens, but Layla's blood is very pure. She's a Chosen. That's going to help you."

John thought of the beautiful blonde. And of her dropping her robe right in front of him to show him her body for his approval. Man, he still couldn't believe she'd done that.

How will I know what to do?

Z craned his neck back and looked at the sky. "Don't need to worry about that. Your body will take charge. It will know what it wants and what it needs." Z's skull-trimmed head came back to level and he glanced over, his yellow eyes piercing the darkness sure as sunlight through a break in the clouds. "Your body is going to own you for a little while."

Though it shamed him he signed, *I think I'm scared.*

"Means you're smart. This is heavy-duty shit. But like I said . . . I'm not going to let anything bad happen to you."

Z turned away like he was feeling awkward, and John studied the male's profile against the backdrop of the trees.

As gratitude welled, Z cut off the thank-you John was gearing up to sign. "We'd better head home."

Crossing back over the river and heading for the compound, John found himself thinking about the biological father he'd never known. He'd avoided asking about Darius, because he'd been Tohr's best friend, and anything connected to Tohrment was hard for the Brothers to talk about.

He wished he had someone he could talk to about his dad.

ELEVEN

When Jane came awake, her neuropathways were like cheap strands of Christmas lights, flickering randomly, then shorting out: Sounds registered and disintegrated and reappeared. Her body was languid, then tense, now twitchy. Her mouth was dry and she felt too warm, but she shivered.

Taking deep breaths, she realized she was partially sitting up. And had a screamer of a headache.

But something smelled good. God, there was an incredible scent all around her . . . it was part tobacco, like the kind her father had smoked, and part dark spices, as if she were in an Indian oils shop.

She cracked an eyelid. Her vision was off, probably because she wasn't wearing her glasses, but she could see enough to know that she was in a dark, barren room that had . . . Jesus, books stacked everywhere. She also discovered that the chair she was in was right next to a radiator, which maybe explained the hot flashes. Plus her head was kinked at a bad angle, which accounted for the headache.

Her first impulse was to sit up, but she was not alone, so she stayed put: Across the room, a man with multicolored hair was standing over a king-size bed that had a body lying on it. The guy was hard at work doing something . . . putting a glove on the hand of—

Her patient. Her patient was on that bed, the sheets down to his waist, his bare chest covered by her surgical dressing. Christ, what had happened? She remembered operating on him . . . and finding an incredible heart anomaly. Then there had been an exchange with Manello in the SICU, and then . . . Shit, she'd been abducted by the man over the bed, a sex god, and someone who wore a Red Sox cap.

Panic flared along with a good dose of pissed-off, but her emotions couldn't seem to connect to her body, the surge of feeling diffusing in the lethargy that clothed her. She blinked and tried to focus without drawing attention to herself—

Her lids popped wide.

The guy in the Red Sox hat came in with an astonishingly beautiful blond woman at his side. He stood close to her, and though they weren't touching, it was clear that they were a couple. They just belonged together.

The patient spoke up in a rasp. "No."

"You've got to," Red Sox said.

"You told me . . . you'd kill me if I ever—"

"Extenuating circumstances."

"Layla—"

"Fed Rhage this afternoon, and we can't get another Chosen here without tangoing with the Directrix. Which would take time you don't have."

The blond woman approached the patient's bed and sat down slowly. Dressed in a black suit with tailored pants, she seemed like a lawyer or a businessperson, and yet she was wildly feminine with her long, luxurious hair.

"Use me." She extended her wrist over the patient's mouth, hovering it just above his lips. "If only because we need you strong so you can take care of him."

There was no question who the "him" was. Red Sox looked sicker than he had when Jane had first seen him, and the clinician in her wondered exactly what the "taking care of" involved.

Meanwhile, Red Sox stepped back until he hit the opposite wall. Wrapping his arms around his chest, he held on to himself.

In a soft voice, the blonde said, "He and I talked about it. You've done so much for us—"

"Not . . . for you."

"He's alive because of you. So that's *everything*." The blonde reached out as if she were going to smooth the patient's hair, but then took her hand back as he flinched. "Let us care for you. Just this once."

The patient looked across the room at Red Sox. When Red Sox nodded, the patient cursed and closed his eyes. Then opened his mouth . . .

Holy shit. His pronounced canines had elongated. Sharply pointed before, now they were positively fanglike.

Okay, clearly this was a dream. *Yup.* Because that just didn't happen to cosmetically enhanced teeth. Ever.

As the patient bared his "fangs," the man with the multicolored hair stepped in front of Red Sox, braced both hands on the wall, and leaned in until their chests almost touched.

But then the patient shook his head and turned away from the wrist. "Can't."

"I need you," Red Sox whispered. "I'm sick from what I do. I need you."

The patient fixated on Red Sox, a powerful yearning flashing in his diamond eyes. "Only for . . . you . . . not me."

"For both of us."

"All of us," the blond woman interjected.

The patient took a deep breath, then—*Christ!*—bit into the

blonde's wrist. The strike was fast and decisive as a cobra's, and as he locked on, the woman jumped, then exhaled with what seemed like relief. Across the room, Red Sox trembled all over, looking bereft and desperate while the one with the multicolored hair blocked his way without coming into contact with him.

The patient's head started to move in a rhythm, as if he were a baby nursing at a breast. But he couldn't be drinking from there, could he?

Yeah, the hell he couldn't.

Dream. This was all a dream. A loony-bin dream. Wasn't it? Oh, God, she hoped it was. Otherwise she was stuck in some kind of Gothic nightmare.

When it was done, her patient eased back onto the pillows, and the woman licked herself where his mouth had been.

"Rest now," she said, before turning to Red Sox. "Are you okay?"

He shook his head back and forth. "I want to touch you, but I can't. I want in you, but . . . I can't."

The patient spoke up. "Lie with me. Now."

"You can't handle it," Red Sox said in a reedy, hoarse voice.

"You need it now. I'm ready."

"The hell you are. And I have to lie down. I'll be back later after I have a rest—"

The door flew open again, light spilling in from what looked like a hallway, and a huge man with black hair down to his waist and wraparound sunglasses on stalked in. This was trouble. His cruel face suggested he might get off on torturing people, and the glare in his eyes made her wonder if he wanted to start in on someone right now. Hoping to avoid his notice, she slammed her lids shut and tried not to breathe.

His voice was as hard as the rest of him. "If you weren't already assed out, I'd put you on the ground myself. What the *fuck* are you thinking, bringing her here?"

"'Scuse us," Red Sox said. There was a shuffle of feet and the door shut.

"I asked you a question."

"Supposed to come with," the patient said.

"Supposed to? *Supposed to?* Are you out of your goddamned mind?"

"Yes . . . but not 'bout her."

Jane cracked an eye open and watched through her lashes as the mammoth guy glanced at the one with all the fabulous hair. "I want everyone in my study in a half hour. We need to decide what the hell to do with her."

"Not . . . without me . . ." the patient said, his tone getting stronger.

"You don't get a vote."

The patient shoved his palms into the mattress and sat up, even though it made his arms shake. "I get *all* the votes when it comes to her."

The towering man pointed a finger at the patient. "Fuck you."

From out of nowhere, Jane's adrenaline kicked in. Dream or no dream, she should be counted in this happy conversation. Straightening in the chair, she cleared her throat.

All eyes snapped to her.

"I want out of here," she said in a voice she wished were less breathy and more ass-kicking. *"Now."*

The big man put a hand to the bridge of his nose, popped up the wraparounds, and rubbed his eyes. "Thanks to him, that's not an immediate option. Phury, take care of her again, would you?"

"Are you going to kill me?" she asked in a rush.

"No," the patient said. "You're going to be fine. You have my word."

For a split second she believed him. Which was nuts. She didn't know where she was, and these men were clearly thugs—

The one with the beautiful hair stepped in front of her. "You're just going to rest for a little bit more."

Yellow eyes met hers and suddenly she was a TV unplugged, her cord yanked out of the wall, her screen blank.

Vishous stared at his surgeon as she slumped down once more in the armchair across the bedroom.

"She all right?" he said to Phury. "You haven't fried her, true?"

"No, but she's got a strong mind. We want to get her out of here ASAP."

Wrath's voice cracked through the air. "She should never have been *brought* here."

Vishous eased gingerly back onto his bed, feeling like he'd been punched in the chest with a cinder block. He wasn't particularly concerned that Wrath had his leathers in a knot. His surgeon had to be here, and that was that. But at least he could tray-up a rationale.

"She can help me recover. Havers is complicated because of the Butch sitch."

Wrath's stare was level behind his shades. "You think she'll want to help you after you had her kidnapped? The Hippocratic oath only goes so far."

"I'm hers." V frowned. "I mean, she'll take care of me because she operated on me."

"You're grasping at straws to justify—"

"Am I? I just had open-heart surgery because I was shot in the chest. Doesn't feel like straws to me. You want to risk complications?"

Wrath glanced at the surgeon, then rubbed his eyes some more. "Shit. How long?"

"Till I'm better."

The king's sunglasses dropped back onto his nose. "Heal fast, brother. I want her scrubbed and *out*."

Wrath left the room, shutting the door with a clap.

"That went well," V said to Phury.

Phury, in his peacekeeping kind of way, murmured something about how everyone was under a lot of stress, blah, blah, blah, then went over to the bureau to change the subject. He came back to the bedside with a couple of handrolls, one of V's lighters, and an ashtray.

"Know you'll want these. What kind of supplies is she going to need to treat you?"

V whipped a list up off the top of his head. With Marissa's blood in him, he was going to be back on his feet fast, as her lineage was nearly pure: He'd just put high-test gas in his tank.

Thing was, though, he found himself not wanting to heal all that fast.

"She'll also need some clothes," he said. "And food."

"I'll take care of it." Phury headed for the door. "You want something to eat?"

"No." Just as the Brother stepped out in the hall, V said, "Will you check on Butch?"

"Of course."

After Phury left, V stared at the human woman. Her looks, he decided, were not so much beautiful as compelling. Her face was square, her features almost masculine: No pouty lips. No thick lashes. No arching, feminine-wile brows. And there were no big breasts pushing against the white physician's coat she had on, no wildly curvy ins and outs as far as he could see.

He wanted her like she was a naked beauty queen begging to be served.

Mine. V's hips rotated, a flush spreading under his skin even though there was no way he should have the energy to get sexed up.

God, the truth was, he had no remorse about kidnapping her. Matter of fact, it was preordained. Just as Butch and Rhage had shown up in that hospital room he'd had his first vision in weeks. He'd seen his surgeon standing in a doorway, framed in glorious

white light. She'd been beckoning to him with love on her face, drawing him forward down a hall. The kindness she'd offered had been as warm and soft as skin, as soothing as calm water, as sustaining as the sunlight he no longer knew.

Still, though he might feel no remorse, he did blame himself for the fear and anger in her face when she'd come to. Thanks to his mother, he'd gotten a nasty look at what it was like to be forced into something, and he'd just done the same thing to the one who'd saved his life.

Shit. He wondered what he would have done if he hadn't gotten that vision, if he hadn't had his curse of seeing the future speak up. Would he have left her there? Yeah. Of course he would have. Even with the word *mine* running through his head, he would have let her stay in her world.

But the fucking vision had sealed her fate.

He thought back to the past. To the first of his visions . . .

Literacy was not of value in the warrior camp, as you couldn't kill with it.

Vishous learned to read the Old Language only because one of the soldiers had had some education and was in charge of keeping some rudimentary records of the camp. He was sloppy about it and bored by the job, so V had volunteered to do his duties if the male taught him how to read and write. It was the perfect exchange. V had always been entranced by the idea that you could reduce an event to the page and make it not transitory, but fixed. Eternal.

He'd learned fast and then scoured the camp for books, finding a few in obscure, forgotten places like under old, broken weapons or in abandoned tents. He collected the battered, leather-bound treasures and hid them at the far edge of the camp where the animal hides were kept. No soldiers ever went there, as it was female territory, and if the females did, it was just to grab a pelt or two for making clothes or bedding. Further, not only was it safe for the books, it was the perfect spot for reading, as the cave ceiling dropped to a low height and the floor was stone: Anyone's approach was instantly heard, as they'd have to shuffle about to get near him.

There was one book, however, that even his hidden place wasn't secure enough for.

The most precious of his meager collection was a diary written by a male who'd come to the camp about thirty years prior. He'd been an aristocrat by birth but had ended up in the camp being trained due to family tragedy. The diary was written in beautiful script, with big words that V could only guess the meanings of, and spanned three years of the male's life. The contrast between the two parts, the one detailing events prior to his coming here and the one covering afterward, was stark. In the beginning, the male's life had been marked with the glorious passing of the glymera's social calendar, full of balls and lovely females and courtly manners. Then it all ended. Despair, the exact thing Vishous lived with, was what tinted the pages after the male's life changed forever just after his transition.

Vishous read and reread the diary, feeling a kinship with the writer's sadness. And after each reading, he would close the cover and run his fingertips over the name embossed in the leather.

DARIUS, SON OF MARKLON.

V often wondered what had happened to the male. The entries ended on a day when nothing particularly significant occurred, so it was hard to know whether he'd died in an accident or left on a whim. V hoped to find out the warrior's fate at some point, assuming he himself lived long enough to get free of the camp.

As losing the diary would make him bereft, he kept it in the one place where not a soul tarried. Before the camp settled herein, the cave had been inhabited by some manner of ancient human, and the prior inhabitants had left crude drawings on the walls. The hazy representations of bison and horses and palm prints and single eyes were considered curses by the soldiers and were avoided by all and sundry. A partition had been erected in front of that portion of the walls, and though the artistry might

have been painted over in its entirety, Vishous knew why his father didn't do away with them. The Bloodletter wanted the camp off balance and edgy, and he taunted soldiers and females alike with threats that the spirits of those animals would possess them or that the eye images and handprints would come to life with fire and fury.

V wasn't afraid of the drawings. He loved them. The animals' simplicity of design had power and grace, and he liked to place his own hands up against the palm prints. Indeed, it was of comfort to know that there were those who had lived here before him. Perhaps they had had it better.

V hid the diary between two of the larger depictions of bison, in a crevice that provided an accommodation just wide and deep enough. During the day, when all were reposed, he would sneak behind the partition and set his eyes aglow and read until his loneliness was eased.

It was a mere year after he found them that Vishous's books were destroyed. His only joys were burned, as he had always feared they would be. And it was no surprise by whom.

He had been feeling ill for weeks, approaching his transition, though he knew it not at the time. Unable to sleep, he had risen and ghosted to the hide pile, settling in with a volume of fairy tales. It was with the book in his lap that he fell asleep.

When he awoke, a pretrans was standing over him. The boy was one of the more aggressive ones, hard of eye and wiry of body.

"How you laze whilst the rest of us work," the boy sneered. "And is that a book in your hand? Mayhap it should be turned in, as it keeps you from chores. I could get more for my stomach by doing so."

Vishous pushed his stack farther behind the hides and got to his feet, saying nothing. He would fight for his books, just as he fought for the scraps of food to fill his belly or the castoff clothing that covered his skin. And the pretrans before him would fight for the privilege of exposing the books. It was always thus.

The boy came in fast, shoving V back against the cave wall. Though his head hit hard and his breath rushed out, he struck back, slamming his opponent in the face with the book. As the other pretrans rushed over and watched, V hit his opponent over and over again. He had been taught to use any weapon at his disposal, but as he forced the other male to the ground, he wanted to cry that he was using this most precious thing to hurt someone else. He had to keep going, though. If he lost the advantage, he might well be beaten and lose the books before he could move them to another hiding place.

At last, the other boy lay still, his face a swollen mess, his breath gurgling as V held him down by the throat. The volume of fairy tales was dripping blood, the leather cover loose on the spine.

It was in the ragged aftermath that it happened. A strange tingling shot down V's arm and tunneled into the hand that held his opponent to the cave floor. Then an eerie shadow was suddenly thrown, created by a glow coming from V's palm. At once, the pretrans under him began to thrash around, his arms and legs flapping against the stone as if his whole body were in pain.

V let go and stared at his hand in horror.

When he looked back at the male, a vision struck like a fist, rendering V stunned and sightless. In a hazy mirage he saw the boy's face in a stiff wind, his hair blown back, his eyes fixed on some distant point. Behind him there were rocks of the kind found on the mountain, and sunlight shone upon both them and the pretrans's motionless body.

Dead. The boy was dead.

The pretrans suddenly whispered, "Your eye . . . your eye . . . what has been done?"

The words came out of V's mouth before he could stop them: "Death will find you on the mountain, and as the wind comes upon you, so shall you be carried away."

A gasp brought V's head up. One of the females was close by, her face drawn in horror as if he had spoken to her.

"What goes on herein?" came a booming voice.

V leaped off the pretrans so he could get back a ways from his father and keep the male in view. The Bloodletter was standing with his breeches undone, having clearly just taken one of the kitchen females. Which explained why he was in this part of the camp.

"What have you in your hand?" the Bloodletter demanded, stepping closer to V. *"Give it unto me this moment."*

In the face of his father's wrath, V had no choice but to proffer the book. It was snatched up with a curse.

"You used this wisely only when you beat him with it." Shrewd dark eyes narrowed on the indention in the hides whereupon V laid his back. *"You have been lazing off against these skins, have you not? You have passed time here."*

When V didn't reply, his father took another step nearer. *"What do you do back here? Read other tomes? I think yes, and I think you shall give them to me. Perhaps I shall like to read instead of being about my useful endeavors."*

V hesitated . . . and received a slap so hearty it knocked him over onto the hides. As he slid down and rolled off the back of the pile, he landed on his knees in front of his three other books. Blood from his nose dropped onto one of the covers.

"Shall I strike you anew? Or will you give me what I asked for?" The Bloodletter's tone was bored, as if either outcome were acceptable, as both would hurt V and thus bring satisfaction.

V put his hand out and stroked a soft leather cover. His chest roared with pain at the good-bye, but the emotion was such a waste, wasn't it. These things he cared about were about to be destroyed in some fashion, and it was going to happen now, regardless of what he might do. They were as good as gone already.

V looked up over his shoulder at the Bloodletter, and saw a truth that changed his life: His father would destroy anything and anyone V cleaved to for comfort. The male had done so countless times and in countless ways before and would continue apace. These books and this episode were just one footprint along an endless trail that would be well trodden.

The realization made all V's pain go away. Just like that. For him, there was now no utility in emotional connection, only an eventual agony when it was crushed. So he would no longer feel.

Vishous picked up the books he'd cradled in gentle hands for hours *and hours and faced his father. He handed what had been a lifeline over without any care or kinship to the volumes at all. It was as if he had never seen his books before.*

The Bloodletter didn't take what was put before him. "Do you give these to me, my son?"

"I do."

"Yes . . . hmm. You know, perhaps I shall not like to read after all. Perhaps I should prefer to fight as a male does. For my species and my honor." His massive arm stretched out, and he pointed to one of the kitchen fires. "Take them there. Burn them there. As it is winter, the heat is of value."

The Bloodletter's eyes narrowed as V calmly went over and tossed the books into the flames. When he turned back around to his father, the male was studying him carefully.

"What said the boy about your eye?" the Bloodletter murmured. "I believe I heard a reference."

"He said, 'Your eye, your eye, what has been done?'" V replied without affect.

In the silence that followed, blood oozed from V's nose, running warm and slow down his lips and off his chin. His arm was sore from the blows he'd thrown, and his head was in pain. None of it bothered him, though. The strangest strength was upon him.

"Do you know why the boy would say such a thing?"

"I do not."

He and his father stared at each other as an audience of the curious gathered.

The Bloodletter said to no one in particular, "It appears as if my son likes to read. As I wish to be well versed in my young's interests, I should like to be apprised if anyone sees him doing so. I would consider it a personal favor to which a boon of note would be attached." V's father pivoted around, grabbed a female by the waist, and dragged her toward the main fire pit. "And now we shall have some sport, soldiers mine! To the pit!"

A rousing cheer rose from the knot of males and the crowd dispersed.

As V watched them all go, he realized he felt no hatred. Usually, when his father's back turned, Vishous gave free rein to how much he despised the male. Now there was nothing. It was as when he had looked upon the books before holding them out. He felt . . . nothing.

V glanced down at the male whom he'd beaten. "If you ever come near me again, I shall break both your legs and your arms and make it so you shall never see right once more. Are we clear?"

The male smiled even though his mouth was swelling up as if bee-stung. "What if I transition first?"

V put his hands on his knees and leaned down. "I am my father's son. Therefore I am capable of anything. No matter my size."

The boy's eyes widened, as the truth was no doubt obvious: Disconnected as Vishous was now, there was nothing he could not stomach, no deed he could not accomplish, no means he would not call forth to reach an end.

He was as his father had always been, naught but soulless calculation covered by skin. The son had learned his lesson.

TWELVE

When Jane came to again, it was out of a terrifying dream, one in which something that didn't exist was in fact alive and well and in the same room with her: She saw her patient's sharp canine teeth and his mouth at the wrist of a woman and him drinking from a vein.

The hazy, off-kilter images lingered and panicked her like a tarp that moved because there was something under it. Something that would hurt you.

Something that would bite you.

Vampire.

She did not get afraid all that often, but she was scared as she sat up slowly. Looking around the spartan bedroom, she realized with dread that the kidnapping part of things hadn't been a dream. The rest of it, though? She wasn't sure what was real and what wasn't, because her memory had so many holes in it. She remembered operating on the patient. Remembered admitting him to the SICU. Re-

membered the men abducting her. But after that? Everything was spotty.

As she took a deep breath, she smelled food and saw there was a tray set up next to her chair. Lifting a silver lid off the . . . Jesus, that was a really nice plate. Imari, like her mother's had been. Frowning, she noted the meal was gourmet: lamb with baby new potatoes and summer squash. A slice of chocolate cake and a pitcher and a glass were off to the side.

Had they kidnapped Wolfgang Puck as well, for kicks and giggles?

She looked over at her patient.

In the glow from a lamp on the bedside table, he was lying still on black sheets, his eyes closed, his black hair against the pillow, his heavy shoulders showing just above the covers. His respiration was slow and even, his face had color in it, and there was no sheen of fever sweat on him. Although his brows were drawn and his mouth was nothing more than a slash, he looked . . . revived.

Which was impossible, unless she'd been out cold for a week straight.

Jane stood up stiffly, stretched her arms over her head, and arched to crack her spine back into place. Moving silently, she went over and took the man's pulse. Even. Strong.

Shit. None of this was logical. None of it. Patients who had been shot and stabbed and who had crashed twice, who then had had open-heart surgery, did not rebound like this. Ever.

Vampire.

Oh, shut up with that.

She glanced at the digital clock on the bedside table and saw the date. Friday. *Friday?* Christ, it was Friday and ten o'clock in the morning. She'd operated on him a mere eight hours ago, and he looked as if he'd had weeks of healing time.

Maybe this was all a dream. Maybe she'd fallen asleep on the train down to Manhattan and would wake up as they pulled into Penn

Station. She'd have an awkward laugh, get a cup of coffee, and go to her interview at Columbia as planned, blaming it all on vending cuisine.

She waited. Hoped a bump in the tracks would lurch her into waking up.

Instead, the digital clock just kept churning through the minutes.

Right. Back to the shit-this-is-reality idea. Feeling utterly alone and scared to death, Jane walked over to the door, tried the knob, and found it locked. *Surprise, surprise.* She was tempted to bang on the thing, but why bother? No one on the other side was going to let her free, and besides, she didn't want any of them to know she was awake.

Casing the place was the directive: The windows were covered by some kind of barrier on the far side of the glass, the panel so thick there wasn't even a glow of day coming through it. Door was obviously a no-go. Walls were solid. No phone. No computer.

Closet was nothing but black clothes, big boots, and a fireproof cabinet. With a lock on it.

The bathroom didn't offer any escape. There was no window and no vent big enough for her to squeeze through.

She came back out. Man, this wasn't a bedroom. It was a cell with a mattress.

And this was not a dream.

Her adrenal glands got kicking, her heart going giddy-ap wild in her chest. She told herself that the police must be looking for her. Had to be. With all the security cameras and personnel at the hospital, someone must have seen them take her and the patient out of there. Plus, if she missed her interview, questions would start rolling.

Trying to get a grip, Jane closed herself in the bathroom, the lock of which had been removed, natch. After using the facilities, she washed her face and grabbed a towel that was hanging off the back of the door. As she put her nose into the folds, she caught an amazing scent that stopped her dead. It was the smell of the patient. He must

have used this, probably before he went out and took that bullet in the chest.

She closed her eyes and breathed in deep. Sex was the first and only thing that came to her mind. God, if they could bottle this, these boys could feed their gambling and drug habits by going legit.

Disgusted with herself, she dropped the towel like it was trash and caught a flash behind the toilet. Bending down to the marble tile, she found a straight-edged razor, the old-fashioned kind that made her think of Western movies. As she picked it up, she stared at the shiny blade.

Now, this was a fine weapon, she thought. A damn fine weapon.

She slipped it in her white coat just as she heard the bedroom door open.

Leaving the bathroom, she kept her hand in her pocket and her eyes sharp. Red Sox was back, and he had a pair of duffels with him. The load didn't seem substantial, at least not for someone as big as him, but he struggled under it.

"This should be a good enough start," he said in a raspy, tired voice, the word *start* pronounced *staht* in classic Bostonian fashion.

"Start what?"

"Treating him."

"Excuse me?"

Red Sox bent down and opened one of the bags. Inside were boxes of bandages and gauze wraps. Latex gloves. Plastic mauve bedpans. Bottles of pills.

"He told us what you'd need."

"Did he." *Damn it.* She had no interest in playing doc. It was a big enough job being Kidnap Victim, thank you very much.

The guy straightened carefully, like he was light-headed. "You're going to take care of him."

"Am I?"

"Yeah. And before you ask, yes, you're going to make it out of here alive."

"Assuming I do the medical thing, right?"

"Pretty much. But I'm not worried. You'd do it anyway, wouldn't you."

Jane stared at the guy. Not much showed of his face underneath the baseball cap, but his jaw had a curve to it she recognized. And there was that Boston accent.

"Do I know you?" she asked.

"Not anymore."

In the silence she ran a clinical eye over him. His skin was gray and pasty, his cheeks hollow, his hands shaking. He looked like he'd been on a two-week bender, weaving on his feet, his breathing off. And what was that smell? God, he reminded her of her grandmother: all denatured perfume and facial powder. Or . . . maybe it was something else, something that took her back to medical school. . . . Yeah, that was more like it. He reeked of the formaldehyde from Gross Human Anatomy.

He certainly had the pallor of a corpse. And ill as he was, she wondered if she might be able to take him down.

Feeling the razor in her pocket, she measured the distance between them and decided to hang tight. Even though he was weak, the door was shut and relocked. If she attacked him, she'd just risk getting hurt or killed and wouldn't be any closer to getting out. Her best bet was to wait next to the jamb until one of them came in. She was going to need the element of surprise, because sure as hell they would overpower her otherwise.

Except what did she do once she was on the other side? Was she in a big house? A little one? She had a feeling that the Fort Knox routine on the windows was standard-issue everywhere else.

"I want out," she said.

Red Sox exhaled like he was exhausted. "In a couple of days you'll go back to your life without remembering any of this."

"Yeah, right. Being kidnapped has a way of sticking with a person."

"You'll see. Or not, as the case will be." As Red Sox went to the bedside, he used the bureau, then the wall to steady himself. "He looks better."

She wanted to shout at him to get away from her patient.

"V?" Red Sox sat down carefully on the bed. "V?"

The patient's eyes opened after a moment, and the corner of his mouth twitched. "Cop."

The two men reached for each other's hands at exactly the same moment, and as she watched them, she decided the two of them had to be brothers—except their coloring was so different. Maybe they were just tight friends? Or lovers?

The patient's eyes slid over to her and ran up and down her body as if he was checking that she was unharmed. Then he looked at the food she hadn't touched and frowned like he disapproved.

"Didn't we just do this?" Red Sox murmured to the patient. " 'Cept I was the guy in the bed? How about we call it even now and not pull this wounded shit anymore."

Those icy bright eyes left her and shifted to his buddy. The frown didn't leave his face. "You look like hell."

"And you're Miss America."

The patient brought his other arm out of the sheets like the thing weighed as much as a piano. "Help me get my glove off—"

"Forget it. You're not ready."

"You're getting worse."

"Tomorrow—"

"Now. We do it now." The patient's voice lowered to a whisper. "In another day you won't be able to stand. You know what happens."

Red Sox dropped his head until it hung like a bag of flour off his neck. Then he cursed softly and reached for the patient's gloved hand.

Jane backed away until she hit the chair she'd been passed out in. That hand had put her nurse flat on the floor with a seizure, and yet the two men were both going about their business like contact with that thing was no big deal.

Red Sox gently worked the black leather free, revealing a hand covered with tattoos. Good God, the skin seemed to glow.

"Come here," the patient said, opening his arms wide to the other man. "Lay with me."

Jane's breath stopped in her chest.

Cormia walked the halls of the adytum, her bare feet silent, her white robe making no sound, her very breath passing in and out of her lungs with nary a sigh to note its travels. It was thus that she ambulated as a Chosen should, casting no shadow to eye nor whisper to ear.

Except she had a personal purpose, and that was wrong. As a Chosen you were to serve the Scribe Virgin at all times, your intentions always for Her.

Cormia's own need was such as to be undeniable, however.

The Temple of Books was at the end of a long colonnade, and its double doors were always open. Of all the sanctuary's buildings, even the one that contained the gems, this held the most prized lot: Herein rested the Scribe Virgin's records of the race, a diary that was of incomprehensible scope, spanning thousands of years. Dictated by Her Holiness to specially trained Chosen, the labor of love was a testament of both history and faith.

Inside the ivory walls, in the glow of white candles Cormia padded over the marble floor, passing countless stacks, walking faster and faster as she got more anxious. The diary's volumes were arranged chronologically, and within each year by social class, but what she was after wouldn't be in this general section.

Looking over her shoulder to make sure no one was around, she ducked down a corridor and came up to a glossy red door. In the middle of the panels was a depiction of two black daggers crossed at the blades, handles down. Around the hilts in gold leaf was a sacred motto in the Old Language:

THE BLACK DAGGER BROTHERHOOD
TO DEFEND AND PROTECT
OUR MOTHER, OUR RACE, OUR BROTHERS

Her hand shook as she put it on the golden handle. This area was restricted, and if she was caught she would be punished, but she cared naught. Even as she feared the quest she was on, she could no longer bear her lack of knowledge.

The room was of stately size and proportion, its high ceiling gold leafed, its stacks not white but shiny black. The books lining the walls were bound in black leather, their spines marked in gold that reflected the light from candles the color of shadows. The carpet on the floor was bloodred and soft as a pelt.

The air had a smell here that was not usual, the scent recalling certain spices. She had a feeling it was because the Brothers had actually come to this room on occasion and had lingered among their history, taking books out, perhaps about themselves, perhaps about their forebears. She tried to imagine them here and couldn't, as she'd never seen one of them. She had never seen a male in person, actually.

Cormia worked fast to discover the order of the volumes. It appeared that they were arranged by year— *Oh, wait.* There was a biography section, as well.

She knelt down. Each set of these volumes was marked with a number and the name of the Brother, along with his paternal lineage. The first of them was an ancient tome bearing symbols with an archaic variation she recalled from some of the oldest parts of the Scribe Virgin's diary. This initial warrior had several books to his name and number, and the next two Brothers bore him as their sire.

Farther down the line, she randomly took out a book and opened it. The title page was resplendent, a painted portrait of the Brother surrounded by script detailing his name and birth date and induction into the Brotherhood as well as his prowess on the field by weapon and tactic. The next page was the warrior's lineage for generations, followed by a listing of the females he'd mated and the young he'd sired. Then chapter by chapter his life was detailed, both on the field and off.

This Brother, Tohrture, had evidently lived long and fought well. There were three books on him, and one of the last notations was the male's joy when his one surviving son, Rhage, joined the Brotherhood.

Cormia put the book back and kept going, trailing her forefinger over the bindings, touching the names. These males had fought to keep her safe; they were the ones who had come when the Chosen were attacked those decades ago. They were also the ones who kept civilians protected from the *lessers*. Mayhap this Primale arrangement would be well after all. Surely one whose mission was to shield the innocent would not hurt her?

As she had no idea how old her promised was or when he had joined the Brotherhood, she looked at each book. There were so many of them, whole stacks. . . .

Her finger stopped on a spine of a thick volume, one of four.

THE BLOODLETTER
356

The name of the Primale's sire made her go cold. She had read about him as part of the history of the race, and dear Virgin, perhaps she was wrong. If the stories about that male were true, even those who fought nobly could be cruel.

Odd that his paternal line wasn't listed.

She kept going, tracing over more spines and more names.

VISHOUS
SON OF THE BLOODLETTER
428

There was only one volume, and it was thinner than her finger. As she slid it free, she smoothed her palm over the cover, her heart pounding. The binding was stiff as she opened it, as if the book had been rarely breached. Which indeed it had not been. There was no portrait nor carefully penned tribute to his fighting skills, only a birth date that indicated he'd be three hundred and three years old soon, and a notation of when he was inducted into the Brotherhood. She turned the page. There was no mention of his lineage save for the Bloodletter, and the rest of the book was blank.

Replacing it, she returned to the father's volumes and pulled out the third in the set. She read about the sire in hopes of learning something about the son that might allay her fears, but what she found was a level of cruelty that made her pray the Primale took after his mother, whoever that might be. The Bloodletter was indeed the right name for the warrior, for he was brutal on vampires and *lessers* alike.

Flipping to the back, she found on the last page a recording of his death date, though no mention of the manner. She took out the first volume and opened it to see the portrait. The father had had jet-black hair and a full beard and eyes that made her want to put the book away and never open it again.

After replacing the tome, she sat down on the floor. At the conclusion of the Scribe Virgin's sequester the Bloodletter's son would come for Cormia, and he would take her body as his rightful possession. She couldn't imagine what the act entailed or what the male did, and dreaded the sexual lessons.

At least as Primale he would lay with others, she told herself. Many others, some of whom who had been trained to pleasure males. No doubt he would prefer them. If she had any luck at all, she would be rarely visited.

THIRTEEN

As Butch stretched out on Vishous's bed, V was ashamed to admit it, but he'd spent a lot of days wondering what this would be like. Feel like. Smell like. Now that it was reality, he was glad he had to concentrate on healing Butch. Otherwise he had a feeling it would be too intense and he'd have to pull away.

As his chest brushed against Butch's, he tried to tell himself he didn't need this. He tried to pretend that he didn't need this feel of someone beside him, that he wasn't eased as he lay head-to-toe with another person, that he didn't care about the warmth and the weight against his body.

That the healing of the cop didn't heal him.

But that was, of course, all bullshit. As V wrapped his arms around Butch and opened himself up to take in the Omega's evil, he needed it all. With the visit from his mother and the shooting, he craved the closeness of another, needed to feel arms that returned his embrace. He had to have the beat of a heart against his own.

He spent so much time keeping his hand away from others, keeping himself apart from others. To let down his guard with the one person he truly trusted made his eyes sting.

Good thing he never cried or his cheeks would be wet as stones in a river.

As Butch shuddered in relief, Vishous felt the trembling in the male's shoulders and hips. Knowing it was illicit, but unable to stop himself, V took his tattooed hand and buried it deep into Butch's nape. While the cop let out another groan and moved closer, V shifted his eyes over to his surgeon.

She was over by the chair, watching them, her eyes wide, her mouth open slightly.

The only reason V didn't feel awkward as hell was because he knew that when she left she would have no memories of this private moment. Otherwise he couldn't have handled it. Shit like this didn't happen often in his life—mostly because he didn't let it. And he was damned if he'd have some stranger remembering his private biz.

Except . . . she didn't really feel like a stranger.

His surgeon's hand went to her throat, and she sank down into the seat of the chair. As time stretched out languidly, uncurling like a lazy dog on a hazy summer night, her eyes never left his, and he didn't look away either.

That word came back to him: *Mine.*

Except which one was he thinking of? Butch or her?

Her, he realized. It was the female across the room who was bringing that word out of him.

Butch shifted, his legs brushing against V's through the blankets. With a stab of guilt, V recalled the times he'd imagined himself with Butch, imagined the two of them lying as they were now, imagined them . . . well, healing wasn't the half of it. Strange, though. Now that it was happening, V wasn't thinking anything sexual toward Butch. No . . . the sexual drive and the bonding word were directed toward the silent human woman across the room, the one who was clearly shocked.

Maybe she couldn't handle two men being together? Not that he and Butch were ever going to be.

For some ridiculous fucking reason, V said to her, "He is my best friend."

She seemed surprised that he'd offered any explanation. Which made two of them.

Jane couldn't take her eyes off the bed. The patient and Red Sox were glowing together, a soft light emanating from their bodies, and something was happening between them, some kind of exchange. Jesus, that sweet smell was fading, wasn't it.

And best friends? She looked at the patient's hand buried in Red Sox's hair and the way those heavy arms held the man close. Sure they were buddies, but how much further than that did it go?

After God only knew how long, Red Sox let out a long sigh and lifted his head. With their faces separated by a mere matter of inches, Jane braced herself. She had no problem with men being together, but for some insane reason she didn't want to see her patient kiss his friend. Or anybody else.

"Are you okay?" Red Sox asked.

The patient's voice was low and soft. "Yeah. Tired."

"I'll bet." Red Sox got up off the bed in a lithe move. Holy hell, he looked as if he'd spent a month at a spa. His color was back to normal, and his eyes were unclouded and alert. And that air of malevolence was gone.

The patient repositioned himself on his back. Then rolled to his side with a wince. Then tried his back again. His legs scissored under the covers the whole time, as if he were trying to outrun whatever feeling was in his body.

"You in pain?" Red Sox asked. When there was no response, the guy looked over his shoulder at her. "Can you help him, Doc?"

She wanted to say no. She wanted to throw out a couple of curse words and demand to be released again. And she wanted to kick this

member of the Red Sox Nation in the balls for making her patient sicker by whatever just happened.

The Hippocratic oath got her up and moving to the duffels. "Depends on what you brought me."

She dug around and found a Walgreens-load of just about every pain med available. And all of it was straight out of Big Pharma packages, so they clearly had sources on the inside of a hospital: The drugs were sealed up in such a way that they hadn't passed very far through the black market. Hell, these guys probably were the black market.

To make sure she hadn't missed any options, she looked in the second bag . . . and found her favorite pair of yoga sweats . . . and the rest of the things she'd packed to go down to Manhattan for the Columbia interview.

They'd been to her home. These bastards had been in her home.

"We had to take your car back," Red Sox explained. "And figured you'd appreciate some fresh clothes. These were ready to go."

They'd driven her Audi, walked through her rooms, been through her shit.

Jane stood up and kicked the duffel across the room. As her clothes spilled out onto the floor, she shoved her hand into her pocket and gripped the razor, ready to go for Red Sox's throat.

The patient's voice was strong. "Apologize."

She wheeled around and glared at the bed. "For *what*? You take me against my w—"

"Not you. Him."

Red Sox's voice was contrite as he spoke up fast. "I'm sorry we went through your house. Just trying to make this easier on you."

"Easier? No offense, but fuck off with your apology. You know, people are going to miss me. The police will be looking for me."

"We took care of all that, even the appointment in Manhattan. We found the train tickets and the interview itinerary. They no longer expect you."

Rage made her lose her voice for a moment. "How *dare* you."

"They were quite content to reschedule when they heard you were sick." As if this was supposed to make it right.

Jane opened her mouth, ready to have at him, when it dawned on her that she was wholly at their mercy. So antagonizing her captors was probably not a smart move.

With a curse, she looked at the patient. "When are you going to let me go?"

"As soon as I'm on my feet."

She studied his face, from the goatee to the diamond eyes to the tats at his temple. On instinct she said, "Give me your word. Swear on the life I gave back to you. You will let me go unharmed."

He didn't hesitate. Not even to take a breath. "On my honor and the blood in my veins, you'll be free as soon as I'm well."

Berating herself and them, she took her hand from her pocket, bent down, and grabbed a vial of Demerol out of the bigger duffel. "There aren't any syringes."

"I've got some." Red Sox came over and held a sterile pack out. When she tried to take it from him, he kept a grip on the thing. "I know you'll use this wisely."

"Wisely?" She snapped the syringe out of his hand. "No, I'm going to poke him in the eye with it. Because that's what they trained me to do in medical school."

Bending down again, she fished around in the duffel and found a pair of latex gloves, an alcohol towelette packet, and some gauze and packing to change the chest dressing.

Although she'd given the patient prophylactic antibiotics through his IV before surgery, so his risk of infection was low, she asked, "Can you get antibiotics as well?"

"Anything you need."

Yeah, they were definitely hooked up with a hospital. "I might want some ciprofloxacin or maybe some amoxicillin. Depends on what's going on under that surgical packing."

She put the needle and the vial and the other supplies on the bedside table, snapped on the gloves, and tore open the foiled square.

"Hold up for a second, Doc," Red Sox said.

"Excuse me?"

Red Sox's eyes fixed on her like a pair of gun sights. "With all due respect, I need to stress that if you harm him intentionally, I will kill you with my bare hands. In spite of the fact that you're a woman."

As a shot of terror stiffened her spine, a growling sound filled the bedroom, the kind a mastiff made before it attacked.

They both looked down at the patient in shock.

His upper lip was peeled back and those sharp front teeth were twice the size they'd been before. "No one touches her. I don't care what she does or to whom."

Red Sox frowned as if his buddy had lost his marbles. "You know our agreement, roommate. I keep you safe until you can do it yourself. You don't like it? Get your ass healed up and then you can worry about her."

"*No one.*"

There was a moment of silence; then Red Sox looked back and forth between Jane and the patient like he was recalibrating a law of physics—and having trouble with the math.

Jane jumped in, feeling the need to calm them down to a rolling boil. "Okay, okay. Let's cut the macho-shithead posturing, shall we?" The two of them looked at her in surprise and seemed even more astounded as she elbowed Red Sox out of the way. "If you're going to be here, unplug the aggression. You're not helping him." She glared at the patient. "And you—you just relax."

After a moment of dead-fish silence, Red Sox cleared his throat, and the patient pulled on his glove and shut his eyes.

"Thank you," she muttered. "Now, you boys mind if I do my job so I can get out of here?"

She gave the patient a shot of Demerol, and within moments his tight eyebrows eased up like someone had loosened the screws on them. As the tension left his body, she stripped off the bandage on his chest and lifted the gauze and packing off.

"Dear . . . God," she breathed.

Red Sox looked over her shoulder. "What's wrong? It's healed up perfect."

She gently prodded the row of metal staples and the pink seam beneath them. "I could remove these now."

"You need help?"

"This just isn't right."

The patient's eyes opened, and it was obvious he knew exactly what she was thinking: *Vampire*.

Without looking at Red Sox, she said, "Will you get me the surgical scissors and the grips in that duffel? Oh, and bring me the topical antibiotic spray."

As she heard rustling from across the room, she whispered, "What are you?"

"Alive," the patient replied. "Thanks to you."

"Here you go."

Jane jumped like a puppet. Red Sox was holding out two stainless-steel implements, but for the life of her she couldn't remember why she'd asked for them.

"The staples," she murmured.

"What?" Red Sox asked.

"I'm taking out the staples." She took the scissors and the grips and hit the patient's chest with a mist of antibiotic.

In spite of the fact that her brain was doing the twist in her skull, she managed to cut and remove each of the twenty or so metal clips, dropping them in the wastepaper basket next to the bed. When she was finished she swabbed up the tears of blood that welled at each entrance and exit hole, then hit his chest with some more antibacterial spray.

As she met his brilliant eyes, she knew for sure he was not human. She had seen the insides of too many bodies and witnessed the strug-

gle to heal too many times to think otherwise. What she wasn't sure of was where that left her. Or the rest of the human race.

How was this possible? That there was another species with so many human characteristics? Then again, that was probably how they stayed hidden.

Jane covered the center of his chest with a light layer of gauze, which she then taped in place. As she finished up the patient grimaced, and his hand, the one with the glove, went to his stomach.

"You all right?" Jane asked as his face drained of color.

"Queasy." A line of sweat broke out over his upper lip.

She looked at Red Sox. "I think you're going to want to take off."

"Why?"

"He's about to be sick."

"I'm fine," the patient muttered, closing his eyes.

Jane headed for the duffels for a bedpan and talked at Red Sox. "Go on, now. Let me see to him. We aren't going to need an audience for this."

Goddamn Demerol. It worked great on pain, but sometimes the side effects were a real problem for patients.

Red Sox hesitated until the patient groaned and started to swallow compulsively. "Umm, okay. Listen, before I go, can I get you something fresh to eat? Anything in particular you want?"

"You're kidding me, right? Like I'm supposed to forget the abduction and the mortal threat and give you a drive-thru order?"

"No reason not to eat while you're here." He picked up the tray.

God, that voice of his . . . that rough, hoarse voice with the Boston accent. "I know you. I definitely know you from somewhere. Take the hat off. I want to see your face."

The guy went across the room with the wilted food. "I'll bring you something else to eat."

As the door shut and locked she had a childish urge to run at the thing and pound on it.

The patient moaned and she looked at him. "You going to stop fighting the urge to throw up now?"

"Fuck . . . me . . ." Curling over on his side, the patient began retching.

No bedpan was needed, because he didn't have anything in his stomach, so Jane hauled herself into the bathroom, brought back a towel, and put it to his mouth. While he gagged miserably, he held on to the center of his chest as if he didn't want to pop his wound open.

"It's okay," she said as she put her hand on his smooth back. "You're healed up enough. You're not going to tear that scar open."

"Feels . . . like . . . I . . . *Fuck*—"

God, he was suffering, his face strained and red, sweat all over him, body heaving. "It's okay, just let it roll through you. The less you fight it, the easier it will be. Yeah . . . there you go . . . breathe between them. Okay, now . . ."

She stroked his spine and held the towel and couldn't help but keep murmuring to him. When it was over, the patient lay still, breathing through his mouth, his hand with the glove clenched around a tangle of sheets.

"That was so not fun," he rasped.

"We'll find you another painkiller," she murmured, brushing his hair from his eyes. "No more Dem for you. Listen, I want to check your wounds, okay?"

He nodded and eased onto his back, the expanse of his chest seeming as big as the damn bed. She was careful with the adhesive tape, gentle as she lifted the gauze. *Good lord . . .* The skin that had been perforated by the staples just fifteen minutes ago was completely healed. All that remained was a small pink line down his sternum.

"What are you?" she blurted.

Her patient rolled back toward her. "Tired."

Without even thinking about it she started stroking him again, the sound of her hand smoothing up and down his skin making a hushed noise. It wasn't long before she noticed that his shoulders were all hard muscle . . . and that what she was touching was warm and very male.

She took back her palm.

"Please." He caught her wrist with his unmarked hand—even though his eyes were closed. "Touch me or . . . shit, hold on to me. I'm . . . all adrift. Like I'm going to float away. I can't feel anything. Not the bed . . . not my body."

She looked down at where he held on to her, then measured his biceps and the breadth of his chest. She had the passing thought that he could snap her arm in two, but she knew he wouldn't. He'd been ready to rip the throat out of one of his nearest and dearest a half hour ago to protect her—

Stop it.

Do not *feel safe with him. The Stockholm syndrome is not your friend.*

"Please," he said on a shaky breath, shame constricting his voice.

God, she'd never understood how kidnapping victims developed relationships with their captors. It went against all logic as well as the laws of self-preservation: Your enemy cannot be your friend.

But denying him warmth was unthinkable. "I'll need my hand back."

"You have two. Use the other." With that he curled himself around the palm he held on to, the sheets getting pulled farther down his torso.

"Let me switch sides then," she muttered as she slid her hand out of his grip, replaced it, then laid her newly freed palm on his shoulder.

His skin was the golden brown of a summer tan and smooth . . . boy, it was smooth and supple. Following the curve of his spine she went up to his nape, and before she knew it she was stroking his glossy hair. Short in the back, long around his face—she wondered whether he wore it that way to hide the tattoos on his temple. Except they had to be for show—why else would he put them somewhere so noticeable?

He made a noise in the back of his throat, a purr that rolled through his chest and upper back; then he moved away, the shift tugging her arm. Clearly he wanted her stretched out next to him, but as she resisted, he eased off.

Staring at her arm in the tight clutch of his biceps, she thought about the last time she'd been entwined with a man. Long while. And it hadn't been that good, frankly.

Manello's dark eyes came to mind. . . .

"Don't think of him."

Jane jerked. "How did you know who was on my mind?"

The patient released his hold on her and slowly shifted around so he faced away from her. "Sorry. Not my biz."

"How did you know?"

"I'm going to try to sleep now, okay?"

"Okay."

Jane got up and went back to her chair, thinking of his six-chambered heart. His untypeable blood. Those fangs of his in that blonde's wrist. Glancing over to the window, she wondered if what covered the glass panes was not just for security but also to keep out daylight.

Where did it all leave her? Locked in a room with a . . . vampire?

The rational side of her rejected the thought out of hand, but at her core she was logic driven. With a shake of the head, she recalled her favorite quote from Sherlock Holmes, paraphrasing it: If you eliminate all possible explanations, then the impossible is the answer. Logic and biology didn't lie, did they? It was one of the reasons why she'd chosen to become a physician in the first place.

She looked down at her patient, getting lost in the implications. The mind reeled at the evolutionary possibilities, but she also con-

sidered more practical matters. She thought about the drugs in that duffel bag and the fact that her patient had been out in a dangerous part of town when he'd been shot. And hello, they'd kidnapped her.

How could she possibly trust him or his word?

Jane put her hand in her pocket and felt for the razor. The answer to that one was easy. She couldn't.

FOURTEEN

Up in his bedroom at the big house, Phury sat with his back against his headboard and his blue velvet duvet over his legs. His prosthesis was off, and a blunt was smoldering in a heavy glass ashtray next to him. Mozart drifted out of a set of hidden Bose speakers.

The book of firearms in front of him was being used as a lap easel instead of reading material. A thick sheet of white paper was laid out on top of the thing, but he hadn't made any marks on it with his Ticonderoga No. 2 for a while. The portrait was complete. He'd finished it about an hour ago and was working up the courage to wad it up and throw it out.

Even though he was never satisfied with his drawings, he almost liked this one. From out of the blizzard-thick blankness of the page, a female's face and neck and hair had been revealed by strokes of lead. Bella was staring off to the left, a slight smile on her lips, a strand of her dark hair across her cheek. He'd caught sight of the pose at Last

Meal this evening. She'd been looking at Zsadist, which explained the secret lift to her mouth.

In all the poses he'd drawn her in, Phury always sketched her with her eyes elsewhere. If she were staring out of the page, at him, that just seemed inappropriate. Hell, drawing her at all was inappropriate.

He flattened his hand over her face, prepared to crumple the paper.

At the last moment he went for the blunt instead, craving some artificial ease as his heart beat too hard. He was smoking a lot lately. More than ever. And though relying on the chemical calm made him feel dirty, the idea of stopping never crossed his mind. He couldn't imagine getting through the day without help.

As he took another hit and held on to the smoke with his lungs, he thought of his brush with heroin. Back in December the backflip off the H-cliff had been prevented not by his making a good choice, but because John Matthew happened to pick the right time to interrupt.

Phury exhaled and stared at the tip of the blunt. The temptation to try something more hard-core was back. He could feel the urge to go to Rehv and ask the male for another Baggie full of deep nod. Maybe then he'd get some peace.

A knock went off on his door and Z's voice said, "Can I come in?"

Phury stuffed the drawing into the belly of the firearms book. "Yeah."

Z walked in and didn't say another word. With his hands on his hips, he paced back and forth, back and forth, at the end of the bed. Phury waited, lighting up another blunt and tracking his identical twin as Z wore out the carpet.

You didn't push Z to talk any more than you'd try to coerce a fish onto the business end of a hook with a lot of chatter. Silence was the only lure that worked.

Finally the Brother stopped. "She's bleeding."

Phury's heart jumped, and he splayed his hand out over the cover of the book. "How much and for how long?"

"She's been hiding it from me, so I don't know."

"How'd you find out?"

"I found a thing of Always stuffed in the back of the cabinet right next to the toilet."

"Maybe they're old."

"Last time when I got my buzz razor out, they weren't there."

Shit. "She has to go to Havers's, then."

"Her next appointment isn't for a week." Z started up with the pacing again. "I know she's not telling me because she's afraid I'll freak out."

"Maybe what you found is being used for another reason?"

Z stopped. "Oh, yeah. Right. Because those things are multifunctional. Like Q-tips or some shit. Look, would you talk to her?"

"What?" Phury quickly took a drag. "This is private. Between you and her."

Z scrubbed the top of his skull-trimmed head. "You're better with shit like this than I am. The last thing she needs is for me to break down in front of her, or worse, yell at her because I'm scared to death and not being reasonable."

Phury tried to take a deep breath, but he could barely get the air down his windpipe. He so wanted to get involved. He wanted to walk down the hall of statues to the pair's room and sit Bella down and get the story out of her. He wanted to be a hero. But it was not his place.

"You're her *hellren*. You need to do the talking." Phury stabbed out the last half inch of the blunt, rolled up a new one, and flipped open his lighter. The flint wheel made a rasping noise as the flame jumped up. "You can do it."

Zsadist cursed, paced some more, then eventually headed for the door. "Talking about this whole pregnancy thing reminds me that if I lose her, I'm fucked. I feel so goddamned powerless."

After his twin took off, Phury let his head fall back. As he smoked, he watched the blunt's lit tip flare and wondered idly if it was like an orgasm for the hand-rolled.

Jesus. If Bella was lost, both he and Z were going to go into a tailspin the likes of which males didn't come out of.

As the thought occurred to him, he felt guilty. He really shouldn't care that much about his twin's female.

As anxiety made him feel like he'd swallowed a swarm of locusts, he smoked his way through the emotion until he caught sight of the clock. *Shit.* He had to teach a class on firearms in an hour. He'd better hit the shower and try to get sober.

John woke up confused, vaguely aware that his face hurt and that there was some kind of bleating going off in his room.

He lifted his head out of his notebook and rubbed the bridge of his nose. The spiral binding had left behind a pattern of dents that made him think of Worf from *Star Trek: TNG.* And the noise was the alarm clock.

Three fifty in the afternoon. Classes started at four P.M.

John got up from the desk, wobbled into the bathroom, and stood over the toilet. When that felt too much like work, he turned around and sat down.

God, he was exhausted. He'd spent the last couple of months sleeping in Tohr's chair in the training center's office, but after Wrath had put his foot down and moved John up to the big house, he'd been back in a real bed. You'd think he'd be feeling great with all that legroom. Instead, he was whipped.

After he flushed, he turned on the lights and winced in the glare. *Damn.* Bad idea to lose the darkness, and not just because his eyes were killing him. Standing beneath the recessed lighting his little body looked horrible, nothing but pale skin over evident bone. With a grimace, he covered up his thumb-sized sex with his hand so he didn't have to look at the thing and killed the lights.

There was no time for a shower. Quick brush of the teeth, little splash action on the puss with some water, and he didn't bother with his hair.

Out in his bedroom he just wanted to go back between the sheets, but he pulled on jeans that were junior-sized and frowned as he zipped up the fly. The things were loose on his hips, baggy though he'd been trying to eat.

Great. Instead of going through the transition, he was shrinking.

As another round of what-if-it-never-comes-for-me? rolled him over, his eyebrows started to pound. *Crap.* He felt like there was a little man with a hammer in each of his eye sockets, bashing the shit out of his optic nerve.

Grabbing his books off his desk, he shoved them into his backpack and left. The instant he stepped into the hall he put his arm over his face. The sight of the brilliant foyer made his headache roar, and he stumbled back, bumping into a Greek kuroi. Which made him realize he hadn't put a shirt on.

Cursing to hell and gone, he went back to his room, threw one on, and somehow made it downstairs without tripping over his own feet. Man, everything was getting on his nerves. The sound of his Nikes across the foyer was like a band of squeaky mice following him. The clicking of the hidden door into the tunnel seemed loud as a gunshot. His trip through the underground route to the training center went on forever.

This was *not* going to be a great day. His temper was flaring already, and going by the last month or so, he knew that the earlier it kicked in, the harder it would be to hold.

And as soon as he walked into the classroom, he knew he was really in for it.

Sitting in the back row at the loner table John had called home before he got tight with his boys was . . . Lash.

Who now came in the economy-size asshole package. The guy was big and filled out, built like a fighter. And he'd gone through a

G.I. Joe makeover. Before he'd worn flashy couture clothes and a vault's worth of Jacob & Co. jewelry; now he was dressed in black cargo pants and a skintight black nylon shirt. His blond hair, which had been long enough to pull back into a ponytail, was now military short.

It was as if all that pretension had been wiped clean because he knew he had the goods on the inside.

One thing hadn't changed: His eyes were still sharkskin gray and focused on John—who knew without a doubt that if he got caught alone with the guy he was in for a world of hurt. He might have taken Lash down the last time, but it wouldn't happen again, and more than that, Lash was going to get him. The promise of payback was in both the set of those big shoulders and the half smile that had *fuck you* written all over it.

John took a seat next to Blay, feeling a dark-alley kind of dread.

"Hey, buddy," his friend said softly. "Don't worry about that bastard, okay?"

John didn't want to look as weak as he was feeling, so he just shrugged and unzipped his backpack. God, this headache was a killer. But then, the flight-or-fight response on an empty, rolling stomach was hardly a dose of Excedrin.

Qhuinn leaned over and dropped a note in front of John. *We gotchu*, was all it said.

John blinked quickly from gratitude as he got out his firearms book and thought about what they were going to cover today in class. How appropriate it was guns. He felt like one was leveled at the back of his skull.

He looked to the rear of the room. As if Lash had been waiting for the eye contact, the guy leaned forward and put his forearms on the table. His hands slowly cranked into two fists that seemed big as John's head, and when he smiled, his new fangs were sharp as knives and white as the afterlife.

Shit. John was a dead man if his transition didn't come soon.

FIFTEEN

ishous woke up, and the first thing he saw was his surgeon in the chair across the room. Apparently even in his sleep, he'd been keeping track of her.

She was watching him, too.

"How are you?" Her voice was low and even. Professionally warm, he thought.

"I'm better." Although it was hard to imagine feeling worse than he had when he'd been throwing up.

"Are you in pain?"

"Yeah, but it doesn't bother me. More an ache, really."

Her eyes went over him, but again it was with professional purpose. "Your coloring is good."

He didn't know what to say to that. Because the longer he looked like shit, the longer she could stay. Health was so not his friend.

"Do you remember anything?" she asked. "About the shooting?"

"Not really."

Which was only a partial lie. All he had were flashes of the events, partial clippings of the articles instead of the full columns: He remembered the alley. A fight with a *lesser*. A gun going off. And after that ending up on her table and getting evac'd from the hospital by his brothers.

"Why did someone want to shoot you?" she asked.

"I'm hungry. Is there food around?"

"Are you a drug dealer? Or a pimp?"

He rubbed his face. "Why do you think I'm either?"

"You got shot in an alley off Trade. The paramedics said you had weapons on you."

"It didn't occur to you I could be undercover police?"

"Cops in Caldwell don't carry martial-arts daggers. And your kind wouldn't go that route."

V narrowed his eyes. "My kind?"

"Too much exposure, right? Besides, you wouldn't worry much about policing another race."

Man, he didn't have the energy to tackle the species discussion with her. Plus, there was a part of him that didn't want her to think of him as different.

"Food," he said, glancing over at a tray that was set on the bureau. "Can I have some?"

She stood up and planted her hands on her hips. He had a feeling she was going to say something along the lines of *Get it yourself, you freak bastard.*

Instead she walked across the room. "If you're hungry, you can eat. I didn't touch what Red Sox brought me, and there's no sense throwing it out."

He frowned. "I will not take food meant for you."

"I'm not going to eat it. Being kidnapped has killed my appetite."

V cursed under his breath, hating the position he'd put her in. "I'm sorry."

"Instead of doing the 'sorry' thing, how about you just let me go?"

"Not yet." *Not ever*, some crazy-ass voice muttered.

Oh, Christ, not more with the—

Mine.

On the heels of the word, an all-powerful need to mark her lit him up. He wanted to get her naked and underneath him and covered with his scent as he pumped into her body. He saw it happening, saw them skin-to-skin on the bed, him on top of her with her legs split wide to accommodate his hips and his cock.

As she brought the tray of food over his temperature spiked, and what was doing between his legs throbbed like a bitch. Surreptitiously he bunched the blankets up so that nothing showed.

She put the food down and lifted the silver lid off the plate.

"So how much better do you have to be for me to leave?" Her eyes went over his chest, all medical assessment, as if she were measuring what was under the bandages.

Ah, hell. He wanted her to look at him as a male. He wanted those eyes of hers going over his skin not to check a surgical wound, but because she was thinking about putting her hands on him and wondering where to start.

V closed his eyes and rolled away, grunting at the pain in his chest. He told himself the ache was from the surgery. Suspected it was more because of the surgeon.

"I'll pass on the food. Next time they come in I'll ask for some."

"You need this more than I do. And I'm worried about your fluid intake."

Actually, he was fine, because he'd fed. With enough blood vampires could survive a number of days without sustenance.

Which was great. Cut down on the trips to the bathroom.

"I want you to eat this," she said, staring down at him. "As your physician—"

"I will not take from your plate." For God's sake, no male of worth would ever rob his female of food, not even if he was starved to the point of dizziness. Her needs always came first—

V felt like putting his head in a car door and slamming it a couple of dozen times. Where the hell was this manual of mating behavior coming from? It was like someone had loaded new software into his brain.

"Okay," she said, turning away. "Fine."

Next thing he heard was banging. She was pounding on the door.

V sat upright. "What the hell are you doing?"

Butch flew into the room, nearly knocking V's surgeon off her feet. "What's wrong?"

V cut into the drama with, "Nothing—"

The surgeon spoke over them both, all calm authority. "He needs food, and he won't eat what's on that tray. Bring him something simple and easy to digest. Rice. Chicken. Water. Crackers."

"Okay." Butch leaned to the side and looked at V. There was a long pause. "How you doing?"

Fucked in the head, thanks. "Fine."

But at least there was one good thing going. The cop was back to normal, his eyes clear, his stance strong, his scent a combination of Marissa's ocean smell and his bonding mark. He'd obviously been getting busy.

Interesting. Usually when V thought about those two together, his chest felt like it was wrapped in barbed wire. Now? He was just glad his friend was healthy.

"You look great, cop."

Butch smoothed his silk pin-striped shirt. "Gucci can turn any-one into a rock star."

"You know what I mean."

Those familiar hazels grew serious. "Yeah. Thanks . . . as always." In the awkward moment, words hovered in the air between them, things that couldn't be said with any kind of audience. "So . . . I'll be back with chow."

As the door shut Jane glanced over her shoulder. "How long have you been lovers?"

Her eyes met his, and there was no getting out of the question. "We're not."

"You sure about that?"

"Trust me." For no particular reason he looked at her white coat. "'Dr. Jane Whitcomb,'" he read. "'Trauma.'" Made sense. She had that kind of confidence. "So I was in bad shape when I came in?"

"Yeah, but I saved your ass, didn't I."

A wave of awe came over him. She was his *rahlman*, his savior. They were bonded—

Yeah, whatever. Right now his savior was inching away from him, backing up until she hit the far wall. He closed his lids, knowing his eyes were glowing. The retreat, the horror in her face, stung like hell.

"Your eyes," she said in a thin voice.

"Don't worry about it."

"What the hell are you?" Her tone suggested *freak* could easily be the descriptor, and God, wasn't she right about that.

"What are you?" she repeated.

It was tempting to front, but there was no way she would buy it. Besides, lying to her made him feel dirty.

Leveling his stare on her, he said in a low voice, "You know what I am. You're smart enough to know."

Long silence. Then: "I can't believe it."

"You're too smart not to. Hell, you've already alluded to it."

"Vampires do *not* exist."

His temper flared even though she didn't deserve it. "We don't? Then explain why you're in my wonder-fucking-land."

Without taking a breath she shot back, "Tell me something—do civil rights mean anything to your kind?"

"Survival means more," he snapped. "But then, we've been hunted for generations."

"And the ends justify any means for you. How noble." Her voice was as sharp as his. "Do you always use this rationale to snatch humans?"

"No, I don't like them."

"Oh, except you need me, so you'll use me. Aren't I the lucky exception."

Well, shit. This was a turn-on. The more she met his aggression head-on, the harder his body got. Even in his weakened state, his arousal was a demanding throb between his thighs, and in his mind he was picturing her bent over the bed with nothing but that white coat on . . . and him driving into her from behind.

Maybe he should be grateful she was repulsed. Like he needed to get tangled with a female—

All at once the night of his shooting funneled into his brain with total clarity. He remembered his mother's happy little visit and her fabulous birthday present: the Primale. He'd been tapped to be the Primale.

V grimaced and clapped his hands over his face. "Oh . . . *fuck.*"

In a grudging tone, she asked, "What's wrong?"

"My goddamn destiny."

"Oh, really? I'm locked up in this room. At least you're free to go where you choose."

"The hell I am."

She made a dismissive noise, and then neither of them said another word until Butch brought another tray in about a half hour later. The cop had the presence of mind not to say much and move quickly—and also the foresight to keep the door locked the whole time as he made the delivery. Which was smart.

V's surgeon was planning on making a run for it. She tracked the cop like she was measuring a target and kept her right hand in the pocket of her coat.

She had some kind of weapon in there. *Goddamn it.*

V watched Jane closely as Butch put the tray on the bedside table, praying like hell she didn't do anything stupid. When he saw her body tense and her weight shift forward, he sat up, prepared to lunge because he didn't want anyone but himself handling her. Ever.

Nothing came of it, though. She caught his change in position from the corner of her eye, and the distraction was enough to get Butch out of the room and the door relocked.

V settled back against the pillows and measured the hard line of her chin. "Take off your coat."

"Excuse me?"

"Take it off."

"No."

"I want it off."

"Then I suggest you hold your breath. Won't affect me in the slightest, but at least the suffocation will help pass the time for you."

His arousal *pounded*. Oh, shit, he needed to teach her that disobedience carried a price, and what a session that would be. She'd fight him tooth and nail before she submitted. If she submitted at all.

Vishous's spine arched all on its own, his hips swiveling as his erection kicked beneath the sheets. *Jesus* . . . He was so totally and completely sexed he was on the verge of coming.

But he still had to disarm her. "I want you to feed me."

Her eyebrows popped. "You're perfectly capable of—"

"Feed me. Please."

As she came over to the bed she was all business and bad mood. She unrolled the napkin and—

V sprang into action. He took her by the arms and dragged her over his body, the element of surprise shocking her into a surrender he was damn sure was temporary—so he worked fast. He stripped the coat off her, handling her as gently as he could while her body torqued to get free.

Shit, he couldn't help it, but the urge to subdue her took over. Suddenly he was touching her not to keep her hands from whatever was in that pocket, but because he wanted to pin her to the bed and let her feel his power and strength. He took both her wrists in one hand, stretched her arms over her head, and trapped her thighs with his hips.

"Let. Me. *Go!*" Her teeth were bared, fury iridescent in her dark green eyes.

Totally aroused, he arched into her and sucked in a breath . . . only to freeze. Her scent carried no sultry sweetness of a female who wanted sex. She was not attracted to him at all. She was pissed off.

V let her go immediately, rolling away, though making sure he had the coat with him. The instant she was free she shot off the bed like the mattress was on fire and faced off with him. Her hair was tangled at its blunt ends, her shirt wrenched around, one pant leg shoved up to her knee. She was breathing heavily from exertion and staring at her coat.

When he went through it, he found one of his straight-edged razors.

"I can't have you armed." He folded the coat up with care and put it at the foot of the bed, knowing she wouldn't come near him if she was paid to. "If you attacked me or one of my brothers with something like this, you could get hurt."

A curse left her on a hard exhale. Then she surprised him. "What tipped you off?"

"Your hand going to find it as Butch brought in the tray."

She put her arms around herself. "Shit. Thought I'd been more discreet."

"I have some experience with concealed weapons." He reached down and pulled opened the drawer to his bedside table. The razor made a dull thud as he dropped it inside. After he shut the thing in, he triggered a lock with his mind.

When he looked back up she was doing a quick sweep under her eyes. Like she was crying. With a quick twist, she turned away from him and faced into the corner, her shoulders curling in. She made no sound. Her body did not move. Her dignity remained intact.

He shifted his legs over and put his feet on the floor.

"If you come anywhere near me," she said hoarsely, "I will figure out some way to hurt you. Probably won't be much, but I'll take a hunk out of you one way or the other. We clear? Leave me the hell alone."

He propped his arms on the bed and hung his head. He was gutted as he listened to the nothing-at-all sound of her tears. Would rather have been beaten with a hammer.

He had caused her this.

All at once she wheeled around to him and took a deep breath. Except for the red rims around her eyes, he would never have guessed she'd been upset. "Okay. You eating on your own or do you really need help with the fork-and-knife stuff?"

V blinked.

I am in love, V thought as he looked at her. *I have so fallen in love.*

As class progressed, John felt like holy hell on the end of a shovel: Achy. Nauseous. Exhausted and restless. And his head hurt so badly he could have sworn his hair was on fire.

Squinting like he was facing headlights instead of a blackboard, he swallowed through a dry throat. He hadn't written anything down in his notebook for a while and wasn't sure what Phury was lecturing on. Was it still firearms?

"Yo, John?" Blay whispered. "You okay, my man?"

John nodded, because that was what you did when someone asked you a question.

"You want to go lie down?"

John shook his head, figuring it was another appropriate response, and he wanted to spice things up. No reason to get stuck in a nod rut.

God, what the hell was wrong with him. His brain was like cotton candy, a tangle that took up space but was mostly nothing.

Up front, Phury closed the textbook he'd been teaching from. "And now you get to try out some firearms for real. Zsadist is on deck for the shooting range tonight, and I'll see you tomorrow."

As talk sprang up like a gusty wind, John dragged his backpack

onto the table. At least they weren't doing any physical training. As it was, getting his sorry ass out of this chair and down to the range was going to be enough of a production.

The shooting range was located behind the gym, and on the way there it was hard not to notice how Qhuinn and Blay flanked him tight as bodyguards. John's ego hated it, but the practical side of him was grateful. Every step of the way he could feel Lash's stare, and it was like having a lit stick of dynamite in your back pocket.

Zsadist was waiting at the range's steel door, and as he opened it he said, "Line up against the wall, ladies."

John followed the others in and settled back against the white-washed concrete. The place was built along the lines of a shoe box, all long and thin, and it had more than a dozen shooting booths facing outward. The targets were shaped like heads and torsos and hung from tracks stretching down the ceiling. From the master station each one could be manipulated remotely to vary distance or provide movement.

Lash was the last trainee in, and he marched to the end of the line with his head up high, like he knew he was going to kick ass with a pistol. He didn't look anyone in the eye. Except for John.

Zsadist shut the door, then frowned and went for the cell phone on his hip.

"Excuse me." He went over to a corner and talked on the RAZR, then came back, seeming pale. "Change of instructor. Wrath is going to take over tonight."

A split second later, like the king had dematerialized to the door, Wrath came in.

He was bigger even than Zsadist and dressed in black leathers and a black shirt that was rolled up at the sleeves. He and Z talked for a moment; then the king clasped the Brother's shoulder and squeezed like he was offering reassurance.

Bella, John thought. This had to be about Bella and the pregnancy. Shit, he hoped everything was okay.

Wrath shut the door after Z left, then stood in front of the class, crossing his tattooed forearms over his chest and spreading his stance. As he looked the eleven trainees over, he seemed as impenetrable as what John was leaning against.

"Weapon tonight is the nine-millimeter autoloader. The term *semiautomatic* for these handguns is a misnomer. You will be using Glocks." He reached behind to the small of his back and took out a lethal piece of black metal. "Note that the safety on these weapons is on the trigger."

He reviewed the specs of the gun and the bullets as two *doggen* came forward rolling a cart the size of a hospital gurney. Eleven guns of the exact same make and model were laid out on top, and next to each was a clip.

"Tonight we work on stance and aim."

John stared at the guns. He was willing to bet he was going to suck at shooting, just like he sucked at every other aspect of training. Anger spiked, making his head pound even worse.

Just once he'd like to find something he was good at. Just. Once.

SIXTEEN

As the patient stared at her funny, Jane did a quick check of her clothes, wondering if anything was hanging out.

"What," she muttered as she kicked her foot and her pant leg slid back down.

She didn't really have to ask, though. Hard-asses like him usually didn't appreciate women doing the crying thing, but assuming that was the case, he was going to have to suck it up. Anyone would be having trouble in her shoes. Anyone.

Except instead of saying anything about the weakness of weepers in general or of her in particular, he picked the plate of chicken up off the tray and started to eat.

Disgusted with him and the whole situation, she went back to her chair. Losing the razor had taken the starch out of her covert rebellion, and in spite of the fact that she was a fighter by nature, she was resigned to a waiting game. If they were going to kill her outright, they would have; the issue now was the exit. She prayed there was one coming soon. And that it didn't involve a funeral director and a coffee can full of her ashes.

As the patient cut into a thigh, she thought absently that he had beautiful hands.

Okay, now she was disgusted with herself, too. Hell, he'd used them to hold her down and strip her coat off like she was nothing more than a doll. And just because he'd carefully folded what she'd had on afterward didn't make him a hero.

Silence stretched, and the sounds of his silverware softly hitting the plate reminded her of horribly quiet dinners with her parents.

God, those meals eaten in that stuffy Georgian dining room had been painful. Her father had sat at the head of the table like a disapproving king, monitoring the way food was salted and consumed. To Dr. William Rosdale Whitcomb, only meat was to be salted, never vegetables, and as that was his stand on the matter, everyone in the household had had to follow the example. In theory. Jane had been a frequent violator of the no-salt rule, learning how to flick her wrist so she was able to sprinkle her steamed broccoli or boiled beans or grilled zucchini.

She shook her head. After all this time, and his passing, she shouldn't still get pissed off, because what a waste of emotion. Besides, she had other things she should be worried about at the moment, didn't she.

"Ask me," the patient said abruptly.

"About what?"

"Ask me what you want to know." He wiped his mouth, the damask napkin rasping over his goatee and his beard growth. "It'll make my job harder at the end, but at least we won't be sitting here listening to the sound of my silverware."

"What job do you have at the end, exactly?" *Please let it not be buying Hefty bags to put her body parts in.*

"You aren't interested in what I am?"

"Tell you what, you let me go, and I'll ask you plenty of questions

about your race. Until then, I'm slightly distracted with how this happy little vacation on the good ship *Holy Shit* is going to pan out for me."

"I gave you my word—"

"Yeah, yeah. But you also just manhandled me. And if you say it was for my own good, I'm not going to be responsible for my comeback." Jane looked down at her blunt nails and pushed at her cuticles. After getting her left hand done, she glanced up. "So this 'job' of yours . . . you going to need a shovel to get it done?"

The patient's eyes dropped to his plate, and he forked at the rice, silver tines slipping in between the grains, penetrating them. "My job . . . so to speak . . . is to make sure you won't remember any part of this."

"Second time I've heard that, and I've got to be honest—I think it's bullshit. It's a little hard to imagine me breathing and not, I don't know, recalling with the warm and fuzzies how I was draped over some guy's shoulder, hauled out of my hospital, and drafted as your personal physician. Just how do you figure I'm going to forget all of that?"

His diamond-bright irises lifted. "I'm going to take these memories from you. Scrub this whole thing clean. It will be as if I never existed and you were never here."

She rolled her eyes. "Uh-huh, ri—"

Her head started to sting, and with a grimace she put her fingertips to her temples. When she dropped her hands, she looked at the patient and frowned. What the hell? He was eating, but not from the tray that had been here before. Who'd brought the new food in?

"My buddy with the Sox cap," the patient said as he wiped his mouth. "Remember?"

In a burning rush, it all came back: Red Sox walking in, the patient taking her razor, her tearing up.

"Good . . . God," Jane whispered.

The patient just kept eating, as if eradicating memories were no more exotic than the roasted chicken he was sucking back.

"How?"

"Neuropathway manipulation. A patch job, as it were."

"How?"

"What do you mean, how?"

"How do you find the memories? How do you differentiate? Do you—"

"My will. Your brain. That is specific enough."

She narrowed her eyes. "Quick question. Does this magical skill with gray matter come with a total lack of compunction for your kind, or is it just you who were born without a conscience?"

He lowered his silverware. "I *beg* your pardon?"

She so didn't care that he was offended. "First you abduct me, and now you're going to take my memories, and you're not sorry at all, are you? I'm like a lamp you borrowed—"

"I'm trying to protect you," he snapped. "We have enemies, Dr. Whitcomb. The kind who would find out if you knew about us, who would come after you, who would take you to a hidden place and kill you—after a while. I won't let that happen."

Jane got to her feet. "Listen, Prince Charming, all the protective rhetoric is fine and dandy, but it wouldn't be relevant if you hadn't taken me in the first place."

He dropped his silverware into his food and she braced herself for him to start yelling. Instead, he said quietly, "Look . . . you were supposed to come with me, okay?"

"Oh. Really. So I had a 'Jack Me Now' sign pinned on my ass that only you could see?"

He put the plate onto the bedside table, shoving it aside as if he were disgusted by the food.

"I get visions," he muttered.

"Visions." When he said nothing further, she thought about the

Mr. Eraser trick he'd pulled with her head. If he could do that . . . Jesus, was he talking about seeing into the future?

Jane swallowed hard. "These visions, they aren't sugarplum-fairy kind of stuff, are they."

"No."

"Shit."

He stroked his goatee, like he was trying to decide exactly how much to tell her. "I used to get them all the time, and then they just dried up. I haven't gotten one . . . well, I had one of a friend a couple of months ago, and because I followed it I saved his life. So when my brothers came into that hospital room and I had a vision of you, I told them to take you. You talk about conscience? If I didn't have one I would have left you there."

She thought back to him getting aggressive with his nearest and dearest on her behalf. And the fact that even when he'd been stripping her of the razor he'd been careful with her. And then there was him curling up against her, seeking comfort.

It was possible he'd thought he was doing the right thing. It didn't mean she forgave him but . . . well, it was better than his doing a Patty Hearst with no compunction at all.

After an awkward moment she said, "You should finish that food."

"I'm done."

"No, you're not." She nodded at the plate. "Go on."

"Not hungry."

"I didn't ask if you were hungry. And don't think I won't plug your nose and shovel it in if I have to."

There was a short pause and then he . . . Jesus . . . he smiled at her. From the midst of his goatee his mouth lifted at the corners, his eyes crinkling.

Jane's breath stopped in her throat. He was so beautiful like that, she thought, with the dim light of the lamp falling on his hard jaw and his glossy black hair. Even though his long canine teeth were still

a little odd, he looked far more . . . human. Approachable. Desirable—

Oh, no. Not going there. Nope.

Jane ignored the fact that she was blushing a little. "What's up
with flashing all those pearly whites? You think I'm joking about the
food?"

"No, it's just no one talks to me like that."

"Well, I do. You have a problem with it? You can let me go. Now,
eat or I feed you like a baby, and I can't imagine your ego would get
off on that."

The little smile was still on his face as he put the plate back on his
lap and made slow, steady work of the dinner. When he was done,
she went over and picked up the glass of water he'd drained.

She refilled it in the bathroom and brought it back to him. "Drink
more."

He did, finishing the whole eight ounces. When he put the glass
back on the bedside table, she focused on his mouth and the scientist
in her became fascinated by him.

After a moment he curled his lip off his front teeth. His fangs
positively gleamed in the lamplight. Sharp and white.

"They elongate, right?" she asked as she leaned into him. "When
you feed, they get longer."

"Yeah." He closed his mouth. "Or when I get aggressive."

"And then they retract when it passes. Open again for me."

When he did, she put her finger to the hard point of one—only
to have his whole body jerk.

"Sorry." She frowned and took her hand back. "Are they sore from
the intubation?"

"No." As his lids lowered, she figured it was because he was tired—

God, what was that scent? She breathed in deep and recognized the
mix of dark spices that she'd smelled on the towel in his bathroom.

Sex came to mind. The kind that you had when you lost all your
inhibitions. The kind you felt for days afterward.

Stop it.

"Every eight weeks or so," he said.

"Excuse me? Oh, is that how often you . . ."

"Feed. Depends on stress. Activity level, too."

Okay, that totally killed the sex thing. In a gruesome series of Bram Stoker scenes, she imagined him tracking and preying on humans, leaving them chewed raw in alleys.

Clearly her distaste showed, because his voice got hard. "It's natural to us. Not disgusting."

"Do you kill them? The people you hunt?" She braced herself for the answer.

"People? Try vampires. We feed off members of the opposite sex. Of our race, not yours. And there's no killing."

Her brows lifted. "Oh."

"That Dracula myth is such a fucking bore."

Her mind spun with questions. "What's it like? What does it taste like?"

His eyes narrowed, then drifted from her face to her neck. Jane quickly brought her hand to her throat.

"Don't worry," he said roughly. "I'm fed. And besides, human blood doesn't do it for me. Too weak to be of interest."

Okay. Right. Good.

Except, what the hell? Like she wasn't evolutionarily good enough?

Yeah, whoa, she was so totally losing it, and this particular subject matter wasn't helping. "Ah, listen . . . I want to check your dressing. I wonder if we can even remove it altogether by now."

"Suit yourself."

The patient pushed himself up on the pillows, his massive arms flexing under smooth skin. As the covers fell from his shoulders, she had a moment's pause. He seemed to be getting bigger as he recovered his strength. Bigger and . . . more sexual.

Her mind shied away from where she was headed with that thought and latched onto the medical issues he faced like they were a lifeboat. With steady, professional hands, she pulled the covers completely from his chest and eased the adhesive tape off the gauze between his pecs. She lifted the bandage and shook her head. Astounding. The only thing marring the skin was the star-shaped scar that had been there before. The residual marks from the operation were reduced to a slight discoloration, and if she extrapolated, she could assume the inside of him was just as well healed.

"Is this typical?" she asked. "This rate of recovery?"

"In the Brotherhood, yes."

Oh, man. If she could study the manner in which his cells regenerated, she might be able to unlock some of the secrets to the aging process in humans.

"Forget it." His jaw set as he shifted his legs off the far side of the bed. "We're not going to be used as lab rats for your kind. Now, if you don't mind, I'm going to take a shower and have a cigarette." She opened her mouth and he cut her off. "We don't get cancer, so spare me the lecture, okay?"

"You don't get cancer? Why? How does that—"

"Later. I need hot water and nicotine."

She frowned. "I don't want you smoking around me."

"Which is why I'm going to do it in the bathroom. There's an exhaust fan."

As he stood up and the sheet fell from his body, she glanced away fast. A naked man was hardly a new thing for her, but for some reason he struck her as different.

Well, duh. He was six feet, six inches tall and built like a brick shithouse.

As she headed back to her chair and sat down, she heard a shuffling noise, then a thud. She looked up in alarm. The patient was so unsteady on his feet, he'd lost his balance and landed on the wall.

"Do you need help?" *Please say no. Please say—*

"No."

Thank you, God.

He palmed a lighter and what looked like a hand-rolled cigarette from the bedside table and lurched across the room. From her vantage point in the corner she waited and watched, ready to pull a fireman's hold on him if she needed to.

Yeah, and okay, maybe she watched him for a reason other than wanting to keep him from getting a carpet burn all over that face of his: His back was amazing, the muscles heavy yet elegant as they spanned his shoulders and feathered out from his spine. And his ass was . . .

Jane covered her eyes and didn't drop her hand until the door shut. After many years in medicine and surgery, she was pretty clear on the "Thou Shalt Not Mack on Your Patients" part of the Hippocratic oath.

Especially if the patient in question had kidnapped you. *Christ.* Was she really living this?

Moments later the toilet flushed, and she expected to hear the shower come on. When it didn't she figured he was probably having a smoke first—

The door opened and the patient came out, waving like a buoy on the ocean. He grabbed onto the bath's jamb with his gloved hand, his forearm straining.

"Fuck . . . I'm dizzy."

Jane flipped into full doctor mode and rushed over, putting aside the fact that he was naked and twice her size and that she'd eyed his ass like it was up for sale about two minutes ago. She slipped an arm around his hard waist and tucked herself against his body, bracing her hip for the onslaught. When he leaned on her his weight was tremendous, a load that she barely got over to the bed.

As he stretched out with a curse, she reached across him for the sheets and caught an eyeful of the scars between his legs. Given the way he'd healed up without a trace from her operation, she wondered why those had stuck on his body.

He whipped the covers from her with a quick jerk of the duvet, and the comforter settled over him in a cloud of black. Then he put his arm over his eyes, the thrust of his goateed chin all that showed of his face.

He was ashamed.

In the quiet between them he was . . . ashamed.

"Would you like me to wash you?"

His breath stopped, and when he was silent for a long time, she expected to be refused. But then his mouth barely moved. "You would do that?"

For a moment she almost replied in earnest. Except then she had the sense that would make his awkwardness worse. "Yeah, well, what can I say, I'm going for sainthood. It's my new life goal."

He smiled a little. "You remind me of Bu—my best friend."

"You mean Red Sox?"

"Yeah, he's always got the comeback."

"Did you know wit is a sign of intelligence?"

The patient dropped his arm. "I never doubted yours. Not for an instant."

Jane had to catch her breath. There was such respect shining in his eyes, and all she could do as she took it in was curse to herself. There was nothing more attractive to her than when a man was into smart women.

Crap.

Stockholm. Stockholm. Stockholm—

"I would love a bath," he said. Then he tacked on, "Please."

Jane cleared her throat. "Okay. Right."

She went through the medical supply duffels, found a large bedpan, and headed for the bathroom. After she filled the basin full of warm water and grabbed a washcloth, she went back out and set herself up on the bedside table on the left. As she wet the little towel and squeezed off the excess, water chimed through the silent room.

She hesitated. Dipped the washcloth again. Squeezed.

Come on, now, you opened up his chest and went into him. You can do this. No problem.

Just think of him as the hood of a car, nothing but surface area.

"Okay." Jane reached out, put the warm cloth to his upper arm, and the patient flinched. All over. "Too hot?"

"No."

"Then what's with the grimace?"

"Nothing."

Under different circumstances she would have pressed, but she had her own problems. His bicep was damn impressive, his tan skin revealing the very cords of the muscle. The same was true of his heavy shoulder and the slope leading down to his pectoral. He was in sublime physical condition, not an ounce of fat on him, lean as a Thoroughbred, muscular as a lion.

When she crossed the pads of his pecs, she paused at the scar on the left one. The circular mark was embedded in the flesh, as if it had been pounded in.

"Why didn't this heal smoothly?" she asked.

"Salt." He fidgeted as if encouraging her to get on with the bath. "Seals the wound."

"So it was deliberate?"

"Yeah."

She dipped the cloth in the water, wrung it out, and awkwardly leaned over him to reach his other arm. When she drew the cloth downward, he pulled away. "Don't want you near that hand of mine. Even if it's gloved."

"Why is—"

"I'm not talking about it. So don't even ask."

Okaaaay. "It nearly killed one of my nurses, you know."

"I'm not surprised." He glared at the glove. "I'd cut it off if I had the chance."

"I wouldn't advise that."

"Of course you wouldn't. You don't know what it's like to live with this nightmare on the end of your arm—"

"No, I meant I'd have someone else do the cutting if I were you. You're more likely to get the job done that way."

There was a beat of silence; then the patient barked out a laugh. "Smart-ass."

Jane hid the smile that popped up on her face by doing another dip/rinse routine. "Just rendering a medical opinion."

As she swept the washcloth down his stomach, laughter rippled through his chest and belly, his muscles going rock-tight, then releasing. Through the terry cloth she could feel the warmth of his body and sense the potency in his blood.

And suddenly he wasn't laughing anymore. She heard what sounded like a hiss come out of his mouth, and his six-pack flexed, his lower body moving under the bedding.

"That knife wound feeling okay?" she asked.

As he made a noise that sounded like an unconvincing *yes*, she felt bad. She'd been so concerned about his chest, she hadn't paid much attention to the stabbing issue. Lifting the bandage at his side, she saw that he was fully healed, nothing but a faint pink line showing where he'd been injured.

"I'm taking this off." She peeled the white gauze free, folded it in half, and dropped it into the wastepaper basket. "You're amazing, you know that? The healing you can do is just . . . yeah."

While rerinsing the washcloth, she debated whether she wanted to head farther south. Like, way south. Like . . . all the way south. The last thing she needed was more intimate knowledge about how perfect his body was, but she wanted to finish the job . . . if only to prove to herself that he was no different from any of her other patients.

She could do this.

Except when she went to move the covers lower, he grabbed the duvet and held it in place. "Don't think you're going to want to go there."

"It's nothing I haven't seen before." When his lids dropped and he didn't reply, she said in a quiet voice, "I operated on you, so I'm aware that you're partially castrated. I'm not a date, I'm a doctor. I promise that I have no opinion about your body other than what it represents to me clinically."

He winced before he could hide the reaction. "No opinion?"

"Just let me wash you. It's not a big deal."

"Fine." That diamond gaze narrowed. "Suit yourself."

She pulled the sheets away. "There's nothing to be—"

Holy *shit . . . !* The patient was fully erect. Massively erect. Lying straight up his lower belly, stretching from his groin to above his navel, was a spectacular arousal.

"No big deal, remember?" he drawled.

"Ah . . ." She cleared her throat. "Well . . . I'm just going to keep going."

"Fine with me."

Trouble was, she couldn't precisely recall what she was supposed to be doing with the washcloth. And she was staring. She was seriously staring.

Which was what you did when you got a gander at a man who was hung like a Louisville Slugger.

Oh, God, did she really just think that?

"Since you've already seen what was done to me," he said in a dry voice, "I can only guess you're checking my navel for lint."

Yeah. Right.

Jane got back with the program, running the cloth down his ribs. "So . . . how did it happen?"

When he didn't answer, she glanced at his face. His eyes were focused across the room, and they were flat, lifeless. She'd seen that look before in patients who'd been attacked, and knew he was remembering a horror.

"Michael," she murmured, "who hurt you?"

He frowned. "Michael?"

"Not your name?" She took the washcloth back to the bowl. "Why am I not surprised?"

"V."

"I'm sorry?"

"Call me V. Please."

She brought the cloth back to his side. "V it is, then."

She tilted her head and watched her hand rise up his torso, then slide down again. She was stalling, not going lower. Because in spite of his distraction with the ugly past, he was still erect. Totally erect.

Okay, time to get moving downward. Hello, she was an adult. A physician. She'd had a couple of lovers. What she was witnessing was just a biological function that resulted in a pooling of blood in his incredibly large—

That was so not where her thoughts needed to go.

As Jane took the cloth down over his hip, she tried to ignore the fact that he shifted as she went along, his back arching, that heavy arousal on his belly pushing forward, then falling back into place.

The tip of it wept a glossy, tempting tear.

She looked up at him . . . and froze. His eyes were on her throat, and they were burning with a lust that wasn't just sexual.

Any attraction she might have felt for him disappeared. This was a male of another species, not a man. And he was dangerous.

His stare dropped to her hand in the cloth. "I won't bite you."

"Good, because I don't want you to." This she was clear on. Hell, she was glad he'd looked at her like that, because it had jarred her back to reality. "Listen, not that I want to know personally, but does it hurt?"

"Don't know. Never been bitten myself."

"I thought you said that—"

"I feed off females. But no one has ever fed off me."

"Why?" As his mouth closed up tight, she shrugged. "You might as well tell me. I'm not going to remember anything, right? So what will it cost you to talk?"

As silence stretched, she lost her nerve with his pelvic region and decided to try to work her way up from his feet. Down at the end of the bed, she ran the cloth up his soles, then over his toes and he jumped a little like he was ticklish. She moved on to his ankles.

"My father didn't want me to reproduce," the patient said abruptly.

Her eyes shot to his. "What?"

He held up the hand that was gloved, then tapped the temple that had the tattoos around it. "I'm not right. You know, normal. So my father tried to have me fixed like a dog. Of course, there was also the happy correlation of it being one hell of a punishment." As her breath left her on a compassionate sigh, he pointed his forefinger at her. "You show me any pity and I'm going to think twice about the no-bite vow I just gave you."

"No pity. I promise," she lied softly. "But what does that have to do with you drinking from—"

"Just don't like to share."

Himself, she thought. With anyone . . . except maybe Red Sox.

She gently eased the cloth up his shin. "What were you punished for?"

"Can I call you Jane?"

"Yes." She redipped the cloth and eased it under his calf. As he went silent again, she let him have his privacy. For now.

Under her hand, his knee flexed, the thigh above it contracting and releasing in a sensual flow. Her eyes flicked over his erection and she swallowed hard.

"So do your reproductive systems work the same as ours?" she asked.

"Pretty much."

"Have you had human lovers?"

"I'm not into humans."

She smiled awkwardly. "I won't ask you who you're thinking of now, then."

"Good. I don't think you'd feel comfortable with the answer."

She thought of the way he looked at Red Sox. "Are you gay?"

His eyes narrowed. "Why do you ask?"

"You seem rather attached to your friend, the guy in the baseball hat."

"You knew him, didn't you. From before, true?"

"Yeah, he looks familiar, but I can't quite place him."

"Would that bother you?"

She ran the towel up his thigh to the cut juncture of his hips, then skirted away. "You being gay? Not at all."

"Because it would make you feel safer, right?"

"And because I'm open-minded. As a physician, I have a pretty good grip on how no matter our preferences, we're all alike on the inside."

Well, the humans at least. She sat down on the bedside and pushed her hand up his leg again. As she got closer to his arousal, his breath caught and the hard length twitched. While his hips swiveled she looked up. He'd bitten down on his lower lip, his fangs cutting into the soft flesh.

Okay, that was really . . .

None of her business. But, man, he must be running a really hot fantasy about Red Sox right now.

Telling herself this was just a garden-variety sponge-bath situation, and not believing the lie for an instant, she drew her hand over his abdomen, up past the swollen head of him, and down the other side. As the very edge of the washcloth brushed up against his sex, he hissed.

So help her, God, she did it again, going slowly up and around him and letting the erection get stroked just a little.

His hands tightened on the sheets, and in a low rasp he said, "If you keep this up, you're going to find out just how much I have in common with a human man."

Good Christ, she wanted to see him— No, she didn't.

Yes, she did.

His voice dropped deeper. "Do you want me to orgasm?"

She cleared her throat. "Of course not. That would be—"

"Inappropriate? Who's going to know? Just you and me in here. And frankly, I could use some pleasure right about now."

She closed her eyes. She knew on his side none of this was about her. Plus it wasn't as if she was going to jump on the bed and take advantage of him. But did she really want to know how good he looked as he—

"Jane? Look at me." As if he controlled her eyes, they rose slowly to meet his. "Not my face, Jane. You're going to watch my hand. Now."

She complied, because it didn't occur to her not to. And as soon as she did, his gloved palm released its death grip on the bedcovers and fisted his thick arousal. In a rush, the patient's breath left him, and he ran his hand up and down his shaft, the black leather a stark contrast to the deep pink of his sex.

Oh . . . my . . . God.

"You want to do this to me, don't you?" he said roughly. "Not because you want me. But because you wonder what it feels like and what I look like when I come."

As he kept up with the stroking, she numbed out completely.

"Don't you, Jane." His breathing started to quicken. "You want to know what I feel like. What kind of noises I make. What it smells like."

She wasn't nodding her head, was she? *Shit.* She was.

"Give me your hand, Jane. Let me put you on me. Even if you're only clinically curious, I want you to finish me off."

"I thought . . . I thought you don't like humans."

"I don't."

"So what do you think I am?"

"I want your hand, Jane. *Now.*"

She didn't like being told what to do by anyone. Men, women, didn't matter. But when a husky command like that came out of a magnificent male animal like him . . . especially as he was lying sprawled before her, fully aroused . . . it was pretty damn close to undeniable.

She'd resent the order later. But she would follow it now.

Jane put the washcloth in the bedpan and couldn't believe she extended her hand toward him. He took what she offered, took what he'd demanded she give to him, and pulled it forward to his mouth. In a slow, savoring draw, he licked up the center of her palm, his tongue a warm, wet drag. Then he took her flesh and put it to his erection.

They both gasped. He was rock hard and hot as flame and wider than her wrist. As he kicked in her grip, half of her wondered what the hell she was doing and the other half, the sexual part, came alive. Which made her panic. She clamped down on the feelings, using the displacement honed by years of being in medicine . . . and kept her hand right where it was.

She stroked him, feeling the soft, fine skin move over the stiff core. His mouth broke open as he undulated on the bed, and the arching of his body took her eyes on one hell of a ride. *Shit . . .* He was pure sex, totally undiluted by inhibitions or awkwardness, nothing but a gathering storm of orgasm.

She looked down at where she was working him. His gloved hand was so damned erotic as it lay right below where she handled him, the fingers lightly touching his base and covering the ridges of scar tissue.

"What do I feel like, Jane?" he said hoarsely. "Do I feel different than a man does to you?"

Yes. Better. "No. You're just the same." Her eyes went to his fangs as they cut into his full lower lip. The teeth looked as if they'd lengthened, and she had a feeling sex and feeding were linked. "Well, you don't look like them, of course."

Something flickered across his face, some kind of shadow, and his

hand slipped farther down between his legs. At first she assumed he was rubbing what hung below, but then she realized he was shielding himself from her eyes.

A lick of pain went off in her chest like a match strike, but then he moaned low in his throat and his head kicked back, his blue-black hair feathering over the black pillow. As his hips flexed upward, his stomach muscles tightened in a sequential rush, the tattoos at his groin stretching and returning to position.

"Faster, Jane. You're going to do it faster for me now."

One of his legs shifted up and his ribs began to pump hard. Across his luscious, fluid skin, a flush of sweat gleamed in the dim lamplight. He was getting close . . . and the closer he got, the more she realized she was doing this because she wanted to. The clinical-curiosity thing was a lie: He fascinated her for different reasons.

She kept pumping him, focusing the friction at his plum-sized head.

"Don't stop. . . . *Fuck* . . ." He drew the word out, his shoulders and neck straining, his pecs tightening until they threw sharp edges.

Suddenly his eyes flipped open and glowed bright as stars.

Then he bared fangs that had fully dropped and shouted his release. As he came, he stared at her neck, and the orgasm went on and on until she wondered if he'd had two. Or more. God . . . he was spectacular, and in the midst of his pleasure that glorious scent of dark spice filled the room until she breathed it instead of air.

When he was still, she released him and used the hand towel to clean his belly and chest off. She didn't linger on him. Instead she got to her feet and wished she could have some time to herself.

He watched her through low lids. "See," he said gruffly, "just the same."

Not by a long shot. "Yes."

He pulled the duvet over his hips and closed his eyes. "Use the shower if you want."

In an uncoordinated rush, Jane took the bedpan and the washcloth to the bath. Propping her hands against the sink, she thought maybe some hot water and something other than scrubs on her back would clear her head—because right now all she could see was what he'd looked like coming all over her hand and himself.

Overwhelmed, she went back out into the bedroom, got some of her things from the smaller duffel, and reminded herself that this situation was not real, not part of her reality. It was a hiccup, a tangle in the thread of her life, like her destiny had the flu.

This was not real.

After he finished with class, Phury went back to his room and changed from his teaching clothes of a black silk shirt and cream cashmere trousers into his fighting leathers. Technically he was supposed to be off tonight, but with V flat on his back they needed an extra set of hands.

Which worked for him. Better to be out on the streets hunting than getting involved in that sitch with Z and Bella and the pregnancy.

He strapped on his chest holster, slid two daggers in, handles down, and popped a SIG Sauer on each hip. On his way to the door he pulled on his leather coat and patted the inner pocket, making sure he had a couple of blunts and a lighter with him.

As he hit the grand staircase at a fast clip, he prayed no one saw him . . . and got busted just before he made it out of the house. Bella called his name as he stepped into the vestibule, and the sound of her shoes crossing the foyer's mosaic floor meant he had to stop.

"You weren't at First Meal," she said.

"I was teaching." He glanced over his shoulder and was relieved to see she looked good, her coloring bright, her eyes clear.

"Have you eaten at all?"

"Yes," he said, lying.

"Okay . . . well . . . shouldn't you wait for Rhage?"

"We'll meet up later."

"Phury, are you okay?"

He told himself it was not his place to say anything. He'd already closed that door with his pep talk to Z. This was totally none of his—

As always with her, he had no self-control. "I think you need to talk to Z."

Her head eased to one side, her hair falling farther down her shoulder. God, it was lovely. So dark, yet not black. It reminded him of fine mahogany that had been carefully varnished, glowing with reds and deep browns.

"About what?"

Shit, he so shouldn't be doing this. "If you're keeping something from Z, anything . . . you need to tell him."

Her eyes narrowed, then slid away as she changed her stance, her weight shifting from one foot to the other, her arms crossing over her chest. "I . . . ah, I won't ask how you know, but I can assume it's because he does. Oh . . . damn it. I was going to talk to him after I see Havers tonight. I made an appointment."

"How bad is it? The bleeding?"

"Not bad. That's why I wasn't going to say anything until I went to Havers. God, Phury, you know Z. He's nervous as hell about me already, so preoccupied I'm terrified he'll be distracted in the field and get himself hurt."

"Yeah, but see, it's worse now, because he doesn't know what's going on. Talk to him. You have to. He'll be tight. For you he'll stay tight."

"Was he angry?"

"Maybe a little. But more than that he's just worried. He's not stupid. He knows why you wouldn't want to tell him anything was wrong. Look, take him with you tonight, okay? Let him be there."

Her eyes watered a little. "You're right. I know you're right. I just want to protect him."

"Which is exactly the way he feels about you. Take him with you."

In the silence that followed, he knew the indecision in her eyes was hers to contend with. He'd said his piece.

"Be well, Bella."

As he turned away, she grabbed his hand. "Thank you. For not being upset with me."

For a moment he pretended that it was his young inside of her and that he could gather her close and go with her to the doctor's and hold her afterward.

Phury gently took her wrist and pulled her free of him, her hand slipping off his skin on a soft brush that stung like barbs. "You are my twin's beloved. I could never be angry at you."

As he walked out through the vestibule and into the cold, windy night, he thought how true it was that he could never be pissed with her. Himself, on the other hand? Not a problem.

Dematerializing downtown, he knew that he was heading for a collision of some kind. He didn't know where the wall was or what it was made of or whether he was going to drive himself into it or get thrown at it by someone or something else.

But the wall was waiting in the bitter darkness. And part of him wondered whether there wasn't a big, fat *H* painted on it.

SEVENTEEN

watched Jane go into the bathroom. As she pivoted to put her change of clothes down on the counter, the profile of her body was an elegant *S* curve that he needed to get his hands on. His mouth over. His body into.

The door shut and the shower started and he cursed. God . . . her hand had felt so good, taken him higher than any full-on sex had lately. But it had been one-sided. There had been no scent of arousal from her at all. To her it had been a biological function to explore. Nothing more.

If he was honest with himself, he'd thought that maybe seeing him orgasm would turn her on—which was nuts, given what was doing below his waist. No one in their right mind would think, *Oh, yeah, check out the one-balled wonder. Yum.*

Which was why he always kept his pants on when he had sex.

As he listened to the shower run, his arousal softened and his fangs retracted back up into his jaw. Funny, when she'd been handling him, he'd surprised himself. He'd wanted to bite her—not to feed because he was hungry, but because he wanted her taste in his mouth and the mark of his teeth on her neck. Which was pretty fucking out of character. Typically he bit females only because he had to, and when he did, he never particularly liked it.

With her? He couldn't wait to pierce a vein and suck what ran through her heart right down into his gut.

When the shower stopped, all he could think about was being in that bathroom with her. He could just imagine her all naked and wet and pink from the heat. Man, he wanted to know what the back of her neck looked like. And the stretch of skin between her shoulder blades. And the hollow at the base of her spine. He wanted to run his mouth from her collarbone to her navel . . . then have a go between her thighs.

Shit, he was getting hard again. And that was pretty damn useless. She'd satisfied her curiosity with his body, so she wouldn't be up for throwing him a bone and relieving him again. And even if she was attracted to him, she already had someone, didn't she. With a nasty growl he pictured that dark-haired doctor type who was waiting for her back in her real life. The guy was of her kind and no doubt wholly masculine as well.

The very idea of that bastard treating her right, not just during the day but between the sheets at night, made his chest sting.

Shit.

V put his arm over his eyes and wondered exactly when he'd had a personality transplant. Theoretically Jane had operated on his heart, not his head, but he hadn't been right since he'd been on her table. Thing was, he just couldn't help but want her to see him as a mate— although that was an impossibility for a whole host of reasons: He was a vampire who was a freak . . . and he was going to become the Primale in a matter of days.

He thought about what was waiting for him on the Other Side, and even though he didn't want to go into the past, he couldn't stop

himself. He went back to what had been done to him, recalling what had set the wheels in motion for the mauling that had left him half a male.

It was perhaps a week after his father burned his books that Vishous was caught coming out from behind the screen that hid the cave paintings. His undoing was the diary of the warrior Darius. He'd avoided his precious possession for days and days, but eventually he'd given in. His hands had craved the weight of the binding, his eyes the sight of the words, his mind the images it gave him, his heart the connection he found with the writer.

He was too alone to resist.

It was a kitchen whore who saw him, and they both froze when she did. He didn't know her name, but she had the same face that all females had in the camp: hard eyes, lined skin, and a slash of a mouth. There were bite marks layered on her neck from males feeding from her, and her shift was dirty and frayed at the hem. In one hand she had a rough-hewn shovel, and behind her she was dragging a wheelbarrow with a broken wheel. She'd obviously drawn the short straw and been forced to tend to the privy pits.

Her eyes shifted down to V's hand as if she were measuring a weapon.

V deliberately made a fist with the thing. "'Twould be a shame should you say a thing, would it not."

She paled and scurried off, dropping the shovel as she ran.

News of what had happened between him and the other pretrans had been all around the camp, and if it made them fear him, that was all to the good. To protect his only book he wasn't above threatening anyone, even females, and he was unashamed by this. His father's law held that no one was safe in the camp: V was quite confident that female would use what she'd seen to her own benefit if she could. That was the way.

Vishous left the cave through one of the tunnels that had been bored out of the mountain, and emerged in a thicket of brambles. The winter was coming upon them all fast, the cold making the air dense as bone.

Up ahead he heard the stream rushing and wanted a drink, but he stayed hidden as he scrambled up the pine-covered incline. He always kept away from the water for a distance after he came out, not just because it was what he'd been taught to do upon penalty of punishment, but because in his pretrans state he was no match for what might come at him, be it vampire, human, or animal.

At the beginning of every night, the pretrans tried to fill their empty bellies at the stream, and his ears picked up the sounds of the other pretrans who were fishing. The boys had congregated at the wide section of the stream, where the water formed a still pool off to one side. He avoided them, choosing a spot farther upriver.

From out of a leather pouch he took a length of fine-spun thread that had a crude hook and a flashing weight of silver tied on the end. He cast his meager tackle into the rushing water and felt the string go tight. As he sat down on a rock, he wound the string around a shaft of wood and held the thing between his palms.

The waiting was neither here nor there, neither burden nor pleasure, and when he heard an argument downriver, he had no interest. Skirmishes were also the way of the camp, and he knew what the fight amongst the other pretrans was about. Just because you pulled a fish from the water did not mean you could keep it.

He was staring into the rushing current when the oddest sensation touched the back of his neck—as if he'd been tapped upon the nape.

He leaped up, dropping his line on the ground, but there was no one behind him. He sniffed the air, probed the trees with his eyes. Nothing.

As he bent down to retrieve his line, the stick flipped out of his reach and off the bank, a fish having taken the bait. V lunged for it, but could only watch the crude handle skip into the stream. With a curse, he ran after it, jumping from rock to rock, tracking it farther and farther downstream.

Whereupon he met up with another.

The pretrans he'd beaten with his book was coming up the stream with a trout in his hand, one that, given his rapacious satisfaction, had

no doubt been stolen from another. As he saw V, the bobbing stick with V's catch on it went by him and he stopped. With a shout of triumph, he shoved the kicking fish in his pocket and went after what was V's—even though it took him in the direction of his pursuers.

Perhaps because of V's reputation, the other boys got out of the way as he went after the pretrans, the group abandoning the chase and becoming cantering spectators.

The pretrans was faster than V, moving recklessly from stone to stone, whereas V was more careful. The leather soles on his coarse boots were wet, and the moss growing on the backs of the rocks was slick as pig fat. Even though his prey was pulling ahead, he held back to ensure his footing.

Just as the stream widened into the pool the others had been fishing in, the pretrans leaped onto the flat face of a stone and got within reach of V's hooked fish. Except as he stretched out to grab the stick, his balance shifted . . . and his foot popped out from under him.

With the slow, graceful tumble of a feather, he fell headfirst into the rushing stream. The crack of his temple on a rock inches below the surface was loud as an ax striking hardwood, and as his body went limp, the stick and the line spirited along.

As V came up to the boy, he remembered the vision he'd had. Clearly it had been wrong. The pretrans did not die on top of the mountain with the sun upon his face and the wind in his hair. He died here and now in the arms of the river.

It was a bit of a relief.

Vishous watched as the body was pulled into the dark, still pool by the current. Just before sinking below the surface, it rolled over so it was faceup.

As bubbles breached unmoving lips and rose to the surface to catch the moonlight, V marveled at death. All was so calm after it came. Whatever screaming or yelling or action that caused the soul its release unto the Fade, what followed was like the dense quiet of falling snow.

Without thinking, he reached down into the frigid water with his right hand.

All at once a glow suffused the pool, emanating from his palm . . . and the pretrans's face was illuminated as surely as if the sun shone upon it. V gasped. It was the vision realized, exactly as he had foreseen it: the haze that had muddled the clarity was in fact the water, and the boy's hair waved to and fro not from wind, but from the currents deep in the pool.

"What do you do unto the water?" a voice said.

V looked up. The other boys stood lined up on the curving bank of the river, staring at him.

V snatched his hand from the water and put it around his back so no one would see it. Upon its removal, the glow in the pool faded, the dead pretrans left to the black depths as if he'd been buried.

V rose to his feet and stared at what he knew now were not only his competitors for scarce food and comforts, but now his enemies. The cohesion between the gathered boys as they stood shoulder-to-shoulder told him that however contentious they were within the camp's dry womb, they had been bonded over one like mind.

He was an outcast.

V blinked and thought about what had come next. Funny, the turn in the road you anticipated was never the one with the black ice on it. He'd assumed that the other pretrans would drive him out of the camp, that one by one they would go through their change, then gang up on him. But fate liked surprises, didn't it.

He rolled on his side and became determined to get some sleep. Except as the door to the bathroom opened, he had to crack an eyelid. Jane had changed into a white button-down shirt and a pair of loose black yoga sweats. Her face was flushed from the heat of her shower, her hair spiky and damp. She looked amazing.

She glanced over at him briefly, a quick cursory review that told him she assumed he was asleep; then she went over and sat in the chair in the corner. As she drew her legs up, she wrapped her arms around her knees and lowered her chin. She seemed so fragile that way, just a twist of flesh and bone within the embrace of the chair.

He shut his eye and felt wretched. His conscience, which had been all but unplugged for centuries, was awake and aching: He couldn't pretend he wasn't going to be fully healed in another six hours. Which meant her purpose was over and he was going to have to let her go when the sun went down tonight.

Except what about the vision he'd had of her? The one of her standing in the doorway of light? Ah, hell, maybe he'd just been hallucinating . . .

V frowned as he caught a scent in the room. *What the hell?*

Inhaling deeply, he hardened in a rush, his cock thickening, growing heavy on his belly. He looked across the room at Jane. Her eyes were closed, her mouth a little open, her brows down . . . and she was aroused. She might not have felt entirely comfortable with it, but she was definitely aroused.

Was she thinking of him? Or the human male?

V reached out with his mind with no real hope of getting into her head. When his visions had dried up, so too had the running ticker-tape of other people's thoughts, the one that could be forced on him or picked up at his will—

The vision in her mind was of him.

Oh, fuck, yeah. It was so totally him: He was arching on the bed, his stomach muscles tightening, his hips pushing up as she worked his sex with her palm. This was right before he came, when he'd removed his gloved hand from what was doing below his cock and made a grab for the duvet.

His surgeon wanted him even though he was partially ruined and not her kind and holding her against her will. And she was aching. She was aching for *him.*

V smiled as his fangs punched out into his mouth.

Well, wasn't this the time to be a humanitarian. And relieve some of her suffering . . .

*　　*　　*

Shitkickers planted in a wide stance, fists curled at his sides, Phury stood over the *lesser* he'd just knocked stupid with a nasty shot to the temple. The bastard was lying facedown in a dirty slush pile, its arms and legs flopped to the side, its leather jacket torn up the back from the fighting.

Phury took a deep breath. There was a gentlemanly way to kill your enemy. In the midst of war, there was an honorable manner to bring death upon even those you hated.

He looked up and down the alley and sniffed the air. No humans. No other *lessers*. And none of his brothers.

He bent down to the slayer. Yeah, when you took out your enemies, there was a certain standard of conduct to be upheld.

This was not going to be it.

Phury picked the *lesser* up by its leather belt and its pale hair and swung the thing headfirst into a brick building like a battering ram. A muffled, meaty *thunch* lit out as the frontal lobe shattered and the spinal column pierced through the back of the skull.

But the thing was not dead. To kill a slayer you needed to stab him in the chest. If left as it was now, the bastard would just be in a perpetual rotting state until the Omega eventually came back for the body.

Phury dragged the thing by an arm behind a Dumpster and took out a dagger. He didn't use the weapon to stab the slayer back to its master. His anger, that emotion he didn't like to feel, that force that he didn't permit to attach to people or events, had started to roar. And its impulse was undeniable.

The cruelty of his actions stained his conscience. Even though his victim was an amoral killer who had been about to take out two civilian vampires twenty minutes ago, what Phury was doing was still wrong. The civilians had been saved. The enemy was incapacitated. The end should be brought cleanly.

He didn't stop himself.

As the *lesser* howled in pain, Phury stuck with what he was doing to the thing, his hands and blade moving swiftly through skin and vitals that smelled like baby powder. Black, glossy blood ran onto the pavement and covered Phury's arms and oiled up his shitkickers and splashed onto his leathers.

As he kept going, the slayer became a StairMaster for his fury and his self-hatred, an object to work out the feelings. Naturally his actions made him think even less of himself, but he didn't stop. Couldn't stop. His blood was propane and his emotions were flame and the combustion was inescapable now that it had been ignited.

Focused on his gruesome project, he didn't hear the other *lesser* come up from behind. He caught the whiff of baby powder right before the thing struck, and just barely wheeled out of the way of the baseball bat that was aimed for his skull.

His rage shifted from the incapacitated slayer to the one that was up on its feet, and with his warrior DNA screaming in his veins, he attacked. Leading with his black dagger, he ducked low and came up for the abdomen.

He didn't make it. The *lesser* clipped him in the shoulder with the bat, then laid in a solid backswing to Phury's good leg, catching the side of his knee. As he crumpled, he concentrated on keeping hold of his dagger, but the slayer was all José Conseco with that aluminum number. Another swing and the blade went flying away, twirling end over point, then dancing across a stretch of wet pavement.

The *lesser* jumped on Phury's chest and held him down by the throat, squeezing with a one-handed grip that was strong as wire cable. Phury clapped a palm on the thing's thick wrist as his windpipe compressed, but then suddenly he had issues other than hypoxia to worry about. The slayer switched his grip on the bat, choking up until he was holding it in the middle. With deadly focus he lifted his arm high and brought the butt of the bat down square on Phury's face.

The pain was a bomb burst in his cheek and eye, its white-hot shrapnel ricocheting throughout his whole body.

And it was . . . curiously good. It overrode everything. All he knew was the heart-freezing impact and the electric throbbing that came right afterward.

He liked it.

Through the one eye that was still working right, he saw the *lesser* lift the bat up again, piston-style. Phury didn't even brace himself. He just watched the kinetics at work, knowing that the muscles that were coordinating to elevate that piece of polished metal were going to tighten up and bring that thing back down on his face again.

Death blow time, he thought dimly. His orbital bone was already shattered, in all likelihood, or at the very least fractured. One more belt and it wasn't going to protect his gray matter anymore.

An image of the drawing he'd done of Bella came to him, and he saw what he had put to paper: her sitting at the dining room table turned toward his twin, the love between them as tangible and beautiful as silken cloth, as strong and enduring as tempered steel.

He said an ancient prayer for them and their young in the Old Language, one that wished them all to be well until he met them in the Fade at some far, far future point. *Until we live anew,* was the way it ended.

Phury let go of the slayer's wrist and repeated the phrase over and over again, dimly wondering which one of the four words would be his last.

Except there was no impact. The *lesser* disappeared from atop him, just popped off his chest like a puppet whose strings had been pulled.

Phury lay there, barely breathing, as a series of grunts echoed in the alley, and then a bright flash of light went off. With his endorphins kicking in, he had a nice, spacey high that made him glow with what felt like health, but was really evidence he was in deep shit.

Had the death blow already happened? Had that first one been enough to leave his brain hemorrhaging?

Whatever. It felt good. The whole thing felt good, and he wondered whether this was what sex was like. The afterward, that was. Nothing but peaceful relaxation.

He thought about Zsadist coming up to him in the midst of that party months ago, a duffel bag in his hand and a hellacious demand in his eyes. Phury had been sickened at what his twin had needed, but he'd nonetheless gone with Z to the gym and hit the male over and over and over again.

That hadn't been the first time Zsadist had needed that kind of release.

Phury had always hated giving his twin the beatings he'd demanded, had never understood the why of the masochistic drive, but he got it now. This was fantastic. Nothing mattered. It was as if real life were a distant thunderstorm that would never reach him because he'd gotten out of its path.

Rhage's deep voice came from a distance as well. "Phury? I've called for pickup. You need to go to Havers's."

When Phury tried to talk, his jaw refused to do its job, sure as someone had glued it in place. Clearly, the swelling was setting in already, and he settled for shaking his head.

Rhage's face came into his lopsided vision. "Havers will—"

Phury shook his head again. Bella would be at the clinic tonight dealing with the baby issue. If she was on the verge of miscarrying, he didn't want to tip her over the edge by showing up as an emergency case.

"No . . . Havers . . ." he said hoarsely.

"My brother, what you've got going on is more than first aid can handle." Rhage's model-perfect face was a mask of deliberate calm. Which meant the guy was really worried.

"Home."

Rhage cursed, but before he could push for the Havers trip again, a car turned into the alley, its headlights flashing.

"Shit." Rhage flipped into action, hefting Phury up off the pavement and hustling behind the Dumpster.

Which brought them right next to the desecrated *lesser*.

"What the *fuck*?" Rhage breathed while a Lexus with chromed-out twenties eased by them, rap thumping.

When it had passed, Rhage's brilliant teal eyes narrowed. "Did you do that?"

"Bad . . . fight . . . s'all," Phury whispered. "Get me home."

As he closed his eye, he realized he'd learned something tonight. Pain was good, and if garnered under the right circumstances, it was less shameful than heroin. Easier to get, too, as it could be a legitimate by-product of his job.

How perfect.

As Jane sat in the chair across from her patient's bed, her head was down and her eyes were closed. She couldn't stop thinking about what she had done to him . . . and what he had done as a result. She saw him just as he climaxed, his head kicked back, his fangs gleaming, his erection jerking in her grip while his breath went in on a gasp and came out on a groan.

She shifted around, feeling hot. And not because the radiator had kicked on.

God, she couldn't stop herself from replaying the scene over and over again, and it got so bad, she had to part her mouth for breath. At one point during the continuous loop she felt a brief sting in her head, like her neck had settled into a bad position, but then she dozed off.

Naturally, her subconscious took over where memory left off.

The dream started when something touched her shoulder, something warm and heavy. She was eased by the feel of it, by the way it

slowly went down her arm and over her wrist and to her hand. Her fingers were gathered in a grip and squeezed, then splayed out for a kiss placed on the center of her palm. She felt the soft lips, warm breath, and the velvet brush of . . . a goatee.

There was a pause, as if permission had been asked.

She knew exactly who she was dreaming about. And she knew exactly what was going to happen in the fantasy if she allowed things to continue.

"Yes," she whispered in her sleep.

Her patient's hands went to her calves and eased her legs off the chair, then something broad and warm moved in, going between her thighs, splaying them wide. His hips and . . . oh, God, she felt his erection at her core, the rigid length pressing in through the soft pants she had on. The collar of her shirt was dragged aside and his mouth found her neck, his lips latching onto her skin and sucking while his arousal started on a rhythmic push and retreat. A hand found her breast, then skirted down to her stomach. Down to her hip. Down farther, replacing the erection.

As Jane cried out and arched, two sharp points ran up the column of her neck to the base of her jaw. *Fangs.*

Fear flooded her veins. And so did a blast of high-octane sex.

Before she could sort out the two extremes, his mouth left her neck and found her breast through the shirt. As he sucked at her he went after her core, rubbing what was ready for him, hungry for him. She opened her mouth to pant, and something was pushed into it . . . a thumb. She latched on desperately, nursing him while she imagined what else of his could be between her lips.

He was the master of all of it, the driver, the one operating the machinery. He knew exactly what he was doing to her as his fingers used the soft sweats and her wet panties to push her right up to the cliff.

A voice in her head—his—said, "Come for me, Jane—"

From out of nowhere brilliant light hit her face, and she sprang upright, throwing her arms out to shove the patient away.

Except he wasn't anywhere near her. He was in bed. Asleep.

And as for the light, it came from the hall. Red Sox had opened the bedroom door.

"Sorry to wake you guys," he said. "We have a situation."

As the patient sat up, he glanced at Jane. The moment their eyes met, she flushed and looked away.

"Who?" the patient asked.

"Phury." Red Sox nodded over to the chair. "We need a doctor. Like, ASAP."

Jane cleared her throat. "Why are you looking at—"

"We need you."

Her first thought was, the hell she was getting in deeper with them. But then the physician in her spoke up. "What's going on?"

"Real ugly sitch. Run-in with a baseball bat. Can you come with me?"

Her patient's voice got there first, the dead-on growl drawing one hell of a line in the sand: "If she goes anywhere, I'm coming, too. And how bad is it?"

"He got clocked in the face. Bad. Refuses to go to Havers. Said Bella's there about the young, and he doesn't want to upset her by showing up messy."

"Fucking Brother just has to be a hero." V looked at Jane. "Will you help us?"

After a moment, she rubbed her face. *Goddamn it.* "Yeah. I will."

As John lowered the muzzle of the Glock he'd been given, he stared down the range at a target fifty feet away. Slipping the safety back into place, he was utterly speechless.

"Jesus," Blay said.

In total disbelief, John hit a yellow button to his left and the eight-and-a-half-by-eleven sheet of paper whizzed up to him like a dog being called home. In the center, clustered like a daisy, were six perfect shots. *Holy shit.* After having sucked at everything he'd been

taught so far when it came to fighting, he finally excelled at something.

Well, didn't this make him forget about his headache.

A heavy hand landed on his shoulder, and Wrath's voice was proud. "You did good, son. Real good."

John reached out and unclipped the target.

"All right," Wrath said. "That's it for today. Check your weapons, boys."

"Yo, Qhuinn," Blay called out. "You see this?"

Qhuinn gave his gun to one of the *doggen* and came over. "Whoa. That's some real Dirty Harry shit right there."

John folded up the paper and put it in the back pocket of his jeans. As he returned the weapon to the cart, he tried to figure out how to identify it again so he could use it at the next practice. Ah . . . although the serial numbers had been filed off, there was a faint mark on the barrel, a scratch. He could totally find his gun again.

"Move out," Wrath said as he propped his huge body against the door. "Bus is waiting."

When John looked up from returning the gun, Lash was standing right behind him, all menace and loom. In a smooth move the guy leaned in and put his Glock down with the muzzle aimed at John's chest. To make the point, he lingered with his forefinger on the trigger for a moment.

Blay and Qhuinn fell in tight, blocking the way. The move in was all done real casual, like they were just randomly hanging around, but the message was clear. With a shrug, Lash lifted his hand free of the Glock and clipped Blay shoulder to shoulder as he headed for the door.

"Asshole," Qhuinn muttered.

The three buds left for the locker room, where they picked up their books and headed out together. Because John was going to use the tunnel to go back to the mansion, they stopped at the door to Tohr's old office.

As the other trainees walked by, Qhuinn kept his voice low. "We have to go out tonight. I can't wait." He grimaced and shifted his stance like there was sandpaper in his pants. "I'm half-batshit for a female, if you know what I mean?"

Blay flushed a little. "I'm . . . ah, yeah, I could deal with some action. John?"

Pumped from his success on the range, John nodded.

"Good." Blay jacked up his jeans. "We got to hit ZeroSum."

Qhuinn frowned. "How about Screamer's?"

"No, I want ZeroSum."

"Fine. And we can go in your car." Qhuinn glanced over. "John, why don't you get on the bus and go to Blay's?"

Shouldn't I change?

"You can borrow some of his clothes. You have to look good for ZeroSum."

Lash came out of nowhere, like a sucker punch. "So you're going downtown, John? Maybe I'll see you there, buddy."

With a nasty-ass grin, he sauntered off, his body coiled, his muscular shoulders rolling like he was headed into a fight. Or wanted to be.

"Sounds like you want a date, Lash," Qhuinn barked. "Good deal, 'cause you keep that shit up, you're going to get fucked, *buddy*."

Lash stopped and glanced back, the lights from overhead pouring down over him. "Hey, Qhuinn, tell your father I said hi. He always did like me better than you. Then again, I match."

Lash tapped beside his eye with his middle finger and kept going.

In his wake, Qhuinn's face closed up, just went straight to statue.

Blay put his hand on the back of the guy's neck. "Listen, give us forty-five minutes at my house, k? Then we'll pick you up."

Qhuinn didn't respond right away, and when he finally did his voice was low. "Yeah. No problem. Will you excuse me for a sec?"

Qhuinn dropped his books and walked back to the locker room. As the door eased shut, John signed, *Lash's and Qhuinn's families are tight?*

"The two of them are first cousins. Their fathers are brothers."

John frowned. *What's up with Lash pointing to his eye?*

"Don't worry about—"

John gripped the guy's forearm. *Tell me.*

Blay rubbed his red hair like he was trying to rustle up a response. "Okay . . . it's like . . . Qhuinn's dad is a big deal in the *glymera*, right? And so's his mom. And the *glymera* doesn't do defects."

This was said as if it explained everything. *I don't get it. What's wrong with his eye?*

"One's blue. One's green. Because they aren't the same color, Qhuinn's never going to get mated . . . and, you know, his father's been embarrassed by him all his life. Not a good sitch, and that's why we're always at my house. He needs to get away from his parents." Blay looked at the locker room door as if he could see through it to his friend. "The only reason they haven't kicked him out is because they were hoping the transition might clear it up. That's why he got to use someone like Marna. She has very good blood, and I think the plan was that it would help."

It didn't.

"Nope. They're probably going to ask him to leave at some point. I've already got a room ready for him, but I doubt he'd use it. Lot of pride. Rightfully so."

John had a horrible thought. *How did he get the bruise? The one on his face after his transition?*

At that moment the locker room door opened and Qhuinn came out with a solid smile in place. "Shall we, gentlemen?" As he picked up his books, his bravado was back. "Let's bounce before the good ones are taken at the club."

Blay clapped the guy on the shoulder. "Lead on, maestro."

As they headed for the underground parking lot, Qhuinn was in front, Blay behind, John in the middle.

As Qhuinn disappeared up the bus's steps, John tapped Blay on the shoulder.

It was his father, wasn't it?

Blay hesitated. Then nodded once.

EIGHTEEN

kay, this was either cool as hell or scary as fuck.

As Jane walked along, it was like she was going through an underground tunnel in a Jerry Bruckheimer movie. This setup was straight out of high-budget Hollywood: steel, dimly lit from inset fluorescent lights, infinitely long. At any minute Bruce Willis circa 1988 was going to come running by on his bare feet wearing a ratty muscle shirt and a machine gun.

She glanced up at the fluorescent panels in the ceiling, then down to the polished metal floor. She was willing to bet that if she took a drill to the walls they'd be half a foot thick. Man, these guys had money. Big money. More than you could get if you were dealing prescription drugs on the black market or servicing coke, crack, and crank addictions. This was government-scale money, suggesting vampires weren't just another species; they were another civilization.

As the three of them went along, she was surprised they'd left her unrestrained. Then again, the patient and his buddy were armed with guns—

"No." The patient shook his head at her. "You're not in cuffs because you won't run."

Jane's mouth about fell open. "Don't read my mind."

"Sorry. I didn't mean to, it just happened."

She cleared her throat, trying not to measure how great he looked standing up. Dressed in Black Watch plaid pajama bottoms and a black muscle shirt, he was moving slowly, but with a lethal confidence that was a knockout.

What had they been talking about? "How do you know I won't run for it?"

"You won't bail on someone who requires medical attention. It's not in your nature, true?"

Well . . . shit. He knew her pretty well.

"Yeah, I do," he said.

"Cut that out."

Red Sox looked around Jane at the patient. "Your mind reading coming back?"

"With her? Sometimes."

"Huh. You getting anything from anyone else?"

"Nope."

Red Sox repositioned his hat. "Well, ah . . . let me know if you pick up shit from me, k? There are some things that I'd prefer to keep private, feel me?"

"Roger that. Although I can't help it sometimes."

"Which is why I'm going to take up thinking about baseball when you're around."

"Thank fuck you're not a Yankees fan."

"Don't use the Y-word. We're in mixed company."

Nothing else was said as they continued through the tunnel, and Jane had to wonder whether she was losing her mind. She should have been terrified in this dark, subterranean place with two huge

escorts of a vampire nature. But she wasn't. Oddly, she felt safe . . . as if the patient would protect her because of the vow he'd given her, and Red Sox would do the same because of his bond with the patient.

Where the hell was the logic in that, she wondered.

Gimme an S*! A* T*! An* O*! A* C*! Followed by a* K-H-O-L-M*! What's it spell? HEAD FUCK.*

The patient leaned down to her ear. "I can't see you as the cheerleader type. But you're right, we both would slaughter anything that so much as startled you." The patient straightened again, one giant testosterone surge plugged into bedroom slippers.

Jane tapped him on the forearm and crooked her forefinger so he'd lean back down. When he did, she whispered, "I'm scared of mice and spiders. But you don't need to use that gun on your hip to blow a hole in a wall if I run into one, okay? Havahart traps and rolled newspapers work just as well. Plus, you don't need a Sheetrock patch and plaster job afterward. I'm just saying."

She patted his arm, dismissing him, and refocused on the tunnel ahead.

V started to laugh, awkwardly at first, then more deeply, and she felt Red Sox staring at her. She met his eyes with hesitation, expecting to find some kind of disapproval thing going on. Instead, there was only relief. Relief and approval as the man . . . male . . . Christ, whatever . . . looked at her and then his friend.

Jane flushed and glanced away. The fact that the guy was obviously not pulling a best-friend pissing contest with her over V should not have been a bonus. Not at all.

A hundred yards later they came up to a set of shallow stairs that led to a door with a bolt-based locking mechanism the size of her head on it. As the patient stepped up and put in a code, she imagined they were going to walk into a 007 kind of deal—

Well, not hardly. It was a closet with shelves of yellow-lined legal pads and printer cartridges and boxes of document clips. Maybe on the other side . . .

Nope. It was just an office. A regular middle-management kind of office with a desk and a swivel chair and file cabinets and a computer.

Okay, no Jerry Bruckheimer/*Die Hard* here. Try a commercial for Allstate insurance. Or a mortgage company.

"This way," V said.

They went out through a glass door and down an unmarked white corridor to some stainless-steel double doors. Beyond them was a professional-quality gym, one big enough to host a pro basketball game, a wrestling match, and a volleyball exhibition at the same time. Blue mats were laid out across the glossy honey-colored floor, and there were punching bags hanging from under a stacked row of elevated bleachers.

Big money. Huge. And how had they constructed all this without someone on the human side of things catching on? There must be a lot of vampires. Had to be. Workmen and architects and craftsmen . . . all able to pass among humans if they wanted to.

The geneticist in her got a serious case of brain strain. If chimpanzees shared ninety-eight percent of the DNA of humans, how close were vampires? And evolutionarily speaking, when did this other species branch off from apes and Homo sapiens? Yeah . . . wow . . . she'd give anything to get a crack at their double helix. If they were indeed going to clean her mind before they let her go, medical science was missing out on so much. Especially as they didn't get cancer and healed so fast.

What an opportunity.

At the far side of the gym they stopped in front of a steel door marked EQUIPMENT/PT ROOM. Inside there were racks and stacks of weapons: An arsenal of martial arts swords and nunchakus. Daggers that were locked in closets. Guns. Throwing stars.

"Dear . . . God."

"This is just for training purposes," V said with a whole lot of *meh*.

"Then what the hell do you use to fight with?" As all kinds of *War of the Worlds* scenarios marched through her head, she caught the familiar scent of blood. Well, semi-familiar. There was a different tint to the smell, something spicy, and she remembered the same wine-like fragrance when she'd been in the OR with her patient.

Across the way a door marked PHYSICAL THERAPY swung open. The beautiful blond vampire who'd trucked her out of the hospital put his head around the jamb. "Thank God you're here."

All Jane's physician instincts came online as she walked into a tiled room and saw the soles of a pair of shitkickers hanging off a gurney. She pushed ahead of the men, shoving them out of her way so she could get to the guy lying on the table.

It was the one who'd hypnotized her, the one with the yellow eyes and the spectacular hair. And he really needed attention. His left orbital region was crushed inward, the lid so swollen he couldn't open the thing, that side of his face twice the size it should be. She had a feeling the bone above his eye was collapsed, and so was the one on his cheek.

She put her hand on his shoulder and met him in the eye that was open. "You're a mess."

He cracked a weak smile. "You don't say."

"But I'm going to fix you."

"You think you can?"

"No." She shook her head back and forth. "I *know* I can."

She wasn't a plastic surgeon, but given his healing capabilities, she was confident she could address the issues he had without marring his looks. Assuming she had the right supplies.

The door swung wide again, and Jane froze. Oh, God, it was the giant with the jet-black hair and the black wraparound sunglasses. She'd wondered if she hadn't dreamed him, but evidently he was real.

Totally real. And in charge. He carried himself like he owned everything and everybody in the room and could do away with it all in a swipe of his hand.

He took one look at her next to the guy on the gurney and said, "Tell me this is not what's happening."

Instinctively Jane stepped back in the direction of V, and just as she did, she felt him come up behind her. Although he didn't touch her, she knew he was close. And prepared to defend her.

The black-haired one shook his head at the wounded guy. "Phury . . . for fuck's sake, we need to get you to Havers's."

Phury? What the hell kind of name was that?

"No," was the weak response.

"Why the hell not?"

"Bella's there. She sees me like this . . . going to freak . . . She's already bleeding."

"Ah . . . shit."

"And we have someone here," the guy wheezed. His one eye moved over to Jane. "Right?"

As they all looked in her direction, the black-haired one was clearly cranked out. So it was a surprise when he said, "Will you treat our brother?"

The request was nonthreatening and respectful. Evidently he'd been upset primarily that his buddy was down for the count and not getting treated.

She cleared her throat. "Yeah, I will. But what do I have to work with? I'm going to want to knock him out—"

"Don't worry about that," Phury said.

She shot him a level stare. "You want me to put your face back together without general anesthesia?"

"Yes."

Maybe they had a different pain tolerance—

"Are you insane?" Red Sox muttered.

Okay, maybe not.

But enough with the talk. Assuming this boy with the Rocky Balboa puss healed as fast as her patient did, she had to get operating now, before the bones knit together wrong and she had to rebreak them.

Looking around the room, she saw glass-fronted cabinets full of supplies and hoped like hell she could put together a surgical kit from what was around. "I don't suppose any of you have medical experience?"

V spoke up, right at her ear, almost as close as her clothes. "Yeah, I can assist. I'm trained as a paramedic."

She eyed him over her shoulder, a lick of heat going through her. *Get back in the game, Whitcomb.* "Good. You got any kind of local anesthesia?"

"Lidocaine."

"How about some sedatives? And maybe a little morphine. If he flinches at the wrong time, I could blind him."

"Yeah." As V started for the rows of stainless-steel cabinets, she noticed he was wobbly. That walk down the tunnel had been a long one, and even though he seemed healed on the surface, he was still just days out of open-heart surgery.

She grabbed his arm and pulled him back. "You're going to sit down." She glanced over at Red Sox. "Get him a chair. Now." When the patient cracked his mouth to argue, she blew him off by heading across the room. "Not interested in it. I need you on the ball while I operate, and this could take a while. You're better, but you're not as strong as you think you are, so sit your ass down and tell me where to get what I need."

There was a heartbeat of silence, then someone barked a laugh while her patient cursed in the background. The kinglike one started to grin at her.

Red Sox rolled a chair over from the whirlpool bath and shoved it right into the backs of V's legs. "Park it, big guy. On your doctor's orders."

When the patient sat down, she said, "Now, here's what I'm going to want."

She listed the standard scalpel, forceps, and suction supplies, then asked for surgical wire and thread, Betadine, buffered solution to rinse, gauze padding, latex gloves. . . .

She was amazed at how quickly it came together, but then, she and her patient were on the same wavelength. He directed her around the room succinctly, anticipated what she might want, and didn't waste words. The perfect nurse, as it were.

She let out a huge sigh of relief that they had a surgical drill. "And I don't suppose you have a magnifying headset?"

"Cabinet by the crash cart," V said. "Lower drawer. Left side. You want me to scrub in?"

"Yup." She went over and found the set. "We have X-ray capability?"

"No."

"Shit." She put her hands on her hips. "Whatever. I'll go in blind."

As she put the headset on, V got up and went to work on his hands and forearms over the sink in the far corner. When he was done she took his place, then they gloved up.

She came back to Phury, meeting him in his good eye. "This is probably going to hurt even with the local and some morphine. You'll probably pass out, and I hope it happens sooner rather than later."

She went for a syringe and felt the familiar sense of power come to her as she set about fixing what needed to be repaired—

"Wait," he said. "No drugs."

"What?"

"Just do it." There was a gruesome anticipation in his eye, one that was not right on so many levels. He *wanted* to be hurt.

She narrowed her stare. And wondered if he had let this happen to himself.

"Sorry." Jane pierced the rubber seal of the lidocaine vial with the needle. As she drew out what she needed she said, "There is no way in hell I'm going in without you numbed up. You feel strongly to the contrary, find yourself another surgeon."

She put the little glass bottle down on a steel rolling tray and leaned over his face, syringe up in the air. "So what's it going to be? Me and this knockout sauce or . . . gee, no one?"

That yellow stare flared with anger, like she'd cheated him out of something.

But then the kinglike guy spoke up. "Phury, don't be an ass. This is your vision we're talking about. Shut up and let her do her job."

The yellow eye closed. "Fine," the guy muttered.

It was about two hours later that Vishous decided he was in trouble. Big trouble. As he stared at the rows of neat little black stitches in Phury's face, he was overwhelmed to the point of silence.

Yeah. He was in mega trouble.

Jane Whitcomb, M.D., was a master surgeon. An absolute artist. Her hands were elegant instruments, her eyes sharp as the scalpel she used, her focus as fierce and all-consuming as that of a warrior in battle. At times she'd worked with a blurring speed, and at others she'd slowed down until it seemed like she wasn't moving at all: Phury's orbital bone had been broken in a number of places, and Jane had put him back together step by step, removing chips that were white as oyster shells, drilling into the cranium and running wire between fragments, putting a small screw in his cheek.

V could tell she wasn't completely happy with the end result by the hard look on her face as she'd closed. And when he'd asked her what the problem was, she'd told him that she would have preferred to put a plate in Phury's cheek, but as they didn't have that kind of kit handy, she was just going to hope the bone knit fast.

From start to finish she'd been totally in control. To the point where it had turned him on, which was both absurd and shameful.

It was just that he'd never met a female—a woman—like her before. She'd just cared for his brother superbly, with skill V himself couldn't hope to match.

Oh, God . . . He was in such fucking trouble here.

"How's his blood pressure?" she asked.

"Steady," he replied. Phury had passed out about ten minutes in, though his breathing had remained strong and so had his BP.

As Jane wiped off the area around the eye and cheekbone and started to pack it with gauze, Wrath cleared his throat at the doorway. "What about his vision?"

"We won't know until he tells us," Jane said. "I have no way of ascertaining whether his optic nerve has been damaged or whether there was any retinal or cornea damage. If any of that has happened, he's going to have to go to another facility to get it repaired, and not just because of the limited resources here. I'm not an eye surgeon, and I wouldn't even attempt that kind of operation."

The king pushed his sunglasses up a little higher on his straight nose. Like he was thinking of his weak eyes and hoping Phury didn't have to deal with that kind of problem.

After Jane covered the side of Phury's face with gauze, she ran a length of bandage around his head like a turban, then put the instruments she'd used in the autoclave. To keep from watching her obsessively, V got busy throwing out the used syringes, pads, and needles along with the disposable tube from the suction draw.

Jane snapped off her surgical gloves. "Let's talk infection. How susceptible is your kind?"

"Not very." V lowered himself back into his chair. He hated to admit it, but he was tired. If she hadn't made him take a load off, he'd be totally dead on his feet by now. "Our immune systems are very strong."

"Would your doctor have him on antibiotics as a prophylactic?"

"No."

She went over to Phury and stared at him like she was reading his

vital signs without the benefit of a stethoscope and blood pressure
cuff. Then she reached out and smoothed his extravagant hair back.
The ownership in her eyes and the gesture bugged V even though it
shouldn't have: Of course she'd take a special interest in his brother.
She'd just put the side of his face back together.

But *still*.

Shit, bonded males were a pain in the ass, weren't they?

Jane leaned down to Phury's ear. "You did well. It's going to be all
right. You just rest and let that fancy healing of yours go to work,
okay?" After patting his shoulder, she turned off the high-powered
chandelier over the gurney. "God, I'd love to study your kind."

A blast of cold came from the corner, as Wrath said, "Not a
chance, Doc. We aren't playing guinea pig for the likes of the human
race."

"I wasn't getting my hopes up." She glanced around at all of them.
"I don't want him unattended, so either I'm staying with him here or
someone else is. And if I leave, I'm going to want to check on him in
about two hours to see how he's coming along."

"We'll stay here," V said.

"You look like you're about to fall over."

"Not a chance of that."

"Only because you're sitting down."

The idea that he was weak in front of her sharpened his voice.
"You don't worry about me, female."

She frowned. "Okay, that was a statement of fact, not concern.
Do what you want with it."

Ouch. Yeah . . . just ouch.

"Whatever. I'll be out there." He got up and left quick.

In the equipment room he grabbed a bottle of Aquafina from the
cooler, then stretched out on one of the benches. As he cracked the
cap he was dimly aware of Wrath and Rhage coming over and saying
something to him, but he wasn't tracking.

That he wanted Jane to care about him drove him nuts. That he was hurt when she didn't was even more of an ego fuck.

He closed his eyes and tried to be logical. He hadn't slept in weeks. He'd been plagued by that nightmare. He'd almost died.

He'd met his frickin' mommy.

V sucked back most of the water. He was beyond off-kilter, and that had to be why he was catching feelings. It really wasn't about Jane. It was situational. His life was a fruit salad of *fuck-me*s, and that was the reason he was getting chicky about her. Because sure as shit she was giving him nothing to go on. She treated him as a patient and as a scientific curiosity. And that orgasm he'd almost given her? He was damn sure that if she'd been wide-awake it never would have happened: Those images she'd had of him were a woman's fantasy about being with a dangerous monster. They were not about her wanting him in real life.

"Hey."

V opened his eyes and looked up at Butch. "Hey."

The cop shoved V's feet aside and sat down on the bench. "Man, she did a bang-up job with Phury, didn't she?"

"Yeah." V glanced at the open door to the PT suite. "What's she doing in there?"

"Going through all the cabinets. Said she wanted to know what the inventory was, but I really think she's just hanging around Phury and trying to be casual about it."

"She doesn't have to watch him all the time," V muttered.

As the sentence flew out of his mouth, he couldn't believe he was jealous of his injured brother. "What I mean is—"

"Nah. Don't worry. I gotchu."

As Butch started to crack his knuckles, V cursed in his head and thought about leaving. Those popping sounds tended to be the prelude to Meaningful Conversation. "What."

Butch flexed his arms, his Gucci button-down stretching tight

over his shoulders. "*Nada*. Well, other than . . . I do want you to know that I approve."

"Of what?"

"Her. You and her." Butch glanced over, then looked away. "It's a good combo."

In the silence that followed, V traced the profile of his best friend, from the dark hair that fell over a smart forehead to the busted nose to the jutting jaw. For the first time in quite a while he didn't crave Butch. Which should have been classed as an improvement. Instead, he felt worse for a different reason.

"There is no her and me, buddy."

"Bullshit. I saw it right after you healed me. And the connection's getting stronger by the hour."

"Nothing's doing. I'm popping the solid-gold truth to you."

"Okay, well . . . how's that water feeling, then?"

"Excuse me?"

"The Nile warm this time of year?"

As V ignored the jab, he found himself focusing on Butch's lips. In a very quiet voice, he said, "You know . . . I totally wanted to have sex with you."

"I know." Butch's head twisted around, and their eyes met. "Past tense now, huh."

"Think so. Yeah."

Butch nodded toward the PT suite's open door. "Because of her."

"Maybe." V looked across the equipment room and caught sight of Jane as she rifled through a cabinet. His body's response as she bent at the waist was immediate, and he had to shift his hips to keep the head of his erection from being squeezed like an orange. As the pain ebbed, he thought about what he'd felt toward his roommate. "Have to say, I was surprised you were so cool with it. Thought it would creep you out or some shit."

"Can't help how you feel." Butch stared down at his hands, checking the nails. The clasp on his Piaget. The placement of his platinum cuff link. "Besides . . ."

"What?"

The cop shook his head. "Nothing."

"Say it."

"Nope." Butch stood up and stretched, his big body arching. "I'm going to head back to the Pit—"

"You wanted me. Maybe just a little."

Butch settled back on his spine, his arms falling to his sides, his head dropping into place. He frowned, his face crinkling up. "I'm not gay, though."

V dropped his jaw like a quarter and bobble-headed it. "No, really? That's *such* a shocker. I was sure all that I'm-a-good-Irish-Catholic-boy-from-Southie shit was a front."

Butch flipped the bird. "Whatever. And I'm down with homosexuals. Far as I'm concerned people should fuck whoever they want in whatever way gets them off as long as everyone involved is over eighteen and no one gets hurt. I just happen to dig the females."

"Relax. I'm only jerking you."

"You'd better be. You know I'm not a 'phobe."

"Yeah, I know."

"So are you?

"A 'phobe?"

"Gay or bi."

As V exhaled, he wished it was because he had a cigarette between his lips, and on reflex he patted his pocket, comforted by the fact that he'd brought some handrolls with him.

"Look, V, I know you do females, but the way you do them is only the leather-and-wax road. Is it different between you and guys?"

V stroked his goatee with his gloved hand. He'd always felt like there was nothing he and Butch couldn't say to each other. But this . . . this was hard. Mostly because he didn't want anything to

change between them and had always feared that if his sexual endeavors were discussed too openly it would get weird. Truth was, Butch
was a hetero by nature, not just background. And if he'd felt a little
something different here or there for V? It was an aberration that
probably made him uncomfortable.

V rolled the Aquafina bottle between his palms. "How long have
you wanted to ask me the question? About the gay thing."

"For a while."

"Afraid of what I'd say?"

"Nope, because it doesn't matter to me one way or the other. I'm
tight with you whether you like males or females or both."

V looked into his best friend's eyes and realized . . . yeah, Butch
wasn't going to judge him. They were cool no matter what.

With a curse, V rubbed the center of his chest and blinked. He
never cried but he felt as if he could at this moment.

Butch nodded as if he knew exactly what was doing. "Like I said,
my man, it's whatever. You and me? Same as always, no matter who
you screw. Although . . . if you're into sheep, that would be tough.
Don't know if I could handle that."

V had to smile. "I don't do farm animals."

"Can't stand hay in your leathers?"

"Or wool in my teeth."

"Ah." Butch looked back over. "So what's the answer, V?"

"What do you think it is?"

"I think you've done males."

"Yeah. I have."

"But I'm guessing . . ." Butch wagged his finger. "I'm guessing you
don't like them any more than the females you Dom. Both sexes are
irrelevant to you in the long run because you've never really cared
about anyone. Except for me. And . . . your surgeon."

V dropped his eyes, hating that he was so transparent, but not
really surprised by the thin-veil routine he was sporting. He and

Butch were like that. No secrets. And in that vein . . . "I probably should tell you something, cop."

"What?"

"I raped a male once."

Man, you could have heard crickets chirping for the silence.

After a while Butch sank back down on the bench. "You did?"

"Back in the warrior camp, if you beat someone while sparring, you fucked them in front of the rest of the soldiers. And I won the first fight I was in after my transition. The male . . . I guess he'd consented in a way. I mean, he submitted, but it wasn't right. I . . . yeah, I didn't want to do it to him, but I didn't stop." V took out a cigarette from his pocket and stared down at the thin white roll. "It was right before I left the camp. Right before . . . other things happened to me."

"Was that your first time?"

V took out his lighter but didn't strike up a flame. "Helluva way to start, huh."

"Jesus . . ."

"Anyway, after I was out in the world for a while, I experimented with a lot of shit. I was really angry and . . . yeah, just totally pissed off." He looked over at Butch. "There's not much I haven't done, cop. And most of it's been hard-core, if you feel me. There's always been consent, but it was—it still is—on the rails." V laughed tightly. "As well as curiously forgettable."

Butch was quiet for a time. Then he said, "I think that's why I like Jane."

"Huh?"

"When you look at her? You actually *see* her, and when's the last time that's happened for you?"

V geared himself up, then stared hard into Butch's eyes. "I saw you. Even though it was wrong. I saw you."

Shit, he sounded sad. Sad and . . . lonely. Which made him want to change the subject.

Butch clapped V on the thigh, then stood up, as if he knew exactly what V was thinking. "Listen, I don't want you to feel bad. It's my animal magnetism. I'm irresistible."

"Smart-ass." V's smile didn't last long. "Don't get your romantic side fired up about me and Jane, buddy. She's human."

Butch's jaw dropped and he pulled a bobble. "No, really? That's *such* a shocker! And here I thought she was a sheep."

V shot Butch a fuck-ya stare. "She's not into me like that. Not really."

"You sure about that?"

"Yup."

"Huh. Well, if I were you I might test that theory before you let her go." Butch shoved a hand through his hair. "Listen, I . . . shit."

"What?"

"I'm glad you told me. About the sex stuff."

"None of it was a news flash."

"True. But I figure you came out with it because you trust my ass."

"I do. Now drag it back to the Pit. Marissa's got to be coming home soon."

"She is." Butch headed for the door but then paused and looked over his shoulder. "V?"

Vishous raised his stare. "Yeah?"

"I think you should know, after all this deep conversatin' . . ." Butch shook his head gravely. "We still ain't dating."

The two of them busted out laughing, and the cop was still yukking it up as he disappeared into the gym.

"What's so funny?" Jane asked.

V braced himself before looking at her, hoping like hell she didn't know how hard it was for him to front like he was level. "My buddy's just being an ass. It's his life's work."

"Everyone needs a purpose."

"True."

She sat down on the bench across the way, and his eyes ate her up like he'd been in the dark for ages and she was a candle.

"Are you going to need to feed again?" she asked.

"Doubt it. Why?"

"Your coloring is off."

Well, having your chest this tight will do that to a guy. "I'm good."

There was a long silence. Then she said, "I was worried in there."

The exhaustion in her voice made him see past his attraction for her and pick up on the fact that her shoulders were slumped and there were dark circles under her eyes and her lids were low. She was clearly wiped.

You need to let her go, he thought. *Soon.*

"Why were you worried?" he asked.

"Very tricky area to fix in a field situation. Which was what this was." She rubbed her face. "You were great, by the way."

His brows popped. "Thanks."

With a groan, she tucked her feet up under her butt, just as she had back in the bedroom in that chair. "I'm concerned about his sight."

Man, he wished he could rub her back. "Yeah, he doesn't need another liability."

"He has one already?"

"Prosthetic leg—"

"V? Mind if I talk to you for a sec?"

V's head shot around to the doorway in from the gym. Rhage was back, still dressed in his fighting leathers. "Hey, Hollywood. What's up?"

Jane uncurled herself. "I can go into the other—"

"Stay," V said. None of this was going to be permanent for her, so it didn't matter what she heard. And besides . . . there was a part of him—a sappy part that made him want to clap himself on the head with a liquor bottle—that wanted to milk every second he had with her.

As she settled back into place, V nodded at his brother. "Talk."

Rhage glanced back and forth between him and Jane, his teal eyes too shrewd for V's taste. Then the guy shrugged. "I found an incapacitated *lesser* tonight."

"Incapacitated how?"

"Gutted."

"By one of its own?"

Rhage glanced at the PT room door. "Nope."

V looked in that direction and frowned. "Phury? Oh, come on, he would never pull any Clive Barker shit. Must have been one hell of a fight."

"We're talking field-dressed, V. Surgical cuts. And it's not like the thing had swallowed the Brother's car keys and he was looking to get 'em back. I think he did it for no good reason."

Well . . . shit. Among the Brotherhood, Phury was the gentleman, the noble fighter, the one who was Boy Scout–tight about things. He had all kinds of standards for himself, and honor in the combat arena was one of them, even though their enemies didn't deserve the favor.

"I can't believe it," V muttered. "I mean . . . shit."

Rhage took a Tootsie Pop out of his pocket, peeled off the wrapper, and pieholed the thing. "I don't give a crap if he wants to shred those fuckers like tax returns. What I'm not into is what's driving the behavior. If he's knifing like that, there's some high-level frustration going on. Plus if the reason he got cracked in the face tonight was because he was so busy playing *Saw II*, then it's a safety issue."

"You tell Wrath?"

"Not yet. I was going to talk to Z first. Assuming everything goes okay with Bella tonight at Havers's."

"Ah . . . that's Phury's *why*, then, true? Anything happens to that female or the young inside her and we're going to have to deal with both of them like you read about." V cursed to himself, suddenly thinking of all the pregnancies in his future. *Fuck.* That Primale shit was going to kill him.

Rhage bit down on the Tootsie Pop, the crunch muffled by his flawless cheek. "Phury's got to cut that obsession with her."

V looked down at the floor. "No doubt he would if he could."

"Listen, I'm going to go find Z." Rhage pulled the white stick out of his mouth and wrapped it in the purple wrapper. "You two need anything?"

V glanced at Jane. Her eyes were on Rhage and she was sizing him up as a doctor would, taking note of the composition of his body, doing his internal math in her head. Or, at least, V hoped that was what was doing. Hollywood was a good-looking bastard.

As V's fangs throbbed in warning, he wondered if he was ever going to get his calm and cool back. It seemed like he was jealous of everything in pants with Jane around.

"No, we're good," he said to his brother. "Thanks, man."

After Rhage left and closed the door, Jane shifted around on her bench, stretching her legs out. With a ridiculous surge of satisfaction, he realized they were sitting in exactly the same position.

"What's a *lesser?*" she asked.

He called himself a loser as he stared at her. "An undead killer who's trying to hunt my kind into extinction."

"Undead?" Her forehead bunched up, as if her brain were rejecting what she'd heard. Like it was a widget that hadn't passed quality control. "Undead how?"

"Long story."

"We have time."

"Not that much." Not much at all.

"Was that what shot you?"

"Yup."

"And what attacked Phury?"

"Yup."

There was a long silence. "I'm glad he cut one of them up, then."

V's eyebrows danced with his hairline. "You are?"

"The geneticist in me abhors extinction. Genocide is . . . utterly

unforgivable." She got up and went to the door to look in at Phury. "Do you kill them? The . . . *lessers?*"

"That's what we're for. My brothers and I were bred to fight."

"Bred?" Her dark green eyes shifted to his. "What do you mean?"

"The geneticist in you knows exactly what I mean." As the word *Primale* pinged around his skull like a loose bullet, he cleared his throat. Shit, he was so not in a big hurry to talk about his future as the Chosen's stud with the woman he actually wanted to be with. Who was leaving. At, like, sundown.

"And this is a facility for training more of you?"

"Well, soldiers to support us. My brothers and I are a little different."

"How so?"

"Like I said, we were specifically bred for strength and endurance and healing."

"By whom?"

"Another long story."

"Try me." When he didn't reply, she pressed, "Come on. We might as well talk, and I'm really interested in your kind."

Not him. His kind.

V swallowed a curse. Man, if he were any more chicked-out about her, he'd be wearing nail polish.

He really wanted to light the cigarette in his hand, but he wasn't about to around her. "Standard stuff. The strongest males were mated to the shrewdest females. Which resulted in guys like me, who are the best bet for the protection of the race."

"And the female births from these pairings?"

"Were the basis of the spiritual life of the species."

"Were? So that kind of selective breeding doesn't go on anymore?"

"Actually . . . it's starting up again." Damn, he really needed a cigarette. "Will you excuse me?"

"Where are you going?"

"Out to the gym for a smoke." He slipped the handrolled between his lips, stood up, and went just beyond the equipment room's door. Leaning against the gym's concrete wall, he set the Aquafina bottle down at his feet and put his lighter to good use. As he thought about his mother, he exhaled a smoky *fuck*.

"The bullet was strange."

V snapped his head around. Jane was in the doorway, arms across her chest, her blond hair messed up like she'd been pushing a hand through it.

"Excuse me?"

"The bullet that hit you. Do they use different weapons?"

He blew his next stream of smoke out in the opposite direction, away from her. "How was it strange?"

"Normally bullets are conical in shape, the tops either coming to a sharp angle if it's a rifle or being more blunt if it's a pistol. The one in you is round."

V took another draw on his handrolled. "You saw this on the X-ray?"

"Yeah, read like normal lead as far as I could see. The bullet was slightly uneven around the edges, but that was likely caused by it banging around your rib cage."

"Well . . . God only knows what kind of new technology the *less-ers* are tripping with. They have toys just like we have toys." He looked at the tip of the cigarette. "Speaking of which, I should say thank you."

"For what?"

"Saving me."

"You're very welcome." She laughed a little. "I was so surprised at your heart."

"You were?"

"Never seen anything like it before." She nodded to the PT room. "I want to stay here with you guys until your brother's healed up, okay? I have a bad feeling about him. Can't put my finger on it. . . . He looks all right, but my instincts are ringing, and when they go off

like this I'm always sorry if I don't follow them. Besides, I'm not due back to real life until Monday morning anyway."

V froze with the handrolled on the way up to his lips.

"What?" she said. "There a problem with that?"

"Ah . . . no. No problem. At all."

She was staying. A little longer.

V smiled to himself. So this was what winning the lottery felt like.

NINETEEN

As John stood in the line in front of ZeroSum with Blay and Qhuinn, he was not happy and not comfortable. They'd been waiting to get into the club for, like, an hour and a half, and the only good thing was that the night wasn't so cold they froze their balls off.

"I'm so not getting any younger here." Qhuinn stomped his feet. "And I didn't dud up to play wallflower in this wait line."

John had to admit the guy looked tight tonight: black open-collared shirt, black trousers, black boots, black leather jacket. With his dark hair and his mismatched eyes, he was getting a lot of attention from the human females. For example, right now two brunettes and a redhead were strolling down the line, and what do you know, all three of them did a head snap as they went by Qhuinn. He was characteristically shameless as he stared back.

Blay cursed. "My man over here is going to be a menace, aren't you?"

"You'd better believe it." Qhuinn jacked up his pants. "I'm starving."

Blay shook his head, then scanned the street. He'd done this a number of times, his eyes sharp, his right hand in his jacket pocket. John knew what was in that palm of his: the grip of a nine. Blay was armed.

He'd said he'd gotten the gun from a cousin of his and it was all hush-hush. But then, it had to be. One of the rules of the training program was that you weren't supposed to carry when you were out and about. It was a good rule, built on the theory that a little knowledge was a dangerous thing, and trainees shouldn't front like they had half a brain when it came to fighting. Still, Blay had said he wasn't going downtown without some metal, and John had decided to pretend he didn't know what that bulge was about.

And there was also a little part of him that thought if they ran into Lash, it might not be a bad idea.

"Well, hey, ladies," Qhuinn said. "Where you off to?"

John glanced over. A pair of blondes were standing in front of Qhuinn, looking like his body was the candy counter at a movie theater and they were wondering whether to start with the Milk Duds or the Swedish Fish.

The one on the right, who had hair down to her ass and a skirt the size of a paper napkin, smiled. Her teeth were so white they gleamed like pearls. "We were going to Screamer's, but . . . if you're heading in here, we might change our plans."

"Make it easy on all of us and join us in line." He bowed, sweeping his arm in front of him.

The blonde looked at her friend, then pulled a little Betty Boop maneuver, hip and hair swinging. It looked well rehearsed. "I just love a gentleman."

"I'm one to my very core." Qhuinn held his hand out, and when the Betty took it, he pulled her into line. A couple of guys frowned, but one look from Qhuinn and they cut the crap, which was understandable. Qhuinn was taller and wider than them, a semi to their station wagons.

"This is Blay and John."

The girls beamed up at Blay, who flushed the color of his hair, then the two did a cursory pass over John. He got a quick pair of head nods and then the focus was back on his friends.

Putting his hands in the windbreaker he'd borrowed, he moved out of the way so Betty's friend could squeeze in next to Blay.

"John? You okay there?" Blay asked.

John nodded and looked at his friend, signing quickly, *Just zoning out.*

"Oh, my God," Betty said.

John shoved his hands back into his pockets. Shit, she'd no doubt noticed he'd used sign language, and this was going to go one of two ways: She'd either think he was cute. Or she'd pity him.

"Your watch is so hot!"

"Thank you, baby," Qhuinn said. "I just got it. Urban Outfitters."

Oh, right. She hadn't noticed John at all.

Twenty minutes later they finally made it up to the club's entrance, and it was a miracle John got in. The bouncers at the door surveyed his ID with everything but a proton microscope, and they were just starting to shake their heads when a third came up, took one look at Blay and Qhuinn, and let them all in.

Two feet past the door and John decided he wasn't into the scene. There were people everywhere, showing so much skin they might as well have been at the beach. And was that couple over there . . . shit, was that guy's hand up her skirt?

No, it was the hand of the guy behind her. The one she wasn't kissing.

All around, techno music blared, the shrill beats ringing through air that was stuffy with sweat and perfume and something musky that he suspected was sex. Lasers speared the dimness, evidently aim-

ing right for his eyeballs, because wherever he looked they nailed him a good one.

He wished he had sunglasses and earplugs.

He glanced back at the couple—er, threesome. He wasn't sure, but the woman seemed to have her hands down both their pants.

How about a blindfold, too, he thought.

With Qhuinn in the lead, the five of them filed by a roped-off area that was guarded by bouncers the size of cars. On the other side of the steakhead barricade, separated from the riffraff by a wall of falling water, there were fancy people sitting in leather booths, the type who wore designer suits and no doubt drank liquor John couldn't pronounce.

Qhuinn headed for the back of the club like a homing pigeon, picking out a spot against the wall with a good view of the grinding on the floor and easy bar access. He took drink orders from the ladies and Blay, but John just shook his head. This was so not a good environment to get even slightly loose in.

All of it reminded him of the time before he'd come to live with the Brotherhood. When he'd been out in the world alone he'd been used to being the smallest one around, and man, that was true here. Everyone was taller than he was, the crowd looming over him, even the women. And it brought out all of his instincts. If you had few physical resources to protect yourself with, you had to rely on your twitchy senses: Two feet and hauling ass was the strategy that had always saved him.

Well, saved him except for that one time.

"God . . . you are so tight." In Qhuinn's absence, the girls were all over Blay, especially Betty, who seemed to think he was a stroking post.

Blay had no game, evidently, because he had no quick comeback. But he was definitely not brushing them off, letting Betty's hands go wherever they wanted.

Qhuinn sauntered over from the bar to the sound of brass balls clanging. Jesus, he was in his zone, two Coronas in each hand, eyes leveled on the girls. He moved like he was already having sex, his hips shifting with his stride, his shoulders doing the roll of a guy whose parts were in working order and ready to be used.

Man, the girls were eating that shit up, their eyes flaring as he came through the crowd.

"Ladies, I need a tip for my efforts." He slipped Blay one of the beers, took a swig of another, and held the other pair over his head. "Gimme a little of what I want."

Betty was on the ball, putting both her hands on his chest and stretching up. Qhuinn tilted his head a little, but didn't help her much. Which only made her work harder. As their lips met, Qhuinn's lifted into a smile . . . and he reached out and pulled the other girl close. Betty didn't seem to mind in the slightest, and helped draw her friend in.

"Let's go to the bathroom," Betty stage-whispered.

Qhuinn leaned around Betty and laid a French kiss on her friend. "Blay? You want to join us?"

Blay threw back his beer, swallowing hard. "Nah, I'm going to hang out. Just want to chill."

His eyes called his bluff when they flipped to John for a split second.

Which pissed John off. *I don't need a babysitter.*

"I know, buddy."

The girls frowned as they hung from Qhuinn's shoulders like a set of drapes, as if John was being a buzz-kill drama queen. And they looked positively bitched when Qhuinn started to back off from them.

John pegged his buddy with hard eyes. *Don't you fucking dare think of bailing. I will never speak to you again.*

Betty cocked her head, her blond hair slipping over Qhuinn's forearm. "What's wrong?"

John signed, *Tell her nothing is wrong and go get laid. I'm fucking serious, Qhuinn.*

Qhuinn signed back, *Don't feel right leaving you.*

"Is something wrong?" Betty chirped.

If you don't go, I'm leaving. I will walk out of this club, Qhuinn. For real.

Qhuinn's eyes closed briefly. Then before Betty could something-wrong them all again, he said, "Let's go, ladies. We'll be right back."

As Qhuinn pivoted around and the girls shimmied away with him, John signed, *Blay, go get laid. I'll wait here.* When his friend didn't reply, he signed, *Blay? Getcha ass going!*

There was a moment's hesitation. "I can't."

Why?

"Because I . . . ah, I promised I wouldn't leave you."

John went cold. *Promised who?*

Blaylock's cheeks fired up bright as a traffic light. "Zsadist. Right after I went through the change, he took me aside after class and said that if we ever went out with you . . . you know."

Anger seeped into John's head and made his skull hum.

"Just until your change, John."

John shook his head, because that was what you did when you had no voice and you wanted to scream. In a rush, the pounding behind his eyes came back.

Tell you what, he signed. *You're worried about me, give me your gun.*

At that moment a smoking-hot brunette walked by in a bustier and a pair of pants that looked like they'd been put on her with a Spackle trowel. Blay's eyes latched onto her and the air changed around him, his body throwing off heat.

Blay, what is going to happen to me here? Even if Lash brings it—

"He's been banned from this club. That's why I wanted to come here."

How do you . . . Lemme guess—Zsadist. Did he tell you we could only come here?

"Maybe."

Give me the gun. Get moving.

The brunette took up res at the bar and looked over her shoulder. Right at Blay.

You aren't leaving me. We're both in the club. And I'm really getting pissed here.

There was a pause. Then the gun changed hands and Blay downed his beer like he was nervous as shit.

Good luck, John signed.

"Fuck, I have no idea what I'm doing. I'm not even sure I want to do this."

You do want to. And you'll figure it out. Now go before she finds someone else.

When John was finally alone, he leaned back against the wall and crossed his little ankles. Watching the crowd, he envied them.

Not long thereafter, a shock of recognition went through him, as if someone had called his name. He looked around, wondering if Blay or Qhuinn had hollered for him. Nope. Qhuinn and the blondes were nowhere to be seen, and Blay was cautiously leaning into the brunette at the bar.

Except he was sure someone was calling him.

John got serious about the looking, focusing on the crowd in front of him. There were people everywhere, and yet no one in particular around, and he was about to decide he was nuts when he saw a stranger he knew completely.

The female was standing in the shadows at the end of the bar, the pink and blue glow from the backlit liquor bottles barely illuminating her. Tall and built hard as a man, she had supershort dark hair and a don't-fuck-with-me face that announced loud and clear that you screwed with her at your own risk. Her eyes were lethally smart, fighter-serious and . . . leveled on him.

His body went into instant flip-out, like someone was buffing his skin to a high shine while spanking him with a two-by-four: He was instantly breathless and dizzy and flushed, but at least he forgot about his headache.

Sweet Jesus, she was coming over.

Her walk was one of power and confidence, like she was stalking prey, and men who weighed more than her got out of her way quick as mice. As she approached, John fumbled with his windbreaker, trying to make himself look more masculine. Which was *such* a joke.

Her voice was deep. "I'm security at this club, and I'm going to have to ask you to come with me."

She took his arm without waiting for a reply and led him into a dark hallway. Before he knew what was happening, she pushed him into what was obviously an interrogation room and nailed him to the wall like a velvet Elvis.

As her forearm pushed into his windpipe and he gasped, she patted him down. Her hand was fast and impersonal as it went over his chest and down to his hips.

John closed his eyes and shuddered. Holy shit, this was a turn-on. If he'd been able to get an erection, he was quite sure he'd be hammer-hard right now.

And then he remembered that Blay's unmarked gun was in the big back pocket of the pants he'd borrowed.

Shit.

In the equipment room at the compound, Jane sat down on the bench that would let her see the guy she'd operated on. She was waiting for V to finish his cigarette, and the faint whiff of his exotic tobacco tingled in her nose.

God, that dream of him. The way his hand moved between her—

As an ache started, she crossed her legs and squeezed them together.

"Jane?"

She cleared her throat. "Yes?"

His voice was low as it drifted through the open door, a sensual, disembodied drawl. "What are you thinking about, Jane?"

Oh, yeah, right, like she was going to tell him that she was fantasizing—

Wait a minute. "You already know, don't you?" When he was silent, she frowned. "Was that a dream? Or did you . . ."

No reply.

She leaned forward until she could see him through the jamb. He was exhaling while he tucked the butt into a bottle of water.

"What did you do to me?" she demanded.

He screwed the cap on tight, the muscles of his forearms flexing. "Nothing you didn't want me to."

Even though he wasn't looking at her, she pointed her finger at him like it was a gun. "I told you. Stay out of my head."

His eyes flipped to hers. Oh . . . God . . . they were burning white as stars, hot as the sun. The instant they hit her face her sex bloomed for him, a mouth opening wide, ready to be fed.

"No," she said, although she didn't know why she bothered. Her body spoke for itself, and he damn well knew it.

V's lips lifted in a hard smile, and he breathed in deeply. "I love your scent right now. Makes me want to do more than just get in your head."

Okaaaaaaay, evidently he liked women in addition to men.

Abruptly his expression faded. "But don't worry. I won't go there."

"Why not?" As the question popped out, Jane cursed herself. If you told a man you didn't want him, and then he said he wouldn't have sex with you, generally the reaction you wanted to lead with was *not* something that sounded like a protest.

V leaned in through the door and chucked the water bottle across the room. The thing landed in a trash bin with a decisive flare, as if it were returning home from a business trip and damn relieved to be back. "You wouldn't like it with me. Not really."

He was so wrong.

Shut up. "Why?"

Shit! For the love of God, what was she saying?

"You just wouldn't like it with the real me. But I was glad for what happened when you were sleeping. You felt perfect, Jane."

She wished he would stop using her name. Every time it left his lips she felt like he was reeling her in, dragging her through waters she didn't understand into a net she could only thrash about in until she hurt herself.

"Why wouldn't I like it?"

As his chest expanded, she knew he was smelling her arousal. "Because I like control, Jane. Do you understand what I'm saying?"

"No, I don't."

He pivoted toward her, filling the doorway, and her eyes went right to his hips, traitors that they were. Holy shit, he was erect. Fully aroused. She could see the thick detail of him pushing against the flannel pajama bottoms he had on.

She swayed even though she was seated.

"Do you know what a Dom is?" he said in a low voice.

"Dom . . . as in . . ." *Whoa.* "Sexual dominant?"

He nodded his head. "That's how sex is with me."

Jane's lips parted and she had to look away. It was either that or she was going to combust. She had no experience with that whole alternative-lifestyle thing. Hell, she didn't have a lot of time for regular sex, much less to dabble in the fringes.

Damn her, but dangerous and wild with him seemed pretty fricking attractive right now. Although maybe that was because, for all intents and purposes, this was not real life, even though she was awake.

"What do you do?" she asked. "I mean do you . . . tie them up?"

"Yes."

She waited for him to go on. When he didn't, she whispered, "Anything else?"

"Yes."

"Tell me."

"No."

So there was pain involved, she thought. He hurt them before he fucked them. Probably during, too. And yet . . . she remembered him holding Red Sox in his arms so gently. Maybe with men it was different for him?

Terrific. A bisexual dominant vampire with kidnapping expertise. Man, for so many reasons she shouldn't feel like she did about him.

Jane covered her face with her hands, but unfortunately that only kept her from looking at him. It was no escape from what was going on in her head. She . . . wanted him.

"Goddamn it," she muttered.

"What's wrong."

"Nothing." God, she was such a liar.

"Liar."

Great, so he knew that, too. "I don't want to feel like I do right now, okay?"

There was a long pause. "And how do you feel, Jane?" When she said nothing, he murmured, "You don't like wanting me, do you. Is it because I'm a pervert?"

"Yes."

The word just shot out of her mouth, although it wasn't really the truth. If she was honest with herself, the problem was more than that . . . she'd always prided herself on her intelligence. Mind over emotion and logic-driven decision making had been the things that had never let her down. And yet here she was, coveting something that her instincts told her she'd be far, far better off without.

When there was a long silence, she dropped one of her hands and looked to the door. He wasn't standing between the jambs anymore, but she sensed he hadn't gone far. She leaned forward again and caught sight of him. He was up against the wall, staring across the gym's blue mats as if he were looking out over the sea.

"I'm sorry," she said. "I didn't mean it like that."

"Yeah, you did. But it's cool. I am what I am." His gloved hand flexed, and she had a feeling it was unconsciously.

"The truth is . . ." As she let the sentence go, one of his brows cocked, though he didn't look at her. She cleared her throat. "The truth is, self-preservation is a good thing and it should dictate my reactions."

"And it doesn't?"

"Not . . . always. With you, not always."

His lips lifted a little. "Then for once in my life, I'm glad I'm different."

"I'm scared."

He grew instantly serious, his diamond-bright eyes meeting hers. "Don't be. I won't hurt you. And I won't let anything else either."

For a split second her defenses went down. "Promise?" she said hoarsely.

He put his gloved hand over the heart she'd fixed and spoke a beautiful rush of words she didn't understand. Then he translated: "On my honor and by the blood in my veins, I so avow myself."

Her eyes shifted away from him and unfortunately landed on a rack of nunchakus. The weapons hung on pegs, their black handles lying like arms off their chain shoulders, at the ready to do mortal damage.

"I've never been so scared in my life."

"Fuck . . . I'm sorry, Jane. Sorry about all this. And I will let you go. In fact, you're free to leave anytime you want now. You just say the word and I'll take you home."

She looked back at him and stared at his face. His beard had grown in around the goatee, shading his jaw and his cheekbones, making him look even more sinister. With those tattoos around his eye and his sheer size, if she'd run into him in an alley she would have fled in terror even without knowing he was a vampire.

And yet here she was, trusting him to keep her safe.

Were her feelings real? Or was she in fact knee-deep in Stockholm syndrome?

She traced his broad chest and his tight hips and his long legs. God, whichever one it was, she wanted him like nothing else.

He let out a soft growl. "Jane . . ."

"Shit."

He cursed too and then fired up his next cigarette. As he exhaled, he said, "There's another reason I can't be with you."

"Which is?"

"I bite, Jane. And I wouldn't be able to stop myself. Not with you."

She remembered from the dream the feel of his fangs going up her neck with a soft scratching. Her body flooded with heat even as she wondered how she could want such a thing.

V stepped back into the doorway, the cigarette in his gloved hand. Tendrils of smoke rose from the handroll's tip, thin and graceful as a woman's hair.

With their eyes locked, he took his free hand and ran it down his chest, down his belly, down to that heavy erection behind the thin flannel of the pajama bottoms. As he cupped himself, Jane swallowed hard, pure lust slamming into her linebacker style, hitting her so hard she nearly went off the bench.

"If you'll let me," he said quietly, "I'll find you again in your sleep. I'll find you and finish what I started. Would you like that, Jane? Would you like to come for me?"

From out of the PT room, a moan sounded.

Jane tripped as she got up from the bench and headed in to check on her newest patient. The escape was obvious, but whatever—she'd lost her mind, so her pride was hardly a concern at this point.

On the gurney, Phury was twisting in pain, batting at the bandage on the side of his face.

"Hey . . . easy." She put her hand on his arm, stopping him. "Easy. You're okay."

She stroked his shoulder and talked to him until he settled down on a shudder.

"Bella . . ." he said.

Well aware that V was standing in the corner, she asked, "Is that his wife?"

"His twin's wife."

"Oh."

"Yeah."

Jane got a stethoscope and the blood pressure cuff and did a quick vitals check. "Does your kind normally run low for BP?"

"Yeah. Heart rate, too."

She put her hand on Phury's forehead. "He's warm. But your core temperature's higher than ours, right?"

"It is."

She let her fingers drift into Phury's multicolored hair and run through the thick waves, smoothing the tangles out. There was some kind of black oily substance in it—

"Don't touch that," V said.

She whipped her arm back. "Why? What is it?"

"The blood of my enemies. I don't want it on you." He strode over, took her by the wrist, and led her to the sink.

Although it went against her nature, she stood still and obedient as a child as he soaped up her hands and washed them off. The feel of both his bare palm and his leather glove slipping over her fingers . . . and the suds lubricating the friction . . . and the heat of him seeping into her and running up her arm made her reckless.

"Yes," she said as she stared down at what he was doing.

"Yes, what?"

"Come to me again in my sleep."

TWENTY

As head of security for ZeroSum, Xhex did not like any kind of guns in her house, but she especially did not like petty punks with metal fetishes running around armed up to their dime-sized balls.

That was how 911 calls happened. And she hated dealing with the Caldwell PD.

So on that note, she made no apologies as she manhandled the current little shit in question and found the weapon he'd taken from the redhead he'd been standing next to. Yanking the nine-millimeter out of the kid's pants, she popped the clip free and tossed the shell of the Glock on the table. The sleeve of bullets she put in her leathers; then she frisked him for ID. As she patted him down, she could sense he was one of her kind, and somehow that cranked her out even more.

No reason why it should, though. Humans didn't have a lock on being stupid.

She spun him around and shoved him into a chair, holding him down by the shoulder as she flipped open his wallet. Driver's license read John Matthew, and the DOB put him at twenty-three. Address was in an average, nuclear-family part of town that she was willing to bet he'd never set eyes on.

"I know what your ID tells me, but who are you really? Who's your family?"

He opened his mouth a couple of times, but nothing came out because he was clearly scared shitless. Which made sense. Stripped of his flash, he was nothing more than a runt of a pretrans, his brilliant blue eyes wide as basketballs in his pale face.

Yeah, he was a tough one, all right. Click, click, bang, bang, and all that gangsta shit. Christ, she was bored of busting posers like this. Maybe it was time to freelance a little, get back to doing what she did best. After all, assassins were always in demand in the right circles. And as she was half *symphath*, job satisfaction was a given.

"Talk," she said as she pitched the wallet onto the table. "I know what you are. Who are your parents?"

Now he seemed really surprised, although that didn't help with his vocal chops. After he got over his fresh shock, all he did was flap his hands in front of his chest.

"Don't play me. If you're man enough to carry, there's no reason to be a coward now. Or is that what you really are and the metal's there to make you a man?"

In slow motion his mouth closed and his hands dropped into his lap. As if he were deflating, his eyes lowered and his shoulders curled in.

Silence stretched, and she crossed her arms over her chest. "Look, kid, I got all night and a real bitch of an attention span. So you can pull the silent shit for as long as you want. I'm not going anywhere, and neither are you."

Xhex's earpiece went off, and when the bar-area bouncer stopped talking she said, "Good, bring him in."

A split second later there was a knock on the door. When she answered it, her subordinate was front and center with the redheaded vampire who'd given the kid the gun.

"Thanks, Mac."

"No problem, boss. I'm back out by the bar."

She shut the door and eyed the redhead. He was past his transition, but not by much: He carried himself like he didn't have a good sense of his size yet.

As he put his hand into the inside pocket of his suede blazer, she said, "You take out anything other than ID and I will personally put you on a stretcher."

He paused. "It's his ID."

"He already showed me."

"Not his real one." The guy extended his hand. "This is his real one."

Xhex took the laminated card and scanned the Old Language characters that were beneath a recent photo. Then she looked at the boy. He refused to meet her eyes; just sat there wrapped around himself, looking as if he wished he could be swallowed whole by the chair he was on.

"Shit."

"I was told to show this as well," the redhead said. He handed over a thick piece of paper that was folded into a square and sealed with black wax. When she got a load of the insignia, she wanted to curse again.

The royal crest.

She read the damn letter. Twice. "Mind if I keep this, Red?"

"No. Please do."

As she folded it back up she asked, "You got ID?"

"Yeah." Another laminated card came at her.

She checked it out, then gave both cards back. "Next time you come here, you don't wait in the line. You go up to the bouncer and you say my name. I'll come get you." She picked up the gun. "This yours or his?"

"Mine. But I think I'd rather him have it. He's a better shot."

She slammed the clip back into the butt of the Glock and put it out toward the silent kid, muzzle down. His hand didn't shake as he took it from her, but the thing looked way too big for him to handle. "Don't use it in here unless you have to defend yourself. We clear?"

The kid nodded once, lifted his ass from the seat, and disappeared the semi into the pocket she'd taken it out of.

God . . . damnit. He was no mere pretrans. According to his ID this was Tehrror, son of the Black Dagger warrior Darius. Which meant she had to see to it that nothing happened to him on her watch. Last thing she and Rehv needed was the kid turning up damaged on ZeroSum property.

Great. This was like having a crystal vase in a locker room full of rugby players.

And to top it off, he was mute.

She shook her head. "Well, Blaylock, son of Rocke, you look after him, and we will, too."

As the redhead nodded, the kid finally lifted his face to her, and for some reason his brilliant blue stare made her uncomfortable. Jesus . . . he was old. In his eyes he was an ancient, and she was momentarily stunned.

Clearing her throat, she turned and went to the door. As she opened the thing, the redhead said, "Wait, what's your name?"

"Xhex. Drop it anywhere in this club and I'll find you in a heartbeat. It's my job."

As the door shut, John decided that humiliation was like ice cream: It came in a lot of different flavors, gave you the chills, and made you want to cough.

Talk about Rocky Road. Right now he was choking on the shit.

Coward. God, was it so obvious? She didn't even know him and she got him right. He absolutely was a coward. A weak coward whose dead had not been avenged, who had no voice, and whose body was nothing even a ten-year-old would envy.

Blay shuffled his big feet, his boots making a soft noise that seemed as loud as someone yelling in the small room. "John? You want to go home?"

Oh, terrific. Like he was a five-year-old who'd gotten sleepy at the grown-up party.

Rage rolled in like thunder, and John felt its familiar weight ground him, energize him. Oh, man, he knew this well. This was the kind of pissed-off that had put Lash flat on his back. This was the kind of viciousness that had had John beating that kid's face in until the tile had run red as ketchup.

By some miracle, the two neurons in John's head that were still working rationally pointed out that the best thing for him to do was go home. If he stayed here, in this club, he'd just replay what that female had said over and over again, until he got so out-of-the-head mad that he did something truly stupid.

"John? Let's go home."

Fuck. This was supposed to be Blay's big night. Instead he was getting buzz-killed out of his chance to get laid good and hard. *I'll call Fritz. You stay with Qhuinn.*

"Nope. We go together."

Suddenly John felt like crying. *What the hell was on that piece of paper? The one you gave her?*

Blay flushed. "Zsadist gave it to me. He said if we ever got into a crack to show it."

So what was it?

"Z said it was from Wrath as king. Something about the fact that he's your *ghardian.*"

Why didn't you tell me?

"Zsadist said to show it only if I had to. And that included to you."

John rose from the chair and smoothed down his borrowed clothes. *Look, I want you to stay and get laid and have a good time—*

"We come together. We leave together."

John glared at his friend. *Just because Z said you had to babysit me—*

For one of the first times in recorded history, Blay's face got hard. "Fuck you—I'd do it anyway. And before you go all UFC, I'd like to point out that if our roles were reversed, you'd do the same goddamn thing. Admit it. You so fucking would. We're friends. We back up. 'Nuff said. Now cut the shit."

John wanted to kick over the chair he'd been sitting on. And he almost did.

Instead, he used his hands to sign, *Shit.*

Blay took out a BlackBerry and dialed. "I'll just tell Qhuinn I'll come back and pick him up whenever he wants."

John waited and briefly imagined what Qhuinn was doing somewhere dim and semiprivate with one or both of those human women. At least he was having a good night.

"Yo, Qhuinn? Yeah, me and John are heading home. Wha— No, everything's cool. We just had a run-in with security . . . No, you don't have . . . No, everything's tight. No, really. Qhuinn, you don't have to stop— Hello?" Blay stared at his phone. "He's meeting us by the front door."

The two of them left the little room and weeded in and out of hot and sweaty humans until John felt rabid—claustrophobic—like he'd been buried alive and was breathing dirt.

When they finally made it to the front door, Qhuinn was standing to the left against the black wall. His hair was messed up, his shirttail was hanging out, his lips were red and a little swollen. Up close he smelled like perfume.

Two different kinds.

"You okay?" he asked John.

John didn't answer. He couldn't stand it that he'd ruined everyone's night and just kept walking to the door. Until he felt the weird calling again.

He paused with his hands on the push bar and looked over his shoulder. The head of security was there watching him with her smart eyes. She was, once again, in a bank of the shadows, a place he suspected she preferred.

A place he suspected she always used to her advantage.

As his body tingled from head to foot, he wanted to put his fist through the wall, through the door, through someone's upper lip. But he knew that wouldn't get him the satisfaction he craved. He doubted he had enough upper-body strength to punch through the sports section of a newspaper.

The realization naturally pissed him off even more.

He turned his back on her and walked out into the chilly night. As soon as Blay and Qhuinn joined him on the sidewalk, he signed, *I'm going to wander around for a while. You can come with me if you like, but you're not going to talk me out of it. There is no way in hell I'm getting into a car and going home right now. Got it?*

His friends nodded and let him lead the way, staying a couple feet behind him. Clearly, they knew he was a quarter of an inch away from losing it and needed the space.

As they went down Tenth Street, he heard them talking quietly, whispering about him, but he didn't give a shit. He was a bag of anger. Nothing more.

True to his weak nature, his march of independence didn't last long. Pretty damn quick, the March wind ate away the clothes Blay had let him borrow, and his headache got so bad he was gritting his teeth. He'd imagined he'd take his friends all the way to Caldwell's bridge and beyond, that his anger was so strong he would wear them out until they begged him to stop walking just before dawn.

Except, of course, his performance was grossly below expectation.

He stopped. *Let's go back.*

"Whatever you say, John." Qhuinn's mismatched eyes were impossibly kind. "Whatever you want to do."

They headed back for the car, which was parked in an open-air lot about two blocks from the club. As they came around the corner, he noticed that the building next to the lot was being worked on, its construction zone battened down for the night, tarps flapping in the wind, heavy equipment sleeping soundly. To John, it seemed desolate.

Then again, he could have been bathed in sunshine in a field of daisies and all he would have seen was shadows. There was no way the night could have been worse. No. Way.

They were a good fifty yards from the car when the sweet smell of baby powder floated over on the breeze. And a *lesser* stepped out from behind a bucket loader.

TWENTY-ONE

Phury came to but didn't move. Which made sense, given the fact that one side of his face felt like it had been burned off. After a couple of deep breathers, he lifted a hand to the pounding ache. Bandages ran from his forehead to his jaw. He probably looked like an extra on the set of *ER*.

He sat up slowly and his whole head throbbed, like a bicycle pump had been shoved up his nose and someone was working that bitch with a strong arm.

Felt good.

Shifting his feet off the gurney, he pondered the law of gravity and debated whether he had the strength to deal with it. He decided to give it a shot, and what do you know, he managed to weave his way to the door.

Two pairs of eyes flipped over to him, one diamond bright, the other forest green.

"Hi," he said.

V's woman came up to him, and her stare was all doctor-scan. "God, I can't believe how fast you heal. You shouldn't even be conscious, much less upright."

"Do you want to check your handiwork?" When she nodded, he sat down on a bench and she carefully peeled the tape back. As he winced, he looked around her at Vishous. "Did you tell Z about this yet?"

The Brother shook his head. "Haven't seen him, and Rhage tried his phone but it was off."

"So, no news from Havers?"

"Not that I've heard. Although we're about an hour before dawn, so they'd better be back soon."

The doctor whistled under her breath. "It's like I can see the skin knitting back together in front of my eyes. Mind if I put another gauze pack on?"

"Whatever you like."

When she went back into the PT suite, V said, "Gotta talk to you, my man."

"About?"

"I'm thinking you know."

Shit. The *lesser.* And there was no playing dumb with a brother like V. Lying, however, remained an option. "Fight got tight."

"Bullshit. You can't be pulling moves like that."

Phury thought back to a couple months before, when he'd become his twin for a time. Literally. "I've been worked over on one of their tables, V. I can assure you they are not concerned with warfare etiquette."

"But you got cracked tonight because you were going Ginsu on that slayer's ass. Weren't you."

Jane came back in with supplies. *Thank God.*

When she'd finished packing him up, he got to his feet. "I'm going to head to my room now."

"You want help?" V asked in a hard tone. Like he was sucking back a whole lot of need-to-share.

"No. I know the way."

"Well, since we have to go back anyway, let's make this a field trip. And take it slow."

Which was a damn good idea. His head was killing him.

They were halfway through the tunnel when Phury realized that the doctor wasn't being watched or guarded. But, then, hell, she didn't look as if she wanted to bolt. Matter of fact, she and V were walking side by side.

He wondered if either one of them was aware of how much they seemed like a couple.

When Phury got to the door that led into the big house, he said good-bye without meeting V's eyes and went up the shallow steps that led out of the tunnel and into the mansion's foyer. His bedroom seemed like it was all the way across town instead of just up the grand staircase, and the exhaustion he felt told him he needed to feed. Which was such a bore.

Up in his room he took a shower and stretched out on his majestic bed. He knew he should be calling one of the females he used for blood, but he *so* wasn't interested. Instead of picking up the phone, he closed his eyes and let his arms fall to his sides, his hand landing on the firearms book, the one he'd taught class from tonight. The one with his drawing in it.

His door opened without a knock. Which meant it was Zsadist. With news.

Phury sat up so fast, his brain went fish-tank in his skull, sloshing around, threatening to spill out his ears. He put his hand up to the bandage as pain speared into him. "What happened with Bella?"

Z's eyes were black holes in his scarred face. "What the *fuck* were you thinking!"

"Excuse me?"

"Getting jumped because—" As Phury winced, Z cut the volume down on his boom-box routine and shut the door. Relative silence didn't improve his mood. In a hushed voice, he bit out, "I can't fucking believe you played Jack the Ripper and got cracked—"

"Please tell me how Bella is."

Z pointed his finger right at Phury's chest. "You need to spend a little less time worrying about my *shellan* and a little more worrying about your own sorry ass, feel me?"

Swamped by pain, Phury squeezed his good eye shut. The Brother was, of course, right on the money.

"Shit," Z spat into the quiet. "Just . . . *shit*."

"You're absolutely right." Phury noticed that his hand was clutching the firearms book, and he forced himself to let go of the thing.

As a clicking sound started to go off, Phury glanced up. Z was flicking the top of his RAZR phone over and over again with his thumb. "You could have been killed."

"I wasn't."

"Cold comfort. At least for one of us. What about your eye? V's doc save it?"

"Don't know."

Z walked over to one of the windows. Pushing the heavy velvet drape aside, he stared out across the terrace and the pool. The strain in his ruined face was obvious, his jaw clenched, his brows down low over his eyes. Strange . . . before it had always been Z who was on the edge of oblivion. Now Phury was standing on that thin, slippery lip, the worrier having become the cause for concern.

"I'll be okay," he lied, leaning to the side for his bag of red smoke and his rolling papers. He spun a thick one up fast, lit it, and the false calm came right away, like his body had been trained well. "Just had an off night."

Z laughed, though it was a curse more than anything jolly. "They were right."

"Who?"

"Payback is a bitch." Zsadist took a deep breath. "You get yourself killed out there and I'm—"

"I won't." He inhaled again, not willing to take the vow any further than that. "Now please tell me about Bella."

"She's going on bed rest."

"Oh, God."

"No, it's good." Z rubbed his skull trim. "I mean, she hasn't lost the young yet, and if she keeps quiet she might not."

"She in your room?"

"Yeah, I'm going to go get her something to eat. She's allowed to be up for an hour a day, but I don't want to give her excuses to be on her feet."

"I'm glad she—"

"Fuck, my brother. Is this what it was like for you?"

Phury frowned and tapped the blunt over his ashtray. "I'm sorry?"

"I'm fucked in the head all the time. It's like whatever I'm doing moment to moment is only half-real because of all the crap I'm worried about."

"Bella's—"

"It's not just about her." Z's eyes, now back in yellow because he wasn't as pissed off, drifted across the room. "It's you."

Phury made elaborate work of bringing the blunt to his mouth and inhaling. As he let the smoke out, he searched his mind for words to comfort his twin.

He didn't come up with much.

"Wrath wants us to meet at nightfall," Z said, looking back out the window, as if he knew damn well there would be no meaningful reassurance. "All of us."

"Okay."

After Z left, Phury opened the firearms book and took out the drawing he'd done of Bella. He ran his thumb back and forth over his depiction of her cheek, staring at her with his one working eye. The quiet pressed in on him, constricting his chest.

All things considered, it was possible he'd already fallen off the ledge, possible that he was already sliding down the mountain of his destruction, bumping against boulders and trees, bouncing and breaking limbs, a mortal blow awaiting him.

He stabbed out the blunt. Falling into ruin was a bit like falling in love: Both descents stripped you bare and left you as you were at your core.

And in his limited experience, both endings were equally painful.

As John stared at the *lesser* who had appeared out of nowhere, he couldn't move. He'd never been in a car accident before, but he had a feeling that this was what they were like. You were going along and then suddenly everything you were thinking about before the intersection was put on hold, replaced by a collision that became your one and only priority.

Damn, they really did smell like baby powder.

And luckily this one was not pale haired, so he was a new recruit. Which might be the only reason John and his friends got out of this alive.

Qhuinn and Blay got in front, blocking the way. But then a second *lesser* came out of the shadows, a chess piece moved into position by an unseen hand. He was also dark haired.

God, they were big.

The first one looked at John. "Better run along, son. This is no place for you."

Holy shit, they didn't know he was a pretrans. They thought he was just a human.

"Yeah," Qhuinn said, shoving John's shoulder. "You got your dime bag. Now get out of here, punk."

Except he couldn't leave his—

"I said, get the fuck out of here." Qhuinn gave him a hard push, and John stumbled into a stack of tarpaper rolls big as couches.

Shit, if he ran, he was a coward. But if he stayed he was going to be worse than no help. Hating himself, he took off at a dead run, heading straight for ZeroSum. Like an idiot, he'd left his backpack at Blay's, so he couldn't call home. And it wasn't like he could waste time looking for one of the Brothers on the off chance they might be hunting nearby. There was only one person he could think of who would help them.

At the club's entrance he went right up to the bouncer at the head of the wait line.

Xhex. I need to see Xhex. Get me—

"What the hell are you doing, kid?" the bouncer said.

John mouthed the word *Xhex* over and over again while signing.

"Okay, you are pissing me off." The bouncer loomed over John. "Get the hell out of here or I'm calling your mommy and daddy."

Snickers from the wait line made John more frantic. *Please! I need to see Xhex—*

John heard a distant sound that was either a car peeling out or a scream, and as he wheeled around toward it, the dull weight of Blay's Glock bumped into his thigh.

No phone to text from. No way to communicate.

But he had a six-pack of lead in his back pocket.

John ran back to the lot, dodging around parallel-parked cars, breathing hard, legs flying as fast as they could. His head was hammering at him, the exertion making the pain so bad he went nauseous. He rounded the corner, skidding on loose gravel.

Fuck! Blay was on the ground with a *lesser* sitting on his chest, and the two were fighting for control of what looked like a switchblade. Qhuinn was holding his own against the other slayer, but the pair were too evenly matched for John's taste. Sooner or later one of them was—

Qhuinn took a right hook to the face and spun out, his head twirling on his spine like a top, carrying his body into a pirouette.

In that moment something came into John, came in through the back way, entered sure as if a ghost had stepped into his skin. Old

knowledge, the kind that came with experience he hadn't yet had enough years to gain, carried his hand deep into his back pocket. He palmed the Glock, popped it free, and double-handed it.

One blink had him bringing the weapon level. A second had the muzzle trained on the *lesser* fighting with Blay over the blade. A third had John squeezing the trigger . . . and blowing a barn door in that *lesser's* head. A fourth had him swinging his stance around to the slayer standing over Qhuinn and rearranging the brass knuckles on his fist.

Pop!

John dropped that *lesser* with one shot to the temple, black blood spraying out in a fine cloud. The thing crumpled at the knees and fell face-first onto Qhuinn . . . who was too dazed to do anything other than push the body off him.

John glanced at Blay. The guy was staring up in shock. "Jesus Christ . . . John."

The *lesser* by Qhuinn let out a gurgling breath, like a coffeepot that had just finished brewing.

Metal, John thought. He needed something metal. The knife that Blay had been fighting over was nowhere in sight. Where could he find—

A torn-open box of roofing spikes was by the bucket loader.

John went over, picked one out of the bunch, and approached the *lesser* by Qhuinn. Lifting his hands high, John threw all of his weight and his anger into the slice downward, and in a flash reality shifted like sand: He was holding a dagger, not a length of steel . . . and he was big, bigger than Blay and Qhuinn . . . and he had done this many, many times.

The spike went into the *lesser's* chest, and the flare of light was brighter than John had expected, shooting into his eyes and running throughout his body in a burning wave. But his job was not done. He stepped over Qhuinn, moving across the asphalt without feeling the ground beneath his feet.

Blay watched, motionless, speechless, as John lifted the spike again. This time, as he brought it down, John opened his mouth and yelled without making a sound, a war cry no less powerful for the fact that it was not heard.

In the aftermath of the light burst he became dimly aware of sirens. No doubt some human had called the police when they heard the gunshots.

John let his arm ease to his side, the spike falling from his hand and clattering across the pavement.

I am not a coward. I am a warrior.

The seizure came on him fast and hard, taking him to the ground, pinning him with invisible arms, making him bounce around in his own skin until he blacked out, the roar of oblivion overtaking him.

TWENTY-TWO

hen Jane and V were back in the bedroom, she took a seat in what she was coming to think of as her chair, and V stretched out on the bed. Man, this was going to be a long night—er, day. She was tired and twitchy, not a good combination.

"You need food?" he asked.

"You know what I wish I had?" She yawned. "Hot chocolate."

V picked up the phone, hit three buttons, and waited.

"You're ordering me some?" she said.

"Yeah. As well as— Hey, Fritz. Here's what I need. . . ."

After V hung up, she had to smile at him. "That's quite a spread."

"You haven't eaten since—" He stopped himself, as if he didn't want to bring up the abduction part.

"It's okay," she murmured, feeling sad for no good reason.

No, there was a good reason. She was leaving soon.

"Don't worry, you won't remember me," he said. "So you won't feel anything after you leave."

She flushed. "Ah . . . exactly how do you read minds?"

"It's like catching a radio frequency. It used to happen all the time whether I wanted it to or not."

"Used to?"

"Guess the antennae broke." A bitter expression bled into his face, sharpening his eyes. "I heard from a good source it's going to fix itself, though."

"Why did it stop?"

"Why is your favorite question, isn't it?"

"I'm a scientist."

"I know." The words were spoken on a purr, like she'd just told him she was wearing sexy lingerie. "I love your mind."

Jane felt a rush of pleasure, then got all tangled in herself.

As if he sensed her conflict, he buried the moment with, "I used to see the future, too."

She cleared her throat. "You did? In what way?"

"Dreamscapes, mostly. No time line, just events in random order. I specialized in deaths."

Deaths? "Deaths?"

"Yeah, I know how all my brothers die. Just not when."

"Jesus . . . Christ. That must be—"

"I have other tricks, too." V lifted up his gloved hand. "There's this thing."

"I've wanted to ask about that. It knocked out one of my nurses when you were in my ER. She was taking your glove off, and it was like she'd been struck by lightning."

"I wasn't conscious when it happened, right?"

"You were out cold."

"Then that's probably the only reason she survived. This little legacy from my mother is goddamned deadly." As he clenched up a

fist, his voice became hard, his words clipped into place. "And she's claimed my future as well."

"How so?" When he didn't answer, some instinct had her saying, "Let me guess, an arranged marriage?"

"Marriages. As it were."

Jane winced. Even though his future meant nothing in the larger scheme of her life, for some reason the idea of him becoming someone's husband—a lot of someones' husband—made her stomach roll.

"Um . . . like how many wives?"

"I don't want to talk about it, okay?"

"Okay."

About ten minutes later an old man in an English butler's uniform came in rolling a tray full of food. The spread was right off the Four Seasons' room service menu: There were Belgian waffles with strawberries, croissants, scrambled eggs, hot chocolate, fresh fruit.

The arrival was truly a thing of beauty.

Jane's stomach let out a roar, and before she knew what she was doing, she was tucking into a heaping plate like she hadn't seen food in a week. Halfway through her second helping and her third hot chocolate, she froze with her fork to her mouth. God, what V must think of her. She was making a pig out of—

"I love it," he said.

"You do? You actually approve of me wolfing back food like a frat boy?"

He nodded, his eyes glowing. "I love seeing you eat. Makes me ecstatic. I want you to keep going until you're so full you fall asleep in your chair."

Captivated by his diamond eyes, she said, "And . . . then what would happen?"

"I'd carry you to this bed without waking you and watch over you with a dagger in my hand."

Okay, that caveman stuff shouldn't be so attractive. After all, she could take care of herself. But man, the idea someone would look after her was . . . very nice.

"Finish your food," he said, pointing at her plate. "And have more cocoa from the thermos."

Damn her, but she did what he said. Including pouring the fourth cup of hot chocolate.

As she settled back in the chair with the mug in her hands, she was blissfully replete.

For no particular reason, she said, "I know about the legacy thing. Father was a surgeon."

"Ah. He must be psyched about you, then. You are superb."

Jane dipped her chin down. "I think he would have found my career satisfactory. Especially if I end up teaching at Columbia."

"Would have?"

"He and my mother are dead." She tacked on, because she felt as if she had to, "It was a small plane crash about ten years ago. They were on the way to a medical conference."

"Shit . . . I'm really sorry. You miss them?"

"This is going to sound bad . . . but not really. They were strangers who I had to live with when I wasn't in school. But I've always missed my sister."

"God, she's gone, too?"

"It was a congenital heart defect. Went quick one night. My father always thought that I went into medicine because he inspired me, but I did it because I was mad about Hannah. Still am." She took a sip from the mug. "Anyway, Father always thought medicine was the highest and best use for my life. I can remember him looking at me when I was fifteen and telling me I was lucky I was so smart."

"He knew you could make a difference, then."

"Not his point. He said given my looks, it wasn't as if I would marry particularly well." At V's sharp inhale, she smiled. "Father was a Victorian living in the seventies and eighties. Maybe it was his

English background, who the hell knows. But he thought women should get married and look after a big house."

"That was a shitty thing to say to a young girl."

"He would have called it honest. He believed in honesty. Always said Hannah was the pretty one. Of course, he thought she was flighty." God, why the hell was she talking like this? "Anyway, parents can be a problem."

"Yeah. Get that. So fucking get that."

When they both fell quiet, she had a feeling that he was doing the family-album flip-through in his head, too.

After a while, he nodded to the flat-screen TV on the wall. "You want to watch a movie?"

She twisted around in the chair and started to smile. "God, yes. I can't remember the last time I did that. What have you got?"

"I wired the cable so we have everything." In an offhand kind of way, he nodded to the pillows next to him. "Why don't you sit here? You won't really be able to see from where you are."

Shoot. She wanted to be over next to him. She wanted to be . . . close.

Even as her brain cramped up over the situation, she went to the bed and settled next to him, crossing her arms over her chest and her legs at the ankles. God, she was nervous the way you were when you were on a date. Butterflies. Sweaty palms.

Hello, adrenal glands.

"So what kind of stuff do you like to watch?" she asked as he palmed a remote that had enough buttons on it to launch the space shuttle.

"Today I'm into something boring."

"Really? Why?"

His diamond eyes shifted over to her, the lids so low it was hard to read his stare. "Oh, no reason. You look tired, is all."

On the Other Side, Cormia sat on her cot. Waiting. Again.

She unfolded her hands in her lap. Refolded them. Wished she had a book in her lap to distract her. As she sat in silence, she pondered briefly what it would be like to have a book of her own. Maybe she would put her name in the front so that others would know it was hers. Yes, she would like that. *Cormia.* Or even better, *Cormia's Book.*

She would lend it out if her sisters wanted to borrow it, of course. But she would know, as it found other palms to be held in and other eyes to read its print, that the binding and the pages and the stories in it were hers. And the book would know it as well.

She thought of the Chosen's library, with its forest of stacks and its lovely leathery-sweet smell and its overwhelming luxury of words. Her time there truly was her haven and her joyous reclusion. There were so many stories to know, so many places that her eyes could never hope to behold, and she loved learning. Looked forward to it. Hungered for it.

Usually.

This hour differed. As she sat on her cot and waited, she did not want the teaching that was coming for her: The things she was about to know were not what she wanted to learn.

"Greetings, sister."

Cormia looked up. The Chosen who was holding back the doorway's white veil was a model of selflessness and service, a truly upstanding female. And Layla's expression of calm contentment and inner peace was one Cormia envied.

Which you were not permitted to do. Envy meant you were separate from the whole, that you were an individual, and a petty one at that.

"Greetings." Cormia stood up, her knees loose with dread at where they were going. Though she had often wanted to see what was inside the Primale's temple, now she wished never to set foot in its marble confines.

They both bowed to each other and held the poses. "It is my honor to be of aid."

In a low voice, Cormia replied, "I am . . . I am grateful for your instruction. Lead onward, if you will."

As Layla's head came back to level, her pale green eyes were knowing. "I thought perhaps we would talk here for a bit instead of going to the temple right away."

Cormia swallowed hard. "I would favor that."

"May I take ease, sister?" When Cormia nodded, Layla went over to the cot and sat down, her white robe slitting open to mid thigh. "Join me."

Cormia sat down, the mattress beneath her feeling as hard as stone. She could not breathe, could not move, barely blinked.

"Sister mine, I would seek to allay your fears," Layla said. "Truly, you shall come to enjoy your time with the Primale."

"Indeed." Cormia drew the lapels of her robe closer. "Yet he will visit others, won't he?"

"You will be his priority. As his inaugural mate, you will hold special court with him. For the Primale there is a rare hierarchy within the whole, and you shall be first among all of us."

"But how long until he goes to the others?"

Layla frowned. "It would be up to him, although you may have a say in it. If you please him well, he may stay with only you for a time. It has been known to happen before."

"I could tell him to find others, however?"

Layla's perfect head tilted to the side. "Verily, my sister, you will like what passes between the two of you."

"You know who he is, yes? You know the identity of the Primale?"

"In fact, I have seen him."

"You have?"

"Indeed." As Layla's hand went to her chignon of blond hair, Cormia took the gesture as a sign the female was choosing her words with care. "He is . . . as a warrior should be. Strong. Intelligent."

Cormia narrowed her eyes. "You withhold to soothe my fears. Do you not?"

Before Layla could respond, the Directrix swept the curtain aside. Without a word to Cormia, she went to Layla and whispered something.

Layla stood up, a flush blooming on her cheeks. "I shall go right away." She turned to Cormia, an odd excitement in her eyes. "Sister, I bid you good leave until my return."

As was custom, Cormia rose and bowed, relieved that she had a reprieve from the lesson for whatever reason. "Be well."

The Directrix, however, did not depart with Layla. "I shall take you to the temple and proceed with your instruction."

Cormia wrapped her arms around herself. "Shall I not wait for Layla—"

"Do you question me?" the Directrix said. "Indeed, you do. Perhaps then you shall desire to set the agenda for the lesson as well, knowing as much as you do about the history and significance of the position for which you have been chosen. For truth, I should enjoy learning from you."

"Forgive me, Directrix," Cormia replied in total shame.

"What is there to forgive? As the Primale's first mate, you shall be free to order me about, so mayhap I should acquaint myself with your leadership now. Tell me, would you prefer me to walk steps arrear of you as we go forth unto the temple?"

Tears welled. "Please, no, Directrix."

"Please, no, what?"

"I would follow you," Cormia whispered with bent head. "Not lead."

Ishtar was the perfect choice, V thought. Boring as hell. Long as the year. As visually arresting as a saltshaker.

"This is the worst load of crap I've ever seen," Jane said while yawning again.

God, she had a nice throat.

As V's fangs unsheathed and he imagined pulling a classic Drac-

ula and rearing up over her prone body, he forced himself to look back at Dustin Hoffman and Warren Beatty trudging through the sand. He'd picked the POS in hopes of getting her to knock out—so he could tunnel into her mind and get all over her.

He was jonesing to have her come against his mouth, even if it was only in the ether of a dream.

While he waited for her to be bored into REM sleep, he found himself staring at the desertscape and perversely thinking of winter . . . winter and his transition.

It was but a few weeks after the pretrans fell and died in the river that V went through his change. He had been aware of the differences in his body for quite some time before it hit: He was plagued by headaches. Constantly hungry yet nauseous if he took food. Unable to sleep though exhausted. The only thing that remained alike was his aggression. The camp's demands meant you always had to be prepared to fight, so the sharpening in his temper was not marked by any overt shift in his behavior.

It was in the depths of a cruel early snowstorm that he was born into his male self.

As a result of the plunge in temperature the cave's stone walls were frigid, the floor sufficed to freeze your feet in fur-lined boots, the air so cold the breath from your mouth was a cloud without a sky. As the onslaught prevailed, the soldiers and the kitchen's females slept in great heaps of bodies, not for sex, but for shared warmth.

V knew the change was upon him, for he awoke hot. At first the ease of the heat was a boon, but then his body raged with fever as an agonizing hunger swept through him. He writhed on the ground, hoping for relief, finding none.

After forever, the Bloodletter's voice pierced through the pain. "The females will not feed you."

From amidst his stupor, V opened his eyes.

The Bloodletter knelt down. "Surely you know why."

V swallowed through the fist that was his throat. "I do not."

"They say the cave paintings have possessed you. That your hand has been o'ertaken by the spirits trapped upon the walls. That your eye is no longer your own."

When V did not answer, the Bloodletter said, "You do not deny?"

Through the morass in his head, Vishous tried to calculate the effect of his two conceivable responses. He went with the truth, not for veracity's sake, but for self-preservation. "I . . . deny."

"Do you deny what they say elsewise?"

"What . . . say . . . they?"

"That you killed your comrade at the river with your palm."

'Twas a lie, and the other boys who had been there knew it to be so, as they had seen the pretrans fall of his own fault. The females must be making the assumption on the fact that the death had occurred and V had been in the vicinity. Because why would the other males be desirous of passing along evidence of V's strength?

Or mayhap it was to their benefit? If V had no female who would feed him, he would die. Which was not a bad outcome for the other pretrans.

"What say you?" his father demanded.

As V needed the appearance of strength, he mumbled, "I killed him."

The Bloodletter smiled broadly through his beard. "I suspected. And for your effort I shall bring you a female."

Indeed, one was brought to him and he did feed. The transition was brutal, long and draining, and when it was through, he overflowed his pallet, his arms and legs cooling on the cold cave floor like meat from a fresh kill.

Although his sex had stirred in the aftermath, the female who had been forced to feed him wanted nothing to do with him. She gave him just enough blood to see him into the change; then she left him to his bones snapping and his muscles stretching until they ripped. No one at-

tended to him, and while he suffered he called out in his mind to the mother who had birthed him. He imagined her coming unto him aglow with love and stroking his hair and telling him that all was well. In his pathetic vision, she called him her beloved lewlhen.

Gift.

He would have liked to have been someone's gift. Gifts were valued and cared for and protected. The diary of the warrior Darius had been a gift to V, the giver perhaps not knowing that in leaving it behind he had done a kindness, but still.

Gift.

When V's body had finished with its change, he had slept, then awoken to hunger for meat. His clothes had been torn from him by the transition, so he wrapped himself up in a hide and walked barefoot to the kitchen area. There was little to be had: He gnawed on a thighbone, found some breadcrusts, ate a handful of flour.

He was licking the white residue off his palm when his father said from behind him: "Time to fight."

"What are you thinking about?" Jane asked. "You're all tense."

V jerked back to the present. And for some reason didn't lie. "I'm thinking about my tattoos."

"When did you get them?"

"Almost three centuries ago."

She whistled. "God, you live that long?"

"Longer. Assuming I don't get cracked dead in a fight and you fool humans don't blow up the planet, I'll be breathing for another seven hundred years."

"Wow. Gives a whole new context for AARP, huh." She sat forward. "Turn your head. I want to see the ink on your face."

Rattled from his memories, he did as she asked because he wasn't coherent enough to think why he shouldn't. Still, as her hand came up, he flinched.

She dropped her arm without touching him. "These were done to you, weren't they. Probably at the same time as the castration, right?"

V recoiled on the inside, but didn't move away from her. He was wholly uncomfortable with the female-sympathy routine, but the thing was, Jane's voice was factual. Direct. So he could respond factually and directly.

"Yeah. At the same time."

"I'm going to guess they're warnings, as you have them on your hand, your temple, your thighs and your groin. I'm guessing they're about the energy in your palm, the second sight, and the procreation issue."

Like he should be surprised at her hyperdeduction? "True."

Her voice grew low. "That's why you panicked when I told you I'd restrain you. Back at the hospital in the SICU. They tied you down, didn't they."

He cleared his throat.

"Didn't they, V?"

He picked up the clicker for the TV. "You want to watch something else?"

As he started flipping through movie channels, there was a whole lot of silence.

"I threw up at my sister's funeral."

V's thumb paused on the remote, stopping on *The Silence of the Lambs*. He looked over at her. "You did?"

"Most embarrassing, shameful moment of my life. And not just because of when it happened. I did it all over my father."

As Clarice Starling sat on a hard chair in front of Lechter's cell, V craved information on Jane. He wanted to know the whole course of her life from birth to present, and he wanted to know it all now.

"Tell me what happened."

Jane cleared her throat as if bracing herself, and he couldn't ignore the parallel to the movie, with himself as the caged monster and Jane

as the source of good, giving away bits and pieces of herself for the beast's consumption.

But he needed to know like he needed blood to survive. "What happened, Jane?"

"Well, see . . . my father was a big believer in oatmeal."

"Oatmeal?" When she didn't go on, he said, "Tell me."

Jane crossed her arms over her chest and stared at her feet. Then her eyes met his. "Just so we're clear, the reason I'm bringing this up is so you'll talk about what happened to you. Tit for tat. It's like sharing scars. You know, like the ones from summer camp when you fell off the bunk bed. Or, like, when you cut yourself on the metal edge of a Reynolds Wrap box or when you hit yourself on the head with a—" She frowned. "Okay . . . maybe none of that is a good analogy, considering the way you heal, but work with me."

V had to smile. "I get the point."

"I figure fair is fair, though. So if I spill, you do. We agree?"

"Shit . . ." Except he had to know about her. "Guess we do."

"Okay, so my father and the oatmeal. He—"

"Jane?"

"What?"

"I like you. A lot. Had to get that in."

She blinked a couple of times. Then she cleared her throat again. *Man, that blush looked good on her.*

"You're talking about the oatmeal."

"Right . . . so . . . as I said, my father was a great believer in oatmeal. He made us all eat it in the morning, even in the summer. My mother and my sister and I had to choke that shit down for him, and he expected you to finish what was in your bowl. He used to watch us eat, like we were playing golf and in danger of getting our swing wrong. I swear, he measured the angle of my spine and my hold on the spoon. At dinner he used to—" She paused. "I'm rambling."

"And I could listen to you talk for hours, so don't focus on my account."

"Yeah, well . . . focus is important."

"Only if you're a microscope."

She smiled a little. "Back to the oatmeal. My sister died on my birthday, on a Friday night. The funeral was put together quickly, because my father was leaving to present a paper in Canada the following Wednesday. I found out later he'd scheduled that presentation the day Hannah was found dead in her bed, no doubt because he wanted to move things along. Anyway . . . day of the funeral, I get up and I feel horrible. Just wretched. Nothing but nausea. Hannah . . . Hannah was the only real thing in a house full of nice and pretty. She was messy and loud and happy and . . . I loved her so much, and I couldn't bear that we were putting her in the ground. She would have hated being caged like that. Yeah . . . anyway, for the funeral, my mother went out and got me one of those coatdress getups in black. Trouble was, the morning of the funeral, when I went to put it on, it didn't fit. It was too small, and I felt like I couldn't breathe."

"Naturally made the stomach worse."

"Yup, but I got down to the breakfast table with only the dry heaves. Jesus, I can still remember what the two of them looked like sitting on either end, facing each other without making eye contact. Mother was like a china doll with quality-control problems—her makeup was on, her hair was in place, but everything was a little off. Her lipstick was the wrong color, she had no blush on, her chignon was showing bobby pins. Father was reading the newspaper, and the sound of those flapping pages was loud as a shotgun going off. Neither of them said a word to me.

"So I sat in my chair and couldn't stop looking at the empty seat across the table. Bowl of oatmeal comes in for a landing. Marie, our maid, laid her hand on my shoulder as she put it in front of me, and

for a moment I almost broke down. But then my father snapped that paper of his like I was a puppy who'd shit on the rug, and I picked up my spoon and started eating. I forced that oatmeal down until I gagged from it. And then we went to the funeral."

V wanted to touch her, and he nearly reached out for her hand. Instead he asked, "How old were you?"

"Thirteen. Anyway, we get to the church and it's packed, because everyone in Greenwich knew my parents. My mother was being desperately gracious, and my father was all frozen stoic, so that was pretty much business as usual. I remember . . . yeah, I was thinking the two of them were just as they always were except for my mother's piss-poor makeup job and the fact that my father kept playing with the change in his pocket. Which was so out of character. He hated ambient noise of any kind, and I was surprised that the restless chiming of coins didn't bother him. I guess it was okay because he was in control of the sound. I mean, he could stop at any time if he wanted to."

As she paused and stared across the room, V wanted to try and get into her mind and see exactly what she was reliving. He didn't— and not because he wasn't sure it would work. The revelations she chose to share with him freely were more precious than anything he could take from her.

"Front row," she murmured. "At the church, we were seated in the front row, right in front of the altar. Closed casket, thank God, though I imagine Hannah was perfectly beautiful. She had strawberry-blond hair, my sister did. The luxurious, wavy kind that came on Barbies. Mine was stick-straight. Anyway . . ."

V had a passing thought that she used the word *anyway* like an eraser on a crowded chalkboard. She said it whenever she needed to clear off the things she'd just shared to make room for more.

"Yeah, front row. Service started. Lots of organ music . . . and the thing was, those pipes vibrated up through the floor. Have you ever been in a church? Probably not . . . Anyway, you can feel the bass of the music when it really gets rolling. Naturally, the service was in a big formal place with an organ that had more pipes than Caldwell's city sewer system. God, when that thing played, it was like you were on an airplane that was taking off."

As she stopped and took a deep breath, V knew the story was wearing her down, taking her to a place she didn't go willingly or often.

Her voice was husky as she continued. "So . . . we're halfway through the service and my dress is too tight and my stomach is killing me and that fucking oatmeal of my father's has sprouted vile roots and is grafting itself to the inside of my gut. And the priest comes up to the lectern to do the eulogy. He was straight out of central casting, white haired, deep voiced, dressed in ivory-and-gold robes. He was the Episcopal bishop for all of Connecticut, I think. Anyway . . . he gets to talking about the state of grace that awaits in heaven, and all this horseshit about God and Jesus and the Church. It seemed more like an ad for Christianity than anything to do with Hannah.

"I'm sitting there, not really tracking, when I look over and see my mother's hands. They were clasped together in her lap, totally white-knuckled . . . like she was on a roller-coaster ride, even though she wasn't moving. I turned to my left and looked at my father's. His palms were on his knees and all of his fingers were digging in except for the pinkie on the right, which was out for a jog. The thing was tapping against the fine wool of his slacks with a Parkinsonian tremble."

V knew where this was going. "And yours," he said softly. "What about yours?"

Jane exhaled on a little sob. "Mine . . . mine were utterly still, utterly relaxed. I felt nothing but that oatmeal in my stomach. Oh . . . God, my sister was dead and my parents, who were about as emotionless as you could get, were upset. Me? Nothing. I remember thinking Hannah would have cried if I had been lying on satin in a coffin. She would have cried for me. Me? I couldn't.

"So when the priest finished his infomercial on how great God was, and how Hannah was all lucky to be with Him and yadda, yadda, yadda, the organ lit off. The vibration of those bass pipes rose up from the floor through my seat and hit just the right frequency. Or the wrong one, I suppose. I threw up that oatmeal all over my father."

Fuck it, V thought. He reached out and took her hand. "God-damn . . ."

"Yeah. So my mother stands up to take me away, but my father tells her to stay put. He walked me over to one of the church ladies, told her to take me to the bathroom, then went into the men's room. I got left alone in a stall for about ten minutes, then the church lady came back, put me in her car, and drove me home. I missed the burial." She sucked in a breath. "When my parents came home, neither of them checked on me. I kept expecting one of them to come in. I could hear them moving around the house until it was all silent. Eventually, I went down, got something out of the fridge, and ate standing up at the counter, because we weren't allowed to take food upstairs. I didn't cry then either, even though it was a windy night, which always scared me, and the house was mostly dark and I felt like I'd ruined my sister's funeral."

"I'm sure you were in shock."

"Yeah. Funny . . . I was worried she'd be cold. You know, cold autumn night. Cold ground." Jane batted her hand around. "Anyway, next morning my father left before I got up, and he didn't come home for two weeks. He kept calling and telling my mother he was going to consult on another complex case somewhere else in the country. Meanwhile, Mother woke up every day and got dressed and took me to school, but she wasn't really there. She became like a newspaper. The only things she talked about were the weather and what had gone wrong with the house or the staff while I was at school. My father came back eventually, and you know how I knew his arrival was imminent? Hannah's room. Every night I went into

Hannah's room and sat with her stuff. The thing I couldn't get was how her clothes and her books and her drawings were still there, but she wasn't. It just didn't compute. Her room was like a car without an engine, everything where it should be, except all it was was potential. None of it was going to get used again.

"The night before Father returned, I opened that bedroom door and . . . everything was gone. Mother had had it all cleaned out and the bedspread changed and the draperies switched. It went from being Hannah's room to a guest room. That was how I knew my father was coming home."

V rubbed his thumb over the back of her hand. "Jesus . . . Jane . . ."

"So that's my revelation. I threw up oatmeal instead of crying."

He could tell she was jumpy and wishing she'd throttled back, and he knew how she felt, because he did the same thing on those few occasions he got personal. He kept up with the petting of her hand until she looked over at him. As silence stretched out, he knew what she was waiting for.

"Yeah," he murmured. "They held me down."

"And you were conscious through the whole thing, weren't you."

His voice got reedy. "Yeah."

She touched his face, running her palm down his now bearded cheek. "Did you kill them for it?"

He lifted up his gloved palm. "This took over. Glow flashed throughout my body. They all had their hands on me, so they went down like stones."

"Good."

Shit . . . He so totally loved her. "You would have made a fine warrior, you know that?"

"I am one. Death is my enemy."

"Yeah, it is, isn't it." God, it made such sense that he'd bonded with her. She was a fighter . . . like him. "Your scalpel's your dagger."

"Yup."

They stayed like that, linked by their hands and their eyes. Until, without warning, she brushed his lower lip with her thumb.

As he inhaled with a hiss, she whispered, "I don't have to be asleep, you know."

TWENTY-THREE

When John regained consciousness, he had a raging fever: His skin was made of flames, his blood a lava flow, his bone marrow the furnace that drove it all. Desperate to get cool, he rolled over and went to pull off his clothes, except he had no shirt on, no pants. He was naked as he writhed.

"Take my wrist." The female voice came from above and to the left, and he tilted his head toward the sound, sweat running like tears down his face. Or maybe he was crying?

Hurts, he mouthed.

"Your Grace, take my wrist. The scoring is done."

Something pressed against his lips and wet them with wine, rich wine. Instinct rose like a beast. The fire was, in fact, a hunger, and what was being offered was the sustenance he needed. He grabbed at what turned out to be an arm, opened wide, and drank in hard sucks.

God... The taste was of the earth and of life, heady and potent and addicting. The world began to twirl, a dancer *en pointe*, a carni-

val ride, a whirlpool without end. In the midst of the spinning he
swallowed with desperation, knowing without being told that what
was going down his throat was the only antidote to dying.

The feeding lasted for days and nights, whole weeks passing. Or
was it the blink of an eye? He was surprised that there was an end to
it after all—wouldn't have been shocked to learn that the rest of his
life would be passed at the wrist that had been given to him.

He loosened his sucking hold and opened his eyes.

Layla, the blond Chosen, was sitting beside him on his bed, her
robe white as sunlight to his tender eyes. Over in the corner Wrath
was standing with Beth, the two of them wrapped in each other's
arms, looking concerned.

The change. *His* change.

He lifted up his hands and signed like a drunk, *Is this it?*

Wrath shook his head. "Not yet, it's coming."

Coming?

"Take some deep breaths," the king said. "You're going to need
them. And listen, we're right here, okay? We're not going to leave you."

Shit, that was right. The transition was a two-parter, wasn't it.
And the hard part was yet to come. To combat his fear, he reminded
himself that Blay had made it through. So had Qhuinn.

So had all the Brothers.

So had his sister.

He met Beth's dark blue eyes, and from out of nowhere a hazy
vision came to him. He was in a club . . . in a Goth club with . . .
Tohrment. No, he was watching Tohr with someone, a big male, a
Brother-sized male, whose face John could not see.

John frowned, wondering why in the world his brain would
cough up something like that. And then he heard the stranger speak:

She's my daughter, Tohr.

She's a half-breed, D. And you know how he feels about humans.
Tohrment shook his head. *My great-great-grandmother was one, and
you don't see me yakking that up around him.*

They were talking about Beth, weren't they . . . which meant the stranger with the blurred features was John's father. *Darius.*

John strained to get the vision in focus for a single look into his dad's face, praying for clarity as Darius lifted his hand to catch a waitress's eye before pointing at his empty bottle of beer and Tohrment's nearly dry glass.

I'm not going to let another of my children die, he said. *Not if there's a possibility I can save her. And anyway, there's no telling whether she'll even go through the change. She could end up living a happy life, never knowing about my side. It's happened before.*

Had their father even known about him? John wondered. Probably not, given that John had been born in a bus stop bathroom and left for dead: A male who cared so much for his daughter would have cared for a son as well.

The vision started to fade, and the harder John tried to hold on to it, the faster it disintegrated. Just before it disappeared he looked at Tohr's face. The military haircut and the strong bones and the clearsighted eyes made John's chest ache. So too did the way Tohr stared across the table at the male sitting with him. They were close. Best friends, it seemed.

How wonderful it would have been, John thought, to have had both of them in his life—

The pain that hit was cosmic, a big bang that splintered John apart and sent his molecules spinning from his core. All thought, all reasoning was lost, and he had no choice but to submit. Opening his mouth, he screamed without making a sound.

Jane could not believe she was looking into the face of a vampire and praying that he'd have sex with her. And yet at the same time she'd never been so sure of something in her life.

"Close your eyes," V said.

"Because you're going to kiss me for real?" *Please, God, let that be the case.*

V reached up and ran his ungloved hand down her face. His palm was warm and broad and smelled of dark spice. "Sleep, Jane."

She frowned. "I want to do it awake."

"No."

"Why?"

"Safer that way."

"Wait, you mean you could get me pregnant?" And what about STDs?

"It's been known to happen with humans on occasion, but you aren't ovulating. I'd smell it. As for transmittable diseases, I don't carry any, and you couldn't give me any, but none of that's the point. It's safer for me to take you when you're not awake."

"Says who?"

He shifted on the bed, impatient, restless. Sexed. "Sleep's the only way it can happen."

Man, just her luck he was determined to be a gentleman. The bastard.

Jane pulled back and got to her feet. "Fantasies don't interest me. If you don't want us to be together for real, then let's not go there at all."

He pulled part of the duvet over his hips, covering an erection that was straining against his flannels. "I don't want to hurt you."

She shot him a glare that was part sexual frustration, part Gertrude Stein. "I'm tougher than I look. And to be honest, the whole male-driven, I'm-looking-out-for-your-best-interests bullshit gives me the scratch."

She turned away with her chin up, but then realized there was nowhere really to go. *Way to make an exit.*

Confronted with an utter lack of alternatives, she went into the bathroom. As she paced between the shower and the sink, she felt like a horse in a stall—

With no warning at all she was tackled from behind, pushed face-first into the wall and held in place by a rock-hard body twice the size of her own. Her gasp was first one of shock, then one of sex as she felt V grind into her ass.

"I tried to tell you no," he growled as his hand buried itself in her hair and locked on, pulling her head back. As she cried out she ran wet between her legs. "Tried to be nice."

"Oh . . . *God*—"

"Praying's not going to help. Too late for that, Jane." There was regret in his voice—as well as erotic inevitability. "I gave you a chance to have it on your terms. Now we'll do this on mine."

She wanted this. She wanted him. "Please—"

"Shh." He cranked her head to the side with a twist of his wrist, exposing her throat. "When I want you to beg, I'll tell you." His tongue was warm and wet as it rode up her neck. "Now ask me what I'm going to do to you."

She opened her mouth, but could only pant.

He tightened the hold on her hair. "*Ask me.* Say, 'What are you going to do to me?'"

She swallowed. "What . . . what are you going to do to me?"

He wheeled her to one side, all the while keeping his hips tight to her ass. "You see that sink, Jane?"

"Yes . . ." Holy shit, she was going to orgasm—

"I'm going to bend you over that sink and make you hold on to the sides. Then I'm going to pull your pants off."

Oh, Jesus . . .

"Ask me what's next, Jane." He licked up her throat again, then clamped what she knew was a fang onto her earlobe. There was a delicious lick of pain, followed by another rush of heat between her legs.

"What's . . . next?" she breathed.

"I'm going to get on my knees." His head went down and he nipped her collarbone. "Say to me now, 'And then what, V?'"

She nearly sobbed, so aroused her legs started to fail her. "And then what?"

He tugged on her hair. "You forgot the last part."

What was the last part—what was the last . . . "V."

"No, you start over. From the beginning." He pushed his arousal into her, a hard ridge that clearly wanted in her *now*. "Start over, and do it right this time."

From out of nowhere an orgasm came bearing down on her, the momentum carried forward by the rasp of his voice in her—

"Oh, no, you don't." He backed off from her body. "You don't come now. When I say you can, you will. Not before."

Disoriented and aching, she sagged as the need to release receded.

"Now say the words I want to hear."

What were they? "And then what . . . V?"

"I'm going to get on my knees, run my hands up the backs of your thighs, and spread you open for my tongue."

That orgasm rushed back at her, making her legs tremble.

"No," he said in a growl. "Not now. And only when I say."

He maneuvered her to the sink and did exactly what he'd told her he would. He bent her over, planted her hands on either side of the basin, and commanded, "Hold on."

She tightened her hands up good and hard.

He used both his palms on her, running them up under her shirt, cupping her breasts. Then they were down over her stomach and around to her hips.

He yanked her pants down with one sharp pull. "Oh . . . *fuck*. This is what I want." His leather-clad hand gripped her ass and massaged it. "Lift this leg."

She did, and her yoga sweats disappeared off her foot. Her thighs were pushed apart and . . . yes, his hands, one gloved, one not, coasted upward. Her core was running hot and needy as she felt herself bared to him.

"Jane . . ." he whispered reverently.

There was no prelude, no easing into what he did to her. It was his mouth. Her core. Two sets of lips meeting. His fingers dug into her cheeks and kept her in place as he went to work, and she totally lost track of what was his tongue or his goateed chin or his mouth. She could feel herself being penetrated between lapping drags, hear the sounds of flesh on flesh, knew the mastery he had over her.

"Come for me," he demanded against her core. "Right now."

The orgasm arrived in a devastating blast that had her bucking against the sink until one of her hands slipped off. She was saved from falling only because V's arm shot out and gave her something to grab onto.

His mouth released her, and he kissed both her cheeks, then slid his palm up her spine as she drooped onto her arms. "I'm going to come inside you now."

The sound of his pajamas being wrenched down was louder than her breath, and the first brush of his erection against the top of her hips nearly made her lose it all over again.

"I want this," he said in a guttural voice. "God . . . I want this."

He entered in a single hard thrust that brought his hips right to her backside, and though she was the one absorbing the tremendous girth of him, he was the one who cried out. With no pause whatsoever, he started to pump in her, leveraging her at the hips, moving her forward and back to meet his thrusts. With her mouth open, her eyes open, her ears eating up the delicious sounds of the sex, she braced herself against the sink and another orgasm rolled her over. As she came again, her hair was flopping into her face, her head bobbing, their bodies smacking against each other.

It was like nothing she'd ever known. It was sex to the millionth power.

And then she felt his gloved palm grip her shoulder. As he pulled her upright, he kept riding her hard, in and out, in and out. His hand moved up her throat, locked onto her chin, and tilted her head back.

"Mine," he growled, pounding into her.

And then he bit her.

TWENTY-FOUR

When John woke up, the first thought that went through his mind was that he wanted a hot-fudge sundae with bacon bits on top. Which was just nasty, really.

Except, damn . . . chocolate and bacon would be heaven right about now.

He opened his eyes and was relieved to be staring at the familiar ceiling of the room he slept in, but he was confused as to what had happened. It was something traumatic. Something momentous. But what?

He lifted his hand up to rub his eyes . . . and stopped breathing. The thing that was attached to his arm was *huge*. A giant's palm.

He raised his head and looked down his body or . . . someone's body. Had he been a head donor sometime during the day? 'Cause sure as hell his brain hadn't been plugged into the likes of this before.

The transition.

"How you feel, John?"

He glanced toward Wrath's voice. The king and Beth were by the bed, looking utterly exhausted.

He had to concentrate to make his hands form the words, *Did I make it through?*

"Yeah. Yeah, son, you did." Wrath cleared his throat, and Beth stroked his tattooed forearm as if she knew he was struggling with emotion. "Congratulations."

John blinked quick, his chest constricting. *Am I still . . . me?*

"Yes. Always."

"Shall I go?" a female voice said.

John turned his head. Layla was standing in a dim corner, her perfectly beautiful face and her perfectly beautiful body in the shadows.

Instant. Hard-on.

Like someone injected steel into his cock.

He fumbled to make sure he was covered up, and thanked God when there was a blanket already over him. As he settled back on the pillow, Wrath was talking, but John's sole focus was the throb between his legs . . . and the female across the room.

"It would be my pleasure to stay," Layla said with a deep bow.

Staying was good, John thought. Her staying was . . .

Wait, the *hell* it was good. He wasn't going to have sex with her, for God's sake.

She stepped forward, into the pool of illumination thrown by the lamp on the bedside table. Her skin was white as moonlight, smooth as a satin sheet. It would be soft, too . . . under his hands, under his mouth . . . under his body. Abruptly John's upper jaw tingled on both sides, right in front, then something protruded into his mouth. A quick stroke of his tongue and he felt the sharp points of his fangs.

Sex roared through his body until he had to look away from her.

Wrath chuckled a little, as if he knew what John was all about. "We'll leave you two. John, we're right down the hall if you need anything."

Beth leaned down and barely brushed his hand with hers, as if she knew exactly how sensitive his skin was. "I'm so proud of you."

As their eyes met, what came to him was, *And I of you.*

Which made absolutely no sense. So he signed in a sloppy way, *Thank you,* instead.

They were gone a moment later, the door shutting him and Layla in together. Oh, this was not good. He felt he was on a bucking bronco, for all the control he had over his body.

As it wasn't safe to look at the Chosen, he glanced over to the bathroom. Through the jambs, he saw the marble shower and got a serious case of the joneses.

"Would you care to wash, Your Grace?" Layla said. "Shall I run the water for you?"

He nodded to get her busy with something while he tried to figure out what to do with himself.

Take her. Fuck her. Have her twelve different ways.

Okay, yeah, that was not what he should be doing.

The shower came on and Layla came back, and before he knew what was doing, the blanket came off his body. His hands shot up to cover himself, but her eyes got to his erection first.

"May I help you into the bath?" Her voice was husky, and she stared at his hips as if she approved.

Which inflated that huge weight under his palms even more.

"Your Grace?"

Just how was he supposed to sign in this condition?

Whatever. She wouldn't understand him anyway.

John shook his head, then sat up, keeping one hand on himself and planting the other on the mattress for stability. Shit, he felt like a table whose screws had all been loosened, his constituent parts not fitting together well anymore. And the trip into the bathroom seemed like an obstacle course, even though there was nothing in his way.

At least he wasn't solely focused on Layla anymore.

Keeping himself cupped, he stood and wobbled into the bathroom, trying not to think about how he was mooning Layla. While he went along, images of newborn foals played through his head, particularly the ones where their spindly legs bent like wires as they struggled to keep off the ground. He so got that. It seemed like at any moment his knees were going to take a vacation and he was going to yard-sale like an idiot.

Right. He was in the bathroom. *Good job.*

Now if he could just keep from hitting the bald marble. Although, God, getting clean would be worth the contusions. Except even the shower he wanted so badly was trouble. Stepping under the warm, gentle spray was like getting lashed with a whip, and he jumped back—only to catch Layla disrobing out of the corner of his eye.

Holy Christ . . . She was beautiful.

As she joined him he was speechless, and not because he had no voice box. Her breasts were full, the rosy nipples tight in the midst of their lush weight. Her waist looked small enough for him to circle it with his hands. Her hips were a perfect balance to her narrow shoulders. And her sex . . . her sex was bare to his eyes, the skin smooth and hairless, the little slit made up of two folds he was desperate to part.

He clamped both of his hands to himself, as if his cock were liable to leap right off his pelvic girdle.

"May I wash you, Your Grace?" she said as steam swirled between them like fine cloth in a soft breeze.

The arousal behind his hands jerked.

"Your Grace?"

His head nodded. His body throbbed. He thought of Qhuinn talking about what he'd done with the female he'd had. *Oh, Jesus* . . . And now it was happening to John.

She picked up the soap and massaged it between her palms, rolling the bar around and around, suds foaming up white and dripping onto the tile. He imagined his cock in between her hands and had to breathe through his mouth.

Look at her breasts sway, he thought as he licked his lips. He wondered if she'd let him kiss her there. What would she taste like? Would she let him go between her—

His cock jumped, and he let out a plaintive moan.

Layla put the soap back in the little dish on the marble wall. "I'll be gentle, as you are sensitive now."

He swallowed hard and prayed he didn't lose control as her frothy hands came toward him and settled on his shoulders. Unfortunately the anticipation was far more enjoyable than the reality. Her light touch was like sandpaper on a sunburn . . . and yet he craved the contact. Craved her.

With the smell of French-milled soap wafting up in the moist, hot air, her palms traveled down his arms, then back up and over his now tremendous chest. Suds ran past his belly and onto his hand, threading between his fingers before dripping off his sex in soft clumps.

He stared into her face as she lingered on his chest, finding it beyond erotic that her pale green eyes roamed over his new, big body.

She was hungry, he thought. Hungry for what he was holding in his hands. Hungry for what he wanted to give her.

She took the soap out of the dish again and knelt before him, knees on the marble. Her hair was still up in its chignon, and he wanted to take it down, wanted to see what it looked like wet and plastered to her breasts.

As she put her hands on his lower leg and started north, her eyes lifted up. In a flash he saw her giving him head, his erection stretching her mouth wide, her cheeks sucking in and out as she worked him.

John moaned and swayed, bumping his shoulder.

"Drop your arms, Your Grace."

Even though he was terrified of what was going to happen next, he wanted to obey her. Except what if he made a fool out of himself? What if he came all over her face because he couldn't hold back? What if—

"Your Grace, drop your arms."

He slowly let his hands fall away from himself, and his arousal jutted straight out of his hips, not so much defying gravity as being totally outside of its reach.

Oh, Jesus. Oh, Jesus . . . Her hand was lifting up toward—

The instant she touched his cock, the erection deflated: From out of nowhere he saw himself in a grungy stairwell. Held at gunpoint. Violated while he cried silently.

John jerked away from her hold and stumbled out of the shower, his wet feet and his loose knees making him slip on the floor. To keep from falling over, he ass-planted it on the toilet.

Not dignified. Not manly. How fucking typical. He was finally in a big body, but he was no more a male than when he'd been in a little one.

The water shut off and he heard Layla covering herself with a towel. Her voice quavered. "Would you like me to go?"

He nodded, too ashamed to even look at her.

When he glanced up much later, he was alone in the bathroom. Alone and cold, the heat of the shower lost, all that glorious steam gone as if it had never been.

His first time with a female . . . and he'd lost his erection. God, he wanted to throw up.

V broke Jane's skin with his fangs, penetrating her throat, tapping into her vein, latching on with his lips. As she was human, the rush of power at the drinking came not from the composition of her blood, but the fact that it was her. Her taste was what he was after. Her taste . . . and his consumption of a piece of her.

When she cried out, he knew it wasn't from pain. Her body was lush with her arousal, and that scent got even stronger as he took what he wanted from her, took her sex with his cock, took her blood with his mouth.

"Come with me," he said hoarsely, releasing her throat and letting her prop herself up against the sink again. *"Come . . . with . . . me."*

"Oh, *God . . .*"

V locked into her hips as he started to orgasm, and she went over the edge with him, her body sucking on his erection just as he had worked at her neck. The exchange felt fair and satisfying; she was now in him and he was in her. It was right. It was good.

Mine.

After it was over, they were both breathing hard.

"Are you all right?" he asked on a gasp, very aware that the question had never before come out of his mouth following sex.

When she didn't reply, he eased back from her a little. On her pale skin he could see the marks he'd left on her, red blushes from his rough handling. Nearly everyone he'd ever fucked had ended up with them because he liked it rough, needed it rough. And he'd never been bothered by what he'd left behind on other people's bodies.

The marks bothered him now. Bothered him even more as he wiped his hand across his mouth and came away with a smudge of her blood.

Oh, Jesus . . . He'd used her too hard. It had been way too hard. "Jane, I'm so—"

"Amazing." She shook her head, her cap of blond hair swinging at her cheeks. "That was . . . amazing."

"Are you sure I didn't—"

"Just amazing. Although I'm afraid to let go of this sink because I'll fall over."

Relief went to his head, a drunken buzz. "I didn't want to hurt you."

"You overwhelmed me . . . but in the way that if I had a good girlfriend I would call her up and be like, 'Oh, my God I just had the sex of my life.'"

"Good. That's . . . good." He so didn't want to leave her core, especially if she was talking like that. But he moved his hips back and slipped his erection free so she had a break.

From the back she was exquisite. Temple-pounding beautiful. Totally takeable. His arousal beat like a heart as he pulled his pajama bottoms up and stuffed himself into the flannel.

V straightened Jane slowly and looked at her face as it came up in the mirror. Her eyes were glassy, her mouth open, her cheeks flushed. On her neck his bite mark was just where he wanted it: right where everyone could see.

He turned her around to face him and ran his gloved forefinger up her throat, catching the thin trail of blood from the punctures. He licked the black leather clean, savoring the taste of her, wanting more.

"I'm going to seal this closed, okay?"

She nodded, and he dipped his head. As he delicately ran his tongue over the holes, he closed his eyes and got lost nuzzling her. Next time he wanted to go between her legs and tap into the vein that ran down the juncture of her hips, tap into it so he could alternate between sucking at her blood and licking at her sex.

He leaned to the side and turned the shower on, then stripped off the button-down shirt she wore. Her breasts were covered in white lace, the pink tips visible through the lovely pattern. Bending down, he suckled one of her nipples through the fine weave and was rewarded with her hand easing into his hair and a moan bubbling up her throat.

He growled and slipped his palm between her legs. What he'd left behind was on the inside of her thighs, and though it made him a crass bastard, he wanted it to stay there. He wanted to leave that stuff where it was and put more inside of her.

Ah, yes, the instincts of the bonded male. He wanted her to wear him like she did her own skin: all over.

He took her bra off her and eased her into the shower, holding her by the shoulders, getting her under the spray. He stepped in, his pajama bottoms getting wet, his feet feeling the smooth marble floor. Sweeping his hands over her hair and taking the short blond waves back from her face, he looked into her eyes.

Mine.

"I haven't kissed you yet," he said.

She arched against him and used his chest for balance, just as he wanted her to. "Not on the mouth, no."

"May I?"

"Please."

Shit, he was nervous as he looked at her lips. Which was so strange. He'd had so much sex over the course of his life, all different kinds and combinations, but the prospect of kissing her properly wiped all of that away: He was the virgin he'd never been, clueless and weak-kneed.

"So are you going to?" she asked as he stalled out.

Oh . . . shit.

With a smile like the Mona Lisa's, she put her hands to his face. "Come here."

She pulled him down to her, tilted his head, and brushed her lips against his. Vishous's body shuddered. He had felt power before—his own in his muscles, his godforsaken mother's in his destiny, his king's in his life, his brothers' in his job—but he'd never let any of it overcome him.

Jane overcame him now. Held total sway as she cradled his face in her palms.

He gathered her close and pressed his lips tighter on hers, the communion a sweetness he never would have believed he'd want, much less revere. When they broke apart, he soaped up her sleek curves and rinsed her off. Shampooed her hair. Cleaned between her legs.

Handling her with care was like breathing . . . an automatic function of his body and brain that he didn't have to think about.

He shut off the water, toweled her dry, then picked her up and carried her back to the bed. She sprawled out on his black duvet, arms over her head, legs slightly parted, nothing but flushed female skin and muscle.

She stared at him from underneath lowered lids. "Your pajamas are wet."

"Yeah."

"You're hard."

"I am."

She arched on the bed, the undulation riding up her torso from her hips to her breasts. "You going to do anything about it?"

He bared his fangs and hissed. "If you'll let me."

She moved one of her legs to the side, and his corneas nearly started bleeding. She was glistening at her core, and not from the shower.

"Does this look like a no to you?" she said.

He ripped off his bottoms and was on her in a heartbeat, kissing her deep and long, lifting his hips, positioning himself, sinking in. She was so much better like this, in reality, not a dream state. As she came for him once, twice . . . more . . . his heart broke.

For the first time he was having sex with someone he loved.

He felt a momentary blind panic at his exposure. How the fuck had this happened?

But, then, this was his last—well, only—shot at the love thing, wasn't it. And she wasn't going to remember a thing, so it was safe: Her heart wasn't going to be broken at the end.

Plus . . . well, her lack of memory made it safe for him, too, didn't it. Kind of like that night he and Wrath had gotten shit-faced and V had talked about his mother.

The less people knew about him, the better.

Except damn, why the hell did the thought of cleaning out Jane's mind make his chest hurt?

God, she was going so soon.

TWENTY-FIVE

On the Other Side, Cormia stepped out of the Primale's temple and waited as the Directrix shut the enormous gold doors. The temple was on top of a raised knoll, a gilded crown on the head of a small hill, and from here the whole of the Chosen's compound was visible: the white buildings and the temples, the amphitheater, the covered walkways. The stretches between landmarks were carpeted with cropped white grass that never grew, never changed, and as always, the vista offered little in the way of horizon, just a diffused blurring of the distant white forest boundary. The only color to the composition was the pale blue of the sky, and even that faded at the edges.

"Thus ends your lesson," the Directrix said as she divested her neck of her graceful chain of keys and locked the doors. "In accordance with tradition you shall present yourself for the first of the cleansing rituals when we come for you. Until then you shall ponder the grace you have been given and the service you will provide for the benefit of us all."

The words were spoken in the same hard tone the Directrix had used to describe what the Primale would do to Cormia's body. Over and over again. Anytime he wished.

The Directrix's eyes held a calculating light as she put her necklace back on, a chiming sound rising up as the keys settled between her breasts. "Fare thee well, sister."

As the Directrix walked down off the hill, her white robe was indistinguishable from both ground and buildings, another splash of white differentiated solely because it was in motion.

Cormia put her hands to her face. The Directrix had told her—no, vowed to her—that what would transpire beneath the Primale would be painful, and Cormia believed it. The graphic details had been shocking, and she feared there was no way she could get through the mating ceremony without breaking down—to the disgrace of the whole of the Chosen. As the representative of them all, Cormia had to perform as expected and with dignity, or she would tarnish the venerable tradition she was in service to, contaminating it in its entirety.

She glanced over her shoulder at the temple and put her hand on her lower belly. She was fertile, as all Chosen were at all times on this side. She could beget a young of the Primale from her very first time with him.

Dear Virgin in the Fade, why had she been chosen?

When she turned back around, the Directrix was down at the bottom of the hill, so small in comparison to the towering buildings, so tremendous in practicality. More than anyone or anything else, she defined the landscape: The Scribe Virgin was whom they all served, but it was the Directrix who ran their lives. At least until the Primale arrived.

The Directrix did not want that male in her world, Cormia thought.

And that was why Cormia had been the one nominated to the Scribe Virgin for choosing. Of all the females who might have been picked and would have been thrilled, she was the least welcoming, the least accommodating. A passive-aggressive declaration against the change in supremacy.

Cormia started down the knoll, the white grass texture without temperature under her bare feet. Nothing save food and drink possessed heat or coldness.

For a moment she thought of escaping. Better to be gone from all she knew than to endure the picture the Directrix had painted. Except she had no knowledge of how to get to the far side. She knew you had to pass through into the Scribe Virgin's private space, but what then? And what if she were caught by Her Holiness?

Unthinkable. More frightening than being with the Primale.

Deep in her private, sinful thoughts, Cormia ambled without purpose through the landscape she'd known all her life. It was so easy to be lost here in the compound, because everything looked the same and felt the same and smelled the same. With no contrast, reality's edges were too smooth to grab onto for purchase, either mentally or physically. You were never grounded. You were air.

As she passed by the Treasury, she stopped on its regal steps and thought of the gems inside, the only true color she'd ever seen. Beyond the locked doors there were whole baskets full of precious stones, and though she had seen them only once or twice, she remembered the colors so clearly. Her eyes had been shocked by the vivid blue of the sapphires and the dense green of the emeralds and the blood strength of the rubies' red. The aquamarines had been the color of the sky, so they had fascinated her less.

Her favorites had been the citrines, the lovely yellow citrines. She'd sneaked in a touch of those. It had been only a quick push of her hand into the basket when no one had been looking, but oh, how glorious to see the light flicker in their cheerful facets. The feel of them shifting against her palm had been a lively chatter to her hand's great content, a fanciful, tactile rush made all the more exciting by its illicit nature.

They had warmed her, though they were in fact no warmer than anything else.

And the gems weren't the only reason that entry to the Treasury was an extraordinary treat. There were objects from the other side kept there in glass cases, things that had been collected either because they played a pivotal role in the history of the race or because they had ended up in the keeping of the Chosen. Even if Cormia hadn't always known what she was looking at, it had been such a revelation. Colors. Textures. Foreign things from a foreign place.

Ironically, though, the thing she'd been most drawn to had been an ancient book. On the battered front, in faded embossed letters, it had read: DARIUS, SON OF MARKLON.

Cormia frowned and realized she'd seen that name before . . . in the Black Dagger Brotherhood room in the library.

A diary of a Brother. So that was why it had been preserved.

As she stared at the locked doors, she wished she had been around in the olden days, when the building had been kept open and one could go inside as freely as one could enter the library. But that had been before the attack.

The attack had changed everything. It seemed inconceivable that rogue members of the race had come over from the far side bearing weapons and looking to loot. But they had entered through a portal that was now closed and had rushed the Treasury. The previous Primale had died protecting his females, besting the three civilians but dying thereafter.

She supposed he'd been her father, hadn't he.

After that horrible interlude, the Scribe Virgin had closed that portal of entry and routed through her private courtyard all who sought to come. And as a precaution, the Treasury had always been locked, except for when the jewels were needed for the Scribe Virgin's sequester or for certain ceremonies. The Directrix held the key.

She heard a shuffling and looked toward a colonnaded walkway. A fully draped figure limped along, one leg dragging behind a black robe, covered hands holding a stack of towelings.

Cormia looked away quickly and hurried along, wanting both distance from that particular female as well as the Primale's Temple. She ended up as far away from both as one could go, all the way at the reflection pool.

The water was clear and perfectly still, a mirror that showed the sky. She wanted to put her foot in, but that was not allowed—

Her ears picked up on something.

At first she wasn't sure what she heard, if anything at all. There was no one nearby that she could see, nothing but the Tomb of the Youngs and the white-treed woods that marked the edges of the sanctuary. She waited. When the sound did not come again, she dismissed it as her imagination and continued on.

Though she was afeared, she was drawn toward the tomb where infants who did not survive birth were enshrined.

Anxiety rode up her spine. This was the one place she never visited, and it was the same for rest of the Chosen. All avoided this solitary square building with its white fencing. Sorrow hung 'round therein, sure as the black satin ribbons that were tied upon the door's handles.

Dear Virgin in the Fade, she thought, her destiny would soon be entombed here, as even Chosen had a high rate of infant deaths. Verily, parts of her would rest here, little chips of her being deposited until there was nothing but a husk left. The fact that she could not choose the pregnancies, that *no* was not a word or even a thought she was permitted, that her offspring were trapped in the same role she was made her visualize herself inside this solitary tomb, locked among the littlest dead.

She pulled the lapels of her robe closer to her neck and shivered as she stared through the gates. Before now, she had found this place disconcerting, feeling as if the tender ones were lonely even though they were in the Fade and should have been happy and at peace.

Now the temple was a horror.

The sound she'd heard came again, and she jumped back, ready to run from the woeful spirits who dwelled herein.

Except, no, that wasn't the spectral young. It was a catching of breath. Not at all ghostly, but very real.

She went around the corner silently.

Layla was sitting on the grass with her knees to her chest and her arms around herself. Her head was tucked in, her shoulders shaking, her robe and hair wet.

"My sister?" Cormia whispered. "How fare thee?"

Layla's head shot upright, and she quickly scrubbed her cheeks until they were free of tears. "Leave. Please."

Cormia went over and knelt down. "Tell me. What has happened?"

"Nothing of which you need be—"

"Layla, speak unto me." She wanted to reach out but you were not permitted to do so and she did not want to add to the upset. Instead of touch, she used gentle words and tone. "My sister, I would ease you. Please talk to me. Please."

The Chosen's blond head went back and forth, her ruined chignon falling further apart. "I failed."

"How?"

"I . . . failed. This night I failed to please. I was turned away."

"From what?"

"The male whose transition I saw through. He was ready to mate, and I touched him and he lost his impulse." Layla's breath went in on a sob. "And I . . . I shall have to report unto the king what transpired, as is tradition. I should have done so before I left, but I was so horrified. How will I tell His Majesty? And the Directrix?" Her head dropped down again, as if she hadn't the will to hold it up. "I was trained by the great ones to please. And I failed us all."

Cormia took a chance and laid her hand on Layla's shoulder, thinking it was always thus. The burden of the whole Chosen fell

upon each sole female when she acted in an official capacity. There was, therefore, no private and personal disgrace, only the great weight of monumental failure.

"My sister—"

"I shall go into reflection after I speak to the king and the Directrix."

Oh, no . . . Reflection was seven cycles of no food, no light, no contact with others, meant for atonement of infractions of the highest order. The worst of it, or so Cormia had heard, was the lack of illumination, as Chosen craved light.

"Sister, are you sure he did not desire you?"

"Males' bodies lie not in that regard. Merciful Virgin . . . perhaps it is for the best. I may well have not pleased him." Pale green eyes shifted over. "It is well and good I was not your instructor. I am trained in theory, not practice, so I could have imparted no visceral knowledge unto you."

"I would rather have had you."

"Then you are unwise." The Chosen's face abruptly grew old. Ancient. "And I have learned my lesson. I shall take myself out of the pool of *ehros*, as I am clearly incapable of upholding their sensual tradition."

Cormia didn't like the dead shadows in Layla's eyes. "Perhaps it was he who was at fault?"

"There is no issue of fault on his side. He was not pleased by me. My burden, not his." She wiped a tear away. "I shall say unto you, there is no failure such as the sexual one. Nothing cuts so deep as the denial of your nakedness and your instinct for communion by one you would wish to mate. . . . To be shunned in your skin is the worst sort of refusal. So I should leave the *ehros*, not just for their fine tradition, but for me. I would not go through this again. Ever. Now please go, and say nothing. I must collect myself."

Cormia wanted to stay, but arguing didn't seem right. She stood and removed her outer robe, draping it around her sister.

Layla looked up in surprise. "Verily, I am not cold."

This was said as she drew the cloth tight to her neck.

"Fare thee well, my sister." Cormia turned and walked up past the reflecting pool.

As she looked up at the milky blue sky she wanted to scream.

Vishous rolled off Jane's body and positioned her so she was tucked into his chest. He liked her up close on his left side, with his fighting hand free to kill for her. Lying here now, he'd never felt more focused, never had his life's purpose so clear: His one and only priority was keeping her alive and healthy and safe, and the strength with which he held that directive made him feel whole.

He was who he was because of her.

In the short time they'd known each other, Jane had barged into that secret chamber in his chest, shoved Butch out of the way, and slammed herself in good and tight. And it felt right. The fit felt right.

She made a little murmuring noise and wheedled her way in even closer to him. As he stroked her back, he found himself thinking, for no good reason, about the first fight he'd had, a face-off that was closely followed by the first time he'd had sex.

In the war camp, males just through their transitions were given a limited amount of time to find their strength. And yet as Vishous's father stood before him and pronounced that he was to fight, V was surprised. Surely he should have had a day to recover.

The Bloodletter smiled, showing fangs that were always distended. "And you shall pair off with Grodht."

The soldier V had stolen the deer leg from. The fat one whose prowess was of the hammer.

With exhaustion weighing upon him, and his pride all that kept him on his feet, V proceeded over to the fighting ring that was set back from where the soldiers slept. The ring was an uneven circular sinkhole in the cave's floor, like a giant had pounded its fist into the earth out of frustra-

tion. Waist deep, with its sides and bottom dark brown from blood having been spilled, you were expected to fight until you couldn't stand. No conduct was barred, and the only rule pertained to the loser and what he had to present himself for to address his deficiency in combat.

Vishous knew he wasn't ready to fight. Virgin in the Fade, he could barely get down into the ring without falling over. But then, that was the purpose in this, was it not? His father had engineered the perfect power maneuver. There was only one way V could hope to win, and if he used his hand, the whole camp would see for themselves what they had only heard in rumor and shun him completely. And if he lost? Then he would not be perceived as any threat to his father's dominion. So either way the Bloodletter's supremacy would remain intact and unchallenged by his son's new maturity.

As the fat soldier jumped in with a lusty shout and the swing of a hammer, the Bloodletter loomed at the lip of the ring. "What weapon shall I give my son?" he asked the assembled crowd. "I think perhaps . . ." He looked over at one of the kitchen females, who was leaning on a broom. "Give me."

The female fumbled to comply and dropped the thing at the Bloodletter's feet. As she bent over to pick it up, he kicked her aside as one would a tree branch that was in one's path. "Take this, my son. And pray to the Virgin it is not what is used in you when you lose."

As the throng of witnesses laughed, V caught the wooden handle.

"Engage!" the Bloodletter barked.

The crowd cheered, and someone threw the dregs of their ale at Vishous, the warm splash hitting his bare back and dripping down his naked arse. The fat soldier opposite him smiled, revealing fangs that had extended out of his upper jaw. As the male began to circle V, the hammer swung on the end of its chain, a low whistle rising up.

V was clumsy while he tracked his opponent, finding it difficult to control his legs. He focused primarily on the male's right shoulder, the one that would tense before the hammer was thrown out, while with his *peripheral vision he kept track of the crowd. Mead would be the least of what they might pitch at him.*

It turned out not to be as much a fight as a dodging contest, with V on the shoddy defensive and his opponent all showy aggression. Whilst the soldier displayed his proficiency with his weapon of note, V learned the predictability of the male's actions as well as the hammer's rhythm. Even as strong as the soldier was, he had to brace his feet square before the hammer's head-sized spiked ball was sent forward. V waited for one of the pauses in action and then struck, flipping the broom around and jamming the handle directly into the bulbous soldier's groin.

The male roared, lost hold of the hammer, and clapped his knees together, cupping himself. V didn't waste a moment. He lifted the broom over his shoulder and swung with his full reach, catching his opponent in the temple and knocking him senseless.

The cheering dried up until all there was was the fire's crackling chatter and the sound of V's ragged breathing. He dropped the broom and stepped over his opponent, ready to get out.

His father's boots planted on the lip of the circle, blocking his way.

The Bloodletter's eyes were narrow as blades. "You haven't finished."

"He shall not rise."

"Not the point." The Bloodletter nodded to the soldier on the floor. "Finish him."

As his opponent moaned, Vishous assessed his father. If V said no, the game his father was playing would be fulfilled, the alienation the Bloodletter was after complete, though not in the way the male had probably expected: V would become a target for the simple staple that he would be perceived as weak for not punishing his opponent. If he finished, however, his position in the camp would be as stable as it could be—until the next test.

Exhaustion overtook him. Would his life always be based on such a crude and unforgiving scale of balances?

The Bloodletter smiled. "This bastard who calls himself my son has no

spine, it appears. Perhaps the seed that his mother's womb ate was of another?"

Laughter rippled through the crowd, and someone yelled out, "No son of yours would hesitate at such an hour!"

"And during a fight no true son of mine would be so cowardly as to attack a male's vulnerable place as such." The Bloodletter met the eyes of his soldiers. "The weak must be devious, as strength is not available to them."

The sensation of being strangled locked onto Vishous's throat, sure as if his father's hands were wrapped around his neck. As his breath quickened anew, anger swelled in his chest and his heart pounded. He looked down at the fat soldier who had beaten him . . . then thought of the books his father had made him burn . . . and the boy who had gone after him . . . and the thousands of cruel and graceless acts that had been done to him over the course of his life.

V's body quickened from the anger that burned in him, and before he knew what he was doing he was rolling the soldier over onto his fat belly.

He took the male. In front of his father. In front of the camp.

And he was brutal about it.

When it was over, he disengaged and stumbled back. The soldier was covered with V's blood and sweat and the remnants of his rage.

With a scramble like a goat he got himself out of the ring, and though he knew not what time of day it was, he ran through the camp to the main way out of the cave. As he burst free, the cold night was just gaining its hold on the land, and the faint glow in the east burned his face.

He bent over at the knees and threw up. Again and again.

"So weak you are." The Bloodletter's voice was bored . . . but only on the surface. There was a depth of satisfaction in his words caused by a mission completed: Although Vishous had done what he had to the soldier, his retreat afterward had been precisely the kind of cowardice his father had sought.

The Bloodletter's eyes narrowed. "You shall never best me, boy. Just as you shall never be free of me. I shall rule your life—"

On a surge of hatred, V sprang up from his crouch and attacked his father head-on, leading with his glowing hand. The Bloodletter went rigid as the electrical blast went through his massive body, and the two of them fell upon the ground, with Vishous on top. Going on instinct, V locked his bright white palm on his father's thick throat and squeezed.

As the Bloodletter's face turned brilliant red, V's eye stung briefly and a vision replaced what was before him.

He saw the death of his father. As clearly as if it happened in front of him.

Words left his mouth, though he was not conscious of speaking them: "You shall see your end in a wall of fire caused by a pain you know. You will burn until you are nothing but smoke, and be cast upon the wind."

His father's expression turned to abject horror.

V was peeled off by another soldier and held by the armpits, feet dangling above the snowy ground.

The Bloodletter leaped up, his face ruddy, a line of sweat beading above his upper lip. He breathed like a horse ridden hard, clouds of white shooting out of his mouth and nostrils.

V fully expected to be beaten to death.

"Bring me my blade," his father snarled.

Vishous scrubbed his face. To avoid thinking about what happened next, he thought about how that first time with the soldier had never sat well with him. Three hundred years later it still felt like a violation of the other male, even though that had been the way of it at the camp.

He looked at Jane curled up next to him and decided that, as far as he was concerned, tonight was when he'd finally lost his virginity. Though his body had done the act in many different ways to many different people, sex had always been about an exchange of power— power that flowed in his direction, power that he fed off of to reassure himself that no one was ever going to get him flat on his back and tied down and unable to fight while shit was done to him.

Tonight had not fit his pattern. With Jane there had been an exchange: She had given something to him, and he had turned over a piece of himself in return.

V frowned. A piece, but not everything.

To do that they would need to go to his other place. And . . . shit, they would go there. Even though he got a case of the cold clammies just thinking about it, he vowed that before she left his life, he'd give her the one thing he had never let anyone have.

And would never give to anyone else.

He wanted to repay the trust she gave to him. She was so strong as a person, as a woman, and yet she put herself in his sexual care— even while knowing that he had hard-core Dom tendencies and she was no match for him physically.

Her trust brought him to his knees. And he needed to return the faith before she left.

Her eyes blinked open and met his, and they both spoke at the same time:

"I don't want you to go."

"I don't want to leave you."

TWENTY-SIX

When John woke up the following afternoon, he was afraid to move. Hell, he was afraid to open his eyes. What if it had been a dream? Bracing himself, he lifted his arm, cracked his lids, and . . . oh, yeah, there it was. Palm as big as his head. Arm longer than his thighbone had been before. Wrist thick as his calf once had been.

He made it.

He reached for his cell phone and sent texts to Qhuinn and Blay, who hit him back at a dead run. They were totally pumped for him, and he grinned a big fat-bastard smile . . . until he realized that he had to use the bathroom, and glanced at the open door. Looking through the jambs, he saw the shower.

Oh, God. Had he really choked in there last night with Layla?

He tossed the phone onto the comforter, even though the thing was beeping that there were texts waiting for him. Rubbing his strangely broad chest with his new Shaquille O'Neal hand, he felt

like hell. He should apologize to Layla, but for what? Being a lame-ass who went soft? Yeah, that was a conversation he was dying to have, as she was no doubt totally unimpressed with him and his performance.

Was it better to let it go? Probably. She was so beautiful and sensual and perfect in every way, there was no chance she'd ever think it was her fault. All he'd do would be embarrass himself into an aneurysm as he wrote what he'd say if he'd had a voice box.

He still felt like hell, though.

His alarm clock went off, and it was just too fricking weird to reach over with this man arm and silence the thing. When he stood up it was even more freaky. His vantage point was totally different, and everything seemed smaller: the furniture, the doors, the room. Even the ceiling was shorter.

Just how big was he?

As he tried to take a few steps, he felt like one of those circus stilt-walkers: gangly, loose, in danger of falling. Yeah . . . a circus walker who had had a stroke, because the commands his brain gave weren't received properly by his muscles and bones. On his way to the bathroom he lurched all over the place, hanging on to drapes, the molding around windows, a dresser, the doorjamb.

For no particular reason he thought about crossing the river on his walks with Zsadist. As he went along now, the stationary objects he used as crutches were like the stones he jumped one to another to stay out of rushing water, little aids of big importance.

The bathroom was pitch dark, as the shutters were still down for the day and he'd turned all the lights off after Layla left. With his hand on the switch he took a deep breath, then flipped on the recessed lights.

He blinked hard, his eyes supersensitive and way more acute than they'd been before. After a moment, his reflection came into focus like an apparition, emerging from the glare, like a ghost of himself. He was . . .

He didn't want to know. Not yet.

John shut the lights off and went to the shower. As he waited for the hot water to get running, he settled back against the cold marble, wrapping his arms around himself. He had this absurd need to be held at the moment, so it was a good thing he was alone. Although he'd hoped the change would make him stronger, it appeared to have nancied him out even more.

He thought back to killing those *lessers*. Right after he'd stabbed them he'd gotten such clarity as to who he was and what kind of power he had. But that had all faded, so much so that he wasn't sure he'd ever really felt that way.

He pushed open the shower door and stepped inside.

Christ, ow. The fine spray was like needles going into his skin, and when he tried to soap up his arm that French-milled stuff Fritz bought stung like battery acid. He had to force himself to wash his face, and though it was cool to have stubble on his jaw for the first time in recorded history, the idea of taking a razor to his puss was utterly repellent. Like drawing a cheese grater down his cheeks.

He was washing his body off, being as gentle as he could, when he got to his privates. Without thinking much of it he did what he had done all of his life, a quick sweep under his sac, then down himself—

This time the effect was different. He got hard. His . . . cock got hard.

God, that word seemed weird to use, but . . . well, that thing was definitely a cock now, something a man had, something a man used—

The erection came to a halt. Just stopped swelling and lengthening. The curling ache in his lower belly went away, too.

He rinsed the soap off himself, determined not to open the can of worms about him and sex. He had enough problems. His body was a remote-controlled car whose antenna was broken; he was going to class, where everyone was going to stare at him; and it dawned on

him that Wrath must know about the gun he'd had on him down-town. After all, he'd been brought back here somehow, and Blay and Qhuinn would have had to explain what was doing with the scene. Knowing Blay, the guy would try to protect John about the nine and cop to its being his, but what if that got the guy kicked out of the program? No one was supposed to have weapons when they were out and about. No one.

When John got out of the shower, toweling off wasn't an option. Even though it was cold as hell he let himself air-dry as he brushed his teeth and clipped his nails. His eyes were superacute in the dark, so finding what he wanted in the drawers wasn't a problem. Avoiding the mirror was, though, so he went into his bedroom.

Opening up his closet, he took out a bag from Abercrombie & Fitch. Fritz had turned up at his door with the thing weeks ago, and when John had taken a gander at the clothes he'd figured the butler had lost his mind. Inside were a pair of brand-new distressed jeans, a fleece the size of a sleeping bag, an XXXL T-shirt, and a pair of size-fourteen Nike Air Shox in a shiny new box.

Turned out Fritz, as usual, had been right. All of it fit. Even the boat-sized shoes.

As John stared down at his feet, he thought, man, those Nikes needed to come with PFDs and a frickin' anchor, they were so big.

He left his room, his legs working in a gawky gait, his arms swing-ing loose, his balance off.

As he got to the head of the grand staircase he lifted his eyes to the ceiling, with its depictions of great warriors.

He prayed he would be one. But he just couldn't see how in the hell he'd pull that off.

Phury woke up to the sight of the female of his dreams. Or maybe he was dreaming?

"Hi," Bella said.

He cleared his throat, and still his voice was reedy as he replied, "Are you really here?"

"Yes." She took his hand and sat on the edge of his bed. "Right here. How are you feeling?"

Shit, he'd worried her, and that was not good for the young.

With what little energy he had he did a fast mental mop-up, an OxiClean of his brain, sweeping out the dredges of the red smokes he'd fired up, as well as the lethargy of injury and sleep.

"I'm fine," he said, bringing his hand up so he could rub his good eye. Not a great idea. In his fist was his drawing of her, crumpled up like he'd been hugging it in his sleep. He shoved the piece of paper under the covers before she could ask what it was. "You should be in bed."

"I get to be up a little each day."

"Still, you should—"

"When do the bandages come off?"

"Ah, now, I suppose."

"Would you like me to help?"

"No." The last thing they needed was for her to find out he'd been blinded at the same moment he did. "But thank you."

"Can I bring you something to eat?"

Kindness from her hit harder than a tire iron to the ribs. "Thank you, but I'll call Fritz in a little bit. You should go back and lie down."

"I have forty-four minutes left." She checked her watch. "Forty-three."

He pushed himself up on his arms, tugging the sheets higher so less of his chest showed. "How do you feel?"

"Good. Scared but good—"

The door swung open without a knock. As Zsadist walked in, his eyes locked on Bella as if he were trying to gauge her vital signs in her face.

"I thought I'd find you here." He bent down and kissed her on the mouth, then on both sides of the neck over her veins.

Phury looked away during the greeting—and realized that his hand had burrowed under the covers and found his drawing. He forced himself to let it go.

Z's whole attitude was much more relaxed. "So how are you, my brother?"

"Good." Although if he heard that question one more time from either of them, he was going to pull a *Scanners*, because his head would explode. "Good enough to come out tonight."

His twin frowned. "You get cleared by V's doc?"

"Not up to anyone but me."

"Wrath might have a different opinion."

"Fine, but if he disagrees, he's going to have to chain me down to keep me here." Phury throttled back, not wanting to get tense with Bella around. "You teaching the first half of tonight?"

"Yeah, figured I'd make some more progress on firearms." Z ran his hand down Bella's mahogany hair, stroking it and her back at the same time. He did this without seeming to notice, and she accepted the touch with the same loving disregard.

Phury's chest ached until he had to open his mouth to breathe. "Why don't I meet you guys down at First Meal, okay? I'm going to shower, get the bandages off, dress."

Bella stood up and Z's hand moved to her waist and tucked her into him.

God, they were a family, weren't they? The two of them together with their young in her belly. And in just over a year, if the Scribe Virgin saw fit, they would stand like this with their infant in their arms. Later, years later, their child would be by their side. And then their son or daughter would be mated, and another generation of their blood would carry the race forward: a family, not a fantasy.

To hurry them along, Phury shifted around like he was about to get up.

"I'll see you down in the dining room," Z said, his palm sliding around to his *shellan*'s lower belly. "Bella's going back to bed, aren't you, *nalla*?"

She checked her watch. "Twenty-two minutes. I'd better get my bath in."

Various good-bye-like words were exchanged, but Phury didn't pay much attention because he was dying for them to leave. When the door finally shut, he reached for his cane, got out of his bed, and went straight to the mirror over his dresser. He eased off the bandage's tape, then peeled free the layers of gauze. Underneath his lashes were so tangled and matted that he went into the bathroom, ran some water, and rinsed his face a number of times before he could get them apart.

He opened his eye.

And saw perfectly.

His total lack of relief at his fine and dandy sight was eerie. He should have cared. He *needed* to care. About both his body and himself. He just didn't.

Disturbed, he took a shower and shaved, then put his prosthesis on and dressed in his leathers. He was on his way out with his blade and gun holsters in his hand when he paused by the bed. That drawing he'd done was still wadded up in his sheets; he could see the white, crinkled edges in the folds of blue satin.

He pictured his twin's hand on Bella's hair. Then on her lower belly.

Phury went over, picked up the drawing, and flattened it out on the bedside table. He took one last look at it, then ripped it into small pieces, put the pile in an ashtray, and struck a match head with his thumb. With the flame flaring, he leaned into the paper.

When there was nothing but ash, he got up and left his room.

It was time to let go, and he knew how to do it.

TWENTY-SEVEN

V was blissfully happy. Wholly complete. A Rubik's Cube solved. His arms were around his female, his body pressed up close to hers, her scent in his nose. Though it was nighttime, it was as if the sun were shining upon him.

Then he heard the gunshot.

He was in the dream. He was asleep and in the dream.

The horror of the nightmare unfolded as it always did, and yet it was fresh as the first time it had come to him: Blood on his shirt. Pain ripping through his chest. A descent to the ground until he was on his knees, his life over—

V shot upright in bed, screaming.

Jane launched herself at him to calm him down just as the door flew open and Butch rushed in with gun drawn. Both of their voices mixed together, a fruit salad of words spoken fast.

"What the fuck!"

"Are you okay?"

V fumbled with the sheets, tearing them off his torso so he could see his chest. The skin was unmarked, but he ran his hand down it anyway. "Jesus Christ . . ."

"Was it a flashback from your shooting?" Jane asked as she urged him to lie down in her arms.

"Yeah, fuck . . ."

Butch lowered his muzzle and jacked up his boxers. "Scared the piss out of me and Marissa. You want some Goose to chill?"

"Yeah."

"Jane? Anything for you?"

She was shaking her head when V cut in with, "Hot chocolate. She'd like some hot chocolate. I had Fritz bring some mix over. It's in the kitchen."

When Butch left, V scrubbed his face. "Sorry about that."

"God, don't apologize." She ran her hand up and down his chest. "You okay?"

He nodded. Then, like a total sap, he kissed her and said, "I'm glad you're here."

"Me, too." She wound her arms around him and held him like he was precious.

They were quiet until Butch came back a little later with a glass in one hand and a mug in the other. "I want a nice tip. I burned my pinkie on the stove."

"You want me to look at it?" Jane tucked the sheet under her arms and reached forward for the cocoa.

"I think I'll live, but thanks, Doc Jane." Butch handed the Goose to V. "How about you, big guy? You cool now?"

Not hardly. Not after the dream. Not with Jane leaving. "Yeah."

Butch shook his head. "You're a bad liar."

"Fuck you." There was no heat to V's words at all. And no conviction as he tacked on, "I'm tight."

The cop went over to the door. "Oh, speaking of strong, guess Phury showed up at First Meal, all ready to go out and fight tonight.

Z stopped by here a half hour ago on the way to class to thank you, Doc Jane, for everything you did. Phury's face looks good and the Brother's eye's working just fine."

Jane blew over the top of the mug. "I'd feel better if he'd go see an optometrist to be sure."

"Z said he pushed for that and got shut down. Even Wrath took a shot at it."

"I'm glad our boy came out okay," V said, and truly meant it. Trouble was, Jane's only excuse to stay had just vaporized.

"Yeah, me too. I'll leave you two alone. Later."

As the door shut, V listened to the sound of Jane blowing across her hot cocoa again.

"I'm going to bring you home tonight," he said.

She stopped blowing. There was a long pause then she took an inhaling sip. "Yes. It's time."

He swallowed half the Goose in the glass. "But before I do, I'd like to take you somewhere first."

"Where?"

He wasn't sure how to tell her what he wanted to happen before he let her go. He didn't want her to bolt, especially as he contemplated the years and years ahead of him and all of the dishonest, disinterested sex he was going to have to have.

He finished his Goose. "Somewhere private."

As she drank from the mug, her brows dropped down low. "So you're really going to let me go, huh?"

He stared at her profile and wished they had met under different circumstances. Except how in the fuck would that have ever happened?

"Yeah," he said quietly. "I am."

Standing in front of his locker three hours later, John wished Qhuinn would shut his damn piehole. Even though the locker room was loud from the sounds of metal doors banging shut and clothes flapping and shoes dropping, he felt like his buddy had a bullhorn stapled to his upper lip.

"You're flippin' huge, J.M. For real. Like . . . ginormous."

That is not a word. John shoved his backpack in like he usually did and realized none of the clothes he was crushing would fit him anymore.

"The hell it isn't. Back me up, Blay."

Blay nodded as he pulled on his *ji*. "Yeah, you fill out? You're going to be, like, Brother-sized."

"Gigundous."

Okay, also not a word, asshole.

"Fine, really, really, really big. How's that?"

John shook his head as he put his books on the floor and deep-sixed the little duds in the nearest trash can. As he came back over, he sized up his friends and realized he was bigger than both of them by a good four inches. Hell, he was as tall as Z.

He glanced down the aisle at Lash. Yup, topped Lash, too.

The bastard looked over as he took his shirt off, as if sensing John's stare. In a smooth move, the guy deliberately flexed his shoulders, the muscles curling up tight under his skin. He had a tattoo across his stomach that hadn't been there two days before, a word in the Old Language John didn't recognize.

"John, getcha ass out in the hall for a sec."

The whole place went silent, and John jerked his head around. Zsadist was standing in the door to the locker room, all business.

"Shit," Qhuinn whispered.

John put his backpack away, shut his locker, and tugged his shirt into place. He walked over to the Brother as quickly as he could manage, stepping around other guys as they pretended to keep doing what they were doing.

Z held the door wide as John went out into the hallway. After the thing was closed, he said, "Tonight, you and me are meeting before dawn, just like usual. We're only going to skip the walking. You'll come to the weight room while I lift. We need to talk."

Shit was right. John signed, *Same time?*

"Four A.M. As for training tonight, I expect you to sit it out in the gym, but participate at the shooting range. Feel me?"

John inclined his head, then grabbed Z's arm as the male turned away. *Is it about last night?*

"Yup."

The Brother walked away, punching open the double doors to the gym. When the two halves shut they made a clanking sound.

Blaylock and Qhuinn came up behind John.

"What's doing?" Blay asked.

I'm going to get shit for capping that lesser, John signed.

Blay pushed a hand into his red hair. "I should have covered for you better."

Qhuinn shook his head. "John, we'll take up for you, my man. I mean, it was my idea to go to the club."

"And my gun."

John crossed his arms over his chest. *It's going to be okay.*

Or at least he hoped it would. He was on the thin edge of getting kicked out of the program as it stood.

"By the way . . ." Qhuinn put his hand on John's shoulder. "Haven't gotten a chance to thank you."

Blay nodded. "Me neither. You were righteous last night. Totally righteous. You fucking saved us."

"Shit, you totally knew what you were doing."

John felt his face go red.

"Well, ain't this cozy," Lash drawled. "Tell me something, do you three draw straws to decide who'll be on the bottom? Or is it always John?"

Qhuinn smiled, baring his fangs. "Has anyone ever shown you the difference between good touch and bad touch? 'Cause I'd love to demonstrate. We could start right now."

John stepped in front of his friend, going face-to-face with Lash. He said nothing, just looked down at the guy.

Lash smiled. "You got something to say to me? No? Wait, you still have no voice? God . . . what a bummer."

John could feel Qhuinn gearing up for a lunge, the heat and the impulse rolling off his friend. To stop the collision from happening, John reached behind and put a hand on his buddy's abs to keep him in place.

If anyone was going after Lash, it was John.

Lash laughed and tightened the belt on his *ji*. "Don't front like you have game, John-boy. The transition doesn't change you on the inside or fix your physical defects. Right, Qhuinn?" As he turned away, he said under his breath, "Mismatched motherfucker."

Before Qhuinn could jump the guy, John wheeled around and grabbed him around the waist just as Blay locked onto one of the guy's arms. Even with their combined weight, it was like keeping back a bull.

"Chill," Blay grunted. "Just *relax*."

"I'm going to kill him one of these days," Qhuinn hissed. "I swear to God."

John glanced over as Lash sauntered into the gym. Taking a vow to himself, he marked the guy for a beating, even if it got him kicked out of the program for good.

He'd always felt that if you fucked with his friends, you were going to get served. End of story.

Thing was, now he had the equipment to deliver the job.

TWENTY-EIGHT

round midnight Jane found herself in the back of a black Mercedes on her way home. Up front, on the other side of the partition that was in place, the uniformed driver was that butler who was older than God and as cheerful as a terrier. Beside her V was dressed in black leather, as silent and grim as a tombstone.

He hadn't said much. But he wouldn't let go of her hand.

The car's windows were darkened to such a degree she felt like she was in a tunnel, and in an effort to ground herself she hit a button on the door next to her. As her slice of glass went down, a shocking rush of cold pushed inside and replaced the warmth, a bully scattering the good kids at a playground.

She stuck her head out into the breeze and looked at the pool of illumination thrown by the headlights. The landscape was blurry, like a photograph out of focus. Although by the downward angle of the road she knew they were coming off a mountain. Thing was, she couldn't get any sense of where they were headed or where they had been.

In a weird way the disorientation was appropriate. This was the interlude between the world she'd been in and the one she was returning to, and stretches of neither here nor there should be hazy.

"I can't see where we are," she murmured as she put the window back up.

"It's called *mhis*," V said. "Think of it as a protective illusion."

"A trick of yours?"

"Yeah. Mind if I light up, as long as I let in some fresh air?"

"That's fine." It wasn't like she was going to be around him for much longer.

Crap.

V gave her hand a squeeze, then put his window down a quarter of an inch, the soft drone of wind flaring up over the quiet hum of the sedan. His leather jacket creaked as he took out a hand-rolled and a gold lighter. The flint made a little rasp, and then the faint smell of Turkish tobacco made her nose tingle.

"That smell is so going to—" She stopped.

"What?"

"I was going to say, 'remind me of you.' But it won't, will it?"

"Maybe in a dream."

She put her fingertips on her window. The glass was cold. Just like the center of her chest.

Because she couldn't stand the silence, she said, "These enemies of yours, what exactly are they?"

"They start as humans. Then they're turned into something else."

As he inhaled, she saw his face aglow in orange light. He'd shaved before leaving, using the razor she'd once wanted to turn against him, and his face was impossibly handsome: arrogant, masculine, hard as his will. The tattoos at his temple were still beautifully done, but now she hated them, knowing them for the violation they were.

She cleared her throat. "So tell me more?"

"The Lessening Society, our enemy, chooses its members through a careful screening process. They look for sociopaths, murderers, amoral Jeffrey Dahmer types. Then the Omega steps in—"

"The Omega?"

He looked down at the tip of his hand-rolled. "Guess the Christian equivalent is the devil. Anyway, the Omega gets his hands on them . . . as well as other things . . . and presto, change-o, they wake up dead and moving. They are strong, virtually indestructible, and can be killed only by a stab wound to the chest with something steel."

"Why are they your enemies?"

He inhaled, again his brows going down low. "I suspect it might have something to do with my mother."

"Your mother?"

The hard smile that stretched his lips was more a curve than anything else. "I'm the son of what you'd probably consider a god." He lifted his gloved hand. "This is from her. Personally, as baby gifts go, I'd have preferred one of those silver rattles, or maybe some paste to eat. But you don't get to pick what your parents give you."

Jane looked at the black leather that stretched over his palm. "Jesus . . ."

"Not according to our lexicon or my nature. I'm not the savior type." He put the cigarette between his lips and pulled off the glove. In the dimness of the backseat, his hand glowed with the soft beauty of moonlight reflecting off of fresh snow.

He inhaled one last time, then took the cigarette and pressed the lit tip down right to the center of his palm.

"No," she hissed. "Wait—"

The butt was ashed in a flare of light, and he blew off the residue, a fine powder that dispersed in the air. "I would give anything to get rid of this piece of shit. Although I will say, it's damn handy when I don't have an ashtray."

Jane felt woozy for a whole host of reasons, especially as she thought about his future. "Is your mother forcing you to get married?"

"Yup. I sure as fuck wouldn't volunteer for it." V's eyes shifted to her and for a split second she could have sworn he was going to say that she'd be the exception to that rule. But then he glanced away.

God, the idea of him with someone else, even if she wouldn't remember him, was like being kicked in the gut.

"How many?" Jane asked hoarsely.

"You don't want to know."

"Tell me."

"Don't think about it. I sure as hell try not to." He looked over at her. "They're going to mean nothing to me. I want you to know that. Even though you and I can't . . . Yeah, well, anyway, they won't mean jack."

It was horrible of her to be glad of that.

He put the glove back on, and they were silent as the sedan ghosted through the night. Eventually they stopped. Started up again. Stopped. Started up again.

"We must be downtown, huh?" she said. "Because this feels like a lot of traffic lights."

"Yeah." He leaned forward, hit a button, and the partition went down so she could see out the windshield.

Yup, downtown Caldie. She was back.

As tears speared into her eyes, she blinked them away and stared down at her hands.

A little later the driver stopped the Mercedes in front of what looked like the service entrance to a brick building: There was a sturdy metal door marked PRIVATE in white paint, and a concrete ramp that went up to a loading dock. The place was clean in the way well-kept urban places were. Which was to say it was grungy, but without any loose trash around.

V opened his door. "Do not get out yet."

She put her hand on the duffel bag with her clothes in it. Maybe

he'd decided to just take her back to the hospital? Except this was no entry she knew of at St. Francis.

Moments later he opened the door and reached in with his bare hand. "Leave your things. Fritz, we'll be back in a while."

"It is my pleasure to wait," the old man said with a smile.

Jane got out of the car and followed V over to a set of concrete stairs next to the ramp. The whole time he was on her like a slipcover, tight against her back, guarding her. Somehow he opened the sturdy metal door without keys; he simply put his hand on the push bar and stared at the thing.

Oddly, once they were inside he didn't relax at all. He led her quickly down a corridor to a freight elevator, checking left and right as they went along. She had no idea they were in the luxurious Commodore Building until she read a notice from the property managers that was posted on the concrete wall.

"You have a place here?" she asked, even though it was self-evident.

"Top floor's mine. Well, half of it." They got in a service elevator and stood on worn linoleum under caged lights. "I wish I could take you in the front way, but that's too public."

There was a lurch as the lift engaged, and she reached out for the elevator wall. V caught her upper arm first, holding her steady, and he didn't let go. She didn't want him to.

V remained tense when they came to a jerking halt and the elevator opened. The plain hallway was nothing special, with just two doors and a stairway exit to give it purpose. The ceiling was high but not ornate, and the carpeting was the kind of low-napped, multicolored variety she recognized from the hospital's waiting rooms.

"I'm down here."

She followed him to the end of the corridor and was surprised to see him take out a gold key to unlock the door.

Whatever was on the other side was pitch-black, but she went inside with him without fear. Hell, she felt like she could walk into a firing squad with him by her side and come out all right. Plus, the place smelled nice, like lemon, as if it had recently been cleaned.

He didn't turn on any lights. Just took her hand and urged her forward with a tug.

"I can't see anything."

"Don't worry. Nothing will hurt you, and I know the way."

She hung onto his palm and wrist and shuffled along behind him until he stopped. With the way their footsteps echoed, she had a sense of great space, but no idea of the contours of the penthouse.

He turned her to face to the right and then stepped away.

"Where are you going?" She swallowed hard.

A candle flared over in the far corner, some forty feet away from her. It didn't illuminate much, however. The walls . . . the walls and the ceiling and . . . the floor . . . it was black. All black. As was the candle.

V stepped into the lee of the light, nothing but a looming shadow. Jane's heart pounded.

"You asked about the scars between my legs," he said. "How they happened."

"Yes . . ." she whispered. So that was why he wanted everything dark as night. He wasn't going to want her to see his face.

Another candle came on, this one on the opposite side of what she realized was a vast room.

"My father had it done to me. Right after I almost killed him."

Jane inhaled sharply. "Oh . . . God."

Vishous stared at Jane but saw only the past and what had come after him taking his father down to the ground.

"Bring me my blade," the Bloodletter said.

V fought against the soldier who was holding his arms and got nowhere. As he struggled two more males appeared. Then another pair. Now three others.

The Bloodletter spat on the ground as someone put a black dagger into his hand, and V braced himself for the stabbing that was coming . . . except the Bloodletter just streaked the blade across his palm, then sheathed the knife in his belt. Bringing both hands together, he rubbed them one against the other, then slammed his right one into the center of V's chest.

V looked down at the print on his skin. Expulsion. Not death. But why?

The Bloodletter's voice was hard. "You shall be ever unknown to those who dwell herein. And death shall come to any who aid you."

The soldiers started to let Vishous go.

"Not yet. Bring him into the camp." The Bloodletter turned away. "And get the blacksmith. It is incumbent upon us to warn others of this male's evil nature."

V bucked wildly as another soldier swept up his legs and he was carried like a carcass into the cave.

"Behind the screen," the Bloodletter told the blacksmith. "We shall do this afore the painted wall."

The male blanched, but took his rough wooden tray of tools around the partition. Meanwhile, V was laid out on his back with a soldier at the end of each of his limbs and one holding his hips down.

The Bloodletter stood over V, his hands dripping bright red. "Mark him."

The blacksmith looked up. "In what manner, great one?"

The Bloodletter spelled out the warnings in the Old Language, and the soldiers held V down as his temple and his groin and his thighs were tattooed. He fought the whole of it, but the ink sank into his skin, the characters permanent. When it was finished he was utterly drained, weaker than when he'd come out of his transition.

"His hand. Do it upon his hand as well." The blacksmith started to shake his head. "You will do it or I will get another blacksmith for the camp, as you will be dead."

The blacksmith shook all over, but was of care not to touch V's skin so the marking was completed without incident.

When it was done, the Bloodletter stared down at V. "There is one more necessary task, methinks. Spread wide his legs. I shall do the race a favor and ensure he never procreates."

V felt his eyes pop as his ankles and his thighs were yanked apart. His father once more unsheathed the black dagger from his belt, but then paused. "No, something else is needed."

He ordered the blacksmith do the deed with a pair of pliers.

Vishous screamed as he felt the metal clamp onto his thinnest skin. There was a spearing pain and a tearing and then—

"Sweet *Jesus*," Jane said.

V shook himself back to the present. He wondered how much he'd said out loud, and decided that, going by the look of horror on her face, it had been pretty much everything.

He watched the candlelight flicker in her dark green eyes. "They weren't able to finish."

"Not out of decency," she said softly.

He shook his head and raised his gloved hand. "Even though I was about to pass out, my whole body lit up. The soldiers who were holding me down were killed instantly. So was the blacksmith—he was using a metal tool, and it conducted the energy right into him."

She closed her eyes briefly. "Then what happened?"

"I rolled over, threw up some more, and dragged myself to the exit. The whole camp watched me go in silence. Not even my father got in the way or said a thing." V cupped himself loosely, remembering the mind-numbing pain. "The, ah . . . the cave floor was covered with this loose, powdery kind of dirt that had various minerals in it—one of which must have been salt. The wound sealed up so I didn't bleed out, but that's how I got the scars."

"I am . . . so sorry." She lifted her hand as if she wanted to reach out, but then dropped her arm. "It's a wonder you survived."

"I barely made it through that first night. It was so cold. I ended up using a branch to help me walk, and went as far as I could in no

particular direction. Eventually I collapsed. My will to keep going was there, my body was not. I'd lost blood, and the pain was exhausting.

"Some civilians of my race found me just before dawn. They took me in, but only for a day. The warnings . . ." He tapped his temple. "The warnings on my face and my body did what my father wanted them to. They made me a freak to be feared. At nightfall I left. I wandered alone for years, sticking to the shadows, staying out of people's way. I fed from humans for a while, but that just didn't sustain me for long enough. A century later I ended up in Italy, working as a hired thug for a merchant who dealt with humans. In Venice there were whores of my kind who would let you feed, and I used them."

"So lonely." Jane put her hand to her throat. "You must have been so lonely."

"Hardly. I didn't want to be with anyone. I worked for the merchant for a decade or so. Then one night, in Rome, I ran into a *lesser* who was in the process of killing a female vampire. I took the bastard out, but not because I particularly cared about the female. It was . . . See, it was her son. Her son was watching in the shadows of the dark street, crouched next to a cart. He was like . . . shit, definitely a pretrans, and a young one at that. I saw him first, actually, then caught the action across the way. I thought of my own mother, or at least the image I had made up about her, and was like . . . hell, no, was this little boy going to watch the female who'd birthed him die."

"Did the mother live?"

He winced. "She was gone by the time I could get to her. Bled out from a throat wound. But I promise you, that *lesser* got shredded. Afterward I didn't know what to do with the kid. I ended up going to the merchant I killed for, and he put me in touch with some folks who took the boy in." V laughed in a short burst. "Turned out the mother who died was a fallen Chosen, and that pretrans? Well, he ended up being the father of my brother Murhder. We got a small world, true?

"So because I saved a kid of warrior blood, word got out, and my brother Darius ended up finding me and introducing me to Wrath. D . . . D and I had a certain connection, and he was probably the only one who could have gotten my attention at that point. When I met Wrath, he wasn't into being king, and he was no more interested in ties than I was. Which meant the two of us clicked. Eventually I was inducted into the Brotherhood. And there . . . shit, yeah, there you have it."

In the silence that followed he could only guess what was going through her mind, and the idea that she pitied him made him want to do something to prove he was strong.

Like bench-press a car.

Except instead of going all soft on him and making him feel even more rattled, Jane just looked around, even though he knew she could see nothing but the two candles that were lit. "And this place . . . this place means what to you?"

"Nothing. Means nothing more than any other."

"Then why are we here?"

V's heart rate spiked.

Shit . . . Standing here with her now, after spilling his guts, he wasn't sure he could go through with what he'd planned.

TWENTY-NINE

s Jane waited for V to speak, she wanted to wrap her arms around him. She wanted to throw a whole lot of very sincere, ultimately lame words at him. She wanted to know whether his father had died and in what way. She hoped the bastard had gone badly and with pain.

When the silence continued, she said, "I don't know if this will help . . . probably won't, but I have to say something here. I can't stomach oatmeal. To this day, it makes me sick." She prayed she wasn't going to say the wrong thing. "It is okay that you're still struggling with everything that was done to you. Anyone would. It doesn't make you weak. You were violently maimed by someone who should have protected and nurtured you. The fact that you're still standing is a miracle. I respect you for it."

V's cheeks went pink. "I, ah . . . don't really see it that way."

"Fine. But I do." To give him a break, she cleared her throat and said, "You going to tell me why we're here?"

He rubbed his face like he was trying to clear his brain. "Shit, I want to be with you. Here."

She exhaled in relief and sadness. She wanted a good-bye with him, also. A good-bye that was sexual and private and not in the bedroom they'd been locked in together. "I want to be with you, too."

Another candle came to life over by a bank of curtains. Then a fourth by a wet bar. A fifth next to a big bed with black satin sheets on it.

She started to smile . . . until the sixth one lit up. There was something hanging off the wall . . . something that looked like . . . chains?

More candles flared. Masks. Whips. Canes. Gags.

A black table with restraints that hung down to the floor.

She wrapped her arms around herself, chilled. "So this is where you do the tying-up."

"Yeah."

Oh, Jesus . . . She didn't want that kind of good-bye. Trying to stay calm, she said, "You know, it makes sense, given what happened to you. That you'd like that." Shit, she couldn't handle this. "So . . . is it men or women? Or, like, a combination?"

She heard the creaking of leather and turned back to him. He was taking off his jacket, and a set of guns she hadn't seen were next. Followed by two black knives that had been hidden as well. Christ, he'd been totally armed.

Jane tightened the hold on herself. She wanted to be with him, but not tied down and masked while he pulled a *9½ Weeks* on her head and whipped the shit out of her body. "Listen, V, I don't think—"

He took his shirt off, his back muscles flexing up his spine, his pecs pumping fully, then settling. He kicked off his boots.

Holy . . . shit, she thought, as it dawned on her what this was really about.

His socks and his leathers were next, and, as he'd gone commando, there were no boxers to get rid of. In total silence he padded

across the glossy marble floor and got up on the table in a coordinated surge. Stretching out, he was utterly magnificent, his body heavy with muscle, his movements elegant and masculine. He took a deep breath, his rib cage rising and falling.

Fine tremors licked over his skin . . . or maybe it was the candlelight?

He swallowed hard.

No, it was fear that was making him twitch.

"Pick out a mask for me," he said in a low voice.

"V . . . no."

"A mask and a ball gag." He turned his head toward her. "Do it. Then put the cuffs on me." When she didn't move, he nodded at what hung on the wall. "Please."

"Why?" she asked, watching the sweat break out over his body.

He closed his eyes, and his lips barely moved. "You've given me so much—and not just a weekend of your life. I tried to think of what I could give you in return—you know, fair-trade shit, throwing up oatmeal for deets on my scars. The only thing I've got is me and this. . . ." He tapped the rack's hard wood with his knuckles. "This is as exposed as I could ever be, and that's what I want to give you."

"I don't want to hurt you."

"I know." His lids flipped open. "But I want you to have me as no one else has or will. So pick out the mask."

As he swallowed, she watched his Adam's apple roll along the column of his thick throat. "This is not the kind of gift I want. Or the kind of good-bye."

There was a long silence. Then he said, "Remember I told you about the arranged-marriage thing?"

"Yes."

"It's going down in a matter of days."

Oh, now she really didn't want this. To think she was with someone else's fiancé—

"I haven't met the female. She hasn't met me." He looked over at Jane. "And she's the first of about forty."

"Forty?"

"I'm supposed to sire all their children."

"Oh, *God.*"

"So here's the thing. Sex is all about biological function from here on out. And see, I haven't really ever put myself out there, true? I want to do this with you because . . . Well, anyway, I just do."

She looked at him. The cost of laying himself out like this was in his wide, bouncing eyes and his pale face and the sweat that beaded his chest. To say no was to degrade his courage.

"What . . ." *Holy shit.* "What exactly do you want me to do to you?"

When V finished telling her, he turned away and stared at the ceiling. The candlelight played across the broad, black expanse, making it look like a pool of oil. As he waited for Jane's response, he was hit by vertigo, feeling as if the room had flipped itself over and he was suspended above the ceiling, about to be dropped into it and swallowed by Quaker State's best.

Jane didn't say a word.

Jesus . . . Nothing like offering yourself raw and being shut down. Then again, maybe she didn't like vampire sushi.

He jumped as her hand came to rest on his foot. And then he heard the metal-on-metal sound of a buckle being lifted. He looked down his naked body as a four-inch leather strap looped around his ankle. At the sight of her pale hands working to restrain him, his cock punched into an erection.

Jane's face was all concentration as she put the end of the leather tongue through the buckle and tugged to the left. "Is this okay?"

"Tighter."

Without glancing up she gave a good solid pull. As the strap bit into his skin, V's head dropped back on the wood and he moaned.

"Too much?" she asked.

"No . . ." He trembled outright as she anchored his other leg, both terrified and really fucking aroused. The feelings intensified as she did one wrist, then the other.

"Now the gag and the mask." His voice was hoarse because his blood was running hot and cold, and his throat was as tight as the restraints.

She looked at him. "You sure?"

"Yeah. One of the masks is the kind that just goes over the eyes, and that will fit."

When she came back to him she had a red rubber ball in a head halter and the mask in her hands.

"The gag first," he told her, opening his mouth wide. Her eyes shut for a moment, and he wondered if she was going to stop, but then she leaned forward. The ball tasted like latex, a stinging, bitter bite on his tongue. As he lifted his head so she could strap it on him, his breath whistled through his nose.

Jane shook her head. "I can't do the mask. I need to see your eyes. I can't . . . Yeah, I won't do this without eye contact. Okay?"

It was probably a good idea. The gag was doing what it should, making him feel suffocated . . . and the restraints were doing what they should, making him feel trapped. If he couldn't see and know that it was her, he'd probably totally fucking lose it.

When he nodded she dropped the mask onto the floor and took off her coat. Then she went over and picked up one of the black candles.

V's lungs burned as she came at him.

She took a deep breath. "You sure?"

He nodded again even as his thighs twitched and his eyes bugged out. With dread and excitement, he watched as she extended her arm over his chest . . . and tipped the candle.

Black wax dripped onto his nipple, and he ground his teeth into the ball gag, straining against what kept him on the table until the leather creaked. His cock jumped on his belly, and he had to suck back the orgasm.

She did exactly what he'd told her he wanted, going down lower and lower on his torso, then skipping over his privates to start at his knees and work her way up. The pain had a cumulative effect, at first nothing more than bee stings, later growing intense. Sweat rolled down his temples and ribs, and he panted through his nose until his whole body was bowing up from the table.

He came the first time when she put the candle away, picked up a length of cane . . . and touched the head of his erection with the end of it. He barked against the gag and ejaculated all over the hardened black wax on his stomach.

Jane froze, as if the reaction surprised her. Then she ran the cane through the mess he'd made, coating his chest with what had come out of him. The bonding scent flooded the penthouse, and so did his groans of submission as she stroked up and down his torso, then onto his hips.

He came a second time when she slipped the cane between his legs and stroked the insides of his thighs with it. Fear and sex and love filled out his skin from the inside, becoming the muscles and bones that made him up; he was nothing but emotion and need, with her as the driver of him.

And then she brought the cane down across his thighs with a slice of her arm.

Jane couldn't believe she was getting hot, considering what she was doing. But with V stretched out and pinned and orgasming for her, it was hard not to jump on him.

She used the cane lightly on him, no doubt less than he wanted, but hard enough to leave marks on his thighs and his belly and his chest. She couldn't believe he liked it like this, considering what he'd been put through, but in fact he loved it. His eyes were focused on her and glowing bright as bulbs, casting white shadows over the but-

tery light of the candles. As he came yet again, that dark, spicy scent she associated with him wafted up anew.

God, it shamed and fascinated her that she wanted to go even further with what was available . . . that she eyed the box of metal clips and the whips on the wall no longer as aberrant but as representative of a host of erotic possibilities. It wasn't that she wanted to hurt him. She just wanted him to feel as intensely as he did now. The point was taking him to his sexual limit.

Eventually she got so worked up she pulled off her pants and her underwear. "I'm going to fuck you," she told him.

He moaned desperately, hips swiveling and pushing upward. His erection was still rock-solid in spite of the number of times he'd ejaculated, and it pulsed as if he were going to go again.

As she got up onto the rack and split her thighs over his pelvis, he breathed through his nose with such force she grew alarmed. With his nostrils sucking in and out, she reached forward to undo the gag, but he jerked his head away and shook it.

"You sure?" she asked.

When he nodded fiercely, she eased down onto his semen-slicked hips and settled on the hard ridge of his arousal, her core parting over him, gripping him. His eyes rolled back in their sockets and his lids fluttered like he was about to pass out as he rocked against her to the extent he could.

While she rode back and forth on him, she took off her shirt and pushed her bra's cups to the side so that they molded her up and out. There was a mighty creak as V strained against the binds. If he'd been free, she was quite sure he would have had her on her back underneath him in the work of a moment.

"Watch me take you," she said, running one of her hands up to her neck. When her fingers coasted over the remnants of his bite mark, V's lips pulled back from the ball gag and his fangs elongated, digging into the red latex as he growled.

She kept touching herself where he'd bitten her while she rose on her knees and stood up his arousal. She sat on him good and hard, and he orgasmed as soon as he entered her, kicking deep inside, flooding her. He was still fully erect afterward, even as he stopped twitching.

Jane had never felt more sexual in her life as she began to grind on top of him. She loved that he was smeared with wax and the result of his orgasms, that his skin was gleaming with sweat and flaming red in places, that there was going to be a mess to clean up. She had done the whole of it to him, and he adored her for what had happened, and that was why it felt right.

As her own release came barreling in, she looked into his wide, wild eyes.

She wished she didn't ever have to leave him.

THIRTY

As Fritz pulled the Mercedes into the short driveway of a condo and put it in park, V looked out through the front windshield.

"Nice place," he said to Jane.

"Thank you."

He fell quiet, getting lost in what had gone down back at his penthouse for the last two hours. The things she'd done to him . . . Christ, nothing had ever been that erotic. And nothing had been so sweet as the aftermath. When the session was finished, she'd released him and taken him into the shower. Under the spray of the water his come had rinsed away and the wax had flaked off, but the cleansing had really been on the inside.

He wished the red marks she'd left on his body would stay. He wanted them in his skin permanently.

God, he couldn't stand to let her go.

"So how long have you been here?" he asked.

"Since my residency. So, ten years."

"Good area for you. Close to the hospital. How're the neighbors?" Such nice cocktail, blah-blah conversation. Meanwhile, the house the party was in was on fire.

"Half of the people are young professionals and the other half are old. Joke is that you leave either because you get married or you go into a nursing home." She nodded to the unit next to hers on the left. "Mr. Hancock pulled out two weeks ago into assisted living. The new neighbor, whoever-it-is, will probably be just like him, because the one-floor units tend to go to the elderly. By the way, I'm rambling."

And he was stalling. "Like I said, I love your voice, so feel free."

"I don't do it except around you."

"Which makes me lucky." He glanced at his watch. Shit, time was draining out like water from a bath, leaving a whole lot of cold in its absence. "So can I have a tour?"

"Absolutely."

He got out first and scanned the area before stepping aside and letting her stand up. He told Fritz to take off, as he'd just dematerialize back home, and while the *doggen* pulled out of the driveway, V let her lead up the walkway.

Jane opened the door with nothing but a single key and a twist of the knob. No security system. Only one lock. And on the inside no dead bolt or chain. Even though she didn't have enemies like he did, this was not safe enough. He was going to—

No, he wasn't going to remedy it. Because in another few minutes he was going to be a stranger.

To keep from losing it, he looked around. Her furniture didn't make sense. Against the ivory walls of the condo, all the mahogany and the oil paintings made the place feel like a museum. From the Eisenhower era.

"Your furniture . . ."

"Was my parents'," she said as she put down her coat and duffel.

"After they died, I moved what could fit here from the house in Greenwich. It was a mistake—I feel like I'm living in a museum."

"Um . . . I can see your point."

He walked around her living room, checking out the kind of stuff that belonged in a doctor's Colonial house in a Bruce Wayne part of town. The shit dwarfed the condo's lines, choking rooms that might otherwise have been airy.

"Don't know why I'm keeping it all, really. I didn't like living with it when I was growing up." She took a little spin, then stalled out.

Shit, he didn't know what to say, either.

He knew what to do, though. "So . . . your kitchen is that way, true?"

She walked over to the right. "It's not much."

But it was nice, V thought as he walked in. Like the rest of the condo, the kitchen was white and cream, but at least here you didn't feel like you needed a docent: The table and chairs in the breakfast nook were pale pine and the right size for the space. The granite countertops were sleek. The appliances were stainless steel.

"I did it over last year."

There was more cocktail blah-blahing as they both ignored the fact that GAME OVER was flashing on their screen.

V went over to the stove, and taking a chance, he opened the upper cupboard to the left. Bingo. The hot chocolate mix was right there.

He snagged it, put it on the counter, then went to the refrigerator.

"What are you doing?" she asked.

"You got a mug? Pan?" He grabbed a container of milk from the icebox, cracked the top, and gave it a sniff.

As he walked back to the stove, she told him the where's-what in a low voice, like she was suddenly having trouble holding it together. He was ashamed to admit it, but he was glad she was upset. Made him feel less pathetic and alone in the midst of this hellacious good-bye.

Man, he was an asshole.

He took out an enameled saucepan and a thick diner-style mug, then popped up a low flame on the stove. As the milk heated, he stared at the assembled crap on the counter and felt his brain go on a little vacation: The setup looked like a commercial for Nestlé, the kind of thing where Suburban Mom was holding down the fort while the Kids played in the snow until they got red noses and cold hands. He could just picture it: the chilly crew would come screaming in just as the self-satisfied mominator put out the kind of warm-up spread capable of cranking Norman Rockwell into a saccharine submission hold.

He could just hear the voice-over: *Nestlé makes the very best.*

Yeah, well, no kids or mom here. No happy hearth either, though the condo was nice enough. This was real-life cocoa. The kind you gave someone you loved because you couldn't think of anything else to do and both of you were a mess. It was the kind you stirred while your gut was knotted and your mouth was dry and you were thinking seriously of crying, but you were too much of a male for that kind of display.

It was the kind you made with all the love you hadn't expressed and might well not have the voice or the chance to speak of.

"I won't remember anything?" she asked roughly.

He added a little more powder and circled the spoon, watching the swirl of chocolate get absorbed in the milk. He couldn't reply, just couldn't say it.

"Nothing?" she prompted.

"From what I understand, you might get feelings once in a while that are triggered by an object or a scent, but you won't be able to place them." He stuck his forefinger in to test for temperature, sucked it clean, and kept stirring. "You're more likely to have vague dreams, though, because your mind is so strong."

"What about the missing weekend?"

"You won't feel as if you missed it at all."

"How's that possible?"

"Because I'm going to give you a weekend to replace it."

When she didn't say anything further, he glanced over his shoulder. She was standing against the refrigerator, arms wrapped around herself, eyes shimmering.

Fuck. Okay, he changed his mind. He didn't want her to feel as bad as he did. He'd do anything to keep her from being this heart-broken.

And he had it in his power to fix her, didn't he.

He tested what he was warming, approved of the temp, and killed the flame. As he filled the mug, the gentle gurgle promised the relaxation and satisfaction he wanted for his female. He brought the mug over to her, and when she didn't take it, he reached out and unhinged one of her forearms. She palmed the hot chocolate only because he made her, and she didn't drink it. She cradled it to her collarbone, curling her wrist in, twisting her arm around the thing.

"I don't want you to go," she whispered, tears in the achy pitch of her voice.

He put his bare hand to her cheek and felt the softness and warmth of her face. He knew that when he pulled out of here, he was leaving his stupid fucking heart with her. Sure, something would beat behind his ribs and keep his blood moving around, but it would just be a mechanical function from now on.

Oh, wait. It had been like that before. She'd just given the thing flesh and life for a short time.

He pulled her into his arms and rested his chin on the top of her head. Holy hell, he was never again going to smell chocolate and not think of her, not pine for her.

Just as he closed his eyes a tingle ran up his spine, trembling along the back of his neck and shooting to the anchor of his jaw. The sun was coming up, and that was his body telling him the time to go was no longer a future thing, but a now thing . . . an urgent now thing.

He pulled back and pressed his lips to hers. "I love you. And I'm going to keep loving you even after you don't know I exist."

Her lashes flickered, catching her tears until there were too many to hold. He brushed his thumbs over her face.

"V . . . I . . ."

He waited for a heartbeat. When she didn't finish, he took her chin in his palm and looked into her eyes.

"Oh, God, you're going to do it," she said. "You're going to—"

THIRTY-ONE

Jane blinked and looked down at the hot chocolate she was holding. Something was dripping into it.

Jesus . . . Tears were pouring down her face, falling into the mug, getting her button-down shirt wet. Her whole body was shaking, her knees weak, her chest screaming in pain. For some crazy reason she wanted to fall to the floor and wail.

Wiping her cheeks off, she glanced around her kitchen. There was milk and cocoa mix and a spoon on the counter. The pan on the stove still had a little steam rising up from it. The cabinet to the left wasn't shut all the way. She couldn't remember taking the stuff out or making what was in her mug, but then, that was often the case with repetitive, habitual actions. You space-shotted them—

What the hell? Through the windows on the other side of the breakfast nook, she saw someone standing in front of her condo. A man. A huge man. He was just outside the glowing pool of a street lamp, so she couldn't see his face, but she knew he was staring at her.

For no evident reason her tears ran harder and faster. And the outpouring got worse as the stranger turned away and walked off down the street.

Jane all but threw the mug onto the counter and bolted out of her kitchen. She had to catch him. She had to stop him.

Just as she came to her front door, a vicious headache took her down to the floor sure as if she'd been tripped off her feet. She sprawled out on the foyer's cold white tile, then twisted onto her side, grinding her fingers into her temples and gasping.

She lay there for God only knew how long, just breathing and praying for the pain to back off. When it finally did she eased her upper body off the floor and leaned against her front door. She wondered if she'd had a stroke, but there had been no cognitive interruptions or visual disturbances. Just one hell of a quick-onset headache.

Must be remnants of the flu she'd had all weekend. That virus that had been around the hospital for weeks had taken her out like a dead rosebush. Which made sense. She hadn't been sick in a long time, so she'd been overdue.

Speaking of overdue . . . Shit, had she even called to reschedule her interview at Columbia? She had no clue . . . which meant she probably hadn't. Hell, she didn't even remember leaving the hospital on Thursday night.

She wasn't sure how long she made like a doorstop, but at some point the clock on the mantel started to chime. It was the one that had been in her father's study in Greenwich, an old-fashioned Hamilton made of solid brass that she'd always sworn rang the hours in with a British accent. She'd hated the damn thing forever, but it kept good time.

Six o'clock in the morning. Time to go to work.

Good plan, but when she stood up, she knew without a doubt she wasn't going into the hospital. She was light-headed, weak, exhausted. There was no way she could administer care in her condition; she was still sick as a dog.

Damn it . . . she had to call in. Where were her pager and her phone . . . ?

She frowned. Her coat and the bag she'd packed to go down to Manhattan were sitting next to the front hall closet.

No cell, though. No pager.

She dragged her sorry ass upstairs and checked by her bed, but the pair weren't there. Back down on the first floor she went through the kitchen. Nothing. And her shoulder bag, the one she always took to work, was missing, too. Could she have left the thing in the car all weekend?

She opened the door into the garage and the automatic light came on.

Weird. Her car was parked headfirst. Usually she backed it in.

Which just proved how out-of-it she'd been.

Sure enough her bag was in the front seat, and she cursed herself as she went back into the condo while dialing. How could she have gone for so long without calling in? Even though she was covered by other attendings, she was never out of touch for more than five hours.

Her service had a number of messages, but luckily none of them was urgent. The important ones concerning patient care had been turfed to whoever was on call, so the rest of it was stuff she could handle later.

She was heading out of the kitchen, making a beeline for her bedroom, when she looked at the mug of chocolate. She didn't have to touch it to know it had gone cold, so she might as well ditch the thing. She went and picked it up, but paused over the sink. For some reason she couldn't bear to throw it out. She left it right where it was on the counter, though she did return the milk to the refrigerator.

Upstairs in her bedroom she ditched her clothes, letting them land where they did, pulled on a T-shirt, and got in bed.

She was settling between her sheets when she realized her body was stiff, especially her inner thighs and lower back. Under different circumstances she would have said she'd had a lot of terrific sex . . . either that or climbed a mountain. But instead it was just the flu.

Shit. Columbia. The interview.

She'd call Ken Falcheck later this morning, apologize for what she hoped was the second time, and reschedule. They were hungry for her to come onboard, but not showing for an interview with the chairman of the department was insulting as hell. Even if you were sick.

Rearranging herself against her pillows, she couldn't get comfortable. Her neck was tight, and she reached up to massage it, only to frown. There was a sore spot on the right side in front, a real . . . What the hell? She had a pattern there, some raised bumps.

Whatever. Rashes were not unheard-of with the flu. Or maybe a spider had done her in.

She closed her eyes and told herself to rest. Resting was good. Resting would get rid of this bug faster. Resting would bring her back to normal, a reboot for her body.

Just as she drifted off, an image came to mind, an image of a man with a goatee and diamond eyes. His mouth was moving as he looked at her, framing the words . . . *I love you.*

Jane struggled to hold on to what she saw, but she was sliding fast into sleep's dark arms. She fought to stay with the image and lost the battle. The last thing she was aware of were tears flowing onto her pillow as the blackness stole her away.

Well, wasn't this awkward.

John sat on the bench-press in the weight room and watched as Zsadist did bicep curls across the way. The huge loads of iron made a subtle clinking sound as they went up and down, and that was it for noise. There had been no talking so far; it was just like one of their walks, only without the woods. The convo was coming, though. John could sense it.

Z put the weights down on the mats and wiped his face. His bare chest gleamed, his nipple rings rising and falling as he breathed.

His yellow eyes shifted over.

Here we go, John thought.

"So about your transition."

Okaaaay . . . so they were going to ease into the *lesser* thing. *What about it?* he signed.

"How you feeling?"

Good. Wobbly. Different. He shrugged. *You know when you, like, clip your nails, and your fingertips are weird for a day, all supersensitive? It's like that all over me.*

Oh, what the hell was he going on about? Z had been through the change. He knew what was doing afterward.

Zsadist dropped the towel and picked up the weights for his second set of reps. "You got any physical problems?"

Not that I know of.

Z's eyes locked on the mats as he alternated lifting his left forearm, then his right. Left. Right. Left. It seemed strange that such heavy weights could make that gentle sound.

"So, Layla reported in."

Oh . . . shit.

What did she say?

Please . . . not the shower . . .

"She said you two didn't have sex. Even though it appeared that you wanted to at one point."

As John's brain shut down, he mindlessly kept track of Z's reps. Right. Left. Right. Left. *Who knows this?*

"Wrath and me. That's it. And it's no one else's biz. But I'm bringing it up in case there's something physical going on that you need to get checked out."

John stood up and paced around in his gangly way, nothing but sloppy arms and legs and a drunk's sense of balance.

"Why did you stop, John?"

He glanced over at the Brother, about to give some kind of blow-off, no-big-deal answer, when he realized to his horror that he wouldn't be able to do that.

Z's yellow eyes glowed with knowledge.

Holy fuck. Havers had spilled, hadn't he. That therapist session at the clinic when John had talked about what had happened to him in that stairwell had gotten out.

You know, John signed with fury. *You fucking know, don't you?*

"Yeah, I do."

That cocksucking therapist told me it was confidential—

"A copy of your medical records was sent over here when you started the program. It's standard procedure for all trainees in case something happens in the gym, or in the event the transition starts while you're on-site."

Who's read my file?

"Just me. And no one else will, not even Wrath. I locked it up, and I'm the only one who knows where it is."

John sagged. At least there was consolation in that. *When did you read it?*

"About a week ago, when I figured your change was going to hit any day now."

What . . . what did it say?

"Pretty much everything."

Fuck.

"That's why you won't go to Havers, right?" Z put the weights down again. "You figure the guy's going to snatch and drag you into another therapy hour."

I don't like to talk about it.

"I don't blame you. And I'm not asking you to."

John cracked a little smile. *You're not going to hit me with all kinds of talk-is-good-for-you shit?*

"Nah. I'm not a talker myself. Can't recommend it to others." Z put his elbows on his knees and leaned forward. "Here's the deal,

John. I want you to have absolute faith that that shit's going no-where, okay? If someone wants to see your record, I'm going to make it so they don't, even if I have to burn the fucker to ash."

John swallowed through a sudden lump in his throat. With stiff hands, he signed, *Thank you.*

"Wrath wanted me to talk to you about the Layla thing because he was worried there might be something wrong with your post-transition plumbing. I'm going to tell him that you were nervous and that was the why of it, deal?"

John nodded.

"Have you jerked off yet?"

John blushed from eyebrow to ankle and considered passing out. As he measured the distance to the ground, which seemed like a hundred yards, he figured this was not a bad place to keel over. Plenty of mats to land on.

"Have you?"

He shook his head slowly.

"Do it once to make sure nothing is wrong." Z got up, toweled his torso off, and pulled on his shirt. "I'm going to assume you'll take care of it in the next twenty-four hours. I will not ask you what happens. If you say nothing, I'll take it that everything's cool. If it isn't, you come to me and we'll deal with it. We solid?"

Um, not really. What if he couldn't do it? *I guess.*

"Last thing. About the gun and the *lessers?*"

Fuck, his head was already spinning, and now he had to deal with the shit about that nine? He lifted his hands to make excuses—

"I don't care that you were packing. In fact, I want you armed if you go to ZeroSum."

John stared at the Brother, stunned. *That's against the rules.*

"Do I look like the kind of guy who worries about that shit?"

John smiled a little. *Not really.*

"If you get in the crosshairs of one of those slayers again, you do him just like you did. From what I understand, that was some impressive shit you pulled, and I'm proud of you for taking up for your boys."

John flushed, his heart singing in his chest: Nothing on the face of the planet, except Tohrment's safe return, could have made him happier.

"By now I'm guessing you know what I hooked Blaylock up with? About your papers and ID and only going to ZeroSum?"

John nodded.

"I want you to keep hitting that club if you hang downtown, at least for the next month or so, until you're strong. And though I'm willing to stroke you on what went down last night, I don't want you out hunting for *lessers*. I hear that's going on, I'm going to ground your ass like a twelve-year-old. You have a lot of training ahead of you, and you've got no idea how to work that body of yours. You fuck around and get yourself killed, I'm going to be really pissed off. I want you to give me your word, John. Right now. No going after those bastards until I say you're ready. We down?"

John took a deep breath and tried to think of the most solid vow he could offer. Everything seemed flimsy so he just signed, *I swear I will not hunt them.*

"Good. Okay, we're done tonight. Go hit the sack." As Z turned away, John whistled to get his attention. The Brother looked over his shoulder. "Yeah?"

John had to force his hands to sign what was in his mind . . . because he doubted he'd have the courage to do it again.

Do you think less of me? Because of what happened back then . . . you know, in the stairwell? And be honest.

Z blinked once. Twice. A third time. And then in a voice that was curiously thin, he said, "Never. It was *not* your fault, and you did *not* deserve it. You heard me? It was *not* your fault."

John winced as tears stung his eyes, and he had to look away, glancing down his big body at the mats. For some reason, though he was far from the ground, he felt shorter than ever.

"John," Z demanded, "you heard me on that? Not your fault. Did not deserve it."

John didn't really have a reply, so he shrugged. Then he signed, *Thanks again for not telling. And for not making me talk about it.*

When Z didn't say anything, he glanced up. Only to take a step back.

Zsadist's whole face had changed, and not just because his eyes had gone black. His bones seemed more prominent, his skin tighter, his scar shockingly evident. A cold blast emanated from his body, chilling the air, turning the locker room into a freezer.

"No one should have their innocence raped from them. But if they do? They get to pick how they deal with it, because it's no one else's biz. You never want to say another fucking word on the subject, you're getting no lip from me."

Z stalked off, the drop in temperature easing off as the door shut behind him.

John took a deep breath. He never would have guessed that Z would end up being the Brother he was closest to. After all, the two of them had nothing in common.

But he sure as hell was going to take his friends where he found them.

THIRTY-TWO

$\mathfrak{A}$ couple of hours later, Phury leaned back into the sofa in Wrath's pansy-ass study and crossed his legs at the knee. The Brotherhood meeting was the first they'd had since V had gotten shot, and so far everything had been stilted. Then again, there was a big frickin' pink elephant in the room that hadn't been addressed yet.

He glanced over at Vishous. The brother was against the double doors and staring straight ahead, his blank fixation the kind of thing you caught on someone's face when they watched old Westerns on TV. Or a Lifetime movie.

The living-dead affect was easy to recognize because it had made an appearance in this room before. Rhage had sported the breathing-corpse routine when he thought he'd lost Mary forever. So had Z when he'd been determined to let Bella go.

Yeah . . . bonded male vampires without their females were empty vessels, nothing but muscle and bone held in by a thin skin. And

though you had to mourn for anyone who was like that, given the load of shit V was carrying with the Primale thing, the loss of Jane seemed especially cruel. Except how the hell could it have possibly worked long-term between those two? Human doctor. Warrior vampire. No middle ground.

Wrath's voice rang out. "V? Yo, Vishous?"

V's head jerked up. "What?"

"You're going to the Scribe Virgin this afternoon, right?"

V's mouth barely moved: "Yeah."

"You're going to need a rep from the Brotherhood to go with you. I'm assuming Butch, right?"

V glanced over at the cop, who was sitting in a pale blue love seat. "You mind?"

Butch, who was clearly worried about V, immediately manned up. "Of course not. What do I need to do?"

When V said nothing, Wrath filled the void. "Human equiv's probably best man at a wedding. You'll go for the viewing today and then the ceremony, which'll be tomorrow."

"Viewing? Like this woman is a painting or some shit?" Butch grimaced. "I'm so not feeling this whole Chosen thing, I gotta be honest."

"Old rules. Old traditions." Wrath rubbed his eyes under his sunglasses. "Lot needs to change, but it's the Scribe Virgin's territory, not mine. All right . . . so . . . rotation. Phury, I want you sitting out tonight. Yeah, I know you're tight after being hurt, but I just noticed you missed your last two scheduled breaks."

When Phury just nodded, Wrath cocked a smirk. "No fight on that?"

"Nope."

Actually, he had something he had to do. So it was fucking perfect.

On the Other Side, in the sacred marble bathing chamber, Cormia wished she could leave her own skin. Which was a bit ironic, as it had been so carefully prepared for the Primale. One would think she would wish to stay within it now that it was so purified. She had been steeped in a dozen different ritual baths . . . had her hair cleansed and recleansed . . . had her face put in masks of rose-smelling unguents, then ones that smelled of lavender, then still others of sage and hyacinth. Oil had been rubbed all over her, while incense had burned in honor of the Primale and prayers were chanted. The process had made her feel like something in a ceremonial buffet. A piece of meat, seasoned and prepared for consumption.

"He will be here on the hour," the Directrix said. "Waste not the time."

Cormia's heart stopped in her chest. Then pounded. The numb state induced by all the steam and the warm waters retreated, leaving her painfully and horribly aware that her last moments of life as she had always known it were about to be over.

"Ah, the robing is here," one of the Chosen said with excitement.

Cormia looked over her shoulder. Across the vast marble floor a pair of Chosen came through gold doors with a white hooded robe hanging between them. The garment was embroidered with diamonds and gold, and it shimmered in the candlelight, alive with color. Behind them another Chosen held a stretch of translucent cloth in her arms.

"Bring the veil forward," the Directrix commanded. "And put it on her."

The diaphanous sheath was draped over Cormia's head, and it landed upon her with the weight of a thousand stones. As it fell before her eyes, the world around her fogged.

"Stand," she was told.

She got to her feet and had to steady herself, her heart beating hard behind her ribs, her palms growing sweaty. The panic grew worse as the heavy robing was borne forward by the two Chosen. As the ceremonial dress was laid upon her from behind, it clamped onto her shoulders, not so much settling onto her frame as locking onto

her body. She felt as though some giant stood at her back with his massive, pawlike hands pressing her down.

The hood was lifted over her head and everything went black.

The front of the robe was buttoned in place over the tail end of the hood, and Cormia tried not to think about when and in what manner those fastenings were going to be freed again. She tried to take slow, deep breaths. Fresh air came in through some vents at her neck, but it wasn't enough. Not by a measure and a half.

Under her dressings all sound was muffled, and it would be difficult for anyone to hear her speak. But then, she had no personal role in either the presentation ceremony or the mating ritual that was to come. She was a symbol, not a female, so her individual response was not required or encouraged. The traditions reigned supreme.

"Perfect," one of her sisters said.

"Resplendent."

"Worthy of us."

Cormia opened her mouth and whispered to herself, "I am me. I am me. I am me. . . ."

Tears welled and fell, but she couldn't reach her face to wipe them off, so they ran down her cheeks and her throat, getting lost in the robing.

With no warning, her panic suddenly got away from her, a wild animal set loose. She wheeled around, hobbled by the heavy robes, but driven by a need to flee that she could not harness. She took off in the direction she thought was the door, dragging the weight with her. Dimly she heard shrieks of surprise echoing in the bathing chamber, along with crashing sounds as bottles and bowls and jars were knocked asunder.

She flailed around, trying to strip off the robing, desperate for relief.

Desperate to be free of her destiny.

THIRTY-THREE

In downtown Caldwell, in the northeast corner of the St. Francis hospital complex, Manuel Manello, M.D., hung up the phone on his desk without having dialed anything on it or having answered a call that had come through to him. He stared at the NEC console. The thing was jacked up with buttons, right out of a Circuit City junkie's wet dreams with all its bells and whistles.

He wanted to throw it across the room.

He wanted to, but he didn't. He'd given up throwing tennis rackets, TV remotes, scalpels, and books when he decided to become the youngest chief of surgery in St. Francis hospital history. Since then, his palm punting involved only empty bottles and vending machine wrappers snapped into trash cans. And that was just to keep his aim up.

Shifting back in his leather chair, he pivoted himself around and stared out the window of his office. It was a nice office. Big, fancy as shit, all mahogany-paneled and Oriental-rugged up, the Throne

Room, as it was known, had served as the head surgeon's landing pad for fifty years. He'd been sitting pretty in the digs for about three years now, and if he ever got a break in the action he was going to give the place a makeover. All the Establishment gloss made him scratch.

He thought of the damn phone and knew he was going to make a call he shouldn't. It was just so fucking weak, and it was going to come across that way, even if he was all his usual macho arrogance.

Still, he was going to end up letting his fingers do the walking.

To put off the inevitable, he blew some time staring out the window. From his vantage point he could see the front of St. Francis's landscaped entrance, as well as the city beyond. Hands down this was the best view on hospital grounds. In the spring cherry trees and tulips bloomed in the median of the entrance's drive. And in the summer, on either side of the two lanes maples leafed up green as emeralds until they faded to peach and yellow in the fall.

Usually he didn't spend a lot of time enjoying the scenery, but he did appreciate knowing it was there. Sometimes a man needed to corral his thoughts.

He was having one of those moments now.

Last night he'd called Jane's cell phone, figuring she'd be home from that damn interview. No answer. He'd called her this morning. No answer.

Fine. If she didn't want to spill about that fucking interview at Columbia, he was going to go directly to the source. He'd call the chief of surgery down there himself. Egos being what they were, his former mentor wouldn't hesitate to share some details, but, man, this was going to be an ass burner of a fishing expedition.

Manny twisted around, punched out ten digits, and waited, tapping a Montblanc pen on his blotter.

When the ringing was answered, he didn't wait for a hello. "Falcheck, you raiding dickhead."

Ken Falcheck laughed. "Manello, you have such a way with words. And me being your elder, I'm especially shocked."

"So how's life in the slow lane, old man?"

"Good, good. Now tell me, baby boy, they letting you eat solid foods yet or are you still on the Gerber?"

"I'm up to oatmeal. Which means I'll be well fortified to do your hip replacement anytime you get bored with that walker."

This was all utter bullshit, of course. At fifty-eight Ken Falcheck was in great shape, and a ballbuster right up Manny's lane. The two had gotten along ever since Manny had gone through the guy's training program fifteen years ago.

"So, with all deference to the elderly," Manny drawled, "why are you macking on my trauma surgeon? And what did you think of her?"

There was a slight pause. "What are you talking about? I got a message Thursday from some guy saying she had to reschedule. I thought that was why you were calling. To gloat that she blew me off and you were keeping her."

A nasty sensation wrapped around the back of Manello's neck, like someone had slapped a palmful of cold mud on him.

He kept his voice level. "Come on, would I do that?"

"Yeah, you would. I trained you, remember? You get all your bad habits from me."

"Just the professional ones. Hey, the guy who called—you get his name?"

"Nope. Figured it was her assistant or something. Obviously wasn't you. I know your voice, plus the guy was polite."

Manny swallowed hard. Okay, he needed to dump this call right away. Jesus Christ, where the hell was Jane?

"So, Manello, can I assume you're keeping her?"

"Let's face facts, I've got a lot of things I can offer her." Himself being one of them.

"Just not the chairmanship of a department."

God, at the moment, all this bullshit medical politicking didn't matter. Jane was MIA, as far as Manny was concerned, and he needed to find her.

With perfect timing, his assistant poked her head through his door. "Oh, sorry—"

"No, wait. Hey, Falcheck, I've got to go." He hung up as Ken was still saying good-bye and immediately started dialing Jane's house. "Listen, I need to make a phone—"

"Dr. Whitcomb just called in sick."

Manny looked up from the phone. "Did you speak to her? Was she the one who called?"

His assistant looked at him a little funny. "Of course. She's been down all weekend with the flu. Goldberg's going to cover her cases today and man the chute. Hey, are you okay?"

Manny put the receiver down and nodded even though he felt light-headed as hell. Shit, the idea that something had happened to Jane thinned his blood to water.

"You sure, Dr. Manello?"

"Yeah, I'm good. Thanks for the info on Whitcomb." As he stood up, the floor only weaved a little. "I'm due in the OR in an hour, so I'm going to food up. You got anything else for me?"

His assistant ran through a couple of issues with him, then left.

As the door shut Manny sank back into his chair. Man, he needed to gather the reins in his head. Jane Whitcomb had always been a distraction, but this shaky relief that she was fine surprised him.

Right. He needed to go eat.

Kicking himself in the ass, he got to his feet again and picked up a stack of residency applicant files to read in the lounge. In the process of taking them in hand, something slipped off the desk. He bent over and picked it up, then frowned. It was the printout of a photograph of a heart . . . that had six chambers.

Something flickered in the back of Manny's mind, some kind of shadow that moved around, a thought on the verge of actualization, a memory about to crystallize. Except then he got a sharp, shooting pain right at the temples. As he cursed, he wondered where the hell the photograph had come from, and checked the date and time at the bottom. It had been taken here, on his premises, in his OR, and the print job had been done in his office: His machine had a hiccup in it that left an ink dot on the lower left-hand corner, and the mark was there.

He turned to his computer and did a search of his files. No such photograph existed. *What the fuck?*

He checked his watch. No time to keep digging, because he really did have to eat before he went to operate.

As he left his big-cheese office, he decided he was going to be an old-fashioned doctor this evening.

Tonight he was going to pay a house call, the first of his professional career.

Vishous pulled on a pair of loose black silk pants and a matching top that looked like a smoking jacket from the forties. After he put the godforsaken Primale medallion around his neck, he left his room while lighting up. On his way down the hall he heard Butch swearing out in the living room, the rolling, under-the-breath litany marked by a lot of *F*-words and an interesting twist on *a-hole* V was going to have to remember.

V found the guy on the couch, glowering over Marissa's laptop. "What's doing, cop?"

"I think this hard drive has bitten it." Butch glanced up. "Jesus Christ . . . you look like Hugh Hefner."

"So not funny."

Butch winced. "I'm sorry. Shit . . . V, I'm s—"

"Shut up and let me look at the PC." V picked the thing up off Butch's lap and did a quick maintenance scan. "Dead."

"Should have known. Safe Place is in a cluster fuck of IT shit. Their server's down. Now this. Meanwhile Marissa's up at the man-

sion with Mary trying to figure out how to hire more staff. Man, she doesn't need this."

"I put four new Dells in the supply cabinet outside Wrath's study. Tell her to go get one, true? I'd set it up for her now, but I gotta go."

"Thanks, man. And yeah, I'll get ready to come with you—"

"You don't have to be there."

Butch frowned. "Fuck that. You need me."

"Someone else can stand in."

"I'm not abandoning you—"

"Wouldn't be abandonment." Vishous wandered over to the foosball table and spun one of the rods. As the row of little men did backflips, he exhaled. "It's kind of like . . . I don't know, if you're there, it's all too fucking real."

"So you want somebody else to back you?"

V spun the rod again, a whirring noise rising up from the table. He'd chosen Butch on a knee-jerk, but the truth was, the male was a complication. V was so damned close to the guy it was going to be harder to front his way through the presentation and the ritual.

V looked across the living room. "Yeah. Yeah, I think I want someone else."

In the short silence that followed, Butch assumed the look of someone holding a plate of food that was too hot: uneasy and insecure. "Well . . . as long as you know I would be there for you, no matter what was doing."

"I know you're solid." V went to the phone, thinking over his choices.

"Are you su—"

"Yes," he said, dialing. When Phury answered his call, V said, "You mind standing in with me today? Butch is going to hang back. Yeah. Uh-huh. Thanks, man." He hung up. It might be an odd choice, because the two of them had never been particularly close. But then, that was the point. "Phury's going to do it, no problem. I'm going to bounce to his room now."

"V—"

"Shut it, cop. I'll be back in a couple hours."

"I wish like hell you didn't have to—"

"Whatever. This isn't going to change things." After all, Jane would still be gone; he would still be a bonded male without his mate. So yup, yup, nothing different, nothing mattered.

"You're absolutely positive you don't want me to go?"

"Just be here with the Goose when I get back. I'm going to need a drink."

V left the Pit through the underground tunnel, and as he walked over to the mansion, he tried to give himself some perspective.

This Chosen he was mating was just a body. Same as he was. The two of them were going to do what needed to be done, when it was necessary. It was just male parts meeting female parts, then thrust and repeat until the male ejaculated. And as for his complete and utter lack of arousal? Not a problem. The Chosen had salves to en-sure an erection and incense that made you come. So even though he had absolutely no interest in sex, his body would do what it was born and bred to do: ensure that the best lines in the species sur-vived.

Shit, he wished it could be clinical, all cup-and-baster. But vam-pires had tried IVF in the past, to no success. Young had to be con-ceived the good old-fashioned way.

Man, he did not want to think of how many females he was going to have to be with. He just couldn't go there. If he did, he was going to—

Vishous stopped in the middle of the tunnel.

Opened his mouth.

And screamed until his voice gave out.

THIRTY-FOUR

When Vishous and Phury crossed over to the other side together, they took form in a white courtyard surrounded by a white arcade of Corinthian columns. In the center was a white marble fountain that splashed crystal-clear water into a deep white cistern. In the far corner, on a white tree with white blossoms, a flock of rainbow-colored songbirds was gathered as if they'd been sprinkled on top of a cupcake. The sweet calls of the finches and the chickadees harmonized with the chiming sound of the fountain, as if both cadences were in the same key of joy.

"Warriors." The Scribe Virgin's voice came from behind V and made his skin pull like plastic over his bones. "Kneel and I shall greet you."

V ordered his knees to bend, and after a moment they hinged like rusty legs on a card table. Phury, on the other hand, didn't seem to be suffering from a case of the stiffs and went down smoothly.

Then again, he wasn't hitting the floor in front of a mother he despised.

"Phury, son of Ahgony, how fare thee?"

In a perfectly eloquent voice, the brother replied in the Old Language, "I fare well, for I am before thee with purity of devotion and depth of heart."

The Scribe Virgin chuckled. "A proper greeting in the proper way. Lovely of you. And surely more than I will get from my son."

V felt rather than saw Phury's head whip toward him. *Oh, sorry,* V thought. *Guess I forgot to mention that happy little fact, my brother.*

The Scribe Virgin drifted closer. "Ah, so my son has not told you his maternal lineage? Out of decorum, I wonder? Concern for upsetting the generally held principle of my so-called virginal existence? Yes, that is why, is it not, Vishous, son of the Bloodletter."

V lifted his eyes, though he hadn't been invited to. "Or maybe I just refuse to acknowledge you."

It was exactly what she expected him to say, and he could sense this not from reading her thoughts, but because on some level the two of them were one and the same, indivisible in spite of the air and space between them.

Yay.

"Your reticence to concede my maternity of you changes nothing," she said in a hard tone. "A book unopened alters not the ink on its pages. What is there is there."

Without permission, V stood and met his mother's hooded face, eye for eye, strength for strength.

Phury was no doubt blanching white as flour, but whatever. He'd match the decor that way. Besides, the Scribe Virgin wasn't going to toast her future Primale or her precious little boy. No way. So he didn't give a fuck.

"Let's get this over with, *Mom*. I want back to my real life—"

V found himself flat on his back and not breathing in the blink of an eye. Though there was nothing on top of him and his body

didn't seem to be compressed, he felt like he had a grand piano on his chest.

As his eyes bugged out and he fought to drag some air into his lungs, the Scribe Virgin floated over to him. Her hood lifted from her face of its own volition, and she stared down at him with a bored expression on her ghostly, glowing face.

"I would have your word that you will comport yourself with respect toward me whilst we are before my assembled Chosen. I concede that you have some liberties by definition, but I will not hesitate to determine you a worse future than the one you wish to forsake if you reveal them in public. Are we in agreement?"

Agreement? *Agreement?* Yeah, right, that kind of shit presupposed free will, and from everything he'd learned over the course of his life, it was clear he had none.

Fuck. Her.

Vishous exhaled slowly. Relaxed his muscles. And embraced the suffocation.

He held her stare . . . as he began to die.

After about a minute into the self-imposed drowning, his autonomic nervous system kicked in, his lungs punching against his chest walls, trying to drag down some oxygen. He locked his molars, pressed his lips together, and tightened his throat so that the draw reflex was rendered impotent.

"Oh, Jesus," Phury said in a shaky voice.

The burn in V's lungs spread throughout his torso as his vision started to fuzz and his body shook in the battle between mental will and the biological imperative to breathe. Eventually the war became less a fuck-you to his mother and more a fight to gain what he wanted: peace. Without Jane in his life, death was really his only option.

He began to black out.

All at once the nonexistent weight was lifted; then air shot through his nose and into his lungs sure as if it were a solid and an invisible hand had shoved the shit into him.

His body took over, hammering back his self-control. Against his will he sucked in oxygen like it was water, curling over on his side, breathing in great drafts, his vision gradually clearing until he could focus on the hem of his mother's robes.

When he finally peeled his face off the white floor and looked up at her, she was no longer the bright form he was used to. She had dulled, as if her glow were on a dimmer switch and someone was trying to pull off mood lighting.

Her face was the same, though. Translucent and beautiful and hard as a diamond.

"Shall we proceed in for the presentation?" she said. "Or perhaps you would like to receive your mate lying prostrate on my marble?"

V sat up, dizzy but not caring if he passed the fuck out. He supposed he should feel some kind of triumph for winning the fight with her, but he didn't.

He glanced at Phury. The guy was freaked, his yellow eyes peeled like grapes, his skin sallow and pasty. He looked like he was standing in the middle of a gator pool wearing steaks for shoes.

Man, going by how his brother was handling this little family spat, V couldn't imagine the Chosen would deal any better with open conflict between him and his Joan Crawford mother-mare. And V might not have any affinity for that bunch of females, but there was no reason to rile them up.

He got to his feet, and Phury stepped in at just the right time. As V listed to one side, the Brother caught him under the armpit and steadied him.

"You will follow me now." The Scribe Virgin led the way to the arcade, floating above the marble, making neither sound nor any particular movement, a tiny apparition of solid form.

The three of them proceeded down the colonnade to a pair of

gold doors V had never been through before. The things were massive and marked with an early version of the Old Language, one that bore enough relation to the current written symbology that V could translate:

Behold the sanctuary of the Chosen, sacred domain of the Race's past, present and future.

The doors opened unhanded, revealing a pastoral splendor that under other circumstances might have calmed the shit out of even V. Except for the fact that everything was white, it could have been any Ivy League–type college campus, the buildings Georgian-formal and spread out widely amidst rolling, milky grass and albino oak and elm trees.

A runner of white silk had been stretched out, and he and Phury walked on it while the Scribe Virgin ghosted along about a foot above the thing. The air was at the perfect temperature and so absolutely calm there was no sensation of it passing over exposed skin. Although gravity still held V down, he felt lighter and somewhat buoyant . . . as if, with a running start, he could go bounding off across the lawn like those pictures of men on the moon.

Or, shit, maybe this lunar-walk sensation was because he had some brain-fry going on.

When they crested a hill, an amphitheater was revealed down below. As were the Chosen.

Oh, Jesus . . . The forty or so females were dressed in identical white robes with their hair up and their hands gloved. Their coloring varied from blond to brunette to redhead, yet they seemed to be all the same person because of their long, lean builds and those matching robes. Split into two groups, they lined either side of the amphitheater, presenting themselves at a three-quarter turn with their right feet out slightly. They reminded him of the caryatids of Greek architecture, those sculptures of females that supported pediments or roofs on their regal heads.

Staring at them now, he wondered whether they had hearts that beat and lungs that pumped. Because they were as still as the air.

See, this was the problem with the Other Side, he thought. Nothing ever moved here. There was life . . . without life.

"Come forward," the Scribe Virgin commanded. "The presentation awaits."

Oh . . . God . . . He couldn't breathe again.

Phury's hand landed on his shoulder. "You need a minute?"

Fuck a minute; he needed centuries—although even assuming he had that kind of time, it wasn't going to change the outcome. With a sense of destiny, he pictured that civilian vampire he'd found in the alley, the one who he'd come upon that night he'd been shot, the one who he'd killed that *lesser* to avenge.

They needed more warriors in the Brotherhood, he thought as he started to walk again. And it wasn't like the stork was going to get the job done.

Down in front there was only one seat in the house, a golden thronelike production that was positioned up close to the lip of the amphitheater's stage. From this vantage point, he realized that what he'd assumed was a blank white wall at the back was really a vast white velvet curtain that hung down as motionless as if it had been painted on a mural.

"You. Sit," the Scribe Virgin said to him, obviously beyond sick of his ass.

Funny, he felt the same way about her.

V planted it as Phury took root like a tree behind the throne.

The Scribe Virgin floated over to the right, assuming a position at the side of the stage, a Shakespearean director, the driver of all the drama.

Man, what he wouldn't give for an asp right about now.

"Proceed," she called out in a clipped voice.

The curtain split down the middle and retracted, revealing a female covered in jeweled robes from head to foot. Flanked by two

Chosen, his intended seemed to be standing at an odd angle. Or maybe she wasn't standing. Jesus, it appeared as though she was on some kind of slab that had been tilted upright for viewing. Like a butterfly mounted.

As she was rolled forward, it became clear that she was in fact fixed on something. There were bands around her upper arms, ones that were camouflaged with jewels to match her robes, ones that appeared to be holding her up.

Must be part of the ceremony. Because what was under that robe was not only prepared for this presentation and the mating ritual that would follow, but no doubt was psyched as hell to be the number one female: The Primale's first Chosen had special rights, and he could only imagine what a rocking good time that would be for her.

Even though it might not be fair, he resented the hell out of what was under that splendor.

The Scribe Virgin nodded, and the Chosen to the left and the right of his intended started to undo the robing. As they went to work, a rush of energy rippled through the stillness of the amphitheater, the culmination of decades of the Chosen waiting for the old ways to start up again.

V watched with no care whatsoever as the jeweled robes were pulled back to reveal a stunningly beautiful female form draped in a gossamer-thin sheath. His intended's face was kept hooded, according to tradition, for it was not her that was being given but all of the Chosen.

"Is she to your liking?" the Scribe Virgin asked dryly, as if she knew that the female was utter perfection.

"Whatever."

A murmur of disquiet went through the Chosen, a chilly breeze through stiff reeds.

"Perhaps you shall choose your words anew?" the Scribe Virgin snapped.

"She'll do."

After an awkward pause, a Chosen came forward with an incense burner and a white feather. As she chanted, she wafted smoke over the female from hooded head to bare feet, going around once for the past, once for the present, once for the future.

As the ritual progressed, V frowned and leaned forward. The front of his intended's gossamer-thin sheath was wet.

Probably oils from when she'd been prepared for him.

He eased back in the throne. Shit, he hated the ancient ways. Hated this whole fucking thing.

Underneath the hood, Cormia was in a state of desperation. The air she breathed was hot and wet and smothering, worse in that regard than having nothing at all to inhale. Her knees were loose as blades of grass, her palms wringing wet. If not for the restraints, she would have crumpled.

Following her panicked bid for escape in the baths, and her eventual capture, a bitter drink had been forced down her throat at the Directrix's command. It had calmed her for a time, but the elixir was now wearing weak, and her fear was spiking once again.

As was the degradation. When she'd felt hands going down the front of the robing to free the golden toggles, she'd wept for the violation of a stranger's gaze upon her private skin. Then the two heavy halves of the robe had been pulled apart from her body and she'd felt coolness on her skin, something that was in no way a relief from the weight of what had been draped all over her.

The Primale's eyes had been upon her as the Scribe Virgin's voice had called out: "Is she to your liking?"

Cormia had waited for the Brother's response, praying for some warmth within it.

There was absolutely none: "Whatever."

"Perhaps you shall choose your words anew?"

"She'll do."

Upon hearing the reply, Cormia's heart stopped beating, fear re-

placed by terror. Vishous, son of the Bloodletter, had a cold voice, one that suggested proclivities far worse than even his father's reputation had detailed.

How would she survive the mating, much less represent well the venerable Chosen during the course of it? In the bath, the Directrix had been brutal in her wording of all that Cormia would disgrace if she did not comport herself with appropriate dignity. If she didn't carry out her responsibility. If she was not the proper representative of the whole.

How could she bear this all?

Cormia heard the Scribe Virgin speak again: "Vishous, your stead has not tendered his gaze. Phury, son of Ahgony, you must view the Chosen that is offered as the Primale's witness."

Cormia trembled, afeared of yet another set of unknown male eyes upon her form. She felt unclean, though she had been so carefully washed; dirty, though no filth dripped from her. Under the hood she wished she were small, so small she would shame the head of a pin.

For if she were small, their eyes wouldn't find her. If she were tiny, she could hide amongst larger things . . . disappear from all of this.

Phury's eyes were glued to the back of the golden throne, and he really didn't want them anywhere else. This whole thing was wrong. All wrong.

"Phury, son of Ahgony?" The Scribe Virgin pronounced his father's name as if the weight of the family's entire lineage rested on whether Phury got with the program.

He flipped his lids up to the female—

Every one of his mental processes ground to a halt.

His body was what responded. Instantly. He thickened in his silk pants, his erection popping up fast as a breath even as he was utterly ashamed of himself. How could he be so *cruel*? He dropped his lids, crossed his arms over his chest, and tried to figure out how he could manage to kick his own ass and still remain standing.

"How find you her, warrior?"

"Resplendent." The word came out of his mouth from nowhere. Then he added, "Worthy of the fairest tradition of the Chosen."

"Ah, now, that is the proper response. As acceptance has been made, I pronounce this female as the Primale's selection. Complete the incense bathing."

In his peripheral vision, Phury was aware of two Chosen coming out with staffs that had smoky white trails drifting from them. As they began to sing in high, crystal voices, he breathed in deep, sifting through a garden's bloom of female scents.

He found the intended's. Had to be hers, because it was the only one in the whole place that was spelling out pure terror—

"Stop the ceremony," V said in a hard voice.

The Scribe Virgin's head twisted over to him. "They shall finish it."

"The hell they will." The Brother got up out of his throne and marched onto the stage, having obviously caught the scent as well. As he came forward, the Chosen let out squeaks of alarm and broke ranks. While the females scattered and their white robes whipped around, Phury thought of a stack of paper napkins at a picnic, blowing away all willy-nilly, skipping along the grass.

Except this was no Sunday in the park.

Vishous yanked the intended's jeweled robing back together, then tore free the binds. As she sagged, he caught her by the arm and held her up. "Phury, I'll meet you back home."

Wind began to rip around, emanating from the Scribe Virgin, but V held his own, facing off with his . . . well, his mother, apparently.

Mother. Christ, never saw that one coming.

V had a death grip on the poor female and a face full of hatred as he stared at the Scribe Virgin. "Phury, get the *fuck* out of here."

Even though Phury was a peacekeeper at heart, he knew better than to intercede in this kind of family squabble. The best he could to was pray his brother didn't come back in an urn.

Before he took off, he had one last look at the female's hooded form. V was now holding her with both hands, as she appeared to have passed out. *Jesus Christ* . . . What a mess.

Phury turned and beat feet back down the white silk runner toward the Scribe Virgin's courtyard. First stop? Wrath's study. The king was going to have to know what went down. Even though clearly the biggest part of the story had yet to play out.

THIRTY-FIVE

When Cormia came to, she was stretched out flat on her back, the robing still on, the hood in place. She didn't think she was on that board she'd been strapped to, however. No . . . she wasn't on—

It all came back to her: The Primale stopping the ceremony and freeing her. A vast wind blowing through the amphitheater. The Brother and the Scribe Virgin starting to argue.

Cormia had passed out at that point, missing what ensued. What had happened to the Primale? Surely he had not survived, as no one defied the Scribe Virgin.

"You want any of that off?" a hard male voice said.

Fear shot up her spine. Merciful Virgin, he remained herein.

Instinctively she curled into a ball to protect herself.

"Relax. I'm not going to do anything to you."

Going by his harsh tone of voice, she could not trust the words: Anger marked the syllables he spoke, turning them into verbal

blades, and though she could not see his form, she could sense the awesome power in him. He was indeed the warrior son of the Blood-letter.

"Look, I'm going to take the hood off so you can breathe, okay?"

She tried to get away from him, tried to crawl from wherever she lay, but the robing tangled and trapped her.

"Hold up, female. I'm just trying to give you a break here."

She went dead still as his hands fell upon her, sure she would be beaten. Instead he merely loosened the top two fastenings and lifted the hood.

Sweet, clean air swept onto her face through the thin veil, a luxury like food to the hungry, but she couldn't draw much in. She was tight all over, her eyes squeezed shut, her mouth drawn in a grimace as she braced herself for only the Virgin knew what.

Except nothing happened. He was with her still . . . she could catch his fearsome scent . . . and yet he touched her not, spoke no other words.

She heard a rasping sound and an inhale. Then she smelled something tangy and smoky. Like incense.

"Open your eyes." His voice was all command as it came from behind her.

She lifted her lids and blinked a number of times. She was on the stage at the amphitheater, facing outward toward an empty golden throne and a white silk runner that led up the hilly rise.

Heavy footsteps came around.

And there he was. Towering over her, bigger than anything she'd seen that breathed, his pale eyes and hard face so cold she recoiled.

He brought a thin white roll to his lips and inhaled. As he spoke, smoke came out of his mouth. "Told you. I'm not going to hurt you. What's your name?"

Through a tight throat, she rasped, "Chosen."

"That's what you are," he snapped. "I want your name. I want to know *your* name."

Was he allowed to ask her that? Was he— What was she thinking? He could do anything he wanted. He was the Primale. "C-C-Cormia."

"Cormia." He inhaled on the white thing again, the orange tip flaring up brightly. "Listen to me. Don't be scared, Cormia, okay?"

"Are you—" Her voice cracked. She wasn't sure whether she could question him, but she had to know. "Are you a god?"

His black eyebrows came down low over his white eyes. "Hell, no."

"But then how did you—"

"Speak up. I can't hear you."

She tried to make her voice stronger. "How then did you intercede with the Scribe Virgin?" As he glowered, she rushed to apologize. "Please, I mean not to offend—"

"Whatever. Look, Cormia, you're not into this mating thing with me, are you?" When she said nothing, his mouth compressed with impatience. "Come on, talk to me."

She opened her mouth. Nothing came out.

"Oh, for the love of God." He pushed a gloved hand through his dark hair and started pacing.

Surely he was a deity of some kind. He looked so fierce she wouldn't have been surprised if he called lightning from the sky.

He stopped and loomed over her. "I told you, I'm not going to hurt you. Goddamn, what do you think I am? A monster?"

"I have never seen a male before," she blurted. "I know not what you are."

That stopped him cold.

Jane woke up only because she heard a garage door squeaking, the high-pitched whine coming from the condo to the left of hers. Rolling over, she looked at the clock. Five in the afternoon. She'd slept most of the day.

Well, kind of slept. For the most part, she'd been trapped in a bizarre dreamscape, one in which images that were half-formed and

hazy tormented her. A man was involved somehow, a big man who felt at once a part of her and yet utterly alien. She'd been unable to see his face, but she knew his smell: dark spices, up close, in her nose, all around her, all over her—

That bone crusher of a headache flared up, and she dropped what she was thinking of like it was a hot poker and she was holding the wrong end. Fortunately, the pain behind her eyes eased off.

At the sound of a car engine, she lifted her head off the pillow. Through the window next to the bed she saw a minivan back down the driveway beside hers. Someone had moved in next door, and God, she hoped it wasn't a family. The walls between units were not as thin as an apartment building's, but they weren't bank-safe solid by a long shot. And screaming kids she could do without.

Sitting up, she felt beyond wretched and into a whole new category of dreck. Her chest was aching something fierce, and she didn't think it was muscular. Shifting around from side to side, she had some inclination that she'd felt like this once before, but she couldn't place when or where.

Showering was an ordeal. Hell, just making it into the bathroom was a chore. The good news was that the soap-and-rinse routine revived her a little, and her stomach seemed open to the idea of some food. Leaving her hair to air-dry, she went downstairs and fired up some coffee. The plan was to get her head into first gear, then return some phone calls. Come hell or high water she was going to work tomorrow, so she wanted to clear the decks as best she could before she went into the hospital.

With mug in hand, she headed into the living room and sat down on the couch, cradling her coffee between her palms, hoping Captain Caffeine would come to her rescue and help her feel human. As she glanced down at the silk cushions, she winced. These were the ones her mother had smoothed out so often, the ones that had served as a barometric meter of whether All Was Well or not, and Jane wondered when she'd sat on the damn things last. God, she supposed that would be never. For all she knew, the last butt that had taken a load off here might well have been one of her parents'.

No, probably a guest's. Her parents had sat only on the matching chairs in the library, her father on the right with his pipe and his newspaper, her mother on the left with a square of petit point on her lap. The two had been like something out of Madame Tussaud's wax museum, part of an exhibit on affluent husbands and wives who never spoke to each other.

Jane thought of the parties they'd thrown, all those people milling around that big Colonial house with uniformed waiters passing crepes and things stuffed with mushroom paste. It had been the same crowd and the same conversation and the same kind of little black dresses and Brooks Brothers suits every time. The only difference had been the seasons, and the only break in the rhythm occurred after Hannah's death. Following her burial, the soirees had stopped for about six months on her father's orders, but then it was right back on the bandwagon. Ready or not, those parties started up again, and even though her mother had seemed brittle enough to crack, she'd put on her makeup and her little black dress and stood by the front door, all fake-smiled-and-pearled-up.

God, Hannah had loved those parties.

Jane frowned and put a hand over her heart, realizing when she'd felt this kind of chest pain before. Not having Hannah anymore had created the same kind of achy pressure.

Odd that she would wake up out of the blue and be in mourning. She hadn't lost anyone.

Taking a sip of the coffee, she wished she'd made hot chocolate—

A blurry image of a man holding out a mug came to her. There was hot cocoa in the thing, and he'd made it for her because he was . . . he was leaving her. Oh . . . God, he was leaving—

A sharp pain shot through her head, cutting off the tumbling vision—just as her doorbell went off. As she rubbed the bridge of her

nose, she shot a glare down the hall. She was *so* not feeling social right now.

The thing went off again.

Forcing herself to her feet, she shuffled to the front door. As she flipped the lock free, she thought, man, if this was a missionary, she was going to give them a communion with—

"Manello?"

Her chief of surgery was standing on her front stoop with his typical bravado, like he belonged on her welcome mat just because he said so. Dressed in surgical scrubs and crocs, he was also sporting a fine suede coat that was the rich brown color of his eyes. His Porsche took up half of her driveway.

"I came to see if you were dead."

Jane had to smile. "Jesus, Manello, don't be such a romantic."

"You look like shit."

"And now with the compliments. Stop. You're making me blush."

"I'm coming in now."

"Of course you are," she muttered, stepping aside.

He looked around while he shucked his coat. "You know, every time I come in here, I always think this place is so not you."

"You expect something pink and frilly then?" She shut the door. Locked it.

"No, when I first came in, I expected it to be empty. Like my place."

Manello lived over in the Commodore, that ritzy high-rise of condos, but his home was just an expensive locker, really, decor by Nike. He had his sports equipment, a bed, and a coffeepot.

"True," she said. "You're not exactly *House Beautiful* material."

"So tell me how you are, Whitcomb." As Manello stared at her, his face showed no emotion, but his eyes burned, and she thought back to the last conversation she'd had with him, the one where he'd told her he felt something for her. The details of what had been said were kind of hazy and she had some vague impression it had been up in a SICU room over a patient—

Her head started to hurt again, and as she winced Manello said, "Sit down. Now."

Maybe that was a good idea. She headed back for the couch. "You want coffee?"

"In the kitchen, right?"

"I'll get—"

"I can pour my own. Had years of training. You couch it."

Jane sat back down on the sofa and pulled the lapels of her robe closer as she rubbed her temples. Shit, was she ever going to feel like herself again?

Manello came in just as she leaned forward and put her head in her hands. Which naturally sent him into full doctor mode. He put his mug down on one of Jane's mother's books on architecture and knelt on the Oriental.

"Talk to me. What's happening here?"

"Head." Jane groaned.

"Let me see your eyes."

She tried to sit up straight again. "It's fading—"

"Shut up." Manello gently took her wrists in his hands and eased her arms away from her face. "I'm going to check your pupils. Lean your head back."

Jane gave up, just gave the hell up and relaxed against the couch. "I haven't felt this horrid in years."

Manny's thumb and forefinger went to her right eye and carefully peeled her lid wide while he brought up a penlight. He was so close she could see his long lashes and his five-o'clock shadow and the fine pores of his skin. He smelled good. Cologne.

What kind was it? she wondered in a fuzzy mess.

"Good thing I come prepared," he drawled, clicking on the little beam.

"Yeah, you're a Boy Scout all right— Hey, watch it with that thing."

She tried to blink as he shone the beam in her eye, but he didn't let her.

"Make your head worse?" he said, going over to the left side.

"Oh, no. That feels great. Can't wait for you to— Damn, that's bright."

He clicked the light off and tucked the thing back into the breast pocket of his scrubs. "Pupils dilate properly."

"What a relief. Guess if I want to read under a klieg light I'm good to go, right?"

He took her wrist, put his forefinger on her pulse, and brought his Rolex up.

"Is there going to be an insurance copay with this exam?" she asked.

"Shh."

"'Cause I think I'm out of cash—"

"*Shh.*"

It was awkward being treated like a patient, and keeping her mouth shut made it worse. Man, there was something to be said for hiding awkwardness behind words—

A dark room. A man in a bed. Her talking . . . talking about . . . Hannah's funeral.

Another sharp shooter nailed her in the head and she sucked some air in. "Shit."

Manello let her wrist go and laid his palm on her forehead. "You don't feel hot." He put his hands on the sides of her neck, right under her jaw.

While he frowned and prodded, she said, "I don't have a sore throat."

"Well, you don't have any swollen glands." His fingers went down the column of her neck until she winced, and he tilted her head to the side. "Shit . . . what the hell?"

"What?"

"There's a bruise here. Or something. God*damn*, what bit you?"

She put her hand up. "Oh, yeah, I don't know what that is. Or when I got it."

"Seems to be healing up okay." He palpated the base of her neck, right over her collarbones. "Yeah, no swelling here, either. Jane, I hate to break it to you, but you do not have the flu."

"Sure I do."

"No, you don't."

"You're an ortho guy, not an infectious-disease czar."

"You're not having an immune response here, Whitcomb."

She felt her own throat. Thought about the fact that she wasn't sneezing, coughing, or throwing up. But, hell, where did that leave her?

"I want to have a CAT scan on your head."

"Bet you say that to all the girls."

"The ones who present with your symptoms? Absolutely."

"And here I thought I was special." She shot him a weak smile and closed her eyes. "I'll be okay, Manello. Just need to get back to work."

There was a long silence, during which she realized that his hands were on her knees. And he was still up close, leaning over her.

She lifted her lids. Manuel Manello was looking at her not as a doctor would, but as a man who cared about her would. Shit, he was attractive, especially like this . . . except something was off. Not with him—with her.

Well, duh. She had a headache.

He inched forward and stroked her hair back. "Jane . . ."

"What?"

"Will you let me set up a CAT scan for you?" As she started to shut him down, he interjected, "Consider it a favor to me. I couldn't forgive myself if there was something wrong and I didn't push on this."

Shit. "Yeah. Okay. Fine. But I don't need—"

"Thank you." There was a moment's pause. And then he leaned in and kissed her on the mouth.

THIRTY-SIX

On the Other Side, Vishous stared down at Cormia and wanted to shoot himself in the foot. Following her wobbly revelation that she'd never seen a male before, he felt god-awful. It had never dawned on him that she'd known only females, but if she'd been born just after the last Primale died, how could she have ever met the opposite sex?

Of course she'd be terrified of him.

"Jesus Christ," he muttered, drawing hard on his hand-rolled, then tapping on it. He was ashing on the amphitheater's marble stage, but he didn't give a fuck. "I totally underestimated how hard this would be for you. I assumed . . ."

He'd assumed she'd be hot to trot for him or some shit. Instead, she was no better off than he was.

"Yeah, I'm damn sorry."

As her lids peeled back in surprise, the jade color of her eyes gleamed.

In what he hoped passed for a gentler tone, he said, "Do you want this . . . ?" He moved the hand that held the cigarette back and forth between them. "This mating?" When she stayed quiet, he shook his head. "Look, I can see it in your eyes. You want to run from me, and not just because you're scared. You want to run from what we're going to have to do, right?"

She brought her hands to her face, the heavy folds of the robe riding down her thin arms and choking the crooks of her elbows. In a small voice she said, "I couldn't bear to let down the Chosen. I . . . I will do what I must for the good of the whole."

Well, wasn't that the theme song for the both of them.

"As will I," he murmured.

Neither of them said another word and he didn't know what to do. He was no good with females to begin with, and he was even worse now that he was damaged goods from letting Jane go.

Abruptly he whipped his head around, aware that they were not alone. "You, behind the column. Come out. *Now*."

A Chosen stepped into view, head bowed, body tense beneath her traditional white wrap. "Sire."

"What are you doing here?"

As the Chosen stared meekly at the marble floor, he thought, Lord save him from the subservience. Funny, during sex he'd demanded it. Now the shit annoyed the hell out of him.

"You'd better have come to comfort her," he growled. "If it's anything other than that, you need to get the hell out of here."

"It is for comfort," the Chosen said softly. "I worry for her."

"What's your name?"

"Chosen."

"For fuck's sake!" As both she and Cormia jumped, he forced his temper deep into his gut. "What is *your* name?"

"Amalya."

"Okay, then, Amalya. I want you to take care of her until I get back. That's an order." As the Chosen did some bowing and vowing,

he took a last drag on the hand-rolled, then licked two of his fingers and pressed them to the tip. As he put the butt in the pocket of his robe, he wondered for no good reason why in the hell everyone had to wear fucking pajamas on the other side.

He glanced at Cormia. "See you in two days."

V left without looking back, walking up the white grass of the hill, avoiding the white silk path that had been laid out. When he came to the Scribe Virgin's courtyard, he prayed like hell he didn't run into her, and thanked God she wasn't around. The last thing he needed was a postgame wrap-up with the likes of Momzilla.

Under the watchful eyes of all those songbirds, he launched himself back to the real world, but he didn't go to the mansion.

He went exactly where he didn't need to be: He took form across the street from Jane's condo. It was a bad fucking idea on a skyscraper scale, but he was half-dead from sorrow and not thinking right, and besides, he didn't give a shit about anything. Not even the lines that couldn't be crossed between humans and his kind.

The night was cold, and he was barely dressed in the fakata ceremony clothes, but he didn't care. He was so numbed-out and wrecked in the head, he could have been naked in a sleet storm and not noticed—

What the hell.

There was a car in her driveway. A Porsche Carrera 4S. Same one Z had, only Z's was iron gray and this number was silver.

V hadn't intended to get closer than across the street, but that plan was blown out of the water as he inhaled and caught the scent of a male emanating from the convertible. It was that doctor, the one who'd pulled the lothario shit with her in the hospital room.

V materialized to the maple in her front yard and looked in through the kitchen window. Coffeepot was on. Sugar was out. There were two spoons on the counter.

Oh, hell, no. Hell motherfucking no.

V couldn't see much of the rest of the condo, so he jogged around the side, his bare feet screaming as he crunched through icy snow patches. As an old woman from the condo next door peered out her window as if she'd seen him, he threw some *mhis* around as a precaution—and because he figured he should do something that proved he had a brain.

This stalker routine sure as shit wasn't going to get him on *Jeopardy!*

As he came up to the back windows and got a look-see into the living room, he saw the death of another as clearly as if he'd committed the murder in real time: That human male, that doctor, was on his knees and pressed up close to Jane as she sat on her sofa. The guy had one hand on her face, the other on her neck, and he was focused on her mouth.

V lost his concentration, dropped the *mhis*, and moved without thinking. Without reasoning. Without hesitation. He was nothing but screaming, bonded male instinct as he went for the French doors, prepared to kill—

From out of nowhere Butch stepped in front of him, derailing the attack by grabbing him around the waist and dragging him away from the condo. It was a dangerous move, even between best friends. Unless you were an eighteen-wheeler, you didn't want to get in between a bonded male and the target of this kind of aggression: V's attack instinct shifted its focus instantly. He bared his fangs, hauled off, and punched his nearest and dearest in the side of the head.

The Irishman dropped V like a beehive, whipped back his fist, and threw a low-higher that caught V on the underside of his chin. As his jaw slammed into his skull and his teeth sang like a choir of angels, he caught fire sure as a dry meadow, instantly into overburn.

"*Mhis*, you fucker," Butch spat. "You *mhis* this place first before we do this."

V slammed the visual block down and the two of them went at it hard-core, no holds barred, blood popping from noses and mouths as they pummeled the shit out of each other. Halfway through, V realized this wasn't just about Jane being lost. It was about him being

utterly alone. Even with Butch around, it wouldn't be the same without her, so it was as if V was left with nothing.

When it was all over, he and the cop lay flat on their backs side by side, chests heaving, sweat not so much drying on them as freezing. Shit, V could already feel the swelling: His knuckles and his face were going Michelin Man on him.

He coughed a little. "I need a cigarette."

"I need an ice pack and some Neosporin."

V rolled to the side, spat out some blood, then flopped back to where he'd been. He wiped his mouth with the back of his hand. "Thanks. I needed that."

"No pr—" Butch groaned. "No problem. Damn, did you have to pound out my liver like that? As if the Scotch ain't enough of a problem for the thing."

"How did you know where I was?"

"Where else would you be? Phury came back alone and mentioned shit was going down, so I figured you'd eventually end up here." Butch cracked his shoulder and cursed. "Let's face it, the cop in me's like a radio tower for stupid morons. And no offense, but you're not winning any awards in the smarty division."

"I think I would have killed that man."

"I know you would have."

V lifted his head. When he couldn't see through Jane's windows, he pushed himself up on his elbows to get a clear shot. The sofa was empty.

He let himself fall down onto the ground again. Were the two of them making love upstairs in her bed? Right now? As he lay ruined on her back fucking lawn?

"Shit. I can't deal."

"I'm sorry, V. I really am." Butch cleared his throat. "Listen . . . it might be a good idea not to come here anymore."

"Said the jackass who did drive-bys on Marissa for how many months?"

"It's dangerous, V. For her."

V glared at his best friend. "If you are going to insist on being reasonable, I'm going to stop hanging with you."

Butch popped a misshapen smile—on account of the crack in his upper lip. "Sorry, buddy, you can't shake me even if you tried."

V blinked a couple of times, horrified at what he was about to say. "God, you're going for sainthood, you know that? You've always been there for me. Always. Even when I . . ."

"Even when you what?"

"You know."

"What?"

"Fuck. Even when I was in love with you. Or some shit."

Butch clasped his hands to his chest. "Was? *Was?* I can't believe you've lost interest." He threw one arm over his eyes, all Sarah Bernhardt. "My dreams of our future are shattered—"

"Shut it, cop."

Butch looked out from under his arm. "Are you kidding me? The reality show I had planned was fantastic. Was going to pitch it to VH1. *Two Bites Are Better Than One.* We were going to make *millions.*"

"Oh, for the love."

Butch rolled over on his side and got serious. "Here's the deal, V. You and me? We're in this life together, and not just because of my curse. I don't know if I'm all into divine providence and shit, but there's a reason why we met. And as for that whole you-being-in-love-with-me thing? It was probably more about you just caring about someone for the first time."

"Okay, stop right there. You're giving me hives from this caring/sharing shit."

"You know I'm right."

"Fuck you, Dr. Phil."

"Good, I'm glad we agree." Butch frowned. "Hey, maybe I could have a talk show, since you aren't going to be my June Cleaver anymore. I could call it the O'Neal Hour. Sounds important, doesn't it?"

"First of all, you were going to be June Cleaver—"

"Screw that. No way I'd bottom for you."

"Whatever. And second, I don't think there's much of a market for your particular brand of psychology."

"So not true."

"Butch, you and I just beat the crap out of each other."

"You started it. And actually, it would be perfect for Spike TV. UFC meets *Oprah*. God, I'm brilliant."

"Keep telling yourself that."

Butch's laughter was cut off as a gust of wind whipped through the backyard. "Okay, big guy, as much as I'm enjoying this, I don't think my tan's improving much, considering it's pitch dark."

"You don't have a tan."

"See? This is getting me nowhere. So how about we head home?" There was a long pause. "Shit . . . you're not coming with me, are you?"

"I don't feel like killing anyone anymore."

"Oh. Good. The idea that you might only cripple the guy makes me feel a fuck of a lot better about leaving you here." Butch sat up with a curse. "Mind if I at least see if he's left?"

"God, do I really want to know?"

"I'll be right back." Butch groaned and got up like he'd been in an accident, all creaky and stiff. "Man, this is gonna hurt for a while."

"You're a vampire now. Body'll be fine and dandy before you know it."

"Not the point. Marissa is going to kill us both for brawling."

V winced. "Crap. That's gonna leave a stain, true?"

"Yup, yup." Butch hobbled off. "She's going to knock our heads."

V glanced up to the condo's second story and couldn't decide whether it was a good or a bad sign that there were no lights on. Closing his eyes, he prayed that the Porsche was gone . . . even though he had no expectation that it would be. Man, Butch was right. Him hanging here was a situation with police tape around it. This needed to be the last time—

"He's gone," Butch said.

V exhaled like he was a tire deflating, then realized he'd gotten a reprieve only for tonight. Sooner or later she was going to be with someone else.

Sooner or later she was probably going to be with that other doctor.

V lifted his head, then slammed it back down into the frozen ground. "I don't think I can do this. I don't think I can live without her."

"Do you have a choice?"

Nope, he thought. *No choice at all.*

Come to think of it, that word shouldn't be applied to people's destinies. Ever. *Choice* should be relegated to TV and meals: You could choose NBC over CBS or steak instead of chicken. But take the concept any further than the stove or the remote control and the word just didn't apply.

"Go home, Butch. I'm not going to do anything stupid."

"Stupider, you mean."

"Semantics are for shit."

"As you're someone who speaks sixteen languages, you know that's a lie." Butch took a deep breath and waited. "I guess I'll see you back at the Pit, then."

"Yup." V got to his feet. "I'll be back in a while."

Jane rolled over in her bed, her instincts waking her.

Someone was in her room. She sat up, heart pounding, and saw nothing. Then again, shadows cast by the hall light offered plenty of hiding places behind the bureau and the half-open door and the stuffed chair by the window.

"Who's there?"

No answer came, but she was definitely not alone.

She wished she hadn't gone to bed naked.

"Who's there?"

Nothing. Just the sound of her own breath.

She curled her hands tight on the duvet and took a deep breath. God . . . there was a marvelous smell in the air . . . rich and sultry, sexual and possessive. She breathed in again, and her brain flickered, recognizing it. It was a man's scent. No . . . this was more than a man.

"I know you." Her body warmed instantly, blooming—but then heartbreak landed, a pain so great she gasped. "Oh, God . . . you . . ."

The headache came back, crushing her skull, making her vow to get that CAT scan ASAP. With a moan she grabbed onto her head, bracing herself against what was probably going to be hours of agony.

Except almost immediately the pain floated away . . . and so did she. A blanket of sleep eased over her, coated her, calmed her.

Right after it landed, a man's hand touched her hair. Her face. Her mouth.

His warmth and love healed the bottomless pit in the center of her chest: It was as if her life had been in a car wreck, but now her parts were put back together, her engine rebuilt, her bumper re-attached, her broken windshield replaced.

Except then the touch left her.

In the dream she reached out blindly. "Stay with me. Please stay with me."

A big palm enveloped her hand, but the answer was going to be no. Though the man didn't say a thing, she knew he wouldn't stay.

"Please . . ." Tears welled. "Don't go."

As her hand was dropped, she cried out and reached forward—

The covers rustled and cold air rushed in, as did a mammoth male body. In desperation she grafted herself to the hard warmth and buried her face in a neck that smelled of those dark spices. Thick arms shot around her and held her tight.

When she burrowed even closer . . . she felt an erection.

In the dream Jane moved fast and decisively, as if she had every right in the world to do what she did. She shot her hand down between them and gripped that straining length.

As the big body jerked, she said, "Give me what I want."

Man, did he ever.

She was flipped onto her back, then her legs were spread and her core covered with a heavy hand. She came immediately, torquing up off the mattress, crying out. Before the sensations faded, the sheets were tossed from the bed and a mouth was on her between her thighs. She grabbed onto thick, luxurious hair and gave herself up to what he did to her.

While she orgasmed for the second time, he pulled back. There was the sound of clothes being pushed down and then—

Jane cursed as she was filled nearly to the point of pain, but she loved what was happening . . . especially as a mouth came down on hers and the erection inside of her started to move. She grabbed onto a surging back and followed the rhythm of the sex.

In the midst of the dream, she had some thought that this was what she had been mourning. This man was the cause of the pain in her chest.

Or rather, the loss of him was.

Vishous knew that what he was doing was wrong. The sex was tantamount to stealing, because Jane didn't really know who he was. But he couldn't stop.

He kissed her harder, moved in her more powerfully. His orgasm rolled in like a firestorm, taking him in a burst of heat, consuming him with a burn that was relieved only as his cock jerked and released inside of her. She came as he did, milking him, drawing out the sensations until he shuddered and fell still on top of her.

He pulled back and looked down at her closed eyes, willing her into an even deeper sleep. She would think that what had happened was nothing more than an erotic dream, an enticing, vivid fantasy. She wouldn't know who he was, though. Couldn't. Her mind was strong, and she could well go insane in the tug-of-war between the memories he'd hidden and what she felt when he was around her.

V eased out of her body and slipped from the bed. As he re-arranged the covers and pulled up his silks, he felt like he was shaving his own skin off.

Bending down, he put his lips to her forehead. "I love you. Forever."

Before he left he looked around her bedroom, then wandered into her bathroom. He couldn't stop himself. He had no intention of returning here again and needed images of her private spaces.

The upstairs was more "her." Everything was simple and uncluttered, the furniture unobtrusive, the walls free of fussy pictures. There was one wild extravagance, though, and he loved it, had the same one back in his room: books. There were books everywhere. In her bedroom the shelving ran floor to ceiling, with each level filled with volumes on science and philosophy and math. In the hall there were more stacked in a nine-foot glass-front wardrobe, with works by Shelley and Keats, Dickens, Hemingway, Marchand, Fitzgerald. Even in the bath there was a short lineup of them next to the tub, as if when she was in the thing, she wanted a few favorites nearby.

She liked Shakespeare, too, evidently. Which he approved of.

See, this was his kind of decorating. An active mind didn't need distractions in its physical environment. It needed a collection of outstanding books and a good lamp. Maybe some cheese and crackers.

V turned to leave the bath and caught sight of the mirror over the twin sinks. He pictured her standing in front of it and combing out her hair. Flossing. Brushing her teeth. Clipping her short nails.

Such normal things, which people did all across the planet every day, vampires and humans alike: proof that in certain prosaic activities the two species were not so different after all.

He would have killed to see her do them once.

Better yet, he wanted to do them with her. Her sink. His sink. Maybe they would argue over the fact that he dropped his floss on the edge of the wastepaper basket instead of making sure it got all the way in.

Life. Together.

He reached forward, put his fingertip on the mirror, and ran it over the glass. Then he forced himself to dematerialize without going to her bedside again.

As he disappeared for good this time, he knew that if he'd been a male who cried, he would have been bawling now. Instead he thought of the Grey Goose that was waiting for him back at the Pit. He had every intention of being completely faced for the next two days.

They were going to have to pour him back into these Hugh Hefner silks and hold him up at that fucking Primale ceremony.

THIRTY-SEVEN

At midnight John was lying in bed, staring at the ceiling above him.

It was a fancy ceiling, with a lot of molding and stuff around the edges, so there was plenty to look at. It made him think of a birthday cake, actually. No . . . a wedding cake. Especially because in the middle there was a light fixture with a lot of curlicue thingies around it, kind of like what those little bride and groom dolls would go on.

For some strange reason he liked the way it all came together. He didn't know jack about architecture, but he was drawn to the lushness, the stately symmetry, the balance between the ornate and the smooth—

Okay, maybe he was stalling here.

Crap.

He'd woken up about a half hour ago, hit the bathroom, and then gone back between the sheets. There was no class tonight, and he should be catching up on his work before he went out, but that whole textbook thing so wasn't happening.

He had some business to take care of.

Which at the moment was lying rock-hard on his belly.

He'd been hanging in bed debating whether he could do this. What it felt like. Whether he'd even be into it. What if he lost his erection? God, that conversation with Z hung over him. Like if he wasn't . . . successful at it, there might be something wrong with him.

Oh, for fuck's sake, he needed to jump off the bridge already.

John took his hand and put it on his pec, feeling his lungs expanding and contracting and his heart beating hard. With a wince he moved his palm downward, heading for that throb that was literally talking to him, it was so loud. Man, the damn thing was craving sensation, desperate to boil over. And underneath it? His balls were so tight he felt like they were about to crack open from the pressure. He so had to do this, and not just to check that his plumbing was right. The need to release was past the ache stage and into flat-out pain.

His hand hit his belly and he pushed it farther down. His skin was warm and smooth and hairless and stretched over hard muscle and heavy bone. He couldn't get over how big he was now. His stomach seemed to stretch as far as a football field.

He stopped just before he touched himself. Then, with a curse, he grabbed the thing and pulled it.

A moan rumbled out of his chest and leaped from his mouth as his erection kicked in his hand. Oh, *shit*, that felt good. He repeated the slow tugging motion, sweat breaking out across his chest. He felt like someone had put him under a heat lamp—no, it was more like warmth was radiating from inside of him.

He arched while he stroked himself, feeling guilty and embarrassed and sinfully erotic. *Oh . . . so good . . .* Settling into a rhythm, he shoved the covers off with his foot and looked down his body. With illicit pride, he watched himself, liking the thick head of him, the outrageous size, the way his hand gripped tight.

Oh . . . fuck. Faster. Faster with his hand. A little clicking noise rose up, the result of the clear, slippery lubricant that came out of the tip getting on his palm. The stuff ran down the shaft, making the erection glisten.

Oh . . . fuck.

From out of nowhere the picture of a female came to him. . . . Shit, it was that hard-ass security guard from ZeroSum, and he saw in HD with her man's haircut and her muscled shoulders and her shrewd face and her powerful presence. In a stunning moment of boldness, he imagined the two of them at the club. She had him pressed against the wall, with her hand down his pants and she was kissing him hard, her tongue in his mouth.

Jesus . . . God in heaven . . . his hand moved at blurring speed, his cock hard as marble, his mind filled with the idea of being inside that female.

Critical overload hit when he pictured her breaking off from the kiss and easing down onto her knees. He saw her unzip his pants, take him out, and suck him into his mouth—

Fuck!

John flipped over onto his side, the pillow getting knocked to the floor, his knees coming up. He shouted without making a sound and jerked around as warm jets went everywhere, landing on his chest and the tops of his thighs and getting on his hand. He kept stroking, eyes nailed shut, veins popping out at his neck, lungs burning.

When there was nothing left in him, John swallowed hard, caught his breath, and opened his eyes. He wasn't sure, but he thought he'd come twice. Maybe three times.

Crap. The sheets. He'd made a mess.

Man, it had been worth it, though. That was great. That shit was . . . *great.*

Except he did feel guilty about what he'd pictured in his mind. He would die if she ever found out—

His cell phone went off. Wiping his hand on the sheets, he picked the thing up. It was a text from Qhuinn, telling him to get his ass to Blay's in a half hour so they could hit ZeroSum before the action dried up.

John hardened again as he thought of the security guard.

Okay, this could turn out to be a pain, he thought as he looked at his erection. Especially if he went to the club and saw that female and . . . yeah, threw a whole lot of wood.

But then, hey, he should look on the bright side: At least his parts were in working order.

John sobered. Yeah, everything worked and he had enjoyed it . . . at least by himself. But the idea of having that go down with some-one else?

Still left him cold.

When Phury walked into ZeroSum at about one A.M., he was glad he wasn't with his brothers. He needed some privacy for what he was going to do.

With grim resolve he went to the VIP section, took a seat at the Brotherhood's table, and ordered a martini, hoping like hell none of the Brothers decided to do a fly-by. He would have much preferred to go somewhere else, but ZeroSum was the only place in town that offered what he was looking for. So he was hung.

The first martini was good. His second was better.

As he drank, human women came up to the table. The first was a brunette, so that wasn't happening. Too much like Bella. Next one was blond, which was good . . . but she was the short-haired one Z had once fed from, so that just felt wrong. Then there was another blond who looked so strung out she gave him the guilts, followed by a black-haired one who looked like Xena: Warrior Princess and kind of scared him.

But then . . . a redhead stopped in front of the table.

She was a tiny thing, no more than five-five even with her stripper stillies, but her hair was huge. Dressed in a bubblegum-pink bustier and micromini, she looked like a cartoon character.

"You looking for some play, daddy?"

He shifted in the seat and told himself to quit being picky and get it over with. It was just sex, for God's sake. "Maybe. What's a ticket on the fifty yard line going to cost?"

She lifted up her hand and touched her lips with two fingers. "For a full game."

Two hundred bucks to get rid of his virginity. Which boiled down to less than a dollar a year. What a steal.

Phury was half-dead as he got to his feet. "Sounds good."

As he followed the prostitute to the back of the VIP area, he had some vague thought that in a parallel universe he would be doing this for the first time with someone he loved. Or cared about. Or at least knew. It wouldn't be about a pair of Benjis and a public bathroom.

Unfortunately, he was where he was.

The woman opened a glossy black door and he went in behind her. As he shut them in together the techno music faded a little.

He was nervous as hell as he held out the money.

She smiled up at him as she took it. "I'm not going to mind this with you at all. God, that hair. Is it extensions?"

He shook his head.

When she reached for his belt he took a knee-jerk step back and banged into the damn door.

"Sorry," he said.

She gave him a strange look. "No problem. This your first time with someone like me?"

Try anyone. "Yeah."

"Well, I'm going to take good care of you." She stepped in close to him, and her big breasts pressed into his belly. He glanced down at her head. She had dark roots that showed on top.

"You're a big one," she murmured, tucking one hand into his waistband and tugging him forward.

He went with her with the grace of a robot, all numbed out and unable to believe he was going to do this. But really, how else was it going to happen?

She backed up against the sink and in a quick, practiced hop got herself up on the counter. As she spread her legs, her skirt rose. Her black thigh-highs were topped with lace. She wasn't wearing panties.

"No kissing, of course," she murmured, dragging his fly down. "On the mouth, that is."

He felt cool air slip inside; then her hand went into his boxers. He flinched as she took hold of his cock.

This was what he came here for, he reminded himself. This was what he'd bought and paid for. He could do this.

It was time to move on. From Bella. From the celibacy.

"Relax, lover," the woman said in a raspy voice. "Your wife is never going to know. My lipstick is eighteen-hour smudge-proof, and I don't wear perfume. So you can just enjoy yourself."

Phury swallowed. *I can do this.*

As John got out of the dark blue BMW, he was sporting a spanking-new pair of black trousers, a black silk shirt, and a cream suede jacket built on the lines of a blazer. They weren't his clothes. Like the car that had driven both him and Qhuinn downtown, they were Blay's.

"We are so ready for this," Qhuinn said as they walked across the parking lot.

John glanced back at the place where he'd taken out those *lessers*. He remembered the power he'd felt, the conviction that he was a fighter, a warrior . . . a Brother. That was all gone now, as if something else had been at work inside of him then, like he'd been possessed or something. As he walked with his friends now, he felt like a whole lot of nothing special duded up in his buddy's fancy threads, his body a bag of water, sloshing around with every step he took.

When they came up to ZeroSum, John headed for the back of the

wait line, but Qhuinn spun him to a halt. "We got an in, remember?"

They sure as hell did. The minute Qhuinn dropped the name Xhex, the piece of mountain at the door snapped to attention and spoke into his earpiece. A split second later he stepped aside. "She wants you in the back. VIP. You know the way?"

"Yeah. Sure," Qhuinn said as he slipped the guy a handshake.

The bouncer put something in his pocket. "You come here again, I'll let you right in."

"Thanks, man." Qhuinn clapped the guy on the shoulder and disappeared into the club, smooth as anything.

John followed, not even trying to pull off Qhuinn's swagger. Which was a good thing. As he headed in through the door, he hit the step up wrong, listed to port, then fell backward as he fought to stay upright, slamming into a guy in the wait line. The man, who had his back to the door because he was hitting on a chick, wheeled around, all pissed off.

"What the f—" The guy froze as he looked at John, his eyes popping. "Ah, yeah . . . my bad. Sorry."

John faltered at the reaction until he felt Blay's hand land on the back of his neck. "Come on, John. Let's go."

John let himself get led inside, bracing for the onslaught of the club's vibe, ready to get lost in the crush of people. It was funny, though. As he looked around, everything seemed less overwhelming. Then again, he was measuring the crowd from a vantage point of about six-foot-seven.

Qhuinn looked around. "To the back. Where the hell is the back?"

"I thought you knew?" Blay said.

"Nah. Just didn't want to come off as an idiot— Wait, I think we have a winner." He nodded to a roped-off area that had two huge guys standing in front of it. "That just screams VIP. Ladies, shall we?"

Qhuinn walked over like he knew exactly what he was doing, said two words to the bouncer, and whaddaya know, the rope was down and the three of them were parading in.

Well, Blay and Qhuinn were parading. John was trying not to run into anyone else. He'd lucked out that the guy at the door had been some kind of pansy. Next time he'd probably manage to land on a hit man. Who was armed.

The VIP section had its own private bar and bartenders, and its waitresses were dressed like high-class strippers, showing a lot of skin as they went around on a lot of heel. The male patrons were all in suits, the women in expensive bits of nothing much. It was a fast, flashy crowd . . . that made John feel like a total poser.

There were banquettes on both sides of the room, three of which were open, and Qhuinn picked the one farthest back, in the corner.

"This is the best," he pronounced. "Next to the emergency exit. In the shadows."

There were two martini glasses on the tabletop, but they sat down anyway, and a waitress came over to clear. Blay and Qhuinn ordered beers. John passed, thinking he needed to stay tight tonight.

They'd been chilling for no less than five minutes, Blay and Qhuinn barely getting a start on their Coronas, when they heard a female voice say, "Hey, daddies."

All three of them looked up at the blond Wonder Woman standing in front of them. She was a knockout in a very Pam Anderson kind of way, more breast than anything else.

"Hey, baby," Qhuinn drawled. "What's your name?"

"I'm Sweet Charity." She put both hands on the table and leaned in, flashing her perfect chest and her tanning-salon skin and her gleaming, bleached teeth. "Want to know why?"

"Like I want my next breath."

She bent down a little farther. "Because I taste good and I'm a giver."

Qhuinn's tight smile was all about sex. "Then come over and sit by me—"

"Boys," came a deep voice.

Oh, Jesus. A huge guy had come up to their table, and John didn't think it was a good thing. With a beautiful black suit and a pair of hard amethyst eyes and a cropped Mohawk, he looked like both a thug and a gentleman.

Okay, that was a vampire, John thought. He wasn't sure exactly how he knew, but he was sure of it and not only because of the size thing. The guy just gave off the same vibe as the Brothers did: power in check on a hair trigger.

"Charity, you mine elsewhere, feel me?" the male said.

The blonde seemed a little bummed as she pulled back from Qhuinn—who was looking pissed. Except then she trotted off and . . . well, shit, pulled the same routine two banquettes down.

As Qhuinn's expression lost some of its edge, the Mohawked male bent low and said, "Yeah, she wasn't just after the pleasure of your company, big man. She's a pro. Most of the women you see walking around in this section are. So unless you want to pay for it, go out to the open-access area, pick up a few, and bring them back here, deal?" The guy smiled, flashing a tremendous set of fangs. "By the way, I own this place, so while you're here I'm responsible for your asses. Make my job easy and keep righteous." Before he turned away, he looked at John. "Zsadist said to say hello."

He left on that note, checking out everything and everybody on his way to an unmarked door in the back. John wondered how the guy knew Z, and figured that no matter the connection, that Mohawked brass-baller was definitely someone you wanted on your side.

Otherwise you might want to pick up a Kevlar bodysuit.

Or better yet, leave the country.

"Well," Qhuinn said, "that's an important tip. Shit."

"Um, yeah." Blay shifted in his seat as another blonde strolled by. "So . . . um, you want to head out to the floor?"

"Blay, you little slut." Qhuinn hustled out of the banquette. "Of course I do. John—"

I'm going to hang here, he signed. *You know, save our table.*

Qhuinn clapped him on the shoulder. "Fine. We'll bring something back from the buffet for you."

John frantically shook his head, but his buddies just turned away. *Oh, God.* He should have stayed home. He *so* should have skipped this.

As a brunette waltzed by he glanced down quickly, but she didn't stop, and neither did any of the others—like the owner had told all the women to leave them alone. Which was a relief. Because that brunette? Looked like she could eat a man alive, and not necessarily in a good way.

Crossing his arms over his chest, John leaned back in the leather seat and kept his eyes on the beers. He could feel people staring at him . . . and no doubt they were wondering what the hell he was doing here. Which made sense. He wasn't like Blay and Qhuinn and couldn't front like he was. All the music and the drinking and the sex didn't energize him; they made him want to disappear.

He was thinking seriously of bailing when a blast of heat hit him, like from out of nowhere. He looked up to the ceiling, wondering if he was sitting under an air vent and the furnace had just come on.

No.

He glanced around—

Oh, shit. The head of security was coming through the VIP section's velvet rope.

As the dim overhead lights hit her, John swallowed hard. She was in the same outfit as before, wearing a muscle shirt that showed off her powerful arms and a pair of leathers that were tight over her hips and long thighs. Her hair had been trimmed since he'd seen her, the brush cut gleaming.

The second her eyes met his he looked away, his face the color of a fire engine. In a panic he convinced himself that she was going to know what he'd done when he was thinking of her earlier today. She was going to know he . . . came while she was on his mind.

Damn it, he wished he had a drink to play with. And a cold pack for his cheeks.

He grabbed Blay's beer and took a swig as he sensed she was coming this way. Man, he couldn't decide whether it would be worse if she stopped . . . or didn't stop.

"Back again, but looking different." Her voice was low, like a banked fire. And made his blush worse. "Congratulations."

He cleared his throat. Which was stupid. Like he could say anything?

Feeling the fool, he mouthed the words, *Thank you.*

"Your friends go trolling?"

He nodded and took another pull on the Corona.

"Not you, though? Or are they bringing you something?" That amazing voice of hers was pure sex, making his body tingle . . . and his cock stiffen. "Well, in case you didn't know, the bathrooms back there have some extra room and extra privacy." She laughed a little, as if she knew he was aroused. "Have fun with the girlies, but keep tight. Then you won't have to deal with me."

She walked away, and as she went the crowd parted for her, men big as football players getting out of her way. As John watched her go, he felt a sharp shooter in the front of his trousers and looked down. He was rock-hard. Thick as his frickin' forearm. And as he shifted in the seat, the friction of his pants made him bite down on his lower lip.

He put his hand underneath the table with the intention of moving things around down there so he could get some more room behind his fly . . . but the instant he came into contact with his erection, the image of that security guard popped back in his mind and he nearly lost it. He whipped his palm back so fast it banged into the underside of the table.

John rolled his hips, looking for relief but making the burn worse. He was itchy and dissatisfied, his mood quickly getting a dangerous edge. He thought about the release he'd given himself in his bed and decided that he could use another. Like now.

Like *right now*, before he came again.

Shit, maybe he could take care of himself here. With a frown, he looked over to the hallway that disappeared into the back and had doors on either side.

One of which happened to open.

A small redheaded woman who looked like a professional came out fluffing her hair and rearranging her bright pink getup. Right behind her was . . . *Phury?*

Yeah, that was definitely him, and he was tucking his shirt into the waistband of his slacks. The two didn't say a word to each other: The woman went to the left and started talking up a group of men; the Brother kept walking forward, like he was on his way out.

When Phury looked up, John locked eyes with him. After an awkward moment the warrior lifted his hand in greeting, then took off for a side exit, disappearing outside. John swigged up some more beer, utterly stunned. Sure as hell that woman hadn't been in a bathroom with the guy because she was giving him a backrub. God, he was supposed to be celi—

"And this is John."

John jerked his head around. *Whoa.* Blay and Qhuinn had struck gold. The three human women with them were all very pretty and mostly undressed.

Qhuinn pointed to each of them. "This is Brianna, CiCi, and Liz. Girls, this is our man John. He uses sign language to talk, so we'll translate."

John finished off Blay's beer, feeling like a jerk as the communication barrier reared its ugly-ass head again. He was thinking about how to word his I'm-going-to-bail speech when one of the girls sat next to him, trapping him in the banquette.

A waitress came by and took orders, and after she left all this chat-

ter and giggling sprang up, the girls' high notes mixing in with Qhuinn's deep voice and Blay's shy, low laugh. John kept his eyes down.

"God, you are so good-looking," one of the girls said. "Are you a model?"

The conversation abruptly lagged.

Qhuinn rapped his knuckles on the table in front of John. "Yo, J. She's talking to you."

John lifted his head in confusion, meeting his buddy's mismatched eyes. Qhuinn nodded pointedly toward the girl next to John, then bugged out his peepers, a kind of *Would you get with the program here, my man?*

John took a deep breath and glanced to his left. The girl was staring up at him with . . . shit, absolute starstruck devotion.

" 'Cause you are, like, so beautiful," she said to him.

Holy Christ, what did he do with that?

As the blood hit his face and his body tensed, he signed quickly to Qhuinn, *I'm going to have Fritz pick me up. I've got to go.*

John beat feet out of the banquette, half trampling the girl who'd sat next to him. He couldn't wait to get home.

THIRTY-EIGHT

When Jane's alarm went off at five A.M., she had to hit the snooze button. Twice. Usually she was out of bed and in the shower before knew she was upright, like the *beep-beep-beep* didn't so much wake her up as spring her out of bed like a toaster. Not today. Today she just lay against her pillows and stared at the ceiling.

God, the dreams she'd had during the night . . . dreams of that ghostly lover coming and taking her, riding her hard. She could still feel him on her, in her.

Enough, though. The more she thought of all that, the more her chest hurt, so, with a Herculean pull, she diverted her attention to work. Which, of course, then just got her tangled up about Manello. She couldn't believe he'd kissed her, but he had . . . he'd laid one right on her mouth. And as she'd always wondered in the back of her mind what he'd be like, she hadn't pulled away. So he'd kissed her again.

He was good, which wasn't a surprise. What was a news flash was

the fact that it had felt wrong. Like she was being unfaithful to someone.

The damn alarm went off again, and she cursed as she shut it up
with her hand. Goddamn, she was tired, even though she thought
she'd gone to bed early. At least, she assumed it had been early,
though she wasn't exactly sure when Manny had left. She recalled
him helping her up here and settling her into bed, but her head was
so scrambled she couldn't remember what time it had been or how
long it had taken her to fall asleep.

Whatever.

Throwing off the covers, she headed for the bathroom and started
the shower. As steam boiled up and clouded the air, she shut the
bathroom door, pulled her T-shirt off, and—

Jane frowned as a feeling of wetness welled between her legs. Doing
a quick count of the days, she figured her period must be wonky—

It wasn't her period. She'd had sex.

Cold shock replaced the heat from the steam. Oh, God . . . what
had she done. What *had* she done?

Jane wheeled around, even though she had nowhere to go—only
to clamp her hand over her mouth.

Written on the mirror, revealed by the steam, were the words, *I
love you, Jane.*

She stumbled backward until she hit the door.

Shit. She'd slept with Manny Manello. And hadn't remembered a
thing.

Phury took a seat in Wrath's study, this time on the delicate pale blue
wing chair by the fireplace. His hair was still wet from the shower,
and he had a cup of coffee in his hand.

He needed a blunt.

As the rest of the Brotherhood filed in, he looked at Wrath.
"Mind if I light up?"

The king shook his head. "I'd consider it a public service. We could all use the contact high today."

God, wasn't that the truth. Everyone was off. Zsadist was twitchy over by the bookcases. Butch was distracted by the computer on his lap. Wrath looked exhausted behind a mountain of paperwork. Rhage was pacing around, unable to settle—a sure sign that he hadn't found a fight during the night hours.

And Vishous . . . V was the worst of them. He stood by the door, staring into space. Icy before, he was glacial now, a sinkhole in the room. Shit, he was even more grim than he'd been the night before.

As Phury lit up, he thought about Jane and V and idly wondered what the sex they'd had had been like. He imagined that, while they had had plenty of pummel sessions, there had been lovely moments of communion, too.

Yeah, nothing like the stuff he'd had in that bathroom. With that prostitute.

He pushed his free hand through his hair. Were you still a virgin if you'd been in a female, but hadn't finished? He wasn't sure. Either way, he wasn't going to ask anyone. It was all just too skeevy.

Man, he'd hoped being with someone would help him move on, but it hadn't. He felt even more trapped, especially as the first thing he'd done when he'd walked through the mansion's door was think of Bella: He'd prayed she didn't catch him coming back smelling of that human woman.

Distance was going to require something else, evidently.

Unless . . . damn, maybe it just required itself. He probably should move out of the house.

"Let's do this," Wrath said, convening the meeting. In quick succession he reviewed some issues concerning the *glymera*; then Rhage, Butch, and Z reported on events in the field. Which wasn't much. The slayers had been relatively quiet of late, likely because the *Forelesser* had been killed about two weeks ago by the cop. This was

typical. Any shift in Lessening leadership usually resulted in some downtime in the war, although it never lasted for long.

As Phury lit up his second blunt, Wrath cleared his throat. "Now . . . about the Primale ceremony."

Phury drew in hard as V's diamond eyes lifted. Damn . . . the male looked like he'd aged a hundred and fifty years in the last week, his skin sallow, his brows down, his lips tight. He'd never been a party to begin with, but now he looked death-knell drawn.

"What about it," V said.

"I will be there." Wrath glanced over. "Phury, you too. We'll go at midnight tonight, okay?"

Phury nodded, then braced himself, because it looked as if Vishous was going to say something. The Brother's body tensed up, his eyes darting around, his jaw working . . . but then nothing came out of his mouth.

Phury exhaled a stream of smoke and stamped the blunt out in a crystal ashtray. It was brutal to watch your brother bleed, to know he suffered while you couldn't do anything about it—

He froze, an eerie calm coming over him, one that had nothing to do with the red smoke.

"Christ on a crutch," Wrath said, rubbing his eyes. "Get out of here, all of you. Go relax. We're all losing it—"

Phury spoke up. "Vishous, if it weren't for the Primale shit, you would be with Jane, right?"

V's diamond eyes shifted over and narrowed into slits. "What the fuck does that have to do with anything?"

"You would be with her." Phury looked over at Wrath. "And you would let him, right? I mean, I know she's a human, but you let Mary come into—"

V cut him off, voice hard as his eyes, like he couldn't believe Phury was being so thoughtless. "There's no making it work. So just fucking drop it."

"But . . . there is."

Vishous's eyes flashed violent white. "No offense, but I'm on my last nerve. Backing off would be a *really* good plan for you right about now."

Rhage surreptitiously moved over next to V, while Zsadist came to stand beside Phury.

Wrath rose to his feet. "How about we drop this."

"No, hear me out." Phury got up from the chair. "The Scribe Virgin wants a male from the Brotherhood, right? For the purposes of breeding, right? Why does it have to be you?"

"Who the fuck else would it be?" V growled as he leaned into a charging stance.

"Why not . . . me?"

In the silence that followed, a grenade could have gone off under Wrath's desk and no one would have noticed: The Brotherhood just stared at him like he'd sprouted horns.

"Well, why couldn't I? She just needs DNA, right? So anyone who's a Brother should be able to do it. My line is strong. My blood is good. Why couldn't it be me?"

Zsadist breathed, "Jesus . . . Christ."

"There's *no* reason I couldn't be the Primale."

V's aggression bled out of him, leaving him with an expression like someone had nailed him in the back of the head with a frying pan. "Why would you do that?"

"You're my brother. If I can fix what's wrong, why wouldn't I? There is no female I want." As his throat got tight, he massaged it. "You're the Scribe Virgin's son, right? So you could suggest the change to her. Anyone else she'd probably kill, but not you. Shit, you could maybe even just tell her." He dropped his hand. "And you could reassure her I'll be better at it, because I'm not in love with someone."

V's diamond eyes did not waver from Phury's face. "It's wrong."

"The whole thing is wrong. But that's not relevant, is it?" Phury glanced over to the delicate French desk, meeting the eyes of his king. "Wrath, what say you?"

"Fuck," came the reply.

"Appropriate word choice, my lord, but not really an answer."

Wrath's voice got low, real low. "You can't be serious—"

"I've got a couple centuries of celibacy to make up for. What better way to take the edge off?" It was meant as a joke, except no one laughed. "Come on, who else could do it? All of you are taken. The only other possible candidate would be John Matthew, because of Darius's line, but John's not a member of the Brotherhood, and who knows if he'll ever be."

"No." Zsadist shook his head. "No . . . this will kill you."

"Maybe if I'm fucked to death, yeah. But barring that, I'll be fine."

"You will never have a life if you do this."

"Of course I will." Phury knew exactly what Z was getting at, so he deliberately shifted his attention back to Wrath. "You'll let V have Jane, won't you? If I do this, you'll let them be together."

This was not smooth, of course. Because you didn't give an order to the king, both by custom and law—and also because he'd kick your ass across the whole state of New York. But at the moment Phury wasn't too concerned with protocol.

Wrath pushed his hand under his sunglasses and pulled another rub routine with his eyes. Then he let out a long exhale. "If anyone could manage the security risks inherent in a relationship with a human, it would be V. So . . . yeah, fuck me, but I would allow it."

"Then you'll let me substitute for him. And he'll go to the Scribe Virgin."

The grandfather clock in the corner of the study began to go off, the steady chiming like the beat of a heart. When it ceased to ring, everyone looked at Wrath.

After a moment the king said, "So be it."

Zsadist cursed. Butch whistled low. Rhage bit into a Tootsie Pop.

"Okay, then," Phury said.

Holy shit, what have I just done?

Apparently, everyone else kind of thought the same thing, be-cause no one moved or said a word.

Vishous was the one who broke the deadlock . . . and he came across the study at a dead run. Phury didn't know what hit him. One second he was about to light up another blunt; the next, V pounded over, threw a massive pair of arms around him, and squeezed the breath out of him.

"Thank you," Vishous said hoarsely. "Thank you. Even if she won't let you, thank you, my brother."

THIRTY-NINE

"You're avoiding me, Jane."

Jane looked up from her computer. Manello was planted in front of her desk like a house, hands on his hips, eyes narrowed, nothing but a whole lot of going-nowhere. Man, her office was fairly sizable, but he made it feel tight as a wallet.

"I'm not avoiding you. I'm playing catch-up from being out all weekend."

"Bullshit." He crossed his arms over his chest. "It's four in the afternoon, and by now we usually would have had at least two meals together. What's up?"

She leaned back in her chair. Lying was not something she'd ever been good at, but it was a skill she was sure as hell going to try to develop.

"I still feel like hell, Manello, and I'm buried up to my molars in work." Okay, neither of those were lies. But she said them only to camo the omission she was pulling.

There was a long pause. "Is this about last night?"

With a wince, she gave up the ghost. "Uh, listen, about that. Manny . . . I'm sorry. I can't do anything like that with you again. I think you're great, I really do. But I'm . . ." She let the sentence drift. She had the urge to say something along the lines of her being in love with someone else, but that was absurd. She had no one.

"Is it because of the department?" he said.

No, it just didn't *feel* right somehow. "You know it's not appropriate, even if we kept it quiet."

"And if you leave? Then what?"

She shook her head. "No. I just . . . can't. I shouldn't have slept with you last night."

His brows shot up. "Excuse me?"

"I just don't think—"

"Wait a minute. Where in the hell do you get the idea we slept together?"

"I . . . I assumed that we had."

"I kissed you. It was awkward. I left. No sex. What makes you think there was?"

Jesus Christ . . . Jane waved a shaky hand around. "Dreams, I guess. Really vivid dreams. Um . . . will you excuse me?"

"Jane, what the hell's going on?" He came around the desk. "You look like you're terrified."

As she stared up at him, she knew there was desperate fear in her eyes, but she couldn't hide it. "I think . . . I think it's quite possible I'm losing my mind. I'm serious, Manny. We're talking schizophrenia time. Hallucinations and distorted reality and . . . memory lapses."

Although the fact that she'd had sex during the night was *not* a figment of her imagination. Shit . . . or was it?

Manny bent down and put his hands on her shoulders. In a low voice he said, "We'll find you someone to see. We'll take care of this."

"I'm scared."

Manny took her hands, pulled her to her feet, and wrapped her up tight against him. "I'm here for you."

As she hugged him back hard, she said, "You would be a good man to love, Manello. You really would."

"I know."

She laughed a little, the choking sound getting lost in the crook of his neck. "So arrogant."

"Try accurate."

He pulled back and put his palm on her cheek, his deep brown eyes grave. "It's killing me to say this . . . but I don't want you in the ORs, Jane. Not where you're at in your head right now."

Her first instinct was to fight him, but then she exhaled. "What will we tell people?"

"Depends on how long it lasts. For now? You have the flu." He tucked a piece of hair behind her ear. "Here's the plan. You're going to talk to a friend of mine who's a psychiatrist. He's out in California, so no one will know, and I'm going to go call him now. I'm also scheduling you for a CAT scan. We'll have it done after hours across town at Imaging Associates. No one will know."

When Manello turned to go there was heartbreak in his eyes, and as she thought about the situation, the oddest memory passed through her head.

Three or four winters ago she'd left the hospital late one night, feeling unsettled. Something, some kind of gut instinct, told her to stay and sleep on the couch in her office, but she chalked it up to the fact that the weather was nasty. Thanks to a bitter, freezing rain that had fallen for hours, Caldwell was pretty much a skating rink. Why would anyone want to go out in weather like this?

The nagging sensation wouldn't stop, though. The whole way out to the parking garage, she'd fought against the voice in her head until finally, as she'd put her key in the ignition, she'd had a vision. The damn thing was so clear it was as if the event had already happened and this was her memory of it: She saw her hands gripping the steering wheel as a pair of headlights pierced her windshield straight-on. She felt the stinging pain of impact, the jarring spin as her car whipped around, the burning in her lungs as she screamed.

Creeped out but determined, she'd pulled slowly into the freezing rain. Talk about defensive driving. She regarded every other car as a potential wreck, and would have used the sidewalks instead of the roads if she could have.

Halfway home she'd stopped at a light, praying that no one hit her.

As if it had been preordained, however, a car had come up behind her, lost traction, and started in on the great slide. She'd gripped the steering wheel and looked up into the rearview window . . . and watched as the headlights came toward her.

The car had missed her entirely.

After she was sure no one was hurt, Jane had laughed to herself, taken a deep breath, and headed home. Along the way, she'd reflected on how the brain extrapolated from its environment and jumped to conclusions, how strong thoughts and fears could be mistaken for some kind of prescient ability, how news reports of bad roads could percolate and lead to—

The plumber's truck slammed into her head-on about three miles from her house. As she'd come around the corner to find those head-lights in her lane, her only thought had been, well, shit, she'd been right after all. She'd ended up with a broken collarbone and a totaled car. The plumber and his truck had been fine, thank God, but she'd been out of the OR for weeks.

So . . . as she watched Manello leave her office, she knew what was going to happen, and the clarity of it all was along the lines of that vision of the accident: As immutable as the color of her eyes. As undeniable as the passage of time. As unstoppable as a plumber's truck skidding on black ice.

"My career is over," she whispered in a dead voice. "I'm done."

* * *

Vishous knelt by his bed, put a necklace of black pearls around his neck, and closed his eyes. As he reached out with his mind to the Other Side, he deliberately thought of Jane. The Scribe Virgin might as well know what the hell this was about from the get-go.

It took a while before he got a response from his mother, but then he was traveling through antimatter to the nontemporal realm, taking form in the white courtyard.

The Scribe Virgin was standing before her tree of birds, and one of them, a peach finchy kind of thing, was in her hand. As the hood of her black robe was down, V could see her ghostly face, and he was astonished at the adoration on it as she looked at the little creature in her glowing hand. Such love, he thought.

Never would have assumed she had it in her.

She spoke first. "Of course I love my birds. They are my solace when I am troubled, my greater joy when I am of cheer. The sweet chime of their songs lifts me as nothing else does." She looked over her shoulder. "That human surgeon, is it?"

"Yeah," he said, bracing himself.

Fuck. She was so quiet. He'd expected her anger. Girded himself for a battle. Instead? Nothing but calm.

Which was right before the storm, wasn't it.

The Scribe Virgin blew on the bird, and it responded by crooning and spreading its little wings to bask. "May I assume that if I deny the substitution you will not carry through with the ceremony?"

It killed him to speak. Killed him. "I gave my word. So I will."

"Indeed? You surprise me."

The Scribe Virgin put the bird back, whistling a call as she did. He imagined that if the sound could be translated it would be something along the lines of *I love you.* The bird returned it in kind.

"These birds," his mother said in an odd, distant voice, "are truly mine only delight. Do you know why?"

"No."

"They ask nothing of me and give much."

She turned to him and in her deep voice said, "This is the day of your birth, Vishous, son of the Bloodletter. Your timing is well calculated."

Um, not really. Jesus, he'd forgotten what day it was. "I—"

"And as this day three hundred and three years ago I bore you into the world, I find myself in the mood to grant you the favor you inquire over, as well as the one that has been thus far unspoken, though evident as the risen moon in a vacant sky."

V's eyes flared. Hope, a dangerous emotion in the best of times, flared in his chest with a little spark of warmth. In the background the birds chirped and sang merrily, as if anticipating his happiness.

"Vishous, son of the Bloodletter, I shall grant you the two things you want most. I shall allow the substitution of your brother Phury in the ceremony. He shall be a fine Primale, gentle and kind to the Chosen while proffering a good bloodline unto the species."

V closed his eyes, relief washing over him in such a great wave that he weaved on his feet. "Thank you . . ." he whispered, aware that he was addressing more his destiny's change of course than her, even though she was the driver.

"Your gratitude is appropriate." His mother's voice was utterly level. "And also curious to me. But then, gifts are like beauty, are they not. It is in the eye of the recipient that they find their seat, not in the hand of the giver. I have learned this now."

V looked over at her, trying not to lose it. "He will want to fight. My brother—he will want to fight and to live on the far side." Because no way would Phury be able to handle not seeing Bella again.

"And I shall allow this. At least until the Brotherhood's ranks grow in number."

The Scribe Virgin lifted glowing hands to the hood of her robe and covered her face with it. Then, soundlessly, she floated over the marble to a small white door that he'd always assumed was the entrance to her private quarters.

"If it would not offend," he called out. "The second favor?"

She paused at the little portal. Without facing him, she said, "I renounce you as my son. You are free of me and I of you. Live well, warrior."

She went through the door and closed him out, the panel shutting firmly, then locking. In her wake the birds fell silent, as if her presence was what charmed them into song.

V stood in the courtyard and listened to the fountain's quiet, chiming waterfall.

He'd had a mother for all of six days.

He couldn't say he missed her. Or that he was grateful to her for giving him his life back. After all, she was the one who'd tried to take everything away from him.

As he dematerialized back to the mansion to report in, it dawned on him that even if his mother had said no, he still would have picked Jane over the Scribe Virgin. No matter what it cost him.

And the Scribe Virgin had known that all along, hadn't she. Which was why she'd forsaken him.

Whatever. All he really cared about was getting to Jane. Things were looking up, but he was so not out of the woods yet. She could, after all, still say no. She could very well choose the life she knew over a dangerous half existence with a vampire.

Damn it, though, he wanted her to pick him.

V was taking shape in his bedroom and thinking of the way it had been with Jane the night before . . . when it dawned on him he'd done the unforgivable: He'd finished inside of her. *Goddamn it.* He'd been so in his head, he'd forgotten that he'd left some of himself behind. She must be going mad by now.

He was such a bastard. A thoughtless, selfish bastard.

And he actually thought he had something to offer her?

FORTY

As night fell, Phury pulled on the white silks for the Primale ceremony. He didn't feel them on his skin, and not because they were made of such delicate cloth. He'd been smoking blunts for the last two hours straight, so he was pretty well numbed-out.

Though not so faced that when the knock came on his door, he didn't know exactly who it was.

"Come in," he said, without turning away from the mirror over his dresser. "And what are you doing out of bed?"

Bella let out a laugh. Or maybe it was a sob. "One hour a day, remember. I have fifty-two minutes left."

He picked up the gold Primale medallion and put it around his neck. The weight of it settled onto his chest like someone had a palm between his pecs and was leaning into him. Hard.

"Are you sure about this?" she said softly.

"Yes."

"I guess Z's going with you?"

"He's my witness." Phury stabbed out his hand-rolled. Picked up another. Lit it.

"When will you be back?"

He shook his head as he exhaled. "The Primale lives on the Other Side."

"Vishous wasn't going to."

"Special arrangement. I'll still fight, but I want to stay over there."

As she gasped, he stared at his reflection in the mirror's antique glass. His hair was damp and tangled at the ends, so he grabbed a brush and started yanking it through.

"Phury, what are you . . . You can't go to the ceremony bald—*Stop*. God, you're ripping your hair out." She came up behind him, took the brush from his hand, and pointed to the chaise next to the window. "Sit. Let me do it."

"No, thanks. I can—"

"You're too hard on yourself. Go on now." She gave him a little shove to the left. "Let me do it."

For no good reason, and a lot of bad ones, he went over and sat down, crossing his arms over his chest and bracing himself. Bella started at the bottom of his mane, the brush clipping the ends first, then working its way up until he felt it come down on the crown of his head and slowly get drawn all the way out. Her free palm followed the strokes, smoothing, soothing. The sound of the bristles going through his hair and the tug on his forehead and her scent in his nose were bittersweet pleasures that left him defenseless.

Tears matted his lashes. It seemed so cruel to have met her, to see what he wanted but never be able to have it. Although that was fitting, wasn't it. He'd always lived his life with things out of his reach. First he'd spent decades searching for his twin, sensing that Zsadist was alive in the world but being unable to rescue him. Then he'd freed his brother, only to find that the male was still far from in hand. The century that had followed their escape from Z's Mistress had been a different kind of hell, with him always waiting for Z to lose it, interceding when the Brother did, and worrying when the next round of drama would get started.

Then Bella had come and they'd both fallen in love with her.

Bella was the old torture in a new guise, wasn't she. Because his was a destiny of yearning, of being outside looking in, of seeing the fire but not being able to get close enough to it to be warmed by it.

"Will you ever be back?" she asked.

"I don't know."

The brush paused. "Maybe you'll like her."

"Maybe. Don't stop yet. Please . . . not yet."

Phury rubbed his eyes as the brush resumed its strokes. This quiet time was their good-bye, and she knew it. She was crying too. He could smell the fresh, rainy tang in the air.

Except she didn't cry for the same reason he did. She cried because she pitied him and his future, not because she loved him and her heart was breaking at the thought that she would never, ever see him again. She would miss him, yes. Worry about him, sure. But she wouldn't yearn for him. She never had.

And all this should have snapped his chain and gotten him to cut out the pansy-ass routine, but he couldn't. He was submerged by his sadness.

He would, of course, see Zsadist on the Other Side. But her . . . he couldn't imagine her coming over to see him. And it wouldn't really be appropriate, as he'd be the Primale, and it wouldn't look right if he took private audiences with a female from the outside—even if she was his twin's *shellan*. Monogamy to his Chosen in deed, thought, and appearance was the Primale's pledge.

Then it dawned on him. The baby. He would never get to see her and Z's young. Except maybe in pictures.

The brush tucked under his hair and ran up his nape. Closing his eyes, he gave himself over to the rhythmic pull and release on his head.

"I want you to fall in love," she said.

I am in love. "It's all right."

She stopped and stepped in front of him. "I want you to love someone for real. Not like you think you love me."

He frowned. "No offense. But you can't know what I—"

"Phury, you don't really love—"

He stood up and met her in the eye. "Please pay me the respect of not assuming to know my emotions better than I do."

"You've never been with a female."

"I was last night."

That shut her up for a moment. Then she said, "Not at the club. Please, not at—"

"In a bathroom in the back. It was good, too. Then again, she was a professional." Okay, now he was being an asshole.

"Phury . . . no."

"May I have my brush back? I think my hair's good now."

"Phury—"

"The brush. Please."

After a moment that was long as a century, she extended the thing toward him. When he reached out and took it, they were linked by the wooden handle for a mere breath, then she dropped her hand.

"You deserve better than that," she whispered. "You're better than that."

"No, I'm not." Oh, man, he had to get away from her heartbroken expression. "Don't let your pity turn me into a prince, Bella."

"This is self-destructive. All of it."

"Hardly." He went over to the bureau, picked up his blunt, and took a drag on it. "I want this."

"Do you? Is that why you've been lighting up red smokes all afternoon? The whole mansion smells of it."

"I smoke because I'm an addict. I'm a loose-willed drug addict, Bella, who was with a whore last night in a public place. You should condemn me, not pity me."

She shook her head. "Don't try to make yourself look ugly in front of me. It won't work. You are a male of worth—"

"For fuck's sake—"

"—who has sacrificed much for his brothers. Probably too much."

"Bella, stop it."

"A male who gave up his leg to save his twin. Who has fought bravely for his race. Who is giving up his future for his brother's happiness. You can't get much more noble than that." Her eyes were rock-solid as she stared up at him. "Don't tell me who you are. I see you more clearly than you see yourself."

He paced around the room until he found himself back in front of the dresser. He hoped there were no mirrors on the Other Side. He hated his reflection. Always had.

"Phury—"

"Go," he said hoarsely. "Please just go." When she didn't, he turned around. "For God's sake, don't make me break down in front of you. I need my pride right now. It's the only thing keeping me standing."

She put a hand over her mouth and blinked quickly. Then she shored herself up and spoke in the Old Language. *"Be of good fortune, Phury, son of Ahgony. May your feet follow a level path and the night fall gently upon your shoulders."*

He bowed. *"As for you, Bella, beloved* nalla *of mine blooded brother, Zsadist."*

When the door shut behind her, Phury sank down on the bed and brought the blunt to his lips. As he looked around the room he'd stayed in since the Brotherhood had moved into the compound, he realized it wasn't home to him. It was just a guest room . . . a luxurious, anonymous guest room . . . four walls of nice oil paintings with good carpeting and drapes lush as a female's ball gown.

It would be nice to have a home.

He'd never had one. After Zsadist had been abducted as an infant, their *mahmen* had closed herself in underground, and their father

had gone on the hunt for the nursemaid who'd taken Z. Growing up, Phury had lived among the moving, breathing shadows of the household. Everyone, even the *doggen*, had just gone through the motions of life. There had been no laughter. No happiness. No calendar of ceremonies.

No hugs.

Phury had learned to keep quiet and stay out of the way. It was, after all, the kindest thing he could do. He'd been the replica of what had been lost, the reminder of the heartbreak that was on everyone's mind. He took to wearing hats to hide his face, and he'd walked with a shuffle, curling into himself so as to be smaller, less noticeable.

As soon as he'd gone through his transition, he'd left to find his twin. No one had waved him off. There had been no good-byes. Z's disappearance had used up all of the household's capacity for missing someone, so there was none left over for Phury.

Which had been good, actually. It made everything easier.

About ten years later he'd learned from a distant cousin that his mother had died in her sleep. He'd gone back home immediately, but they'd had the funeral without him. His father had died about eight years later. Phury had made it to that funeral and had spent his last night in the family house. Afterward the property had been sold, the *doggen* had dispersed, and it was as if his parents had never been.

His rootlessness now was not new. He'd felt it since his first moment of consciousness as a child. He was ever the wanderer, and the Other Side was not going to give him a base. He couldn't make a home there because he couldn't have one without his twin. Or his brothers. Or—

He stopped. Refused to let himself think of Bella.

As he stood up and felt his prosthesis bear his weight, he thought it was ironic that a nomad like him was missing a limb.

Tamping out his blunt, he slipped a number of them into his pocket, and was almost out the door when he stopped and turned around. Four strides brought him to his walk-in closet, three clicks of a lock opened a metal door, two hands reached in. One black dagger came out.

He palmed his weapon, feeling the perfect balance and the precision grip that matched only his specs. Vishous had made it for him . . . hell, how long ago? Seventy-five years . . . yeah, it would be seventy-five years this summer since he'd joined the Brotherhood.

He examined the blade in the light. Seventy-five years of offing *lessers*, and not a scratch on the blade. He took out the other one he used. Same diff. V was a master craftsman, all right.

Looking at the weapons, feeling their weight, he pictured Vishous standing in the bedroom's doorway earlier this evening, explaining that the Scribe Virgin was going to allow the substitution of Primales. The icy Brother had had life in his eyes. Life and hope, along with a shining purpose.

Phury tucked one of the daggers into the satin belt that was around his waist and returned the other to the safe. Then he strode to the door with steel in his spine.

Love was worth sacrificing for, he thought as he left his room. Even if it wasn't yours.

At that moment Vishous materialized on the far side of the street across from Jane's condo. There were no lights on inside her place, and he was tempted just to go inside, but he stayed in the shadows.

Goddamn, his head was scrambled. He felt guilty as hell over Phury. Scared to death over what Jane was going to say. Worried about how to manage a future with a human. Hell, he was even concerned about that poor Chosen who was stuck having to man up for the rest of her kind.

He checked his watch. Eight o'clock. He had to imagine Jane would be home soon—

The garage door to the condo next to Jane's trundled up with a whining sound, and a real yawn of a minivan backed out. Its brakes made a little squeak when it reached the ass end of its K-turn, then the driver put it in forward gear.

V frowned, his instincts coming to attention for no apparent reason. He sniffed the air, but he was upwind of the vehicle and couldn't catch a scent.

Great, so he was paranoid, too—which, along with his ambient anxiety and the narcissistic behavior he'd been popping lately, meant he had most of the *DSM-IV* covered tonight.

He checked his watch again just for the hell of it. Two minutes later. *Great.*

When his cell phone rang, he answered it with relief, because he was looking to pass some time. "I'm glad it's you, cop."

Butch's voice was off. "You at her place?"

"Yeah, but she's not. What's doing?"

"There's something going on with your computers."

"As in?"

"One of the tracers you laid down over at the hospital's been triggered. Someone went into the medical file of Michael Klosnick."

"No big deal."

"It was the chief of surgery. Manello."

Man, V hated the sound of the guy's name. "And?"

"He searched his own computer today for the pictures of your heart. Looking for the file Phury corrupted while we were evac'ing you, no doubt."

"Interesting." V wondered what had gotten the guy's attention . . . some printout of the photographs that had a date/time on it, maybe? Even if there was no notation as to the patient, that Manello guy was probably smart enough to trace it to the OR and figure out who had been on Jane's table. On one level it was no BFD, because the medical record showed that Michael Klosnick had checked out AMA following surgery. But still . . . "I think I should pay a visit to the good doctor."

"Um, yeah, I'm guessing we might want to outsource that one. Why don't you let me handle it."

"Because you don't know how to erase memories, do you?"

There was a pause. "Fuck you. But good point."

"Is the guy logged on now?"

"Yeah, he's in his office."

Messy to do a confrontation in a public place, even if it was after hours, but God only knew what else the doc would get into.

Shit, V thought. Look what he had to offer Jane: Secrets. Lies. Danger. He was a selfish, selfish bastard, and what was worse, he was ruining Phury's life just so he could ruin hers.

A car turned onto the street, and as it went under a light he saw it was her Audi.

"Fuck," he said.

"She's come home, huh?"

"I'll deal with Manello. Later."

As he hung up, he wasn't sure he could do this to her. If he left now, he'd still have time to get to the Other Side before Phury took the Primale vow.

Shit.

FORTY-ONE

Jane backed into her garage, put the Audi in park, and just sat there with the engine going. On the passenger seat beside her were the results of the CAT scan Manello and she had sneaked in. Big all-clear. No evidence of tumor or aneurysm or anything out of order.

She should have felt relieved, but the lack of explanation bothered her because her thought processes remained slow and cumbersome. It was almost as if her neuropathways had to work around some kind of obstacle in her head. And her chest still hurt like a bitch—

A man stepped into the beams of her headlights . . . a huge man with dark hair and a goatee and leathers. Behind him the landscape was blurry, as if he had stepped out of a fog.

Jane immediately burst into tears.

This man . . . this apparition . . . he was her shadow, the thing in her mind, the haunting presence that she knew yet couldn't recognize, that she mourned yet couldn't place. It all made sense—

On her next breath pain lanced into her temples, a horrible crushing burden.

But instead of rolling through her, it dissipated, just floated off, leaving not even a sting behind. In its wake images came to her, images of her operating on this man, of her being kidnapped and being held in a room with him . . . of them being together . . . of her . . . falling in love . . . then getting left behind.

V.

The onslaught of memory warped and shifted as her mind struggled to find purchase in a slippery reality. This couldn't be happening. He couldn't be back. He wasn't coming back.

She must be dreaming.

"Jane," the apparition of her lover said. *Oh, God . . .* His voice was the same as it had been, deep and lovely, sliding into her ear like wine-colored silk. "Jane . . ."

Fumbling with the ignition, she turned off the lights and got out of the Audi.

The air was cold on her wet cheeks, and her heart pounded as she said, "Are you real?"

"Yes."

"How do I know?" Her voice cracked, and she touched her temples. "I don't know anything anymore. I can't . . . think right anymore."

"Jane . . ." he breathed. "I'm so sorry—"

"My head's not right."

"It's my fault. It's all my fault." The strain and the sorrow in his proud face pierced her confusion, offering her some ground to stand on.

She took a deep breath and thought of Russell Crowe toward the end of *A Beautiful Mind.* Bracing herself, she walked up to what seemed to be V, put two fingers on his shoulder, and pushed.

He was solid as stone. And he smelled the same . . . dark spices. And his eyes—those brilliant diamond eyes—glowed as they always had.

"I thought you'd left for good," she whispered. "Why . . ."

At this point she only hoped to understand what was going on and why he'd returned.

"I'm not getting mated."

Her breath stopped. "You aren't?"

He shook his head. "I couldn't do it. I can't be with anyone but you. I don't know if you want me—"

Before she had another conscious thought, she jumped up and latched onto him, not giving a shit about the barriers of species and circumstance. She just needed him. The rest was conversation to be figured out later.

"Of course I want you," she said right in his ear. "I love you."

He let loose some kind of hoarse word, and his arms crushed her to him. As she found herself not being able to breathe because he was squeezing her so tight, she thought, Yup, this really was him. And he wasn't going to let her go this time.

Thank. God.

As he held Jane up off the ground, Vishous was wholly happy. Complete in a way that having all your fingers and toes couldn't hold a candle to. With a shout of triumph, he carried her into her condo, pausing only to put the garage door down.

"I thought I was going crazy," she said as he sat her on the counter. "I really did."

Bonded male that he was, he was dying to get inside her, but he held off his baser urges. For chrissakes, he should give them time to talk a little.

Really.

Shit, he wanted her.

"I'm sorry—shit, Jane, I'm sorry I had to erase all that. I really am. I can imagine it was disorienting as hell. Scary, too."

Her hands went to his face as if she were still working on the whole V-is-real thing. "How did you get out of the marriages?"

"One of my brothers took my place." V closed his eyes as her fingers went over his cheeks and nose, his chin, his temples.

"He did?"

"Phury, the one you took care of, is the one who did it. I don't know how I'm going to make it up to him." All at once the bonded male in him muscled his frontal lobe to the ground, plowing over good manners and good sense. "Listen, Jane, I want you to live with me. I want you with me."

Her smile glowed in her voice. "I'd probably drive you nuts."

"Not possible." His mouth parted as her fingertip went over his lower lip.

"Well, we can try it out."

He looked at her. "Thing is, if you stayed with me, you'd have to give up this world. You'd have to give up your work. You'd have to . . . Yeah, it's an all-or-nothing kind of deal."

"Oh . . ." She frowned. "I, ah, I'm not sure—"

"I know. I really can't ask that of you, and truth is, I don't want you to stop your life." And that was God's honest truth. In spite of the bonded-male thing. "So we'll figure it out day by day. I'll come to you, or we could buy another place, somewhere remote where we could spend days off. We'll make it work." He looked around her kitchen. "I'm going to want to wire this place up, though. Make it safe. Monitor it."

"Okay." She shrugged out of her coat. "Do what you have to."

Mm . . . Speaking of doing. His eyes went down her scrubs. And all he could see was her naked.

"V," she said in a low voice. "What are you looking at?"

"My female."

She laughed softly. "You have something on your mind?"

"Maybe."

"What could it be, I wonder?" The dewy scent of arousal came off her, triggering his need to mark sure as if she were naked and spread before him.

He took her hand and put it between his legs. "Guess."

"Oh . . . yes . . . that again."

"Always."

In a smooth surge he bared his fangs with a hiss, bit through the collar of her scrubs, and ripped the cloth right down the middle. Her bra was cotton and white and, bless its little frickin' heart, had a front clasp. He sprang it free, latched onto one of her nipples, and dragged her off the counter.

The trip upstairs to her bedroom was an interesting one, with a lot of pauses that resulted in her being naked by the time he laid her out on her mattress. It was the work of a moment to ditch his leathers and his shirt, and as he mounted her his mouth was open, his fangs fully extended.

She smiled up at him. "Thirsty?"

"Yes."

With an elegant tilt of the chin she gave him access to her throat, and on a growl he penetrated her in two ways, between her thighs and at her neck. As he took her hard, she scored his back with her short nails and wrapped her legs around his hips.

It was a good two hours before the sex was over, and as he lay in the dark beside her, satiated and at peace, he counted the blessings he had, and laughed a little.

"What?" she asked.

"For all my seeing into the future, I never would have predicted this."

"No?"

"This . . . this would have been too much to hope for." He kissed her temple, closed his eyes, and allowed himself to start to slip into slumber.

But it was not to happen. A black shadow crossed over him on his way to repose, tripping his psychic wires, ushering in an intrusion of fear and panic. He told himself he had the heebs because when you narrowly missed the chance to be with the one you loved, it took a little while to chill out.

The explanation didn't stick. He knew it was something else . . . something too terrifying to consider, a bomb in his mailbox.

He feared destiny wasn't finished with them yet.

"You okay?" Jane said. "You're trembling."

"I'm fine." He moved even closer to her. "As long as you're with me, I'm fine."

FORTY-TWO

On the Other Side, Phury came down the slope to the amphitheater with Z and Wrath flanking him. The Scribe Virgin and the Directrix were waiting in the center of the stage, both in black. The Directrix didn't seem thrilled, her eyes narrow, her lips flat, her hands tight on a medallion that hung off her neck. There was no reading the Scribe Virgin. Her face was hidden beneath her robing, but even if it had shown, Phury doubted he'd be able to know what she was thinking.

He stopped in front of the golden throne but didn't sit down. Probably would have been a good idea, though. He felt as if he were floating, his body drifting, not walking, his head somewhere other than on his shoulders. Could be the bale's worth of red smoke he'd inhaled, he thought. Or that fact that he was marrying over three dozen females.

Dear. God.

"Wrath, son of Wrath," the Scribe Virgin pronounced. "Come forward and greet me."

Wrath walked up to the edge of the stage and knelt down. "Your Grace."

"You have something to ask me. Do it now, provided you phrase it correctly."

"If it would not offend, I would ask to have Phury subject to the same arrangement Vishous was provided with in regard to fighting. We are in need of warriors."

"I am inclined to grant this leave for the time being. He shall live over there—"

Phury cut in with a solid, "No." As everyone jerked around toward him, he said, "I will stay here. I will fight, but I will stay here." He tossed in a little bow to make up for his rudeness. "If it would not offend."

Zsadist's mouth opened, a whole lot of what-the-fuck-are-you-thinking on his scarred face—but the Scribe Virgin's short laugh shut him up. "So be it. The Chosen would prefer that, as would I. Now rise, Wrath, son of Wrath, and let us commence."

As the king stood to his full height, the Scribe Virgin lifted her hood. "Phury, son of Ahgony, I would ask you to accept the role of Primale. Do you consent?"

"I do."

"Come forth upon the dais and kneel before me."

He didn't feel his feet as he walked over and ascended a short set of stairs, didn't feel the marble on his knees as he went down in front of the Scribe Virgin. When her hand landed on his head, he didn't tremble, didn't think, didn't blink. He felt as though he were in the passenger seat of a car, subject to the driver's whims as to speed and destination. Giving in was just expedient.

Odd, because he had chosen this, hadn't he. He had volunteered.

Yeah, but God only knew where the decision would take him.

The words the Scribe Virgin spoke over his bent form had echoes of the Old Language, but he couldn't follow all that she was saying.

"Rise and lift thine eyes," the Scribe Virgin pronounced at the end. "Be presented with your mates, over whom you have mastery, their bodies yours to both command and serve."

As he stood, he saw that the curtain had opened and that all of the Chosen were lined up, their robes bloodred, glowing like rubies amidst all the white. As one, they bowed to him.

Holy shit . . . He'd gone and done it.

All of a sudden Z leaped up on stage and grabbed his arm. What the— Oh, right. He was listing to the side. Probably would have keeled over. And wouldn't that have looked bad.

The Scribe Virgin's voice echoed, rebounding with her power. "And so it is done." Her ghostly hand lifted, and she pointed to a temple up on the hill. "Proceed now to the chamber and take the first among the whole, as a male does."

Zsadist's hand bit into his arm. "Christ . . . my brother—"

"Stop it," Phury hissed. "It's going to be fine."

He disengaged from his twin, bowed to the Scribe Virgin and Wrath, then wobbled down the stairs and began the walk up the hill. The grass was soft beneath his feet, and the odd, ambient light of the Other Side surrounded him. He wasn't soothed by either. He could feel the eyes of the Chosen on his back, and their hunger made him go cold even through his red-smoke haze.

The temple on top of the hill had Roman lines, with white columns and a loft to its height. On its grand double doors there were two gold knots for knobs. He turned the right one, pushed, and went inside.

His body instantly hardened from the scent in the air, the heady mix of jasmine and sweet, smoky incense enticing him, sexing him up. As it was supposed to. Up ahead there was a white curtain hanging, and fulminating illumination bled through the fold, the flickering glow coming from what must be hundreds of candles.

He pulled the curtain aside. And recoiled, losing some of his erection.

The Chosen he was to mate with was stretched out on a marble platform with a bedding cushion on it, a curtain falling from the ceiling and pooling at her throat, obstructing her face from view. Her legs were spread and tied down with white satin ribbons, her arms the same. A gossamer-thin sheath covered her naked body.

The basis of the ritual was self-evident. She was the sacrificial vessel, an anonymous representative of the others. He was the holder of the wine, the one who would fill her body. And though it was absolutely unforgivable of him, for a split second all he could think of was taking her.

Mine, he thought. By law and custom and all that was manifest, she was his, as much as his daggers were, as much as the hair growing out of his head was. And he wanted to get inside of her. Wanted to come inside of her.

Except that wasn't going to happen. The decent part of him overrode his instincts, just plowed them down: She was utterly terrified, crying quietly as if she were trying to hide the sound by biting her lip, shaking such that her limbs were horrid metronomes of fear.

"Be at ease," he said in a soft voice.

She jerked. Then the shaking came back worse than before.

All at once he got pissed off. It was appalling that this poor female was put up for his use like an animal, and though he was being used in a similar way, it was his free choice to put himself here: He had serious doubts whether that was true for her, given how she'd been restrained both times.

Phury reached up, grabbed the curtain that hid her face, and ripped it down—

Holy shit. The female's sobs weren't held in by her biting her lip; she was gagged and bound by the forehead to the bed. Tears streaked her blotchy, red face, and the muscles in her neck stood out in rigid relief—she was screaming, though unable to make a sound, her eyes bulging with terror.

He went for what was in her mouth, loosening the tie, removing it. "Be of ease. . . ."

She panted, seemingly incapable of speech, and going on the theory that actions spoke louder than words, he worked off the binding on her forehead and untangled it from her long blond hair.

When he freed her thin arms she covered her breasts and the juncture of her thighs, and on impulse he took the curtain he'd ripped down and covered her before taking off the ties at her feet. Then he stepped back from her, going all the way across the temple and leaning against the far wall. He figured she might feel safer that way.

Dropping his eyes to the floor, he saw only her: The Chosen was pale and blond, her eyes jade green. Her features were fine, the kind that made him think of porcelain dolls, and her scent very much like jasmine. God, she was too delicate to be tortured like this. Too worthy to endure a stranger's rutting.

Christ. What a mess.

Phury let the silence go on, hoping she'd get used to his presence while he figured out what to do next.

Sex was not going to be it, that was for sure.

Jane was not big on *The Sound of Music*, but she was totally Julie Andrews–ing it up as she lay in bed and watched V try to find his clothes. Man, being in love really did make you want to throw out your arms and spin in the sunshine with a big, sappy, happy grin on your face. Plus she had the short blond hair to pull it off. Although she was drawing the line at lederhosen.

There was just one little problem.

"Tell me you aren't going to hurt him," she said as V pulled his leathers up his thighs. "Tell me my boss is not going to end up with a pair of broken legs."

"Not at all." V drew on a black shirt that stretched tight over his pecs. "I'm just going to make sure that he's good and clean and that picture of my ticker is iced."

"You'll let me know how it goes?"

He looked at her from under his brows, an evil little smile on his face. "Don't trust me with lover boy?"

"Not as far as I can throw you."

"Smart woman." V came over and sat down on the edge of the bed, his diamond eyes still glowing from the sex. "When it comes to you, that surgeon needs to watch it."

She took his bare hand, knowing that he hated her getting anywhere near the gloved one. "Manny knows where he stands with me."

"Does he?"

"I told him. Right after the weekend. Even though I couldn't remember you, it just felt . . . wrong."

V leaned in and kissed her. "I'll come back after I leave him, okay? That way you can look into my eyes and know the guy's still breathing. And, listen, I want to get real here. I'd like to send Fritz over this coming afternoon with some supplies so I can wire this place up. Do you have an extra garage door opener?"

"Yeah, in the kitchen. Drawer under the phone."

"Good. I'm taking it." He ran a finger down her neck and circled his newest bite mark. "Every night when you get home I'm going to be here. Every early morning before I have to go back to the compound, I'm going to be here. Every night I'm off, I'm going to be here. We're going to steal the time when and where we can, and we're going to stay in touch on the phone when we're not together."

Just like any normal relationship, she thought, and the idea that there was a prosaic side to things was nice. It took the pair of them out of some great paranormal superstructure and laid them flat on the ground of reality: They were two people who were committed and ready to work at a relationship. Which was about all you could ask of the person you were in love with.

"What's your full name," she murmured. "I just realized I know you only as V."

"Vishous."

Jane's hand squeezed his. "Excuse me?"

"Vishous. Yeah, I know it's odd for you—"

"Wait, wait, wait—how do you spell it?"

"V-i-s-h-o-u-s."

"Good . . . God."

"What?"

She cleared her throat. "Ah, a long, long time ago—a lifetime ago—I sat in my childhood bedroom with my sister. There was a Ouija board between us and we were asking it questions." She looked up at him. "You were my answer."

"To what question?"

"Who . . . Jesus, who I was going to marry."

V smiled nice and slow, the way a man did when he was feeling pretty damn self-satisfied. "You wanna marry me then?"

She laughed. "Yeah, sure. Let's just jack me into a white dress and do the altar thing—"

His expression lost the tease. "I'm serious."

"Oh . . . God."

"I don't suppose that's a yes?"

Jane pushed herself upright. "I . . . I never thought I'd get married."

He winced. "Yeah, okay, that wasn't exactly the reply I was going for—"

"No . . . I mean, I'm just surprised at how . . . easy it feels."

"Easy?"

"The idea of being your wife."

He started to smile, but then lost the expression. "We can do the ceremony in my tradition, but it won't be official."

"Because I'm not one of you?"

"Because the Scribe Virgin hates my ass, so there can't be any presentation to her. But we can do the rest of it." Now he grinned with an edge. "Especially the carving."

"Carving?"

"Your name. My back. I can't fucking wait."

Jane whistled under her breath. "Do I get to do it?"

He barked a laugh. "No!"

"Come on. I'm a surgeon, I'm good with knives."

"My brothers will do it—well, actually, I guess you could do a letter, too. Mmm, that gets me hard." He kissed her. "Man, you are so my kind of girl."

"Do I have to get cut?"

"Hell, no. It's done on the males so everyone knows who we belong to."

"Belong?"

"Yup. I'll be yours to command. Lord over. Do what you want with. Think you can handle it?"

"I already have, remember?"

V's lids dropped and he let out a growl. "Yeah, every fucking minute. When can we go to my penthouse again?"

"Name the when and I'm *so* there." And next time she might find herself a little leather to wear. "Hey, do I get a ring?"

"If you want, I'll buy you a diamond the size of your head."

"Oh, right. Like I'm going to go glam. But how will people know that I'm married?"

He leaned down and nuzzled her throat. "Do you smell me?"

"God . . . yes. I love it."

He brushed his lips on her jaw. "My scent's all over you. It's inside of you. That's how my people will know who your mate is. It's also a warning."

"A warning?" she breathed, languor suffusing her body.

"To other males. It tells them who will come after them with a dagger if they touch you."

Okay, that shouldn't be erotic as hell. But it was. "You take the mate thing seriously, don't you."

"Bonded males are dangerous." His voice was a low purr in her ear. "We kill to protect our females. That's the way it is." He pushed

the covers off her, unzipped his leathers, and palmed her thighs apart. "We also mark what's ours. And as I'm not going to see you for twelve hours, I think I'll leave a little more all over you."

He surged forward with his hips and Jane moaned. She'd had him so many times, but the size of him was always a shock. His hand pulled her head back by her hair, and his tongue shot into her mouth as he churned over her.

Except then he stopped. "Tonight we'll be mated. Wrath will preside. Butch and Marissa will witness. You want a church thing, too?"

She had to laugh. The two of them were both such control freaks, weren't they. Fortunately she was not inclined to fight him on this one. "I'm fine without a service. I don't actually believe in God."

"You should."

She dug her nails into his hips and arched up. "Now is not the time for a theological debate."

"You should believe, Jane."

"The world doesn't need another religious freak."

He brushed her hair back. As his erection twitched inside of her, he said, "You don't have to be religious to believe."

"And you can live a very nice life as an atheist. Trust me." She ran her hands under his shirt, feeling his strong back. "You think my sister's up in heaven, eating her favorite Fudgsicles on a cloud? Nope. Her body was buried years and years ago, and now there's not much left of her. I've seen death. I know what happens after we go, and there's no God to save us, Vishous. I don't know who or what your Scribe Virgin is, but I'm damn sure she's not It."

The barest hint of a smile tilted his lips. "I'm going to love proving you wrong."

"And how are you going to do that? Introduce me to my Maker?"

"I'm going to love you so good and so long you're gonna be convinced no earthly thing could have brought us together."

She touched his face, imagined the future, and cursed. "I'm going to age."

"So am I."

"Not at the same rate. Oh, Jesus, V, I'm going to—"

He kissed her. "You're going to not think about that. Besides . . . there's a way to slow that down. I'm not sure if you'd be into it, though."

"Oh, jeez, let me think. Um . . . yeah, I'm into it."

"You don't know what it is."

"I don't care. If it prolongs my life with you, I'd eat roadkill."

His hips moved into her and retreated. "It's against my race's law."

"Is it kinky?" She arched up to him again.

"For your kind? Yes."

Jane figured it out even before he lifted his wrist to his mouth. When he paused, she said, "Do it."

He bit down and then put the twin punctures to her lips. Jane closed her eyes and opened her mouth and—

Holy shit.

He tasted like port, and it hit her as hard as ten bottles of the stuff, her head going on a spin after the very first swallow. She didn't stop. She drank as if his blood would keep them together, vaguely aware through the roaring in her body that he was pumping into her and making wild growling noises.

Now V was inside of her in all ways possible: in her brain with his words and her body with his arousal and her mouth with his blood and her nose with his scent. She was completely taken over.

And he was right. It was divine.

FORTY-THREE

With the white curtain clutched to her breasts, Cormia stared across the Primale's temple, dumbfounded. Whoever that male was, he was not Vishous, son of the Bloodletter.

But he was definitely a warrior. He was huge against the marble wall, an absolute giant, with shoulders that seemed big as the bed she was upon. His size terrified her . . . until she looked at his hands. He had elegant hands. Long fingered, broad backed. Strong yet graceful.

Those elegant hands had freed her. And done none else unto her.

Still, she waited for him to yell at her. Then she waited for him to say something. Finally, she waited for him to look at her.

He had beautiful hair, she thought in the silence. Down to his shoulders and full of so many colors, the waves golden blond and deep red and dark brown. What color were his eyes?

More silence.

She wasn't sure how fast time was passing. She knew it was, as it passed even here on the Other Side. But how long had they kept at this? Dear Virgin, she wished he would say something, except maybe that was the point. Maybe he was waiting for her.

"You are not who . . ." Her voice gave out as his stare lifted.

His eyes were yellow, a resplendent, warm yellow that reminded her of her favorite gems, the citrines. Truly, she could feel warmth in her body as he looked upon her.

"I'm not who you expected?" Oh . . . his voice. Smooth and low and . . . kind. "Didn't they tell you?"

She shook her head, abruptly without words. And not because she was scared.

"Circumstances changed, and I took my brother's place." He laid his hand upon his broad chest. "My name is Phury."

"Phury. A warrior's name."

"Yes."

"You appear as one."

He put both palms out to her. "But I'm not going to hurt you. I'm never going to hurt you."

She tilted her head to the side. No, he wouldn't, would he. He was a complete stranger and thrice her size, yet she knew with no doubt that he wouldn't harm her.

He was going to mate with her, however. That was the purpose of this time together, and she'd sensed the arousal in him when he'd first come in. Although . . . he wasn't aroused anymore.

She reached up and touched her face. Perhaps now that he'd seen what she looked like he didn't want to follow through? Was she uncomely to him?

Dear Virgin, what was she worrying over? She didn't want to mate with him. With anyone. It was going to hurt; the Directrix had told her that. And no matter how beautiful this Brother was, he was utterly unknown to her.

"Don't worry," he said in a rush, as if he'd read into her expression. "We're not going to . . ."

She pulled the curtain closer to herself. "We aren't?"

"No."

Cormia ducked her chin. "But then all shall know that I failed you."

"You failed . . . Jesus, you aren't failing anyone." He put his hand through his hair, the thick waves catching the light and gleaming. "I'm just not . . . Yeah, it doesn't feel right."

"But that is the purpose of me. To mate with you and bind the Chosen unto you." She blinked quickly. "If we don't, the ceremony is incomplete."

"So what."

"I . . . don't understand."

"So what if the ceremony isn't complete today. There's time." He frowned and looked around. "Hey . . . you want to get out of here?"

Her brows shot up. "And go where?"

"I don't know. A walk. Or something."

"I was told I can't leave unless we—"

"Here's the deal. I'm the Primale, right? So what I say goes." He shot her a level stare. "I mean, you'd know better than me. Am I wrong?"

"No, you have dominion here. Only the Scribe Virgin is higher than you."

He stood up off the wall. "Then let's go for a walk. The least we can do is get to know each other, considering the situation we're in."

"I . . . have no robe."

"Use the curtain. I'll turn away while you arrange it."

He gave her his back, and after a moment she stood up and wrapped the folds of cloth around herself. She would never have foreseen this, she thought, neither his substitution nor his kindness nor his . . . beauty. For indeed he was fair to the eyes. "I . . . I am ready."

He walked to the door, and she followed behind. He was even bigger up close . . . but he smelled lovely. Dark spices that tingled in her nose.

When he opened the doors and she saw the white vista before them, she hesitated.

"What's wrong?"

Her shame was hard to put into words. She felt selfish in her relief. And concerned that her deficiencies would be borne unto the Chosen whole.

Her stomach clenched. "I have not discharged my duty."

"You haven't failed. We've just postponed the s—er, mating. It'll happen at some point."

Except she couldn't get the voices out of her head. Or her fears. "Mayhap you should just get it over with?"

He frowned. "God . . . you really are scared of disappointing them."

"They are all I have. All I know." And the Directrix had threatened to expel her if she didn't uphold tradition. "I am alone without them."

He regarded her for a long moment. "What's your name?"

"Cormia."

"Well . . . Cormia, you're not alone without them anymore. Now you have me. And you know what? Forget the walk. I have another idea."

Breaking into things was one of V's specialties. He was tight with safes, cars, locks, houses . . . offices. Equally facile with the residential and commercial shit. S'all good.

So, cracking wide the door to the St. Francis Medical Center Department of Surgery's palatial suite of offices was no BFD.

Slipping inside, he kept up the *mhis* that fogged out the security cameras and ensured that he was hidden from the few folks who were still in this administrative section of the complex.

Man . . . these were some seriously sweet digs. Big reception area, all stately and shit, with the wood-paneled walls and the Orientals. Couple of ancillary offices marked with—

Jane's office was right over there.

V went over and put his finger on the brass nameplate by the door. Etched into the polished surface was: JANE WHITCOMB, M.D., CHIEF OF TRAUMA DIVISION.

He put his head through the door. Her scent lingered in the air, and there was one of her white coats folded on top of a conference table. Her desk was covered with piles of paperwork and files and Post-it notes, the chair pushed back as if she'd left in a hurry on some kind of emergency. On the wall there were a number of diplomas and certificates, testament to her commitment to excellence.

He rubbed his sternum.

Hell, how was this going to work between them? She pulled long hours. He was limited to night visits. What if that wasn't enough?

Except it had to be. He wasn't about to ask her to leave a lifetime of work and discipline and success for him. That would be like her wanting him to bail on the Brotherhood.

When someone muttered something, he looked across the reception area to where a light glowed at the far end of the suite.

Time to take care of business with Dr. Manello.

Do not kill him, V told himself as he walked over to a half-open door. *It would be a total buzz kill to have to call Jane and tell her that her boss was fertilizer.*

V stopped and glanced around the jamb into the huge office beyond. The human male was seated behind a presidential-looking desk, going through papers even though it was two in the morning.

The guy frowned and looked up. "Who's there?"

Do not kill him. That shit would totally bum Jane out.

Oh, but V wanted to. All he could see was the guy on his knees, reaching out to Jane's face, and the image so did not improve his mood. When it came to someone else macking on their females, bonded males liked closure. Of the coffin-lid variety.

Vishous pushed open the door, reached into the doc's mind, and froze him up good like a side of beef. "You got pictures of my heart,

Doc, and I need them back. Where are they?" He shot a suggestion into the man's mind.

The guy blinked. "Here . . . on my desk. Who . . . are you?"

The question was a surprise. Most of the time humans had no independent reasoning when they were put down like this.

V walked up and looked at the sea of paper. "Where on the desk?"

The man's eyes drifted to the left-hand corner. "Folder. There. Who . . . are you?"

Jane's motherfucking mate, my man, V wanted to say.

Hell, he wanted to tattoo the shit on the guy's forehead so Manello never forgot she was totally taken.

V found the folder and cracked it open. "Computer files. Where are they?"

"Gone. Who . . . are—"

"Never mind who I am." Damn, the SOB was tenacious. Then again, you didn't get to be the chairman of surgery 'cause you were a laid-back Barcalounger kind of boy. "Who else knows about this picture?"

"Jane."

The sound of the name leaving the bastard's mouth did not put V into his happy place, but he let it slide. "Who else?"

"No one that I know of. Tried . . . to send it to Columbia. Didn't . . . go through. Who are you—"

"The bogeyman." V searched through the surgeon's mind, just in case. There was nothing really there. Time to go.

Except he needed to know one other thing.

"Tell me something, Doc. If a woman were married, would you hit on her?"

Jane's boss frowned, then shook his head slowly. "No."

"Well, what do you know. That's the right answer."

As V headed to the door, he wanted to lay down a minefield of triggers in the guy's brain, forge all sorts of neuropathways so that if the bastard thought of Jane sexually he'd feel dread or nausea or

maybe burst into tears like a total sissy. After all, adverse impulse training was a godsend when it came to deprogramming. But V wasn't a *symphath*, so it would be hard to pull off without a serious time commitment, and besides, that kind of shit was likely to drive someone to madness. Especially someone who was as strong-minded as Manello.

V took one last look at his rival. The surgeon was staring up at him with confusion, but not fear, his dark brown eyes aggressive and intelligent. It was hard to admit, but in V's absence the man probably would have made a good mate for Jane.

The bastard.

Vishous was about to turn away when he got a vision so crisp and clear that it was like it had been before his premonitions had dried up.

Actually, it wasn't a vision. It was one word. That made no sense whatsoever.

Brother.

Weird.

V scrubbed the doctor good and clean and dematerialized.

Manny Manello put his elbows on his desk, rubbed his temples, and groaned. The pain in his head had its own heartbeat, and his skull seemed to have turned into an echo chamber. Just as bad, his brain's radio dial was spinning. Random thoughts bounced all around, a tossed salad of little importance: He had to take his car in for service, he needed to finish going through those residency applications, he was out of Sam Adams, his Monday-night b-ball game had been switched to Wednesday.

Funny, if he looked beyond the swarm of nothing special, he had the sense that all the activity was . . . hiding something.

For no particular reason he had an image of the mauve crocheted throw blanket that hung on the back of his mother's mauve couch in his mother's mauve living room. The damn thing was never used for warmth, and God help you if you tried to pull it off. The blanket's sole purpose was to hide a stain from when his father had spilled a plate of Franco-American spaghetti all over the place. After all, there was only so far you could go with a spray bottle of Resolve, and that canned shit had red dye in it. Which was so not a look on a mauve canvas.

Just like that blanket, his scattered thoughts were obstructing some kind of stain in his brain, although damned if he knew what it was.

He rubbed his eyes and glanced at his Breitling. Past two A.M.

Time to go home.

As he packed up, he had the sense that he'd spaced on something important, and he kept looking at the left-hand corner of his desk. There was a paperless stretch there, the grained wood showing through in what was otherwise a snowbank of work.

The empty space was the size of a file folder.

Something had been taken from there. He knew it. He just couldn't figure out what, and the harder he tried to remember, the more his head pounded.

He walked over to the door.

On the way past his private bathroom, he popped in, found his trusty bottle of five-hundred-count Motrin and took two.

He really needed a vacation.

FORTY-FOUR

Maybe this wasn't the best idea, Phury thought as he stood in the doorway of the bedroom next to his at the Brotherhood's mansion. At least the household was otherwise occupied, so he hadn't had to deal with anyone yet. But man, things were looking rocky.

Crap.

Across the way, Cormia sat on the edge of the bed, that drape clutched at her breasts, her eyes like two marbles in a big glass jar. She was so rattled, he wanted to take her back to the Other Side, but what waited for her there was no better. He didn't want her to face the Directrix's firing squad.

Wasn't going to stand for that shit.

"If there's anything you need, I'm just next door." He leaned out and pointed to the left. "I figure you can stay here for a day or so and get some rest. Have a little time to yourself. Sound good?"

She nodded, her blond hair falling over her shoulder.

For no particular reason he noticed it was a nice color, especially in the dim light of the bedside lamp. It reminded him of polished pine, a rich, shiny yellow.

"Would you like anything to eat?" he asked. When she shook her head, he went over to the phone and put his hand on it. "If you do get hungry, just dial star-four and it'll get you the kitchen. Anything you want, they'll bring to you."

Her eyes glanced over, then returned to him.

"You're safe here, Cormia. Nothing bad can happen to you—"

"Phury? You're back?" From the doorway, Bella's voice was a combination of surprise and relief.

His heart stopped. *Busted.* And by the person he most dreaded explaining this whole thing to. She was worse than Wrath, for God's sake.

He gathered himself before he could look at her. "Yeah, I'm back for a little while."

"I thought you were— Oh, hello." Bella's eyes whipped up to his before she smiled at Cormia. "Ah, my name's Bella. And you are . . . ?"

When there was no reply, Phury said, "This is Cormia. She's the Chosen who I . . . mated. Cormia, this is Bella."

Cormia stood and bowed down low, her hair nearly brushing the floor. "Your Grace."

Bella's hand went to her lower belly. "Cormia, it's so nice to meet you. And please, we're not formal in this house."

Cormia straightened and nodded once.

Then there was a stretch of silence as wide as a six-lane highway.

Phury cleared his throat. Well, if this wasn't awkward.

As Cormia stared at the other female, she knew the full story without hearing another word. So that was why the Primale did not mate. This was the female that he really wanted: His need was in the way his eyes locked and held upon her form, the way his voice deepened, the way his body heated.

And she was pregnant.

Cormia shifted her eyes over to the Primale. Pregnant but not with his young. His expression as he stared across the room was one of yearning, not ownership.

Ah, yes. So this was why he'd stepped in when the Bloodletter's son had had a change of circumstance. The Primale wanted to separate himself from this female because he wanted her and couldn't have her.

He shifted his weight from one foot to another while staring across the room. Then he smiled a little. "How many minutes do you have left?"

The female . . . Bella . . . smiled back. "Eleven."

"Helluva trip down the hall of statues. You might want to get started."

"It's not going to take me that long."

The two held eyes. Affection and sadness made hers luminous. And the slight blush on his cheeks suggested he found what he was looking upon beyond lovely.

Cormia pulled the edge of the drape closer to her chin, covering her neck.

"How about I take you back to your room?" Phury said, walking over and offering her his arm. "I want to see Z anyway."

The female rolled her eyes. "You're just using that as an excuse to get me into bed."

Cormia winced as the Primale laughed and murmured, "Yeah, pretty much. How's it working?"

The female chuckled and put her hand in the crook of his elbow. In a slightly hoarse voice she said, "It's working really well. As usual with you . . . it's working really well. I'm so glad you're here for . . . however long you are."

That blush on his cheeks got a little brighter. Then he glanced at Cormia. "I'll go drop her off, then I'll be in my room if you need anything, okay?"

Cormia nodded and watched the door close behind the two of them.

Left on her own, she sat down on the bed again.

Dear Virgin . . . She felt tiny. Tiny on the big mattress. Tiny in the vast room. Tiny against the looming impact of all the colors and the textures around her.

Which was what she'd wanted, wasn't it. During the viewing ceremony it was exactly as she'd wished it to be.

Except invisible was not the balm she'd assumed.

Looking around the room she was unable to comprehend where she was, and she missed her small, white, womblike space on the Other Side.

When they'd come over from the beyond, they'd taken form in the bedchamber next door, the one that he'd said was his. Her first thought had been that she'd loved the way it had smelled. Slightly smoky, with that dark, spicy scent she recognized as his own. Her next was that the crush of color and texture and form was overwhelming.

And that was before he'd walked her out into the hall and she'd been completely overcome. For truth, he lived in a palace, its foyer as big as the larger temples on the Other Side. The ceiling was high as the heavens, its paintings of warriors in battle bright as the gems her eyes had worshiped. When she'd put her hands on the balcony's rail and leaned over, the drop to the mosaic floor below was dizzying, thrilling.

She'd been astounded as he'd led her into the room she was in now.

She did not feel that awe anymore. Now she was in shock from sensory overload. The air was odd on this side, full of foreign smells, and it was dry in her nose. It also moved constantly. Here there were currents that brushed against her face and her hair and the curtain she had wrapped around herself.

She glanced toward the door. There were strange sounds here,

too. The mansion around her creaked, and she could hear voices on occasion.

Huddling closer into herself, she tucked her feet under her and looked to the fancy table to the right of the bed. She wasn't hungry, but wouldn't know what to ask to eat if she were. And she had no idea how to use that object he'd called a phone, either.

Outside of the windows, she heard a roar and whipped her head to the sound. Were there dragons on this side? She'd read about them, and although she trusted Phury that she was safe herein, she worried at the perils of what she could not see.

Mayhap that was merely the wind? She'd read about it before, but she could not be sure.

Reaching out, she picked up a satin pillow that had tassels at each of its four corners. Holding it to her chest, she stroked one of the silky tails, trying to calm herself with the feel of the strands sliding through her hand over and over again.

This was her punishment, she thought as she felt the room press in upon her and overwhelm her eyes. This was the result of her wanting to leave the Other Side and find her way independently.

She was now where she had prayed to be.

And all she wanted was to go home.

FORTY-FIVE

Jane sat in her kitchen nook with a cold mug in front of her. Across the street the sun was coming up, its rays twinkling through the branches of the trees. Vishous had left about twenty minutes ago, and before he took off he'd made her the cocoa she'd just finished.

She missed him with an ache that made no sense, considering how much time they'd spent together during the night. After V had spoken with Manny, he'd come back and reassured her that her boss was still alive with all his limbs attached. Then he'd wrapped his arms around her and held her . . . and made love to her. Twice.

It was just now he was gone, and the sun had to drop like a stone before she saw him again.

Sure, there were phones and e-mail and texting, and they would meet up tonight. It didn't feel like enough, though. She wanted to sleep beside him, and not only for a few hours before he had to go fight or headed back to his house.

And speaking of logistics . . . what did she do about the opportunity at Columbia? It was farther away from him, but did that matter? He could travel anywhere at a moment's notice. Still, it seemed like a bad idea to be too far away. After all, he'd already been shot once. What if he needed her? She couldn't very well poof to his side.

Except then what was she going to do about running her own shop? The need to lead was part of her chemical makeup, and going down to Columbia remained her best bet, even though it could be five years or so before she was up for a chairmanship.

Assuming they still wanted to interview her. Assuming she got the job.

Jane looked at the cold mug with its chocolate-streaked insides.

The idea that came to her was nuts. Absolutely nuts. And she pushed it away as evidence that her head wasn't quite back on track.

Getting up from the table, she put the mug in the dishwasher, and went to shower and change. A half hour later she pulled out of her garage, and as she headed off, a minivan was turning into the short driveway next door.

A family. *Great.*

Luckily, the trip downtown was smooth sailing. There was little traffic as she shot down Trade Street, and she hit every light on green until she got to the one opposite the *Caldwell Courier Journal*'s offices.

As she came to a stop her cell phone went off. No doubt her on-call service.

"Whitcomb."

"Hello, Doctor. It's your man."

She smiled. A big, shit-eating grin. "Hi."

"Hi." There was a muffled shifting of sheets, like V was turning over in bed. "Where are you?"

"On the way to work. Where are you?"

"On my back."

Oh, Jesus, she could just imagine how good he looked in his black sheets.

"So . . . Jane?"

"Yes?"

His voice dropped low. "What are you wearing?"

"Scrubs."

"Mmmmm. That's sexy."

She laughed. "They're one step up from wearing a sack."

"Not on you they're not."

"What are you wearing?"

"Nothing . . . and guess where my hand is, Doctor."

The light changed, and Jane had to remember how to drive. In a breathless voice she said, "Where?"

"Between my legs. Can you guess what it's on?"

Oh . . . sweet . . . Jesus. As she hit the gas, she said, "What?"

He answered her and she nearly drove into a parked car. "*Vishous . . .*"

"Tell me what to do, Doctor. Tell me what I should do with my hand."

Jane swallowed hard, pulled over . . . and gave him detailed instructions.

Phury rolled up some red smoke, licked the paper, and twisted the blunt closed. As he lit it, he leaned back into his pillows. His prosthesis was off and propped up against the bedside table, and he was wearing a royal-blue-and-bloodred silk robe. His favorite.

Making a little peace with Bella had calmed him out. Being back here had calmed him out. More red smoke had calmed him out.

Peeling the Directrix off the ceiling had not.

That female had appeared at the mansion about a half hour after he and Cormia had come over from the Other Side, and she'd been all up around the rafters about one of her Chosen going missing. Phury had taken her into the library and, in front of Wrath, explained that everything was fine: He'd just changed his mind and wanted to come back here for a little bit.

The Directrix had not been charmed. In a haughty voice that had not played well, she'd informed him that as the representative of the Chosen, she demanded to interview Cormia about what had happened in the temple—for the purpose of ascertaining whether or not the Primale ceremony was complete.

Phury had decided he didn't like her at that point. Her shrewd eyes had told him she knew there had been no sex, and he had the clear impression that she wanted deets only because she was looking forward to laying into Cormia.

Like that was going to happen. With a smile on his face, Phury had dropped the P-bomb and reminded the bitch that as the Primale he was not accountable to her, and that he and Cormia would be back on the Other Side when he damn well pleased. And not a moment before.

Huffy didn't begin to describe the reaction, but he had her by the short hairs, and she knew it. Her eyes had been spitting hatred as she'd bowed and dematerialized.

To hell with her, was his attitude, and he was of a serious mind to have her ass fired. He wasn't sure how to make that happen, but he didn't want someone like that in charge. She was mean.

Phury inhaled and held on to the red smoke. He didn't know how long to keep Cormia here. Christ, for all he knew she already wanted to go back. The only thing he knew for sure was that when she went it would be her choice, not anything forced on her by those Chosen wing nuts.

As for him? Well . . . a part of him still wanted to get away from the mansion, but Cormia was a buffer of sorts. Besides, they would head back to the Other Side and stay there at some point.

He exhaled and absently rubbed his right leg where it ended below the knee. It was sore, but then it usually was at the end of the night.

The knock on the door surprised him. "Come in?"

He guessed who it was by the way the thing opened: slowly and just a crack.

"Cormia? That you?" He sat up, pulling the duvet over his legs.

Her blond head poked through, her body staying out in the hall.

"Are you okay?" he asked.

She shook her head. In the Old Language she said, *"If it would not offend, may I please enter your quarters, Your Grace?"*

"Of course. And you don't have to be formal."

She slipped inside and closed the door. She seemed so fragile wrapped in all that white cloth, more like a young, instead of a female who had been through her change.

"What's wrong?"

Instead of answering him, she stayed silent, eyes downcast, arms holding herself.

"Cormia, talk to me. Tell me what's going on."

She bowed low and spoke from that position. *"Your Grace, I am—"*

"No formality. Please." He started to shift off the bed, but then realized he didn't have his leg on. He eased back into place, not sure how she would feel knowing he was missing a piece of his body. "Just talk to me. What do you need?"

She cleared her throat. "I am your mate, am I not?"

"Um . . . yeah."

"So should I not be staying with you in your chamber?"

His brows shot up. "I thought it would be better for you to have your own room."

"Oh."

He frowned. Surely she didn't want to stay with him.

As silence drifted on, he thought, well, evidently she did.

He felt awkward as hell as he said, "I guess, if you want . . . you can stay here. I mean, we could get another bed brought in."

"What is wrong with the one you have?"

She wanted to *sleep* with him? Why— *Oh, right.*

"Cormia, you don't have to worry about the Directrix or any of the others thinking that you're not doing your duty. No one is going to know what you do here."

Or didn't do, as was the case.

"It is not that. The wind . . . at least, I believe it to be the wind . . . it batters the house, does it not?"

"Well, yeah, it is kind of stormy right now. But we're surrounded by a boatload of stone."

As he waited for her to continue and she didn't, it came to him. Man, he was a clueless bastard, wasn't he? He'd taken her out of the only environment she'd ever known and dropped her in a whole new world. She was rattled by things he took as normal. How could she feel safe when she didn't know which sounds were dangerous and which were not?

"Listen, you want to stay here? That's fine with me." He looked around, trying to figure out where to roll in a cot. "There's plenty of room for a rollaway."

"The bed is good for me."

"Yeah, I'll sleep on the cot."

"Why?"

"Because I'd prefer not to sleep on the floor." There was a stretch over between two of the windows. He could have Fritz—

"But the bed is big enough for us both."

Phury slowly turned his head toward her. Then blinked. "Ah . . . yeah."

"We shall share it." Her eyes were still lowered, but there was an intriguing hint of strength in her voice. "And I shall then at least be able to tell them that I lay beside you."

Oh, so that was it. "Okay."

She nodded and went around to the opposite side. After she slid in between the sheets, she curled up into a ball and faced him. Which was a surprise. As was the fact that she didn't squeeze her eyes shut and feign sleep.

Phury stamped out his blunt and figured he'd do them both a favor and sleep on top of the covers. But he needed to hit the loo before he crashed.

Crap.

Well, she was going to have to know about his leg sooner or later.

He moved the duvet aside, put on his prosthesis, and stood up. As he heard her breath go in on a hiss and felt her stare, he thought, *God, she must be horrified.* As a Chosen, she was used to perfection.

"Got no lower leg." *Well, duh.* "It's not a problem, though."

Provided his prosthesis was fitted correctly and functioning well.

"I'll be right back." It was a relief to shut the bathroom door, and he spent longer than he usually did brushing his teeth and flossing and using the toilet. When he started to rearrange the Q-tips and the Motrin in the medicine cabinet, he knew he had to go back out.

He opened the door.

She was right where she'd been before, all the way over on the edge of the bed, facing him with her eyes open.

As he came across the room, he wished she'd stop looking at him. Especially as he took off his leg and stretched out on top of the duvet. Flipping the corner of the comforter over to hide himself, he tried to get settled.

This was not going to work. He was cold with just his lower half covered.

With a quick glance he measured the stretch of mattress between them. Big as a soccer field. So much space she might as well have been in a different room.

"I'm going to turn the light out."

When her head went up and down on the pillow, he turned off the lamp . . . and slid under the covers.

In the black void, he lay rigidly beside her. *Jesus* . . . He'd never slept with anyone before. Well, there had been that time during Bella's needing with V and Butch, but that was because they'd all passed out. Besides, they were males, whereas . . . well, Cormia was definitely not male.

He took a deep breath. Yeah, her jasmine scent was a dead giveaway.

Closing his eyes, he was willing to bet she was just as stiff and awkward as he was. Man, this was going to be a long day. He so should have followed through on the cot idea.

FORTY-SIX

"Vishous, could you stop grinning like that? You're beginning to freak me out."

V flipped Butch the bird across the mansion's kitchen table and went back to his coffee. Night was coming soon, which meant in . . . twenty-eight minutes . . . he was free.

The second he was out, he was going to go to Jane's house and pull some romantic shit. He wasn't sure what, maybe like flowers or something. Well, flowers and him installing that security system. 'Cause nothing said lovin' like a shitload of motion detectors.

God, he was whipped. For real.

She'd told him she was getting home around nine, so he figured he'd doll up her bedroom a little and then have a visit with her until midnight.

Except that only left him five hours to hunt.

Butch rustled the sports section around, leaned over to kiss Marissa on the shoulder, then went back to the *CCJ*. In response she

glanced up from her paperwork for Safe Place, rubbed his arm, and went back to what she was doing. She had a fresh bite mark on her neck and the glow of a very satisfied female in her face.

V winced and looked down into his coffee, stroking his goatee. He and Jane were never going to have that, he thought, because they weren't ever going to live together. Even if he was off from the Brotherhood, he couldn't crash at her place during daylight hours because of the sun thing, and her coming here wasn't an option for different exposure reasons: There was enough risk with her knowing that the race existed. More contact, more details, more time around the Brotherhood was not smart or safe.

As V cradled his mug and leaned back in the chair, he worried about the future. He and Jane were good together, but the forced separations were going to wear on them. He could already feel a strain as he contemplated the good-bye that would have to happen tonight.

He wanted her as close as his own skin twenty-four/seven. Her voice over the phone, while better than nothing, wasn't enough to truly satisfy him. But what were their other options?

There was another rustle of paper as Butch manhandled the *CCJ*. Christ, he had horrible newspaper etiquette, always mashing the pages and being rough with the creases. It was the same with magazines. Butch didn't so much read them as gnaw on them with his hands.

In the process of terrorizing an article on spring training, Butch glanced over at Marissa again, and V knew the two were going to take off soon—but not because they were finished with their coffee.

Funny, he knew what was going to happen from extrapolation, not second sight or because he could read their minds: Butch was letting off the bonding scent, and Marissa loved being with her male. It wasn't like V had a vision of them ending up locked in the butler's pantry or back in bed at the Pit.

Jane's thoughts were the only ones he could read, and then only sometimes.

He rubbed the center of his chest and thought about what the Scribe Virgin had said . . . that his visions and his prescient ability were obscured because of a crossroads in his own life, and that when he was through, they would come back. Thing was, he had Jane now, so wasn't he past that part? He'd found his female. He was with her. End of story.

He swallowed more coffee. Kept up with the rubbing.

The nightmare had been back again this morning.

As he couldn't chalk up that bullshit gunshot sequence to PTSD anymore, he decided it was now an allegory, his subconscious churning over the fact that he still felt out of control in his life. Because falling in love would do that.

That had to be why. Had to.

"Ten minutes," Butch whispered into Marissa's ear. "Can I have ten minutes with you before you go? Please, baby . . ."

V rolled his eyes and was relieved to be annoyed at the lovey-dovey routine. At least all the testosterone in him hadn't dried up.

"Baby . . . please?"

V took a pull on his mug. "Marissa, throw the sap bastard a bone, would you? The simpering wears on my nerves."

"Well, we can't have that, can we?" Marissa packed up her papers with a laugh and shot Butch a look. "Ten minutes. And you'd better make them count."

Butch was up out of that chair like the thing was on fire. "Don't I always?"

"Mmm . . . yes."

As the two locked lips, V snorted. "Have fun, kiddies. Somewhere else."

They'd just left when Zsadist came in at a dead run. "Shit. Shit . . . shit . . ."

"What's doing, my brother?"

"I'm teaching and I'm late." Zsadist grabbed a sleeve of bagels, a turkey leg out of the refridg and a quart of ice cream from the freezer. "Shit."

"That's your breakfast?"

"Shut up. It's almost a turkey sandwich."

"Rocky Road don't count as mayo, my brother."

"Whatever." He beelined back for the door. "Oh, by the way, Phury's here again, and he brought that Chosen with him. Figured you'd want to know in case you see a random female ghosting around here."

Whoa. Surprise. "How's he doing?"

Zsadist paused. "I don't know. He's pretty tight about shit. Not real talkative. The bastard."

"Oh, and you're a candidate for *The View?*"

"Right back at you, Bahbwa."

"Touché." V shook his head. "Man, I owe him."

"Yeah, you do. We all do."

"Hold up, Z." V tossed the spoon he'd used to sugar his coffee across the room. "You're going to want this, true."

Z caught the thing on the fly. "Ah, would have spaced that. Thanks. Man, I got Bella on the brain all'a time, feel me?"

The butler's door flapped shut.

In the silence of the kitchen V took another drink from his mug. The coffee was no longer hot, its warmth having dissipated. In another fifteen minutes it would be icy.

Undrinkable.

Yeah . . . he knew how hard it was to be thinking about your female all the time.

Knew it firsthand.

Cormia felt the bed wiggle as the Primale rolled over. Once again.

It had been thus for hours upon hours. She had not slept all day, and she was sure he had not, either. Unless he moved around a lot whilst in repose.

He let out a mumble and jerked about, his heavy limbs thrashing. It was as if he couldn't get comfortable, and she worried that she was somehow disrupting him . . . although it was unclear how. She had stayed still since she'd gotten in.

It was strange, though. She was comforted by his presence in spite of his restlessness. There was something easing about the knowledge that he was on the other side of the bed. She felt safe with him, though she knew him not.

The Primale lurched again, groaned and—

Cormia jumped when his hand landed on her arm.

As did he. With a low growl he made some kind of questioning sound in his throat, then ran his palm up and down, as if trying to figure out what was in his bed with him.

She expected him to pull back.

Instead he grabbed on.

Cormia's lips parted in shock as he made a noise deep in his throat and waded through the sheets, his hand going from her arm to her waist. As if she'd passed some kind of test he rolled into her, a thick thigh coming against hers, something hard pushing into her hip. His hand started moving, and before she knew it the drapery was loosening and then it was off her body.

He growled louder and pulled her flush to him such that the hard length now lay across her thighs. She gasped, but there was no time to react or think. His lips found her throat and sucked on her skin, the draw causing her body to heat. And then his hips began to move. The forward and backward surging made something between her legs well and tingle, something dark and needy unfurling in her belly.

Without warning, both his arms shot around her and he rolled her onto her back, his luxurious hair falling down over her face. His thick thigh pushed between hers, and he mounted her, that arch and retreat stroking what she knew was his sex against her. He was

huge atop her, but she didn't feel trapped or scared. Whatever this was between them was something she wanted. Something . . . she craved.

Tentatively she put her hands on his back. The muscles along his spine were tremendous, and they rippled with his movements under the satin of his robe. He growled anew when she touched him, as if he liked her hands on him, and just as she wondered what his bare skin felt like he lifted up and disrobed.

Then he leaned to one side, took her palm in his, and put it between their bodies. On himself.

They both gasped as the connection was made, and she had an instant of pure amazement at the heat and the hardness and the size of him . . . as well the softness of his skin . . . and the power that seemed to rest in his staff of flesh. She gripped him in reflex as a shocking bolt of fire speared her at her thighs.

Except then he cried out and his hips pushed forward and what was in her hand started to kick. Warm bursts shot out from somewhere and covered her belly.

Oh, dear Virgin, had she hurt him?

Phury woke up on top of Cormia, with her hand on his cock and an orgasm in full swing. He tried to stop his body, grappled to get a rein on the erotic currents thundering through him, but he couldn't stop the momentum, even as he was aware he was coming all over her.

The second the sensations passed he whipped back. And then everything got worse.

"I'm so sorry," she said, staring up at him with horror.

"For what?" Shit, his voice was shot. And he was the one who should be apologizing.

"I hurt you . . . until you bled."

Oh, sweet Jesus. "Ah . . . that's not blood."

He shoved the covers aside so he could get up, realized he was totally naked, and had to fumble through the bedding to find the robe. He yanked the damn thing on, got his leg in place, and lit off the bed, heading to the bathroom for a towel.

When he came back over to her, he could only imagine how she'd want that stuff off her. He'd made a mess.

"Let me . . ." He caught sight of the drapery on the floor. Oh, great, she was naked, too. *Fantastic.* "Actually, maybe you should clean up."

He looked away and held out the towel. "Take this. Use it."

From the corner of his eye he watched her awkwardly swipe under the covers, and self-loathing swamped him. *Jesus Christ . . .* He was a lecher. Overwhelming the poor female.

When she handed the towel back, he said, "You can't stay with me. It's not right. For as long as we're here, you're going to be in the other room."

There was a slight pause. Then she said, "Yes, Your Grace."

FORTY-SEVEN

As night fell John was underground in the gym, lined up with the rest of trainees, a dagger in his right hand, his feet planted in the ready position. When Zsadist whistled through his teeth, John and everyone else began to move through the exercise: Swipe the weapon across the chest, slice back at an angle, step forward, and stab up under the rib cage.

"John, stay sharp!"

Shit, he was fucking this whole thing up. Again. Feeling utterly blind and mostly useless, he tried to find the rhythm in the positions, but his balance was in the crapper and his arms and legs just wouldn't behave.

"John—stop." Zsadist came up behind him and moved his arms around. Again. "Ladies, back in ready position."

John settled in, waited for the whistle . . . and screwed it all up. Again.

This time when Zsadist walked over, John couldn't look the Brother in the face.

"Let's try something." Z took the blade and put it in John's left hand.

John shook his head. He was right-dominant.

"Just try it. Ladies? Let's do it."

Another ready position. Another whistle. Another fuckup—

Oh, but this time it wasn't. Miraculously, John's body fell into the series of positions like a perfect piano chord. Everything was in sync, all his arms and legs going where they needed to be, the dagger controlled perfectly in his palm, his muscles coalescing and working together.

When the drill was over, he smiled. Until he met Z's eyes. The Brother was staring at him strangely, but then seemed to catch himself. "Better, John. Much better."

John looked down at the blade in his hand. He had a quick, painful memory of walking Sarelle out to her car a couple of days before she'd been killed. As he'd been by her side, he'd wished he had a dagger, had felt like his palm was too light without one. That had been his right hand then. Why the switch after the transition?

"Again, ladies!" Z called out.

They did the sequence twenty-three more times. Then worked on another that had them getting down on one knee and lunging upward. Z patrolled the line, fixing positions, barking out demands.

He didn't have to address John once. Everything just came together, the vein tapped, the gold extracted.

When class was over John headed to the lockers, but Z called him back and led him into the equipment room, over to the locked closet where the training daggers were kept.

"From now on you'll use this." Z handed over one with a blue hilt. "Calibrated for the left hand."

John tried it out and felt even stronger. He was about to thank the Brother when he frowned. Z was looking at him with the same strange expression he'd had out in the gym.

John tucked the blade into the belt of his *ji* and signed, *What? Am I not in good position?*

Z rubbed a hand over his skull trim. "Ask me how many fighters are left-handed."

John's breath stopped, an odd feeling coming over him. *How many?*

"Only known one. Ask me who he was."

Who was he?

"Darius. D was left-handed."

John stared down at his left hand. His father.

"And you move like him," Z murmured. "It's eerie as fuck, to be honest. It's like I'm looking at him."

Really?

"Yeah, he was smooth. Like you are. Anyway. Whatever." Z clapped him on the shoulder. "Lefty. Go figure."

John watched the Brother leave, then looked at his palm again.

Not for the first time, he wondered what his father had looked like. Sounded like. Acted like. God, what he wouldn't give for some information on the male.

Maybe someday he could ask Zsadist, although he was afraid of getting emotional.

A male should always be tight. Especially in front of a Brother.

Jane backed her car into her garage and cursed at the time as she cut the engine. Eleven thirty-four. She was two and a half hours late to meet V at her place.

It had been a prime case of delayed departure. She'd had her coat on and her bag packed, but on the way to the door all sorts of medical staff had come up to her with question after question. Then one of the patients had taken a turn for the worse in the chute, and she'd had to examine the woman, then talk to the family.

She'd texted Vishous that she'd gotten tied up. Then again when she had to stay even longer. He'd hit her back saying it was fine. But then she'd called when she'd gotten stuck on a detour on the way home, and she'd gone to voice mail.

She got out of the car as the garage door eased shut. She was excited to see Vishous, but exhausted too. They'd spent the night before doing a whole lot of not sleeping, and she'd had a long day.

As she came in through the kitchen she called out, "I'm so sorry I'm late."

"It's cool," he said from the living room.

She walked around the corner . . . and stopped. Vishous was sitting on the couch in the dark, his legs crossed. His leather jacket was next to him, and so was a wrapped bunch of calla lilies. He was still as a frozen lake.

Shit.

"Hi," she said as she dumped her coat and bag on her parents' dining room table.

"Hey." He uncrossed his thighs and planted his elbows on his knees. "Everything at the hospital okay?"

"Yeah. Just busy." She sat down next to the flowers. "These are lovely."

"Got them for you."

"I'm really sorry—"

He stopped her with his hand. "You don't have to be. I can imagine how it is."

As she measured him, she knew he wasn't trying to guilt her or anything; he was just disappointed. Which somehow made her feel worse. If he'd been unreasonable, that was one thing, but this quiet resignation from a man as powerful as him was hard to bear.

"You look tired," he said. "I think the kindest thing I can do is put you in bed."

She leaned back and gently stroked one of the flowers with her forefinger. She liked that he didn't go average with roses or even the white kind of calla lily. These were a deep peach tone. Unusual. Beautiful. "I thought about you today. A lot."

"Did you?" Though she wasn't looking at him, she heard the smile in his voice. "What did you think about?"

"Everything. Nothing. How much I wish I were sleeping next to you every night."

She didn't tell him she'd turned down the Columbia opportunity. Letting that go didn't sit right, but then, trying for a position in New York City where she'd have even more responsibility just didn't seem like a smart thing to do if the goal was to spend more, not less, time with V. She still wanted to be in charge, but you had to sacrifice things in life to get what you wanted. And the idea that you could have it all was such a fallacy.

A yawn sprang up her throat and opened her mouth. Shit, she was tired.

V stood and put out his hand. "Up you go. You can sleep next to me for a while."

She let herself be led upstairs, stripped, and pushed into the shower. She waited for him to join her, but he shook his head.

"If I start with that shit, I'm going to keep you up for the next two hours." His eyes latched onto her breasts and flashed with light. "Oh . . . Christ . . . I'll just . . . Fuck, I gotta wait for you outside."

She smiled as he shut the glass shower door and his big black shape stalked off into the bedroom. Ten minutes later she came out, scrubbed, flossed, brushed, and in one of her nightshirts.

Vishous had straightened the duvet, arranged her pillows, and folded the sheets back. "In," he commanded.

"I hate taking orders," she murmured.

"But you'll do it from me. On occasion." He swatted her butt lightly as she slid in. "Get comfortable."

She arranged everything where she wanted it to be as he went around and lay down on top of the bed. When he pushed his arm under her head and cuddled up close, she thought, God, he smelled good. And that soothing hand running up and down her waist was divine.

After a while she said into the darkness, "So, we lost a patient today."

"Shit, I'm sorry."

"Yeah . . . there was no saving her. Sometimes you just know, and with her? I knew it. We still did everything we could, but all along . . . yeah, all along I knew we weren't going to bring her through."

"That must be hard."

"Awful. I was the one who told the family she was slipping, but at least they got to be there when she passed, which was good. Like my sister? Hannah died alone. I hate that." Jane pictured the young woman whose heart had given out in the chute. "Death is weird. Most people think it's an on/off kind of thing, but more often it's a process, really, kind of like closing up a shop at the end of the day. For the most part things fail in a predictable manner, until finally the last light in the place goes out and the door is shut and locked. As a doctor I can jump in and stop the progression by sealing up wounds or giving more blood or forcing the body to regulate its functions with drugs. But sometimes . . . sometimes the shopkeeper just leaves, and you can't stop him no matter what you do." She laughed awkwardly. "Sorry, don't mean to get morbid."

He brushed his hand down her face. "You're not. You're amazing."

"You're biased," she said, before yawning so wide her jaw cracked.

"I'm right." He kissed her forehead. "Now sleep."

She must have followed orders, because sometime later she felt him moving away. "Don't go."

"Have to. I'm patrolling downtown."

He stood up, a giant of a man—er, male, his dark hair catching the dim light from the streetlamps out in front of the condo.

A wave of sadness came over her, and she closed her eyes.

"Hey," he said, sitting down next to her. "None of that. We're not sad. You and me? We're not sad. We don't do sad."

She laughed with a choking sound. "How did you know what I was feeling? Or do I look that pathetic?"

He tapped his nose. "I can smell it. Spring rain is what the scent's like."

"I hate this good-bye shit."

"Me, too." He leaned down and brushed his lips against her forehead. "Here." He shrugged out of his long-sleeved shirt, balled it up, and put it under her cheek. "Pretend this is me."

She breathed in deep, caught the bonding scent, and was calmed a little. As he stood, he looked so strong in just a muscle shirt, invincible, like a superhero. And yet he breathed.

"Please . . . be careful."

"Always." He bent over and kissed her again. "I love you."

As he pulled away, she reached out and grabbed his arm. Words failed, but the silence said enough.

"I hate the leaving, too," he replied roughly. "But I'll be back. I promise."

He kissed her again and then headed for the door. As she listened to him go downstairs to get his coat, she cradled his shirt to her face and closed her eyes.

With perfectly fucking bad timing, the garage door of the condo beside hers started to rumble up. Halfway through, it got stuck, the motor whining loud enough to make her headboard vibrate.

She punched the pillow and rolled over, ready to scream.

Vishous was not a happy camper as he pulled on his dagger holster. He was distracted, vaguely pissed off, achy as shit, and in desperate need to have a smoke and collect his marbles before he went downtown. He felt totally off center, like he had a heavy duffel bag hanging off one shoulder.

"Vishous! Wait!" Jane's voice came from upstairs just as he was going to dematerialize. "Wait!"

Her footsteps bounded down the stairs and she whipped around the corner, his shirt dwarfing her, the tails hanging down almost to her knees.

"What—"

"I have an idea. It's crazy. But it's also smart." With high color in her cheeks and her eyes lit with purpose, she was the most beautiful thing he'd ever seen. "What if I moved in with you?"

He shook his head. "I want you to, but—"

"And functioned as the Brotherhood's private surgeon."

Holy . . . shit . . . "What?"

"You really should have one on-site. You said there are complications with that Havers guy. Well, I could solve them. I could hire a nurse to assist, upgrade the facilities, and be in charge. You said there are at least three to four injuries a week within the Brotherhood, right? Plus, Bella's pregnant and there will probably be more babies in the future."

"Jesus . . . you would give up the hospital, though?"

"Yeah, but I'd get something in return."

He flushed. "Me?"

She laughed. "Well, yeah. Of course. But there's something else."

"What?"

"The chance to systematically study your race. My other great love is genetics. If I got to spend the next two decades fixing you boys up and cataloging the differences between humans and vampires, I'd say my life had been well served. I want to know where you came from and how your bodies work and why you don't get cancer. There are important things to be learned, Vishous. Things that could benefit both races. I'm not talking about you guys as guinea pigs. . . . Well, I guess I am. But not in a cruel way. Not in the detached way I was thinking of before. I love you and I want to learn from you."

He stared at her and did a whole lot of not breathing.

She winced and said, "Please say y—"

He crushed her against his chest. "Yes. Yeah . . . if it's okay with Wrath and you're cool with it . . . *yes.*"

Her arms went around his waist and squeezed hard.

Holy shit, he felt like he was flying. He was whole, complete, solid in his head and his heart and his body, all his little boxes ar-

ranged properly, that Rubik's Cube in out-of-the-wrapper, perfect condition.

He was about to get sappy when his phone went off. With a curse he unclipped it from his belt and barked, "What. Jane's. You want to meet me here? Right now? Yeah. Fuck. Okay, see you in two, Hollywood." He clipped the RAZR shut. "Rhage."

"You think we'll be able to swing a move-in for me?"

"Yeah, I do. Frankly, Wrath would be much more comfortable if you were in our world." He ran his knuckles down her cheek. "And so would I. I just never thought you'd give up your life."

"Not giving it up, though. Living it a little differently, but not giving it up. I mean . . . I really don't have many friends." *Except Manello.* "And there's nothing tying me down—I was prepared to leave Caldwell for Manhattan anyway. Plus . . . I'm just going to be happier with you."

He looked her face over, loving the strong features and the short hair and the piercing forest green eyes. "I never would have asked you, you know . . . to blow everything you have here away for me."

"That's only one of the reasons I love you."

"Will you tell me the others later?"

"Maybe." She slipped her hand between his legs, shocking the shit out of him and making him gasp. "Might show you, too."

He covered her mouth with his and pushed his tongue into her as he backed her up against the wall. He didn't care if Rhage waited on the front lawn for an extra—

His phone went off. And kept ringing.

V lifted his head and looked through the window by the front door. Rhage was on the front lawn, phone to his ear, staring back. The Brother made a show of checking his watch, then flashing his middle finger at V.

Vishous pounded a fist into the Sheetrock and stepped off from Jane. "I'm coming back at the end of the night. Be naked."

"Wouldn't you rather undress me?"

"No, because I'd shred that shirt, and I want you sleeping in it every night until you're in my bed with me. Be. Naked."

"We'll see."

His whole body throbbed at the disobedience. And she knew it, her stare level and erotic.

"God, I love you," he said.

"I know. Now run along and kill something. I'll be waiting for you."

He smiled at her. "Couldn't love you more if I tried."

"Ditto."

He kissed her and dematerialized out front to Rhage's side, making sure some *mhis* was in place. *Oh, great.* It was raining. Man, he'd so much rather be cozied up with Jane than out with his brother, and he couldn't help but shoot a short-stack glare at Rhage.

"Like another five minutes would kill you?"

"Please. You start down that road with your female and I'll be here until summer."

"Are you—"

V frowned and looked at the condo next to Jane's. The garage door was jammed halfway up, the glow of brake lights revealed. There was a slam of a car door, then on the breeze the faintest scent of sweetness drifted over, like powdered sugar had been sprinkled in the cold wind.

"Oh . . . God, *no.*"

At that very moment Jane threw open her front door and came running out, his leather jacket in her hand, his shirt flowing behind her. "You forgot this!"

It was a hideous hole in one, a revelation of all the pieces he'd seen only fragments of: The dream had arrived in real life.

"No!" he screamed.

The sequence played out in a series of seconds that lasted centuries: Rhage looking at him as if he were crazy. Jane running over the grass. Him dropping the *mhis* as fear overwhelmed him.

A *lesser* ducking out from under the garage door with gun drawn.

The shot made no sound on account of the silencer that was in place. V lunged for Jane, trying to shield her body with his. He failed. She was hit in the back, and the bullet came out the other side, busting through her sternum, going into his arm. He caught her as she fell, his own chest blazing with pain.

As they crumpled to the ground, Rhage tore off after the slayer, not that V really noticed. All he knew was his nightmare: Blood on his shirt. His heart screaming in agony. Death coming . . . but not for him. *For Jane.*

"Two minutes," she said between gasps as her hand flopped onto her chest. "Got less than two . . . minutes."

She must have been hit in an artery and knew it. "I'm going to—"

She shook her head and grabbed his arm. "Stay. Shit . . . not going . . . to . . ."

Make it . . . were the words she was going to say. "Fuck that!"

"Vishous . . ." Her eyes watered, her color draining fast. "Hold my hand. Don't leave me. You can't . . . Don't let me go alone."

"You're going to be fine!" He started to pick her up. "I'm taking you to Havers's."

"*Vishous.* Can't fix this. Hold my hand. I'm leaving . . . oh, fuck . . ." She started to weep while gasping. "I love you."

"*No!*"

"I love . . ."

"*No!*"

FORTY-EIGHT

The Scribe Virgin looked up from the bird in her hand, sudden dread startling her.

Oh . . . wretched happenstance. Oh, horrid destiny.

It had come. The thing she had sensed and feared long ago, the breakdown in the structure of her reality had arrived. Her punishment was now manifest.

That human . . . that human woman her son loved was dying at this very moment. She was in his arms and bleeding on him and dying.

With an unsteady arm the Scribe Virgin put the chickadee back on the white-blooming tree and stumbled over to the fountain. Sitting down on its marble edge, she felt the light weight of her robing as if it were heavy chains drawn around her.

The fault of her son's loss was hers. Verily, she had brought this ruination upon him: She had broken the rules. Three hundred years ago she had broken the rules.

At the inception of time she had been granted one act of creation, and accordingly, after her maturity had been reached, one act of creation she had effected. But then she'd done it again. She had borne what she should not have, and in doing so had cursed her begotten. Her son's destiny—the whole of it, from his treatment under his father to the hard, coldhearted male Vishous had matured into to this, his mortal agony—was in fact her castigation. For as he was in pain, so she suffered a thousandfold.

She wanted to cry out for her Father, but knew she could not. Choices that had been made by her were naught of His concern, and the consequences were hers alone to bear.

As she reached through the dimensions and saw what was transpiring unto her son, she knew Vishous's agony as her own, felt the numbing of his cold shock, the fire of his denial, the gut-wrenching twist of his horror. She felt, too, the death of his beloved, the gradual chill coming upon the human as her blood leaked into her chest cavity and her heart began to flutter. And then, yes, then, too, she heard her son's mumbling words of love and smelled the rank, fetid fear that poured out of him.

There was naught she could do. She, who had power beyond measure over so many, was in this moment impotent because fate and the consequence of free will were her Father's sole domain. He alone knew the absolute map of eternity, the compendium of all choices taken and untaken, of paths known and unknown. He was the Book and the Page and the indelible Ink.

She was not.

And He would not come to her now for that reason. This was her destiny: to suffer because an innocent born of a body she should never have assumed would be ever in pain, her son walking the earth as a dead male for the choices she had made.

With a wail the Scribe Virgin let herself lose her form and slipped out of the robes she wore, the black folds falling to the marble floor. She entered the water of the fountain as a light wave, traveling in between and among the hydrogen and oxygen molecules, her misery energizing them, bringing them to a boil, evaporating them. As the transfer of energy continued, the liquid rose up as a cloud, coalesced above the courtyard, and fell back down as tears she was incapable of crying.

Over on the white tree, her birds craned their necks to the falling water droplets as if considering this new occurrence. And then as a flock they left their perch for the first time and flew to the fountain. Lining up around the edge, they faced outward from the glowing, seething water she inhabited.

They guarded her in her sorrow and regrets, guarded her as though each were big as an eagle and just as fierce.

They were, as always, her only solace and friendship.

Jane was aware that she was dead.

She knew it because she was in the midst of a fog, and someone who looked like her dead sister was standing in front of her.

So she was pretty damn sure she'd kicked it. Except . . . shouldn't she be upset or something? Shouldn't she be worried about Vishous? Shouldn't she be thrilled about reuniting with her little sister?

"Hannah?" she said, because she wanted to be sure she knew what she was looking at. "That you?"

"Kinda." The image of her sister shrugged, her pretty red hair moving with her shoulders. "I'm really just a messenger."

"Well, you look like her."

"Of course I do. What you see now is what's in your mind when you think of her."

"Okay . . . this is a little *Twilight Zone*. Or, wait, am I just dreaming?" Because that would be great fucking news, considering what she thought had just happened to her.

"No, you've passed on. You're just in the middle right now."

"In the middle of where?"

"You're in between. Neither here nor there."

"Can you be a little more specific?"

"Not really." The Hannah-vision smiled her precious smile, the angelic one that had brought even Richard the nasty cook around. "But here's my message. You're going to have to let go of him, Jane. If you want to find peace, you're going to have to let go of him."

If the *him* was Vishous, that just wasn't happening. "I can't do that."

"You have to. Otherwise you'll be lost here. You only have so much time you can be neither here nor there."

"And then what happens?"

"You are lost forever." The Hannah-vision got serious. "Let him go, Jane."

"How?"

"You know how. And if you do, you can see the real me on the other side. Let. Him. Go." The messenger or whatever it was evaporated.

Left on her own, Jane looked around. The fog was pervasive, as dense as a rain cloud and as infinite as the horizon.

Fear crawled through her. This was not right. She really didn't want to be here.

Abruptly a sense of urgency grew, as if time was running out, though she didn't know how she knew that. Except then she thought of Vishous. If letting go meant giving up her love for him, that so wasn't possible.

FORTY-NINE

ishous was driving Jane's Audi like a bat out of hell through the rain, halfway to Havers's, when he realized she was not in her car with him.

Her corpse was.

His panic was the only energy in the enclosed space, his heart the only one that pounded, his eyes the only ones that blinked.

The bonded male in him confirmed what his brain had been denying: In his blood, he knew that she was gone.

V let his foot ease off the accelerator, and the Audi coasted for a stretch, then slowed to a stop. Route 22 was empty, probably because of this early spring storm that was blowing, but he would have stayed right in the middle of the road even if there had been rush-hour traffic.

Jane was in the passenger seat. Belted in upright, with the seat belt holding his muscle shirt against her chest wound as packing.

He didn't turn his head.

He couldn't look at her.

He stared straight ahead, down the road's double yellow line. In front of him the windshield wipers flipped back and forth, their rhythmic slapping like the sound of an old-fashioned clock, *tick . . . tock . . . tick . . . tock . . .*

The passage of time was no longer relevant, was it. And neither was his rush.

Tick . . . tock . . . tick . . .

He felt like he should be dead, too, considering the pain in his chest. He had no idea how he was still up and around when it hurt this badly.

Tock . . . tick . . .

Up ahead there was a curve in the road, the forest coming up to the asphalt's shoulder. For no particular reason he noticed that the trees were all crowded in tight together, their leafless branches interlacing, creating the impression of black lace.

Tock . . .

The vision that came to him crept up so quietly, at first he didn't know that what his eyes were registering had changed. But then he saw a wall, a subtly textured wall . . . lit by a bright, bright light. Just as he wondered about the source of illumination . . .

He realized it was a car's headlights.

The blare of a horn snapped him to attention, and he stomped on the gas while wrenching the wheel to the right. The other vehicle fishtailed by on the slippery pavement, then resumed its course, disappearing down the road.

V refocused on the forest and in quick succession received the rest of the vision like a movie. With numb disregard, he watched himself take actions that were arguably unconscionable, witnessing the future as it unfurled, taking notes. When no more was revealed, he took off with a desperate purpose, heading out away from Caldwell proper at twice the speed limit.

As his cell phone went off, he reached into the backseat, where he'd thrown his leather jacket, and took the thing out. He turned it off, then pulled over to the side of the road and cracked the back of the RAZR open. Taking out the GPS chip, he put it on the Audi's dash and crushed it with his fist.

"Where the *fuck* is he?"

Phury hung back as Wrath paced around his study, and the other brothers stayed out of the male's way as well. When the king got all bulldozer like this, you got out of his path or he'd mow you into the carpet.

Except apparently he was looking for a response. "Am I talking to my fucking self, here? Where the hell is V?"

Phury cleared his throat. "We don't really know. The GPS conked out about ten minutes ago."

"Conked out?"

"Just went silent. Usually it'll flicker when he's got the phone with him, but . . . yeah, we're not even getting that."

"Great. Fucking terrific." Wrath popped up his wraparounds and rubbed his eyes while wincing. He'd been getting headaches lately, probably from trying to read too much, and it was obvious that an AWOL Brother was not helping the sitch.

Across the way Rhage cursed and hung up his phone. "He hasn't shown up at Havers's still. Look, maybe he's gone somewhere to bury her? Ground's frozen, but with that hand of his it wouldn't be a problem."

"You really think she's dead?" Wrath muttered.

"From what I saw she was hit in the back. By the time I got back from killing that *lesser*, the two of them were gone, and so was her car. But . . . yeah, I don't think she survived."

Wrath looked at Butch, who had been totally silent since coming into the room. "Do you know how to find any of the females he used for sex and feeding?"

The cop shook his head. "Not a one. He kept that part of his life very private."

"So we can't track him that way. More good news. Is there any reason to think he'd go to that penthouse of his?"

"I stopped there on my way back," Butch said. "He wasn't in and I honestly don't think he'd land there. Not considering what he used the place for."

"And there's only two hours of nighttime left." Wrath sat behind his Louis XVI desk, but braced his arms against the flimsy chair, like he was going to bolt upright at any moment.

Butch's phone went off, and he scrambled to answer the thing. "V? Oh . . . hey, baby. No . . . nothing yet. I will. I promise. Love you."

As the cop hung up, Wrath turned toward the fire in the fireplace and was quiet for a while, no doubt reviewing, as they all were, what kind of options they had. Which were, like . . . none. Vishous could be anywhere at this point, so if the Brothers scattered to the four arms of the compass, they'd be doing the needle-in-the-haystack routine. Besides, it was pretty obvious V had killed the GPS chip. He did not want to be found.

Eventually Wrath said, "The pin's out of the grenade, gentlemen. Now it's just a question of what gets blown."

V picked the place for the car accident with care. He wanted to be close to their destination, but still far enough for discretion, and just when he got within range, a curve in the road offered itself up for use. Perfect. Putting his seat belt on, he stomped on the gas and braced himself. The Audi's engine roared, and its wheels spun faster and faster on the slick road. Pretty damn quick it ceased being a car, morphing into nothing but a fuckload of kinetic energy.

Instead of going with Route 22's sharp turn to the left, V headed straight for the tree line. Like a well-behaved child with no survival instincts, the car flew off the shoulder and held air for a split second.

The landing bounced V right off the driver's seat, knocking his head into the car's sunroof, then slamming him forward. Air bags exploded from the steering wheel and the dashboard and doors as the sedan pummeled through brush and saplings and . . .

The oak tree was immense. Big as a house. Just as sturdy.

The Audi's crash cage was all that saved V from annihilation as the front of the car crumpled into an accordion of metal and engine. The shock of impact snapped V's head on his neck, banging his face into his air bag again as a branch pierced through the windshield.

In the aftermath his ears rang like they had fire alarms going off in them, and his body did a self-scan for broken bits and pieces. Dazed, bleeding from cuts left by the branch, he undid his seat belt, forced his door open, and stumbled out of the car. As he took some deep breaths, he heard the hiss of the engine and the wheezing deflation of the air bags. Rain fell with steady, graceful disinterest, dripping off the trees into shallow puddles on the forest floor.

As soon as he could he went around the car to Jane. The impact had thrown her forward, and her blood now marked the windshield and the dash and the seat. Which was what he'd wanted. He leaned in and released her belt, then picked her up as carefully as if she still lived, arranging her in his arms so she would have been comfortable. Before he started through the woods, he got his leather jacket and draped it over her to protect her from the cold weather.

Vishous began the walk as all walks began. He put one foot in front of another. Then repeated. Then repeated.

He tromped through the forest, getting wetter and wetter until he became as the trees were, just another object for water to fall off of. He took a roundabout way to their destination, until his arms and his back ached from carrying her.

Finally he came up to the entrance of a cave. He didn't bother checking to make sure he wasn't followed. He knew he was alone.

He walked into the earthy well, the sound of the rain receding as he continued farther over the dirt floor. He located from memory the catch in the rock wall and triggered the release. As a nine-foot slab of granite shifted over, he entered the hall that was revealed and ap-

proached a set of iron gates. He released the locking mechanism with his mind, and the barrier parted without a sound as the rock behind him replaced itself.

Inside, it was beyond pitch-black, the air denser in this underground place, as if it were crowded into the space. With a quick thought he flamed up some of the wall torches with his mind, then started down toward the Tomb's place of worship and ritual. On either side of the hall, on shelves that reached up some twenty feet, there were thousands of ceramic jars containing the hearts of *lessers* killed by the Brotherhood. He did not look up at them, as he usually did. He stared straight ahead as he carried his beloved forward, his wet boots leaving tracks on the glossy black marble floor.

Not long thereafter he stepped into the Tomb's belly, the vast, subterranean cave opening up a great hole in the earth. At his will, thick black candles on stanchions lit up, illuminating the daggerlike stalactites that hung down as well as the massive black marble slabs that formed the wall behind the altar.

The slabs were what he had seen in his vision. When he'd stared down Route 22 and looked at the trees, he had pictured this memorial wall: As with the trees' interlocking branches, the inscriptions on the marble, all those names of warriors who had served in the Brotherhood for generations, formed a subtle, gentle pattern, looking like lace from afar.

In front of the wall the altar was crude, but powerful: an enormous block of stone set on two stout lintels. In the center was the ancient skull of the first member of the Black Dagger Brotherhood, the most sacred relic the Brothers had.

He pushed it aside and laid Jane down. She had lost her color, and her limp white hand as it fell off to the side made him shake all over. He carefully returned it to her, putting it on her chest.

He stepped away until his back hit the etched wall. In the candlelight, and with his jacket over her upper torso, he could almost imagine she was sleeping.

Almost.

Surrounded by the subterranean vista, he thought of the cave of the warrior camp. Then he saw himself using his hand on the pretrans who had threatened him, and on his father.

He undid his glove and slid it off his glowing palm.

What he contemplated now went against the laws of both nature and his species.

Reanimation of the dead was not an appropriate or allowable course of action under any circumstances. And not just because it was the Omega's realm. The Chronicles of the race, those volumes and volumes of history, provided only two examples, and neither had resulted in anything but tragedy.

But he was different. This was different. Jane was different. He was doing this out of love, whereas the examples he read about had been done out of hatred: There had been a murderer that someone had brought back to use as a weapon, and a female returned to life as an act of revenge.

And there was more in his favor. He healed Butch on a regular basis, drawing the evil out of the cop when he did his business with the *lessers*. He could do the same for Jane. He absolutely could.

With iron resolve, he pushed from his mind the outcomes of those other forays into the Omega's realm of dark arts. And focused on his love for his female.

The fact that Jane was a human was not an issue, as reanimation was the act of bringing that which was dead back to life, and the dividing line was the same no matter the species. And he had what he needed. The ritual required three things: something of the Omega's, some fresh blood, and a source of electrical energy such as a harnessed lightning bolt.

Or in his case, his fucking curse.

V walked back out to the hall of jars and didn't waste time picking. He took one randomly from the shelf, its ceramic marked by fine cracks and its color a murky brown, which meant it was one of the early ones.

When he returned to the altar, he slammed the jar into the stone, shattering the thing, revealing what it had housed. The heart inside was covered with a black, oily sheen, preserved by what flowed in the Omega's veins. Though the exact nature of the induction into the Lessening Society was unknown, it was clear the Omega's "blood" went in first before the heart was removed.

So Vishous had what he needed from their enemy.

He looked at the skull of the first Brother and didn't think twice about using the sacred relic for what was an unlawful purpose. He took out one of his daggers, scored his wrist, and bled into the sterling silver cup that was mounted in the top of the skull. Then he palmed the *lesser* heart and squeezed it with his fist.

Black drops of distilled evil welled and fell, mixing with the red of his blood. The liquid sin had magic to it, the kind that ran against the rules of the righteous, the kind that turned torture into sport, the kind that enjoyed pain inflicted on the innocent . . . but it had eternity in it, too.

And that was what he needed for Jane.

"No!"

He spun around.

The Scribe Virgin had appeared behind him, her hood down, her transparent face a mask of horror. "You *must* not do this."

He turned away and brought the skull up next to Jane's head. On a fragmentary thought, he found an odd, reassuring parallel that she knew what the inside of his chest looked like and he was about to know the same of her.

"There is no balance in this! No price given!"

V removed his jacket from his female. The bloodstain under it, on his shirt, was like a bull's-eye right in the middle of her chest, between her breasts.

"She will come back not as you know her," his mother hissed. "She will come back evil. That shall be your result."

"I love her. I can take care of her, like I take care of Butch."

"Your love will not change the outcome, nor will your facility with the Omega's remnants. This is forbidden!"

He wheeled on his mother, hating her and her stupid fucking yin-and-yang bullshit. "You want balance? A trade? You want to stick it to me before I can do this? Fine! What's it going to take? You saddled Rhage with his curse for the rest of his fucking life, what are you going to do to me?"

"Parity is not my law!"

"Then whose is it! And how much do I fucking owe!"

The Scribe Virgin seemed to take a moment to collect herself. "This is beyond what I may gift or not. She is gone. There is no return once a body has been left fallow as hers has been."

"Bullshit." He leaned back over Jane, prepared to cut open her chest.

"You shall condemn her ever after. There will be nowhere for her to go but to the Omega, and you will have to send her there. She will be evil and you will have to destroy her."

He looked at Jane's lifeless face. Remembered her smile. Tried to find it in the pasty skin.

He could not.

"Balance . . ." he whispered.

He reached out and touched her cold cheek with his good hand and tried to think of all that he could give, all that he could trade.

"This is not just about balance," the Scribe Virgin said. "Some things are forbidden."

As the solution became clear to him, he didn't hear anything else from his mother.

He lifted up his precious, normal hand, the one he could touch people and things with, the one that was as it should be, not some cursed burden of destruction.

His good hand.

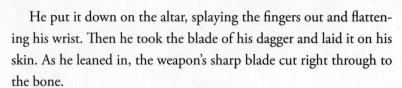

He put it down on the altar, splaying the fingers out and flattening his wrist. Then he took the blade of his dagger and laid it on his skin. As he leaned in, the weapon's sharp blade cut right through to the bone.

"No!" the Scribe Virgin screamed.

FIFTY

ane was out of time. And she knew it in the same way she knew when a patient was taking a turn for the worse. Her internal clock went off, her alarm starting to beep.

"I don't want to let go of him," she said to no one.

Her voice didn't travel far, and she noticed that the fog seemed more dense . . . so dense it was starting to obscure even her feet. And then it dawned on her. They weren't obscured. With cold dread she realized that unless she did something, she was going to dissolve and take her place within the wall of ambient nothing. She would be forever alone and lonely, pining for the love she'd once felt.

A sad, shifting ghost.

Now she was finally struck by emotion, and it was one that brought tears to her eyes. The only way to save herself was to let the yearning for Vishous go; that was the key to the door. But if she did it, she felt as if she were abandoning him, leaving him alone to face

a cold, bitter future. After all, she could imagine how it would be for her if he died.

In a surge the fog grew even thicker and the temperature dropped. She looked down. Her legs were disappearing . . . first up to her ankles, now to her calves. She was leaching out into the nothingness, dispersing.

Jane began to cry as she found her resolve and wept for the selfishness of what she had to do.

How did she let go of him, though?

As the fog crawled up to her thighs, she panicked. She didn't know how to do what she must—

The answer, when it came to her, was painful and simple.

Oh . . . God . . . Letting go meant you accepted what couldn't be changed. You didn't try to hold on to hope in order to coerce a change in fortune . . . nor did you battle against the superior forces of fate and try to make them capitulate to your will . . . nor did you beg for salvation because you assumed you knew better. Letting go meant you stared at what was before you with clear eyes, recognizing that unfettered choice was the exception and destiny the rule.

No bargaining. No trying to control. You gave up and saw that the one you loved was in fact not your future, and there was nothing you could do about it.

Tears fell from her eyes into the swirling mist as she released all pretense of strength and let go of her fight to keep her tie to Vishous alive. As she did, she had no faith or optimism, she was empty as the fog around her: An atheist in life, she found in death she was the same. Believing in nothing, now she was nothing.

And that was when the miracle happened.

A light fell from overhead, sheltering her, warming her, suffusing her with something that was just as the love she had felt for Vishous had been: a benediction.

As she was pulled upward like a daisy plucked from the ground by a gentle hand, she realized that she could still love who she loved, even though she wasn't with him. Indeed, their divergent paths did not dissect and desecrate what she felt. It layered her emotions with a cloak of bittersweet longing, but it didn't change what was in her heart. She could love him and wait for him on the far side of life. Because love, after all, was eternal and not subject to the whims of death.

Jane was free . . . as upward she flew.

Phury was about to lose it.

But he had to get in line if he was going to go mad, because all the Brothers were on a thin edge. Especially Butch, who was pacing around the study like a prisoner in solitary confinement.

No sign of Vishous. No calls. No nothing. And dawn was coming like a freight train.

Butch stopped. "Where would you do a funeral for a *shellan?*"

Wrath frowned. "The Tomb."

"You think maybe he'd take her there?"

"He's never been too keen on the whole ritual deal, and with his mother having forsaken him . . . ?" Wrath shook his head. "He wouldn't go there. Besides, he'd have to know that's one of the places we'd look for him, and he's so damned private. Assuming he's putting her down, he wouldn't want an audience."

"Yeah."

Butch started up with the pacing again as the grandfather clock rang in four thirty A.M.

"You know what?" the cop said. "I'm just going to check it out, if that's cool. I can't stay in here a second longer."

Wrath shrugged. "Might as well. We've got nothing else to go on."

Phury stood up, unable to take the waiting any longer either. "I'm going with you. You'll need someone to show you where the entrance is."

Because Butch couldn't dematerialize, the two of them got in the Escalade, and Phury powered the SUV over the lawn and into the forest. With the sun coming up so soon, he didn't bother with a roundabout way, but gunned right for the Tomb.

The two of them were utterly silent until Phury pulled up to the entrance of the cave and they got out.

"I smell blood," Butch said. "I think we've got them!"

Yeah, there was the barest trace of human blood in the air . . . no doubt from V having carried Jane inside.

Shit. Jogging into the cave, they headed for the back, slipping through the disguised entrance and going down to the iron gates. One side was open, and there was a trail of wet footsteps down the center of the hall of jars.

"He's here!" Butch said, relief carrying his words more than his breath did.

Yeah, except why would V, who hated his mother, bury the female he loved according to the Scribe Virgin's traditions?

He wouldn't.

As they started down the hall, Phury's sense of doom was triggered . . . especially as they got to the end and he saw an empty spot on the shelving, where a *lesser*'s jar was missing. *Oh, no.* Oh . . . God no. They should have brought more weapons. If V had done what Phury feared he had, they were going to need to be armed to the nines.

"Hold up!" He stopped, tore a torch from the wall, and handed it to Butch. After he nabbed one for himself, he grabbed Butch's arm. "Be prepared to fight."

"Why? V might be pissed off that we came, but he's not going to get violent."

"Jane's the one you're going to want to watch for."

"What the fuck are you talking ab—"

"I think he might have tried to bring her back—"

A brilliant flash of light exploded up ahead, turning everything into noontime.

"Fuck!" the cop barked in the aftermath. "Don't tell me he would?"

"If Marissa died and you could pull it off, wouldn't you?"

The two of them took off and burst into the cave. Only to stop dead.

"What is that?" Butch breathed.

"I . . . I have no idea."

On slow, quiet feet they walked down to the altar, transfixed by the sight ahead. Sitting in the middle of the lintel stone was a sculpture, a bust . . . of Jane's head and shoulders. The composition was done in dark gray stone, the likeness so exact it was like a photograph. Or maybe a hologram. Light from candles flickered over the features, casting shadows that seemed to animate them.

At the far right end of the slab there was a smashed ceramic jar, the Brotherhood's sacred skull, as well as what looked like a mangled, oil-covered heart.

On the far side of the altar, V was propped up against the wall of names, his eyes shut, his hands in his lap. One of his wrists was tied up tightly with a strip of black cloth, and one of his daggers was missing. The place smelled like smoke, but there was none in the air.

"V?" Butch went over and knelt down next to his roommate.

Phury left the cop to deal with V and headed for the altar. The sculpture was a perfect likeness of Jane, so real it could have been her as she breathed. He reached out, compelled to touch the face, but the instant his forefinger came into contact with it, the bust lost all form. *Shit.* It wasn't made of stone but ash, and now it was nothing more than a loose mound of what must be Jane's last remains.

Phury looked over at Butch. "Tell me V's alive?"

"Well, he's breathing, at any rate."

"Let's get him home." Phury looked at the ashes. "Let's get them both home."

He needed something to carry Jane in, and he sure as hell wasn't going to use a *lesser* jar. He glanced around. There was nothing.

Phury took off his silk shirt and spread it flat on the altar. It was the best he could do, and they were out of time.

Daylight was coming. And there was no negotiating with its arrival.

FIFTY-ONE

Two days later Phury decided to go over to the Other Side. The Directrix had been hammering for a meeting, and he didn't want to put her off any longer. Besides, he had to get out of the house.

Jane's death had brought a pall to the compound, affecting all the bonded males. The loss of a *shellan*, which was what she'd been even though she and V hadn't been formally mated, was always the greatest fear. But to have her killed by the enemy was nearly unendurable. Worse, to have it happen less than a year after Wellsie was likewise murdered—it was all a horrible reminder of what each of the males knew to be true: Mates of the Brotherhood faced a special threat from the *lessers*.

Tohrment had learned this firsthand. Now so had Vishous.

God, you had to wonder if V was going to stick around. Tohr had taken off right after Wellsie had been killed by a slayer, and no one had seen or heard from him since. Though Wrath maintained

that he could feel that the Brother was still alive, they had all pretty much given up on the idea of him reappearing in this decade or the next. Maybe in some future era he would come back. Or maybe he would die out in the world alone somewhere. But they wouldn't see him again anytime soon, and, hell, the next place might well be the Fade.

Shit . . . Poor Vishous.

Right now V was in his room at the Pit, lying next to the brass urn Phury had eventually put Jane's ashes in. The Brother hadn't spoken or eaten anything, according to Butch, though the guy's eyes were apparently open.

It was clear he had no intention of explaining what had happened in the Tomb. To Jane. Or to his wrist.

With a curse Phury knelt by his bed and put the Primale's medallion around his neck. Closing his eyes he traveled directly to the Chosen's sanctuary, thinking of Cormia along the way. She too stayed in her room, eating little and saying less. He checked on her frequently, though he didn't know what to do for her—other than bring her books, which she seemed to like. She was particularly into Jane Austen, although she didn't quite understand how something could be fiction or, as she put it, a constructed lie.

Phury took form at the amphitheater because he didn't know the layout very well yet and figured it was a good starting point. Man, it felt bizarre to be standing in the middle of all the white. Weirder still to walk around the back of the stage and get a gander at the various white temples. Goddamn, the place was an ad for Clorox. No color anywhere. And it was so quiet. Freaky quiet.

As he picked a direction and started walking, he worried about getting mobbed by a bunch of Chosen and was not exactly in a hurry to go head-to-head with the Directrix. To blow some time, he decided to take a look at what was inside one of the temples. Picking one randomly he went up its shallow marble steps, but found that the double doors were locked tight.

Frowning, he bent down and looked at the large, oddly shaped keyhole. On impulse, he took the Primale medallion off and stuck it into the door.

Well, what do you know. The thing was a key.

The double doors opened without a sound, and he was surprised at what was inside. Lining both sides of the building, and sitting six or eight deep, were bins and bins of precious stones. He walked around the riches, every once in a while stopping and putting his hands into the sparkling gems.

But that wasn't all that was inside. In the back, at the far end, were a series of glass cases such as you would find at a museum. He went over and checked them out. Naturally they were dust-free, although not, he sensed, because they'd been cleaned. He just couldn't imagine there being any pollutants in the air around here, even those of the microscopic variety.

Inside the cases the objects were fascinating, and clearly from the real world. There was an old-fashioned pair of spectacles, a porcelain bowl of Oriental origin, a whiskey bottle with a label from the 1930s, an ebony cigarette holder, a lady's fan made from white feathers.

He wondered how they got over here. Some of the things were quite old, though they were in perfect condition and, of course, everything was sparkly-frickin' clean.

He paused over what looked like an ancient book. "Son . . . of a bitch."

Its leather cover was tattered, but the embossed title was still evident: DARIUS, SON OF MARKLON.

Phury leaned down, astounded. It was D's book . . . probably a diary.

He opened the case, then frowned at the smell inside. Gunpowder?

He looked at the assembled objects. In the far corner there was an old handgun, and he recognized the make and model from the firearms textbook he'd been teaching the trainees from. It was an 1890

Colt Navy .36-caliber, six-cylinder revolver. That had recently been used.

He took the thing out, cocked the chamber open, and palmed one of the bullets. They were spherical . . . and uneven, as if they were handmade.

He'd seen the shape before. When he'd been erasing V's medical results from the computer at St. Francis, he'd looked at a chest X-ray that had been taken . . . and seen a spherical, slightly irregular hunk of lead in his brother's lung.

"Were you here to see me?"

Phury looked over his shoulder at the Directrix. The female was standing in the double doors, dressed in that white robe they all wore. Around her neck, on a chain, was a medallion like his.

"Nice collection of artifacts you have here," he drawled, turning around.

The female's eyes narrowed. "I would think the gems would interest you more."

"Not really." He watched her carefully as he lifted the book in his hand. "This looks like my brother's diary."

As her shoulders eased up ever so slightly, he wanted to kill her. "Yes, that is Darius's diary."

Phury tapped the cover of the book, then waved his hand around at all the gems. "Tell me something—is this place kept locked all the time?"

"Yes. Ever since the attack."

"You and I are the only ones with keys, right? I'd hate to have anything happen to what's in here."

"Yes. Only the two of us. No one may gain entry herein without my knowledge or presence."

"No one."

Her eyes flashed with annoyance. "Order is to be maintained. I have spent years training the Chosen unto their proper ministrations."

"Yeah . . . so a Primale showing up must be a real buzz kill for you. Because I'm in charge now, aren't I?"

Her voice dropped low. "It is right and proper for you to rule herein."

"I'm sorry, could you say that again? I didn't quite hear you."

Her eyes seethed with venom for a split second—which confirmed to him her actions and her motive: The Directrix had shot Vishous. With the gun from the case. She wanted to continue to be in charge, and knew damn well that if a Primale came in at best she would be second in command under a male. At worst she could lose all her power just because the male didn't like the color of her eyes.

When she'd failed to kill V, she backed off . . . until she could try again. No doubt she was smart enough and nasty enough to defend her territory until either the Brothers ran out or the Primale role started to look cursed.

"You were about to say something, weren't you?" he prompted.

The Directrix smoothed the medallion hanging from her throat. "You are the Primale. You are the ruler herein."

"Good. Glad we're both straight on that." He tapped Darius's diary again. "I'm taking this back with me."

"Are we not meeting?"

He walked over to her, thinking that if she had been male he would have snapped her neck.

"Not right now, no. I have something I have to take care of with the Scribe Virgin." He leaned down, putting his mouth next to her ear. "But I'll be back for you."

FIFTY-TWO

Vishous had never cried before. Throughout his life he had never, ever cried. After all the shit he'd been through, it had gotten to the point that he'd decided he'd been born without tear ducts.

The events leading up to now hadn't changed that. When Jane had lain dead in his arms he hadn't wept. When he'd attempted to cut off his hand in the Tomb as a sacrifice and the pain had been astonishing, there had been no tears. When his hated mother had cast him back from the deed he'd been about to do, his cheeks had been dry.

Even when the Scribe Virgin had put her hand upon Jane's body and he'd watched in a daze as his beloved had been reduced to ash, he had not wept.

He did now.

For the first time since his birth, tears rolled down his face and soaked his pillow.

They had started when a vision of Butch and Marissa on the couch in the Pit's living room had come to him. Vivid . . . so vivid. V could not only hear their thoughts in his head, but he knew that Butch was picturing Marissa on their bed in a black bra and blue jeans. And Marissa was imagining him taking off her blue jeans and putting his head down between her thighs.

V knew that in six minutes Butch was going to take the orange juice Marissa had in her hand and put it on the coffee table. He was going to spill it, because the glass was going to land on the corner of a *Sports Illustrated*, and the juice was going to get on Marissa's jeans. The cop was going to use this as an excuse to take her down the hall and get her good and naked.

Except on the way, they would stop by V's door and lose their sexual impulses. With sad eyes, they would go to their mated bed and hold each other in silence.

V put an arm over his face. And wept uncontrollably.

His visions were back, his curse of the future returned to him.

The crossroads in his life was over.

Which meant this was his existence from now on: He was to be nothing but an empty shell that lay next to the ashes of his beloved.

And sure enough, in the midst of his crying he heard Butch and Marissa come down the hall, heard them pause in front of his bedroom, then heard them shut their door. No sounds of sex got muffled by the wall between the rooms, no headboard banged, no throaty cries sounded.

Just as he'd foreseen. In the silence that followed, V wiped his cheeks, then looked at his hands. The left one still throbbed a little from the damage he'd done to it. The right one glowed as it always did—and his tears were white against the backdrop of his inner illumination, white as the irises of his eyes.

He took a deep breath and looked at the clock.

The only thing that was keeping him breathing was nightfall. He absolutely would have killed himself by now—would have taken his

Glock and put it in his mouth and blown the back of his head out—if it weren't for nightfall.

He was making it a personal mission to eradicate the Lessening Society. It was going to take the rest of his life, but that was fucking fine, because there was nothing else out there for him. And he would have preferred to leave the Brotherhood to do it, but Butch would die without him, so he was going to have to stick around.

Abruptly, he frowned and looked toward the door.

After a moment he wiped his cheeks again and said, "I'm surprised you don't just come in."

The door opened without benefit of a hand. On the other side, the Scribe Virgin stood in the hallway, her black robes covering her head to foot.

"I was not sure of my welcome," she said in a low voice as she floated into the room.

He didn't lift his head from the pillow. Had no interest in honoring her in any way. "You know what your welcome is."

"Indeed. So I will get down to the purpose of my visit. I have a gift for you."

"I don't want it."

"Yes. You do."

"Fuck you." Beneath her robes, her head seemed to drop. Not that he gave a shit that her precious little feelings were hurt. "Leave."

"You will want—"

He jerked upright. "You *took* what I wanted—"

A form entered the doorway, a ghostly form. "V . . . ?"

"And I give it back to you," the Scribe Virgin said. "In a certain manner."

Vishous didn't hear a word she said, because he couldn't comprehend what he was looking at. It was Jane . . . kind of. It was Jane's face and Jane's body, but she was . . . a transparent apparition.

"Jane?"

The Scribe Virgin spoke as she dematerialized. "You need not thank me. Just know that your curse is the way you may touch her. Good-bye."

Okay, as romantic reunions went, this one was bizarre and uncomfortable.

And not just because Jane supposed she could be classified as a ghost.

Vishous was looking as if he were going to pass out. Which hurt. It was entirely possible he wouldn't like her like this, and then where would she be? When the Scribe Virgin had come to her in heaven, or whatever that place was, and had given her the option of coming back, the answer had been a real no-brainer. But now that she was standing in front of a completely shocked-out guy, she wasn't so sure she'd made the right choice. Maybe she'd over—

He got up out of bed, walked across the room, and put his glowing hand to her face with hesitation. On a sigh she leaned into the imprint of his palm and the warmth of his flesh.

"Is this you?" he said hoarsely.

She nodded and reached out to his cheeks, which were a little red. "You've been crying."

He captured her hand. "I feel you."

"Me, too."

He touched her neck, her shoulder, her sternum. Brought her arm forward and looked at it . . . well, through it.

"Um . . . so I can sit on things," she said for no particular reason. "I mean . . . while I was waiting out there, I sat on the couch. I also moved a picture on the wall, put a penny back in your change dish, picked up a magazine. It's a little weird, but all I have to do is concentrate." *Shit.* She had no idea what she was saying. "The, ah . . . the Scribe Virgin said I could eat but I didn't have to. She said . . . I could drink, too. I'm not sure how it all works, but she seems to know. Yeah. So. Anyway, I think it's going to take some time to figure out the drill, but . . ."

He put his hand into her hair and it felt the same as it had before.

Her nonexistent body registered the sensations exactly as it had before.

He frowned, then looked downright angry. "She said it required a sacrifice. To bring someone back. What did you give her? What did you bargain with?"

"How do you mean?"

"She doesn't give things away without demanding something in return. What did she take from you?"

"Nothing. She never asked me for anything."

He shook his head and seemed like he was going to speak. But then he wrapped his heavy arms around her and held her against his trembling, glowing body. Unlike the other times when she had to concentrate to find solidity, with V it just happened. Against him, she was corporeal with no effort on her part.

She could tell he was crying by the way he breathed and the fact that he leaned on her, but she knew that if she made any mention of it, or tried to soothe him with words, he would stop on a dime. So she just held him and let him go.

Then again, she was kind of busy holding herself together.

"I thought I would never get to do this again," he said in a voice that cracked.

Jane closed her eyes and squeezed him, thinking about that moment in the fog when she'd let him go. If she hadn't done that, they wouldn't be here, would they?

Fuck free will, she thought. She'd rely on destiny, no matter how much it hurt in the short run. Because love in its many forms always endured. It was the infinite. The eternal. That which sustained. She had no idea who or what the Scribe Virgin was. Had no idea where she herself had been or how she had come back. But she was sure of one thing.

"You were right," she said against V's chest.

"About what?"

"I do believe in God."

FIFTY-THREE

The following evening John didn't have class, so he sat down for First Meal with the Brothers and the females. The mood in the house was considerably lighter than it had been for weeks. But sure as shit, he didn't share in the levity.

"So anyway," Phury was saying, "I went to the Scribe Virgin and told her about the bullet."

"Jesus Christ. The Directrix." Vishous leaned forward, taking Jane's hand with him. "I'd assumed it was a *lesser.*"

V hadn't let go of his doctor since they'd sat down together, as if he were afraid she'd disappear. Which was kind of understandable. John tried not to stare at her, but it was hard not to. She was wearing one of V's shirts and a pair of blue jeans and filling them out as normal. But what was in them was . . . well, a ghost, he supposed.

"Of course you did," Phury said as he turned to Bella and offered her the butter plate. "We all did. But that female had one hell of a motive. She wanted to stay in charge, and yeah, with a Primale on

the scene, that just wasn't going to happen. Classic power-play scenario."

John glanced at the silent blond female who sat on Phury's other
side. Boy, the Chosen was beautiful . . . beautiful in the ethereal way
of angels, with an unearthly glow emanating from her. But she wasn't
happy. She picked at her food and kept her eyes down.

Well, except for when she glanced at Phury. Which was usually
when he spoke to or looked at Bella.

Wrath's voice was hard from the head of the table. "The Directrix
has to die."

Phury cleared his throat as he took the butter plate back from
Bella. "You can consider that . . . taken care of, my lord."

Holy shit. Had Phury—

"Good." Wrath nodded as if understanding perfectly and approv-
ing. "Who's going to replace her?"

"The Scribe Virgin asked who I wanted in the role. But I don't
know any—"

"Amalya," the blond Chosen said.

All heads turned in her direction.

"I'm sorry?" Phury asked. "What did you say?"

As she spoke, the Chosen's voice was lovely in the manner of wind
chimes, sweet and melodic. "If it would not offend, may I suggest
the Chosen Amalya? She is warm and kind and of appropriate se-
niority."

Phury's yellow eyes went over the female, but his face was re-
served, as if he wasn't sure what to say or do with her. "Then that's
who I want. Thank you."

Her eyes lifted to his for a moment, a flush running pink in her
cheeks. But then Phury looked away and so did she.

"All of us are taking the night off," Wrath said abruptly. "We need
some regroup time."

Rhage snorted from across the table. "You're not going to make
us play Monopoly again, are you?"

"Yup." A collective groan rose up from the Brotherhood, one that Wrath ignored. "Right after dinner."

"I have something I have to do," V said. "I'll be back as soon as I can."

"Fine, but you can't be the shoe or the dog then. They always go first."

"I can live with that."

Fritz came in with a massive baked Alaska. "Dessert, perhaps?" the *doggen* said with a smile.

As a universal "Yes, please" filled the room, John folded his napkin and asked to be excused. When Beth nodded, he took off, heading for the tunnel under the grand staircase. The walk to the training center didn't take long, especially as his gait was evening out and he was becoming more comfortable with his body.

When he came out into Tohr's office, he braced himself as he looked around. The place really hadn't changed since the Brother's disappearance. Except for the fact that the ugly-ass green chair was now in Wrath's study, everything was pretty much the same.

John went behind the desk and sat down. Strung across the thing were papers and files, some marked with Post-it notes on which Z had written things in his deliberate way.

John put his hands on the office chair's arms, running them back and forth.

He hated the way he felt right now.

He hated that he was pissed off that V got Jane back, whereas Tohr had lost Wellsie forever. Except it wasn't fair. And not just to Tohr. John would have liked a ghost of Wellsie in his life. He would have liked the only mother he'd ever known to be around.

Except Vishous was the one who'd gotten the boon.

And so had Rhage. With Mary.

What the fuck made them so special?

He put his head in his hands, feeling like the worst kind of person. To begrudge someone happiness and luck was a horrible thing

to do, especially if you loved them. But it was so damn hard to miss Tohr so badly and mourn Wellsie and—

"Hey."

John looked up. Z was standing in the office, though God only knew how he'd managed to make no noise coming through the closet.

"What's on your mind, John?"

Nothing.

"You want to try that again?"

John shook his head and glanced down. Idly he noticed that Lash's folder was on the top of a pile, and he thought of the guy. Man, the two of them were on a collision course. The only open issue was timing.

"You know," Z said, "I used to wonder why me and not Phury."

John looked up with a frown.

"Yeah, wondered why I was the one who got taken and ended up where I did. I wasn't the only one. Phury still kills himself over the fact that it was me, not him." Z crossed his arms over his chest. "Trouble is, getting caught up in why something happens to one person and not another never gets you anywhere."

I want Wellsie to come back.

"I figured that's why you left." The Brother rubbed a hand over his skull trim. "Here's the thing, though. I believe there's a hand that guides us. It just isn't always a gentle one. Or one that seems fair at the time. But I dunno, I try to trust in it now. When I freak, I just try to . . . shit, I guess trust in it. Because at the end of the day, what else can you do? Choice only gets you so far. Reasoning and planning, too. The rest . . . it's up to someone else. Where we end up, who we know, what happens to the people we love . . . we don't have a lot of control over any of it."

I miss Tohr.

"We all do."

Yeah, John wasn't the only one who suffered. He needed to remember that.

"So I have something for you." Z went over to a cabinet and opened it. "Phury gave it to me yesterday. We were going to save it for your birthday, but fuck it. You need it tonight."

Z came back to the desk with an old, battered leather book in his hands. He laid it on top of the piles of paper, his big palm over the front.

"Happy birthday, John."

He lifted his arm and John looked down.

All at once his heart stopped.

With a shaking hand, he reached out and traced the worn lettering that read: DARIUS, SON OF MARKLON.

He gently opened the cover. . . . In a beautiful, formal flourish were words and symbols beyond measure, the reflections of a life that had been led long ago. His father's writing in the Old Language.

John snapped his hand back and covered his mouth, terrified he was going to break down sobbing.

Except when he looked up in shame, he found that he was alone.

Z, with his characteristic grace, had allowed him to have his pride.

And now . . . having given him his father's diary . . . some joy as well.

Right after First Meal, Vishous materialized to the Scribe Virgin's courtyard. He was a little surprised that he got permission, considering the way things were, but he was glad he did.

After he took form, he frowned and looked around at the white marble fountain and the colonnade and the portal into the Chosen's area. Something was different. He wasn't sure what, but something—

"Greetings, sire."

He turned around. A Chosen was standing by what he'd always assumed was the door to the Scribe Virgin's private quarters. Dressed in that white robing with her hair twisted onto the top of her head, he recognized her as the one who'd come to check on Cormia after the presentation ceremony.

"Amalya," he said.

She seemed surprised he remembered her name. "Your Grace."

So this was the one Cormia had recommended as Directrix. Made sense. The female did seem kind.

"I'm here to see the Scribe Virgin." Although he figured she knew that.

"With all due deference, sire, she is not receiving this day."

"Not receiving me or anybody?"

"All comers. Is there a message you would like to proffer her?"

"I'll come back tomorrow."

The Chosen bowed low. "With all due deference, sire, I believe that she will as yet be indisposed."

"Why?"

"I do not inquire why." Her tone was ever so slightly disapproving. As if he shouldn't ask either.

Well, shit. What did he want to say exactly?

"Will you tell her . . . that Vishous came to say . . ."

As words failed him, the Chosen's eyes were wells of compassion. "If I may be so bold, perhaps I shall tell her that her son came to thank her for her generous gift and for her sacrifice for his happiness."

Son.

No, he couldn't go that far. Even with Jane back, the label seemed disingenuous. "Just Vishous. Tell her Vishous came to say thank-you."

The Chosen bowed again, her face saddened. "As you wish."

He watched the female turn away and disappear behind the small, ornate door.

Wait a minute. Had she said *sacrifice?* What sacrifice?

He looked around again, focusing on the fountain. Abruptly the sound of the water struck him as odd. When he'd come before—

V slowly turned his head.

The white tree with the white blossoms was empty. All the songbirds were gone.

That was what was missing. The Scribe Virgin's birds were no more, the tree's branches empty of their color, the still air devoid of their cheerful calling.

In the relative silence, the loneliness of the place sank into him, the hollow sound of water falling amplifying the emptiness.

Oh, God. That was the sacrifice, wasn't it.

She had given up her love for his.

In her private quarters, the Scribe Virgin knew as soon as V left. She could feel his form go back over to the world outside.

The Chosen Amalya approached quietly. "If it would not offend, I would speak."

"You have no need to. I know what he said. Leave me now and return to the sanctuary."

"Yes, Your Highness."

"Thank you."

The Scribe Virgin waited until the Chosen had retreated, then she turned and looked across the white expanse of her suite. The rooms were largely for naught save pacing. As she did not sleep or eat, the bedroom and dining area were but square feet to travel over.

Everything was so silent now.

She floated from room to room, disquieted. She had failed her son in so many ways, and she couldn't blame him his refusal of the name. Yet the hurt was there.

Joining another.

With dread she looked to the far corner of her quarters, to the place she never went. Or least, had not been for two centuries.

She had failed another, hadn't she.

Heavy of heart, she went over to the corner and willed free the double-locked door. On a hiss the seal was broken, a fine mist wafting out from the shift in humidity. Had it truly been so long?

The Scribe Virgin stepped inside and regarded the shadowed form that hovered in suspended animation over the floor.

Her daughter. V's fraternal twin. Payne.

The Scribe Virgin had long subscribed to the notion that it was better and safer for her daughter to so rest. But now she was unsure. The choices she had tried to make for her son had ended badly. Perhaps it was the same for her young of a different sex.

The Scribe Virgin stared at her daughter's face. Payne was not like other females, hadn't been since birth. She had her father's warrior instinct and urge for battle and was no more content to dally with the Chosen than a lion could be caged satisfactorily with mice.

Perhaps it was time to free her daughter, as she had freed her son. It seemed only fair. Protection had indeed proven to be a dubious virtue.

Still, she hated to let go. Especially as there was no reason to expect that her daughter would have any greater love for her than her son did. So she would lose them both.

As she struggled under the weight of her thoughts, her instinct was to go out to the courtyard and be soothed by her birds. There was no succor awaiting her therein, however. No cheerful calls to ease her.

And so the Scribe Virgin stayed in her private quarters, floating through the still, silent air in an endless track through the empty rooms. As she passed the time, the infinite nature of her nonexistence was like a cloak of needles lying upon her, a thousand little pinpricks of pain and sadness.

There was no escape or relief in sight for her, no peace nor kindness nor comfort. She was as she had always been: alone in the midst of the world she'd created.

FIFTY-FOUR

Jane had been in Manny Manello's apartment once or twice. Not often, though. When they'd been together it had always been at the hospital.

Boy, this was serious guy stuff here. *Serious* guy stuff. Any more sports equipment hanging around and it would have been a Dick's.

Kind of reminded her of the Pit.

She went around his living room looking at his DVDs and his CDs and his magazines. Yup, he would get along just fine with Butch and V: He evidently had a lifetime subscription to *Sports Illustrated*, just like they did. And he kept the back issues, just like they did. And he liked his liquor, though he was a Jack man, not into the Goose or the Lag.

As she bent down, she focused her energy so she could pick up the most recent issue of *SI* and realized that she'd been a ghost for exactly one day. It was twenty-four hours ago that she'd appeared with the Scribe Virgin in V's room.

Things were working out. Sex as a member of the undead was just as good as it had been when she'd lived. Matter of fact, she and V were meeting at his penthouse toward the end of the evening. He wanted to be "worked out," as he'd put it, his eyes shining with anticipation—and she was more than willing to indulge her man.

Abso-fucking-lutely.

Jane dropped the magazine and paced around a little more, then took up waiting by one of the windows.

This was going to be hard. Saying good-bye was hard.

She and V had talked over how to handle her departure from the human world. The car accident he'd staged would provide some explanation of her disappearance. Sure, her body would never be found, but the area the Audi had been left in was wooded and mountainous. Hopefully the police would just close her file after a search was conducted, but it wasn't like the consequences were material. She was never going back. So it didn't matter.

As for her shit, the only thing of value in her condo was a picture of her and Hannah. V had gone back and gotten the photograph for her. The rest of her stuff would eventually get sold by the lawyer she'd named executor of her estate two years ago in her last will and testament. The proceeds would go to St. Francis.

She would ache for her books, but V had said he would get her new ones. And although it wasn't quite the same, she had faith she would over time become connected to her new ones.

Manny was the only open issue. . . .

The jangle of keys going into a lock sounded, then the door opened.

Jane stepped back into the shadows as Manny came in, dropped a black Nike bag, and headed for the kitchen.

He looked exhausted. And bereft.

Her first impulse was to approach him, but she knew the better course was to wait for him to go to sleep—which was why she'd come late, hoping he'd already be in bed. Clearly, though, he was working until he couldn't stand up.

When he came out into the hall he had a glass with some water in it. He paused, looked her way with a frown . . . but then kept going to his bedroom.

She heard the shower. Footsteps. Then a soft curse, as if he were stretching out on his bed, but was stiff.

She waited and waited . . . then finally went down the hall.

Manny was on the bed, a towel around his hips, his eyes fixed on the ceiling.

The man was not going to sleep anytime soon.

She stepped into the light thrown by the lamp on the dresser. "Hey."

His head snapped toward her, then he jerked upright. "What—"

"You're dreaming."

"I am?"

"Yeah. I mean, ghosts don't exist."

He rubbed his face. "This feels real."

"Of course it does. Dreams do." She tucked her arms around herself. "I wanted you to know I'm okay. I really am. I'm okay and happy where I ended up."

No reason to mention that she was still in Caldwell.

"Jane . . ." His voice cracked.

"I know. I'd feel the same way if you'd been. . . . taken away."

"I can't believe you died. I can't believe you . . ." He started to blink fast.

"Listen, it's all okay. I promise you. Life . . . well, it ends okay, it really does. I mean, I saw my sister. My parents. Some of the patients we lost. They're all still around, just not where we can see— I mean, you can see them. But it's all right, Manny. You shouldn't be afraid of death. It's just a transition, really."

"Yeah, but you're not here anymore. I have to live without you."

Her chest ached at the tone of his voice and the fact that there was nothing she could do to relieve his suffering. It also hurt because she had lost him as well.

"I'm really going to miss you," she said.

"Me, too." He rubbed his face again. "I mean . . . I miss you already. I'm sick from it. On some level . . . hell, I thought we were going to end up together, you and me. Felt like destiny. Shit, you were the only woman I knew who was as strong as I was. But yeah . . . guess it wasn't meant to be. Plans of mice and men and all that shit."

"There's probably someone out there even better."

"Oh, yeah? Gimme her number before you go back to heaven."

Jane smiled a little, then got serious. "You're not going to do anything stupid, right?"

"You mean kill myself? Nah. But I can't promise you I won't get sloppy drunk a lot over the next couple of months."

"Just do it in private. You have a reputation as a son of a bitch to uphold."

He smirked a little. "What would the department think."

"Exactly." There was a stretch of silence. "I'd better go."

He stared across the room at her. "God, it feels like you're really here."

"I'm not. This is just a dream." She let herself start to fade as tears landed on her cheeks. "Bye, Manny, my dear friend."

He lifted his hand and spoke through what was clearly a tight throat. "Come back and see me sometime."

"Maybe."

"Please."

"We'll see."

Funny, though, as she dissipated, she had the oddest sense that she was going to see him again.

Yeah, it was weird. Just like that vision of the car accident as well as the feeling she'd had that she wasn't going to be at St. Francis anymore, she knew that she and Manny Manello were going to cross paths once more.

The thought eased her. She hated leaving him behind. She really did.

EPILOGUE

One week later . . .

Vishous took the hot chocolate from the stove and turned the burner off. As he poured the cocoa into a mug, he heard a yelp and an "Oh, my God!"

Across the mansion's kitchen he saw Rhage standing halfway inside of Jane, as if she were a pool he'd waded into. The two of them leaped apart just as Vishous bared his teeth and growled at his brother.

Rhage held his hands up. "I didn't see her! Honest!"

Jane laughed. "It's not his fault. I wasn't concentrating, so I faded—"

V cut her off. "Rhage is going to be more careful, aren't you, my brother."

The implication being either the male would be, or he'd end up in traction.

"Yeah, absolutely. Shit."

"Glad you see it my way." Vishous picked up the mug, took it to Jane, and handed it to her. As she blew across the surface, he kissed her on the neck. Then did a little nuzzling.

To him she was just as she always had felt, but to others she was a thing of a different sort. She wore clothes, but if she wasn't keeping herself solid and someone bumped into her, the fabrics compressed like nothing was inside of them, and the person who was in her path basically stepped through her.

It was a little strange. Plus, if it happened to be one of his brothers, V's territoriality got triggered like you read about. The thing was, though, this was the new reality, so everyone had to deal. He and Jane were both making the transition to her new situation, and it wasn't always easy.

But who the fuck cared? They had each other.

"So you're going to Safe Place today?" he asked her.

"Yeah, my first day at my new job. Can't wait!" Jane's eyes shone. "Then I'm coming back here to put in equipment orders for my clinic. I've decided to take on two *doggen* and train them as nurses. I think that's the best thing to do for security purposes. . . ."

As Jane talked about her plans for the Brotherhood's clinic and what she was going to do for Safe Place, V started to smile.

"What?" she said. She glanced down at herself, brushed her white coat off, then looked behind her.

"Come here, female." He pulled her up against him and dropped his head. "I mention lately how sexy your brain is?"

"You were mostly interested in something else this afternoon, so no."

He laughed at her wry smile. "I was a little preoccupied, wasn't I?"

"Mmm, yes."

"I'm going to stop by Safe Place later, true?"

"Good. I think Marissa's got a network problem she wanted to talk to you about."

Without even being aware of doing it, he tucked her in close and just hugged her. This was exactly what he'd wanted, this intermingling of lives, this closeness, this common purpose. The two of them, together.

"Are you okay?" she said softly so no one else could hear.

"Yeah. Yeah, I'm good." He put his mouth next to her ear. "It's just . . . I'm not used to this."

"Used to what?"

"Feeling . . . shit, I don't know." He pulled back, all weirded out that he was so sappy. "Never mind . . ."

"You can't get used to feeling like things are okay?"

He nodded because he didn't trust his voice.

She put her hand on his face. "You'll get used it. Just like I will."

"Sire? I beg your pardon?"

V glanced over at Fritz. "Hey, my man, what's doing?"

The *doggen* bowed. "I have what you asked for. I left it in the foyer."

"Excellent. Thanks." He kissed Jane. "So I'll see you later?"

"Absolutely."

He could feel her eyes on him as he left, and he liked it. He liked everything. He—

Well, shit. He was just full of the joys of spring, wasn't he?

As he emerged into the foyer, he found what Fritz had left for him on the table by the foot of the grand staircase. At first he wasn't sure quite how to handle the thing . . . he didn't want to break it. In the end he held it gently in his hands and went into the library. He shut the double doors with his mind and sent a request to the Other Side.

Yeah, sure, he wasn't following the rules of proper dress, but then, he was a little preoccupied with what was in his hands.

When permission was granted, he dematerialized to the Scribe Virgin's courtyard and was greeted by the same Chosen as the last time he'd been there. Amalya began to bow, but looked up as a chirping sound came from his carefully cupped palms.

"What have you brought?" she whispered.

"Little present. Nothing much." He walked over to the white tree with the white blossoms and opened his hands. The parakeet leaped free and took to a branch as if it knew that was its home now.

The brilliant yellow bird shuffled up and down the pale arm of the tree, its little feet gripping and releasing, gripping and releasing. It pecked at a blossom, let out a trill . . . brought a foot up and pedaled its neck.

V put his hands on his hips and measured how much space there was between all the blossoms on all the branches. He was going to have to bring over a shitload of birds.

The Chosen's voice was rife with emotion. "She gave them up for you."

"Yeah. And I'm bringing her new ones."

"But the sacrifice—"

"Has been made. What's going on this tree is a gift." He looked over his shoulder. "I'm going to fill it up whether she likes it or not. It's her choice what she does with them."

The Chosen's eyes gleamed with gratitude. "She will keep them. And they will keep her from her solitude."

V took a deep breath. "Yeah. Good. Because . . ."

He let the word drift and the Chosen said gently, "You don't have to say it."

He cleared his throat. "So you'll tell her they're from me?"

"I won't have to. Who else but her son would do such a kindness?"

Vishous glanced back at the lone yellow bird in the midst of the white tree. He pictured the branches filled once again.

"True," he said.

Without another word he dematerialized back to the life he'd been given, the life he was leading . . . the life he now, and for the first time, was grateful he'd been born into.